the lost hours

Susan Lewis is the internationally bestselling author of over forty books across the genres of family drama, thriller, suspense and crime – including the novel *One Minute Later*, which was a Richard and Judy pick. She is also the author of *Just One More Day* and *One Day at a Time*, the moving memoirs of her childhood in Bristol during the 1960s. Following periods of living in Los Angeles and the South of France, she currently lives in Gloucestershire with her husband James, and mischievous dogs Coco and Lulu.

To find out more about Susan Lewis:

www.susanlewis.com
www.facebook.com/SusanLewisBooks
@susanlewisbooks

Also by Susan Lewis

Fiction
A Class Apart
Dance While You Can
Stolen Beginnings
Darkest Longings
Obsession
Vengeance
Summer Madness
Last Resort
Wildfire
Cruel Venus
Strange Allure
The Mill House
A French Affair
Missing
Out of the Shadows
Lost Innocence
The Choice
Forgotten
Stolen
No Turning Back
Losing You
The Truth About You
Never Say Goodbye
Too Close to Home
No Place to Hide
The Secret Keeper
One Minute Later

Books that run in sequence
Chasing Dreams
Taking Chances

No Child of Mine
Don't Let Me Go
You Said Forever

Featuring Detective Andee Lawrence
Behind Closed Doors
The Girl Who Came Back
The Moment She Left
Hiding in Plain Sight
Believe in Me
Home Truths
My Lies, Your Lies
Forgive Me

Featuring Laurie Forbes and Elliott Russell
Silent Truths
Wicked Beauty
Intimate Strangers
The Hornbeam Tree

Memoirs
Just One More Day
One Day at a Time

Susan Lewis

the lost hours

HarperCollins*Publishers*

HarperCollins*Publishers* Ltd
The News Building
1 London Bridge Street
London SE1 9GF

www.harpercollins.co.uk

HarperCollins*Publishers*
1st Floor, Watermarque Building, Ringsend Road
Dublin 4, Ireland

Published by HarperCollins*Publishers* 2021
2

A catalogue record for this book
is available from the British Library

ISBN: 978-0-00-828697-2

Typeset in Sabon LT Std by
Palimpsest Book Production Ltd, Falkirk, Stirlingshire

Printed and Bound in the UK using 100%
Renewable Electricity at CPI Group (UK) Ltd

MIX
Paper from
responsible sources
FSC™ C007454

This book is produced from independently certified FSC™ paper
to ensure responsible forest management.

For more information visit: www.harpercollins.co.uk/green

6th September 1999

'They've found her, sir.'

DCI Underwood's heavy grey eyes rose from the file on his desk to the young DC at his door.

'A call's just come in,' the DC explained, 'from a builder. They've started clearing the land over at Embury Vale for the new estate. One of the workmen's found a body, in a derelict railway hut. All indications are that it's our girl.'

Underwood reached for his Nokia and got to his feet. 'You can drive,' he told the DC and started out of the room, wanting to lose no time, in spite of it apparently already being too late.

Karen Lomax, a seventeen-year-old local lass, had vanished from her home a month ago and all leads so far had been up the garden path at best, still open-ended at worst. No one seemed to know what had happened to her, where she'd gone or who could have taken her, although the smart money was on Timbo Jaks, the lowlife she'd been seen with a few times while the fair was on the common. None of her friends had said the relationship was serious, but Underwood would have been failing in his duty if he hadn't tracked the Travellers down to find out if she'd gone with them. There'd been no sign of her,

Jaks had sworn he'd never laid a finger on her, she wasn't his type, but he would say that, wouldn't he? They'd turned the camp upside down, had even hauled Jaks and half a dozen others in for questioning, but in the end they'd been forced to let them go.

Now a body had turned up not half a mile from where the fair had sprawled over the terrain in late July, and Underwood had never been one to believe in coincidences, oblique or otherwise. Karen Lomax had disappeared on 7th August, not two weeks after her last known visit to said fair.

'Someone find out where Timbo Jaks and his lot are now,' he barked to his team as he swept through CID, 'and send a car to pick him up.'

Forty minutes later, Underwood and the young DC were standing on a vast patch of wasteland being drizzled on from above as they watched the SOCOs in hoods, masks, boots and gloves going about their work. Now that Underwood had set eyes on the body he was in no doubt it was Karen, partially decomposed though her once pretty young face was; the clothes, the hair, the build, were all a match. Early examination was suggesting a sharp blow to the back of the head was probably what killed her, but there was still a way to go. Any amount of other injuries, not immediately visible, might be revealed. Later, once the pathologist and forensics had done their jobs, they might know if she'd been beaten, tied up, tortured, starved; possibly if sexual relations had taken place prior to – or even after – her death. There were some sick bastards out there. What would be of more interest to the investigators was whether any identifying fibres, prints, hairs or fluids had been left behind.

Underwood's next stop today was going to be the most difficult of all, breaking the news to the parents, Jess and Eddie Lomax. They owned a wine bar in the old town and lived above it. A nice couple, always friendly, knowledgeable about vintages, generous with the tastings. Honest, law-abiding types, who had closed the bar since the disappearance of their only child. Necessity demanded they were questioned, extensively, but no one had seriously suspected them. Their devastation would have been all but impossible to fake. It had been hard to handle, even for a seasoned detective like him.

Everyone who went into the bar knew their daughter, pretty, flighty, well-developed in all the right places, a proper handful if the truth be told, especially where the opposite sex was concerned. Like plenty of girls her age she was blossoming, growing up too fast, considered herself worldly, all powerful. She'd even batted her saucy eyes at him once or twice and he had a good ten years on her father.

'I always said she'd come to a bad end,' one of the neighbours had claimed. 'That's the trouble with girls these days, they don't even dress decent so who can blame the poor boys for thinking something's on offer when it isn't?'

Though Underwood didn't much appreciate that way of thinking, he had to admit it was an issue that kept coming up, and even he had been known to misunderstand a certain type of flirtation. Not that he'd taken advantage of it, but he couldn't help wishing teenage girls were more aware of the dangers they were putting themselves in with their short skirts, transparent tops and binge-drinking.

'Slappers, the lot of them,' another neighbour had grunted. 'And that Karen . . . The things I've heard about her.'

The gossip had been rife and cruel, but others had spoken about her fondly and loyally, especially her friends. She'd always been generous and caring, they'd said, a shoulder to cry on when things went wrong. She was a good laugh, up for anything, and yes, she liked boys, but who didn't? It was normal, wasn't it, at their age? And she was seventeen, so it wasn't illegal or anything, so why shouldn't she go with whoever she wanted? Yes, she liked them a bit older sometimes, in their twenties or thirties even, but she never went with married men, or not knowingly, anyway.

Timbo Jaks? Yeah, he was cool, and she did hang out with him for a while, but she hadn't come over as upset when the fair shipped out. No one seemed sure if she'd met someone else by then, there were probably a couple she fancied, blokes who came into the bar, or who they met at cafés and nightclubs in town. It was summer, so lots of tourists around and they were all up for holiday romances, no strings, or maybe some if they wanted it. Her friends had never seemed convinced she'd run off with Jaks. 'She wouldn't, not without telling me,' her best mate Lucy had insisted. 'We didn't have any secrets. No reason to. So no, I don't reckon she went off with Timbo. For one thing, she wouldn't do that to her parents, just up and go without even leaving a note, but that's not to say he didn't abduct her and make her go with him. I reckon it's the kind of thing he'd do.'

The thrill of the horror made the girls unreliable witnesses. Their imaginations were so lurid and fertile that even Underwood had felt shocked by some of their suggestions, but he'd never got the impression they were lying about not knowing where she was. They seemed genuinely baffled and even afraid, as if whatever had happened to Karen might be coming for them.

So whether Jaks had or hadn't abducted Karen was a question still to be answered, but Underwood had a very strong feeling that when the forensics came back everything was going to point to that little toerag. And when it did, no one was going to be happier than this detective, because an unsolved killing was not something he wanted hanging over him during his retirement years – any more than the parents needed the torment of not knowing what had happened to their precious girl to drag on any longer than it already had.

CHAPTER ONE

December 2019

Here she was driving across the moor she knew so well, a little too fast as usual, and loving every minute of it. What's not to love about sunshine lighting up the world so gloriously in the middle of December? she might answer, if asked why she was smiling. It was so warm that she'd lowered the convertible's roof and hadn't even bothered to pull on the crazy reindeer hat she usually took with her at this time of year. It was quite possibly the most unstylish item of clothing she possessed and she loved it almost as much as the man who'd given it to her – the man who'd given a shout of laughter when he'd unwrapped his own gift that very same Christmas to discover she'd bought him the same hat. The children, quite predictably, had groaned, rolled eyes and laughed when their parents had put them on and started taking selfies. She wondered what they were going to do this year when they discovered that they too had reindeer hats and were expected to post shots on Instagram and wear them when they went out as a family?

Annabelle grinned to picture what the five of them would look like, some cheesy Christmas card or dorky family trying to get a few laughs. The children would find it funny in spite of themselves, and might even, because they were Crayces, go along with the craziness of it.

'I don't know another family like yours,' her sister-in-law, Julia, would occasionally comment with an affectionate sigh. 'Every one of you unspeakably beautiful, and quite possibly certifiably mad.'

Not mad, just joyful and thankful to be as blessed as they were in so many ways, not least of all in having each other and the incredible life they were able to live all the way up here on this wonderful moor. Sometimes she felt that the billowing, tumbling and soaring mass of it had a life force all of its own, a soul that breathed quietly and steadily beneath the wind-worn landscape, and was nourished by all that came to it.

She wound on through the high hedges, passing the occasional vista of sprawling uplands with her jaunty scarf and pale golden hair streaming out behind her, until she reached the Drang, local-speak for the meeting of roads and pathways. Here she turned into the welcoming, shade-speckled trail that roamed for a quarter of a mile to the wide-open gates of Hanley Combe Estate, aka home. As she swept through and past the quaint stone cottage just inside, she gave a toot of the horn to let her father-in-law know she was back. Although she doubted he was in there. Most likely he was over at the house with his very lively eight-year-old grandson, Quin.

On reaching the divide in the drive where an arc off to the left led to the main residence that she and David had constructed almost twenty years ago in a style that had confounded local planners at the time, she continued to the right and pulled up in the gravelled courtyard of the Byre. This transformed old barn, with its magnificent grey stone walls, black slate roof and grand oak doors, was home to the beating heart of their business. In more recent times it had acquired a glass-fronted wing on one side to house a shop and secure store, and a grand rotunda on the other with a conical roof and floor-to-ceiling windows. This last was used for parties, conferences and anything else it might be found suitable for, such as the upcoming festive Flurry.

As she got out of the car the crack of a gunshot rang through the skies, puncturing nature's benign tranquillity like a wayward thunderbolt and echoing on for a moment or two into silence. No birds stirred, nothing moved at all. Two more explosions boomed into the stillness followed by two more, and yet more.

Reaching into the car's back seat Annie began hauling out the shopping she'd picked up in town, more Christmas decorations, Secret Santa gifts and regular supplies for the Byre's well-equipped kitchen.

'There you are,' a voice called out from the double front doors he was coming through. 'Let me give you a hand with that.'

Happily passing the load to her brother-in-law, Henry, a slightly shorter and darker-haired version of his older brother, a director of the business as well as a landowner in his own right, she said, 'David's still out on the stands?'

'They've just moved down to the tower,' Henry replied, referring to Hanley Combe's new accessory that soared forty metres out of the nearby woods for experienced guns to warm up before high pheasant-shooting days out on the moor. David, being the shooting school's owner and senior coach, usually took these sessions himself, although

Henry was perfectly qualified to do so, as were a handful of freelancers they called on at peak times.

'The phone's been ringing non-stop,' Henry told her, leading the way inside. She couldn't help noticing that his uneven gait seemed slightly more awkward today. That happened at times, usually when he was tired, or the weather was damp; he'd often joshed that having one leg longer than the other made it so much easier for him to get around the steeply rugged terrain of sporting estates, but the car accident that had caused it was very far from being a joke. For almost a fortnight after it had happened they'd lived in daily terror of losing him. David had never left his side, while all the time bracing himself to break the worst of all news to him that his wife, Laura, and four-year-old son, Ryan, hadn't survived the crash.

Although it had happened almost twelve years ago, no one ever made the mistake of thinking Henry was completely over it, not even his second wife, Julia, who'd grown up with the Crayce brothers right here on the moor. Annie was fairly certain Henry had been Julia's first love, but there again it could have been David, given how close they all were; in truth even Julia didn't seem to know for certain. It was well known, however, that Julia had been David and Henry's first love. Although that could also be said for Chrissie, or Sukey, or Rosa, or any one of the gang – aka the Moor-auders – they'd known for most of their lives. All anyone could agree on was that they'd been a pretty wild bunch back in their teens, away at boarding schools during the week, back on the moor for the weekends, until eventually they'd gone their separate ways to uni. It was there that Henry had met Laura, and after that he hadn't often returned to his roots, until the tragedy had forced it. His parents and David and Annie had been there for him throughout his recovery, as had the rest of their friends, many of whom, like David and Annie, had by now made their own way back to Exmoor with various partners and offspring. However, it was Julia, with her easy-going nature and endearing eccentricities, whom Henry had really come to lean on during that time, for her own difficult marriage had been over by then, leaving her much freer than the others to commit to his recovery. And so, it had been a surprise to no one and a joy to all when, four years after the accident, she and Henry had announced they were getting married.

'. . . so the Americans from Oklahoma want to book again for next year,' Henry was telling Annie as he limped across the smart, cavernous barn with its high-beamed ceilings and rug-covered flagstone floor. The uneven, white-washed walls were covered in antlers – most collected from around the moor, although some had been gifted by Gloucestershire's Badminton Estate following a cull. At one end of the room was a vast Inglenook fireplace surrounded by leather sofas and strategically placed drinks tables, and at the opposite end, which they were heading for now, was Annie's welcome desk, large enough to seat four with their laptops and other paraphernalia spread out around them, which it frequently did.

'I've dealt with everything I could,' Henry continued as he turned into the rotunda to drop off his cargo, 'and I've made notes so you can see what's what. Oh, the delivery of Hull cartridges arrived, already in the storeroom, and the new clay trap should be here tomorrow.'

'Great,' she replied, knowing David would be pleased to hear about the trap and stepping over a pile of boxes to get through to the kitchen she dumped the groceries on top of the fridge and flexed her hands. 'Is Julia still with the reporter from *The Field*?' she called out.

'As far as I know,' came the reply.

Pleased to be receiving the coverage, since the last time Hanley Court had featured in the magazine, nine years ago, it had virtually doubled their business, Annie pictured her sprightly sister-in-law chattering away eagerly as she toured the reporter around the best parts of the hundred-acre estate. Only clays were shot here at the school, either for recreation, or to practise for game shoots that were hosted by David and Henry in local as well other highly regarded sporting estates around the country.

'How much longer is David going to be, any idea?' she asked, coming back into the main hall. 'Who's he with again?'

'A bunch of merchant bankers from London,' Henry reminded her, 'and no, that's not rhyming slang. They all seem quite experienced, so it should be a good shoot tomorrow. A couple have their own loaders driving down tonight, so that won't please the local lads too much, but we'll still need half a dozen, plus the regular beaters and picker-uppers.' It was common practice for locals to support the shoots by loading guns, beating the woods and covers to flush out the pheasants and working their dogs to fetch the shot game.

'Is that arranged?' Annie asked.

With a grin he said, 'Are you seriously doubting me?'

'Never,' she laughed. 'And I know their accommodation is sorted, because I booked it myself.'

'OK, so I'm off to relieve himself,' Henry declared, referring to his brother, and looping a set of ear-defenders around his neck. He picked up the unloaded Miroku shotgun he'd left broken on the centre table, grabbed a bag of cartridges and headed out the back door. 'Oh, by the way,' he said, glancing back, 'Jules just texted to say the reporter's about to leave.'

Annie unravelled her scarf and dug around for her mobile phone as it rang.

'Hey Mum.'

'Hey Max,' she responded, adopting the same chirpy tone as her fourteen-year-old son who was growing so fast he'd soon be as tall as his father, and, according to him, twice as handsome. 'Where are you?'

'Same question to you. I've been trying to get hold of someone. Dad's not answering. I guess he's out on a shoot?'

'No, he's here, but he's on the stands with clients at the moment. Anything I can do?'

'Sure, I just wanted to ask if it's OK to come home tomorrow instead of today? Perry Green's invited me and a couple of others to stay over at his place tonight. A kind of pre-Christmas thing.'

'I'm wounded,' she declared, biting into an apple and opening up her emails. 'I thought you couldn't wait to see us.'

'I can't, but you know what they say about anticipation. Sometimes it's the best part.'

That boy was getting too cute for his own good. 'OK, just make sure you have everything before you leave school. We don't want to be driving back there over Christmas to pick up all the presents you have for us.'

'Not going to happen, because I haven't bought any yet. Grandma's promised to take me shopping next week. I'll get the train, OK? You won't have to worry about coming to get me then. Well, you'll have to come into town, obvs, but it's not as far as here. Is Sienna back yet?'

'She got the train too. I met her about an hour ago, but all I've brought home is her luggage. She stayed in town with her friends, so I guess someone will have to go and pick her up later.'

'Cool. I'll give her a call. See you, love you.'

'See you, love you.'

Though mildly disappointed that the two of them were not coming straight home from their boarding schools today, she could live with it since they were around most weekends and more often than not a bunch of teenagers came with them. Sienna, the sixteen-year-old, had plenty of friends, although she was all blissed out at the moment by Grant Peterson who'd apparently invited her to join him and his family in the Caribbean for Christmas and New Year. Annie was sure Sienna had felt tempted, but so far it seemed that even the irresistible Robert Pattinson look-alike hadn't been able to tempt her away from Hanley Combe for the festivities. That was good – Annie really wasn't looking forward to the time when they wouldn't all be together for Christmas, although she was realistic enough to know it would happen one day.

As she sat down at her desk the doors to the woods and shooting areas opened and in wandered her sister-in-law, looking, as she often did in her jodhpurs, long boots and hacking jacket, as if she'd just dismounted from one of her beloved steeds. In fact, she often had, for her and Henry's home – the original Crayce family farm that was now a popular livery stables and refuge for ageing donkeys – was less than three miles away across open moor. It was a journey Julia often made on horseback, although today she'd presumably come by car, as there had been so sign of a trusty mount outside when Annie had pulled up.

'Annie, thank God you're here,' Julia declared, her sweetly plummy voice doing as much as her rosy cheeks, cashmere sweaters and heirloom pearls to make her as gorgeously posh as she was unaffected and girlish. 'Cocktail me up, darling, will you? I'm in sore need.'

Since this was a favourite greeting of Julia's (and generally meant wine) Annie didn't take her seriously, not at this hour anyway. 'Was he that bad?' she grimaced, going to pour two coffees from the machine behind her.

After a moment's confusion Julia caught up and waved a dismissive hand, 'Oh, the reporter. No, he was fine. I'm worrying about Moondance. Would you believe he lost a shoe while we were out this morning and the blasted farrier has just called to say he can't come until tomorrow? Some people just don't understand the meaning of emergency, do they?' Her eyes twinkled self-mockingly. 'Anyway, I guess it's time for me to start my shift in the shop, and I'll take a look at the website while I'm at it. It didn't seem to be downloading properly when I had a go earlier.' Amongst Julia's many and often surprising talents was a gift for understanding technology in a way that eluded the rest of them. So, as well as helping to manage the school, run her stables and refuge, and pander to her mother's beck and call, she also oversaw the smooth running of Hanley Combe's – and her own – website.

As she wandered off to relieve Hans the shop's manager, Annie began reading through Henry's notes and raised her eyebrows to see so many new enquiries. Business really was booming, and everyone was going to be happy for that. Next she checked the free-standing blackboard where details of the Festive Flurry had been artfully chalked up by her father's talented hand, and was about to go and find out what all the jollity was about in the gun shop when the door opened and David came in, as always closely shadowed by his beloved black Lab, Cassie.

It was funny, she thought, as she watched him remove his tweed cap and ear-defenders before running fingers through his mane of thick fair hair, how even after all these years sometimes simply looking at him could do things to her that she'd never want any other man to do. He was handsome, no one could ever say otherwise, and extremely physical, but it wasn't only that which drew people to him, it was the way he could make someone feel the very centre of his attention simply by looking at them as he listened to what they were saying. Knowing him so well, Annie was aware that his thoughts could be miles away, but nothing in his expression showed it; he even managed to respond appropriately when she was sure he'd barely heard what had been said. It was something she often teased him about, only for him to hotly protest his innocence before giving in with a laugh and a promise to get her back one of these days.

Their marriage was strong, full of love and laughter, and very different to how she'd once feared it might be. Thankfully there was never any reason to think back to those dark and distant times now, no need to recall how difficult their first years together had been, when she'd threatened to leave him and had even believed she might. He'd pulled himself together so long ago that even the memories of what he'd put them both through had fallen away, turned to dust, had no more substance than the passing of time. Now, what she probably loved most about him was how central he was to their family, how safe and secure he made them feel, as if nothing could ever matter more than them, and she was sure that nothing did.

She could tell from the way his indigo eyes narrowed as they came to hers that he was feeling the same intimate draw to her right now as she was to him – and this kind of connection was only going to end one way.

Were they not so busy they might have taken themselves over to the house for a while, but as it was they made do with a kiss full of promise made perversely more erotic by the Perazzi shotgun resting against his left shoulder. It wouldn't be loaded, she knew that, but it was a rule around here that all weapons when out of their slips or cases must be broken if not in use, and his was not. However, she wasn't as much interested in that right now as she was in the way their bodies fitted so perfectly together, her slender five-foot nine inches melding into the encompassing embrace of his six-foot three muscular physique, making them seem so right and complete.

'You know what I was thinking about on my way in?' he murmured, gazing into her deep, brown eyes.

'Tell me,' she said huskily.

'This,' he replied, and she had to laugh.

Hearing voices approaching from the far end of the Byre, they broke apart and gave their attention to their various duties.

By the time an hour had passed Annie had made a dozen or more phone calls, responded to twice as many emails and dealt with plenty of enquiries about the Festive Flurry.

'It's a hundred and thirty quid per person,' she'd tell the caller, knowing the details by heart, 'to include four one-hundred-bird flushes, all clays and cartridges, and a midday roast. No alcohol for those on the afternoon session, but there will be drinks at the end of the day.'

While this was happening, Julia signalled that she'd shut up shop and was going over to the main house to find out what scandals were breaking there, while Henry returned from the stands with the eight-gun team he and David were taking over to Combe Sydenham sporting estate in the morning. After serving the clients drinks in front of the fire, Henry and David piled them into the Hanley Combe Range Rovers to drive them to the luxurious accommodation Annie had arranged for while they were on Exmoor. Since they'd arrived by helicopter last night and would return the same way when the shoot was over, they had no transport of their own, so were entirely dependent on the shooting school while they were here. It often happened this way, and Annie knew David would already have liaised with the estate's gamekeeper to make sure everything was in order, from birds, to dogs, to loaders and beaters, to all catering needs for the time they were out. This was his side of the business; hers was behind the scenes. Although she was able to shoot, she just preferred her quarry to be of the clay variety, for she had no great love of blood sports. Strange really that she'd allowed herself to get drawn into setting up this enterprise all those years ago, but since it had been a way of capitalizing on David's expertise while putting to good use the hundred acres of neglected farmland adjacent to his father's, it had seemed to make sense at the time.

And neither of them had ever regretted it.

* * *

By the time David and Henry returned to the Byre at six it had long been dark outside, and a misty rain had begun to drift and thicken through the surrounding trees, working itself up into a fog. Annie had received a text a few minutes ago from Quin urging her to come and find him – a game of hide and seek was often his way of 'tricking' one of his parents into coming home. So she left the men to lock up (always a major operation considering the very expensive firearms on the premises), and let herself out into the dreary night.

Instead of running the couple of hundred yards over to the house she drove, making a mental note to thank whoever had thought to put the roof up before the damp night air had set in. It had to have been David or Henry, or Hans, but her best guess would be Henry. He was thoughtful that way, always noticing what needed to be done and acting without fuss or expectation of appreciation.

Following the unlit drive around the enormous weeping willow, whose dense and delicate foliage had finally fallen from the elegant branches these past few days, she came to a stop outside the rambling old New England-style villa that she and David had spent over a year constructing to an original plan that had finally been approved by the National Parks Authority. With its pale limestone walls, black tiled roof, tall casement windows and white wood wraparound porch, currently decorated with bright Christmas lights and fresh pine garlands, it seemed so proud of itself in its hilltop setting that they could never doubt its character.

Tugging on her reindeer hat to keep off the rain she eschewed the usual back door entrance – Quin would expect her to come in that way – and ran round to the front, up the wide wooden steps with their fairy-lit banisters and pots of creamy hellebores, and on to the veranda where she paused a moment to admire the luxuriant wreath that had appeared on the front door – no doubt put there by her mother.

'Coming ready or not?' she shouted into the brightly lit double-storey entry hall as she went inside and kicked off her boots. She glanced up the staircase with its black filigree railings that hugged two walls in its rise to the first-floor landing. There was no sign of life, although Quin and his grandpa would hardly try to hide in plain sight. Thinking it more likely that they were somewhere on this level – sitting room, snug, dining hall, probably not the kitchen, but maybe downstairs in the games room – she set off on her search. She just hoped it wasn't going to take long because she was more than ready for someone to cocktail her up.

After making a quick scour of the lamplit sitting room with its ash-filled fireplace, many sofas, cosy chairs and colourfully lit Christmas tree, she checked the snug to find no one behind its sofas, desk or giant TV, then headed into the kitchen where her mother, Harriet, and Julia were already partway through a bottle of wine as they prepared something delicious-smelling for dinner.

'Hi darling,' her mother said, glancing up from the Aga that dominated a black tiled recess on the far side of the central island. Her willowy height, pale golden hair and fine-boned features, as well as her manner, were so like her daughter's that Annie didn't need to wonder what she was going to look like in her late sixties – she saw it most days. 'I've no idea what's happened to Quin and Grandpa. We can't find them anywhere.'

Guessing from this that they must be in earshot, Annie groaned, 'They always beat me. I don't know where to look next.'

'Maybe you should try upstairs,' Julia suggested, shaking her head to advise against it.

'What a good idea,' Annie replied, and started to tiptoe around the island towards the pantry door, taking guidance from Julia's laughing grey eyes.

Annie paused, but was directed on to the next door that led to the back stairs, cloakroom and wine cellar. Receiving a nod, she started to turn the handle, preparing to whip it open and make her son jump, but it suddenly sprang from her grasp and she screamed as Quin yelled, 'Found you!'

Laughing at the game's typically bizarre reversal, Annie hugged her son hard, savouring the pleasure of his gangly young limbs in her arms before he wrenched himself free and ran into the kitchen.

'Are you in there?' Annie called out to her father-in-law.

Appearing from the darkness with a dusty bottle in one hand while smoothing the label with the other, he didn't take his eyes from it as he said, 'That son of mine is holding out on me. He's got a 1959 Mission Haut . . . '

Annie quickly grabbed it. 'It's your Christmas present,' she muttered. 'You need to pretend you never saw it.'

Dickie's still handsome, but weathered old face lit up, even as he whispered, 'Never saw it. Putting it back right now.'

Handing it to him, she turned around to find Quin dipping a peeled quail's egg into a saucer of celery salt before stuffing it into his mouth. 'Is Dad coming back for supper?' he asked through a spray of dry yolk.

Cupping her hands around the top of his head and chin, Annie said, 'He'll be here any minute. Who else is staying to eat?'

'Just me and Dickie,' her mother replied. 'Dad's got one of his round-table meetings in town tonight so he's going to get something there.'

'Henry and I are off to see Mommie Dearest and the Delightful Other,' Julia sighed, helping herself to more wine. Though she often looked and sounded pained when talking about her mother and aunt, whose riding stables (the mother's) and boarding kennels (the aunt's) were close to Exford, she was extremely close to them. As was Dickie, whose friendship with Bob Tulley, Julia's father, went back decades, and would probably still have been a mainstay in Dickie's life had it not been brought to a painfully abrupt end when Bob had walked out on his responsibilities as a father and husband to go and live with another woman. The only good thing about that time, more than twenty years ago now, was the fact that Bob hadn't tried to take Blackfare Farm away from Celine, nor should he have when it had come to them through Celine's father. The betrayal and abandonment had, over time, brought the two families even closer together, as if Dickie and his wife, Geraldine, had felt the need to protect Celine and Julia, Ruth too when she'd set up her kennels at Blackfare. And no one knew how they'd have managed during Geraldine's final days without Celine's careful nursing and pragmatic ways.

'BTW,' Julia went on, 'the old dears are wondering if they're invited to stay on after the p.m. Flurry next week? They won't, of course, they're always too busy at the Horse and Hounds,' (Julia's name for her family home) 'but they like to be invited.'

Filling a glass of wine for herself, Annie said, 'Of course they can stay if they'd like to. We hope they do. The more the merrier.'

'I'll tell them you said that when I go over later. They're getting the decorators in after Christmas so they want me to start clearing my old room. What a jolly task that will be.'

'Are you going to have time to do the tree in the Byre?' Annie asked. 'Don't worry if you can't . . . '

'I'll have plenty of time,' Julia confirmed. 'It's being delivered tomorrow and Dickie's going to help decorate it.'

'Me too,' Quin piped up.

'Of course,' Julia agreed, making him grimace as she planted a kiss on his cheek. 'We need someone to be in charge.'

Quin laughed, knowing he was being teased but happy to go along with it. 'I don't know what any of you would do without me,' he informed them, and helped himself to another egg as he climbed on to a stool. 'Mum, where's Max? I thought he was coming home today.'

'He'll be back tomorrow,' Annie assured him. 'Did you text Sienna to find out if she'll be home for dinner?' she asked her mother.

'I didn't realize I had to,' Harriet replied, and drew her phone from the back pocket of her jeans. 'Where is she?'

'In town with friends, which reminds me I need to get her bags out of the boot.'

'I'll go,' Dickie offered.

'All done,' David declared, coming in through the door. 'They're in the hall. I'll take them up later. Hey, Harriet, something's smelling good.'

'Grandma brought the Christmas puddings over today,' Quin told him. 'They smell lush.'

David frowned as he looked down at his younger son. 'Who's that in there?' he asked, parting the curly fringe of thick fair hair, very like his own, and suddenly starting with surprise. 'Goodness, it's you,' he cried.

Laughing, Quin ruffled his own curls as he cried, 'The girls like it long, so I'm keeping it.'

With raised eyebrows David looked at Annie, who shrugged and drank more wine before taking a beer from the fridge for him.

'Where's Henry?' Julia asked, refilling her glass. 'I thought he was with you.'

'He's in the loo. Dad, can we rope you in for some assistance tomorrow? Bashy just rang to say he can't make it.'

'Loading or beating?' his father asked, clearly up for either.

'Beating.'

'Has Bashy's wife given birth yet?' Harriet wanted to know.

'It's imminent, which is why he feels he shouldn't come tomorrow.'

'Good decision,' Julia approved.

Since most men from the villages around acted as loaders and beaters – when not out shooting, hunting or fishing themselves – there was a pretty good number to draw on, but the Crayce family knew how much it meant to Dickie to feel he was coming to the rescue. He was, in fact, a director of the shooting school and could turn his hand to just about anything, and often did now he was no longer running the farm that had been in his family for three generations. He and Geraldine had handed it over to Henry and Julia six years ago, around the time Geraldine had found out her cancer was back, and had moved into the much more manageable cottage near the gates of Hanley Combe – it was where Geraldine had passed three years ago, ripping the hearts from her family. Dickie had remained there, although as often as not he was at the main house with Quin, or at Blackfare Farm, or elsewhere on the Hanley Combe estate helping out where needed. But for him there was nothing like being part of a shoot to make him feel truly valued, especially when it was being run by his sons.

'Any news from Sienna yet?' Annie asked her mother as Harriet checked a text she'd just received.

'No, it's from Dad. I'll give her half an hour and if we haven't heard then I'll ring to chivvy her along.'

'OK, I'm off for a quick shower,' David informed them. 'But before I go perhaps someone can enlighten me as to the whereabouts of my elder son?'

'He's staying with friends tonight, back tomorrow,' Annie replied, starting to lay the table.

'It'll be a girlfriend,' Quin stated knowingly.

Annie and David exchanged glances, aware of how wrong he was about that. His brother's lack of romantic interest in the opposite sex was the source of some frustration for many females of the area, since his smouldering dark eyes and curly black hair had made him the object of several crushes over his fourteen years. He had told Annie and David last year that he was gay and they couldn't have loved him more for feeling able to confide so readily in his parents.

* * *

An hour later Henry and Julia had left for the Horse and Hounds, the Blums and the Rowbothams (old friends from Simonsbath and Monksilver) had popped in for a rowdy few drinks and left, and now the meal was ready but there was still no word from Sienna.

'She can be so inconsiderate at times,' Annie remarked irritably. 'She's probably turned her phone off so she doesn't have to argue about what time to be picked up.'

'We should go ahead and eat,' David decided. 'We can always warm some up for her later.'

'Grandpa, can we go on manoeuvres after supper?' Quin wanted to know. 'It's really cool going out in the rain with our torches and Dad's got a shoot early tomorrow so he can't come.' It was David who'd started the nighttime expeditions over the moor when Max and Sienna were small, teaching them how to set up camp in all winds and weathers, how to start a fire for food and warmth and most of all how to read and follow a map. David set great store by being able to read a map, not that he needed one on Exmoor for he seemed to know it like the back of his hand. If it was summer they'd often 'go on manoeuvres' as a family, for Annie loved the outdoors too, and there was something very romantic about lying under the stars or being huddled in a tent with David, who always seemed to have everything perfectly under control.

'Can we, Grandpa?' Quin asked again.

'It's too foggy,' Annie told him. 'And I thought we were going to write to Santa?'

'I've already done it, and anyway, he's not real. He's Dad.'

David looked shocked, and began checking himself out as if he were starting to morph.

'You're funny,' Quin told him without a laugh.

'So, what are you hoping Santa will bring you?' Harriet asked, starting to dish up the goulash.

Taking no time to think, Quin said, 'I want a Sphero Bolt robot that works with an app.'

Harriet's eyes crossed as David looked at Annie who'd heard this before but still had no idea what it was, so Dickie answered.

'You can order it online from John Lewis,' he informed them, as if he knew all about it.

'You definitely can,' Quin agreed excitedly. 'It costs one hundred and fifty pounds and they can send it next day to make sure it's here in time for Christmas.'

'That's good to know,' David commented, reaching for his mobile as a text arrived. As he frowned, Annie said, 'Is it her?'

'No, Henry,' he replied. 'He's advising us to go into town the back way if we haven't gone for Sienna yet. Apparently there's been an accident on Westleigh Heights and nothing can get through.' As his eyes went to Annie's, she knew they were experiencing the same tangle of apprehension and fear. Was Sienna somehow involved? Grant Peterson had passed his test last month, he might have borrowed his father's car.

'Stop,' her mother chided, as though reading their minds. 'You're jumping to conclusions and that won't get us anywhere. Try calling one of her friends to see if they're with her.'

Annie did, but half the usual suspects weren't answering and the other half hadn't seen her. 'What's going on?' she said to David, as if he ought to know.

'She's being a teenager just freed from school for Christmas,' Dickie decided, tucking into his meal.

'I'll see if I can find out more about this accident,' David said, getting to his feet. 'If nothing else at least it could rule out her being involved.'

Quin was staring round-eyed at his mother. 'Do you think she's dead?' he asked worriedly.

'Oh Quin,' she cried. 'No, of course not. We just need to find out where she is, that's all.'

It turned out a camper van had hit a patch of ice and skidded into a ditch, no other vehicles involved, so at least there was some relief there. But by the time another hour had passed and there was still no news, a palpable sense of concern was creeping into the room.

'This really isn't like her,' Harriet commented for the umpteenth time, and Annie wanted to shout at her to shut up and stop being right. It wasn't helping, it was making things worse because it just wasn't like Sienna to be out of contact for this long, especially when she knew her parents would be worrying.

It was gone ten o'clock and Dickie had taken Quin up to bed by the time David's phone rang and they saw Sienna's name come up.

Annie watched him click on, still not able to relax in case something had happened to her, or someone else was using the phone. David put the call on speaker.

'Dad?'

'Are you OK?' he asked shortly. 'We've been worried.'

'Sorry, I know, I mean . . . '

'Where are you? Why didn't you call?'

'They've only just given me my phone back.'

'What? Who's they?'

'Is Mum with you? She's going to go mental so you've got to be on my side, Dad, OK?'

His eyes went to Annie as he said, 'Just tell me what's happened and we'll take it from there.'

CHAPTER TWO

Sienna might be leggy, beautiful and obsessively proud of her blonde beach waves, but Annie was in no doubt that she wouldn't want to be photographed for Instagram right now. Apart from the smudged mascara and teenage spots showing through the last vestiges of concealer, she looked as guilty and bedraggled as anyone might who'd just come out of police custody – and she didn't smell all that good, either. Kind of earthy, acidy, sweaty and there might even be vomit in the mix.

Annie's father, Francis, had driven her home – they'd caught him before he'd left town – but apparently she hadn't told him anything about what had happened, not only because the fog had meant he needed to focus on the road, but because one of his gossipy old crones was also in the car. He'd dropped her off only minutes ago, collecting Harriet and Dickie at the same time, all of them guessing their granddaughter wouldn't want an audience to the upcoming scene with her parents.

Waiting only until her boots were off and she was seated at the kitchen table, David said, 'Was it drugs?'

Sienna's head snapped up from fussing Cassie. '*No!*' she protested angrily. 'I knew you'd think that! Why do you always think the worst of me?'

In spite of her attitude it was clear she was still worried, and so she should be, Annie thought, her run-in with the law having ended up in custody.

'So, what happened?' David asked, his tone not quite as sharp now. Drugs were his cut-off, he wouldn't tolerate any involvement on any level and his children well knew it, so now that was out of the way he was prepared to adopt a more lenient approach.

'I don't want to talk about it,' she answered sulkily.

Annie said, 'Well that's not an option, I'm afraid, because we do. Now please answer the question.'

Sienna shot her a hostile glance from under wet lashes and continued to stroke the dog's head. 'OK, it was really dumb,' she said finally. 'I didn't want to do it . . . ' Her sky-blue eyes flashed defiantly as they returned to her mother. 'I wasn't even there,' she cried, as if Annie had just accused her of it. 'I was outside . . . '

'Sen,' David interrupted. 'Start from the beginning.'

'I'm trying,' she insisted, 'but I don't really know whose idea it was. It just happened and the next thing, like half an hour later, we were being dragged out of Nando's like we were serious criminals, for God's sake.'

'Had you been drinking?' Annie wanted to know.

'*No!*'

Not sure she believed her, Annie held back as David said, '*Why* did they drag you out?'

'Because we stole a bloody teddy bear,' she cried angrily. 'Can you believe it? A lousy frigging teddy bear and the next thing we know we're being handcuffed and stuffed into the back of a police van like we'd just been rioting or beating up the homeless.'

David and Annie exchanged glances.

'Why on earth did you steal a teddy bear?' Annie asked, confused.

'I didn't! I told you, I waited outside.'

'OK, so, a teddy bear was stolen. Who took it?'

'Camilla and Toby. They wanted to wind up the old grump who owns the shop. You know what he's like, always shouting at people. It's weird that he sells kids' stuff when he's such a misery guts.'

Frowning, David said, 'Let me get this straight, *you* were arrested for *not* stealing a . . . teddy bear?'

'That's right,' Sienna cut in, clearly relieved that at least her father had got it.

'But she was there,' Annie stated quickly, sensing he might be about to laugh. 'She was involved, and that makes her an accomplice to theft.'

'It was just a bloody teddy bear,' Sienna exclaimed indignantly. 'And it wasn't even a big one . . . '

'It doesn't matter what size it was,' Annie shouted over her. 'You were creating mischief and stress for an old man . . . '

'Dad!' Sienna implored. 'Can you please tell her to chill.'

'You're going back there to apologize tomorrow,' Annie informed her.

'No way!'

'I'll take you myself, and I think you should buy a bear – an expensive one – from your savings and then ask him to donate it to a children's charity.'

'Oh puh-lease. As if I'm going to do that.'

'It's exactly what you're going to do, young lady.' Annie's mind was made up and she knew David wouldn't argue with her, no matter how manipulatively Sienna went to work on him. 'You haven't been brought up to treat people like this,' she ranted on. 'What if you'd brought on a heart attack, or he'd slipped coming after you and injured himself? You really didn't think any of it through, did you?'

Sienna appealed to her father again. 'It was just a bit of fun that went wrong,' she whined. 'That's all.'

'But Mum's right,' he replied. 'You need to make amends . . . '

'Even though I wasn't the one who took it?' she protested furiously.

'You were there, and if you do the right thing by going to apologize hopefully the others will too. I take it they've also been released? Hang on, at your age, why weren't we contacted to let us know you were in custody?'

Shamefacedly, Sienna said, 'They called Camilla's mum, so she came to the station. I asked her to let me tell you. Anyway, Grant's as mad as I am about it. He didn't go into the shop either, but it was like we were serious criminals the way we got fingerprinted, photographed, DNA'd and chucked into cells.'

'You've been in a cell?' David laughed.

'You had your DNA taken?' Annie asked.

'I think it's normal procedure following arrest,' David told her. 'I'll call the station tomorrow to find out what, if anything, is going to happen next. Meantime, if you're not going to eat that goulash, Sen, you should go and get out of those clothes and take a shower. You smell like a public toilet.'

'Charming,' she retorted, and getting up from the table she stalked imperiously out of the kitchen.

'And you're grounded until Christmas,' Annie called after her.

'In your dreams,' she was heard to mutter. At the foot of the stairs she shouted, 'Dad, will you come and tuck me in before you go to bed?'

'I've got to be up at five for a shoot,' he told her, 'so I'm going now. If you want to talk it'll have to wait until I'm back tomorrow.'

Knowing how much she would like the last word, they waited for a response, and sure enough it came. 'Funny how I'm never anyone's priority around here,' she commented sourly.

Ignoring her, Annie started to clear up while David let Cassie outside to do her last business of the day.

After David left at five the next morning, Annie turned over and snuggled back into the duvet, thrilled she didn't have to get up in the dark. She must have drifted off for a while, because when she opened her eyes again the first glimmers of daylight were creeping through the curtains and she could hear a number of cars coming and going outside. Guessing that one or more of their freelance instructors were about to hit the stands with clients, she finally got up, and sure enough, by the time she'd pulled on her running gear and jogged over in that direction, six regular shooters were doing their best to blast clay pigeons out of the early morning mist. Pull, bang! Pull, bang! It was a sound as familiar to her as her children's voices.

She ran on, following a trail alongside the woods, the trees glistening gold and amber in breakthroughs of sunlight, past the clay rabbit shoot, the high tower and the quad bike park until she reached the lily pond Geraldine had created, where her memorial bench was now nestled between two rhododendron bushes.

How she still missed her mother-in-law; how they all did.

Starting out on to more open moorland she began to climb.

It was hard for her to put into words how much she loved it here, being so close with nature – sometimes feeling as though she could touch the sky, or hear the ground swelling and breathing beneath her feet. The bitingly cold air, the dank, acrid scents of moss and lichen, the vast swaths of gorse and heather, the dip and rise of harshly rugged terrain, the gush of streams and twittering of birds; there was always so much for her senses to feast on that time and miles could pass with her hardly noticing.

She couldn't be out for long this morning. There was a lot to do today, but as she reached the peak of their land and took a moment to drink in the view she spotted a fully grown stag loping slowly across the heath. He appeared so mighty and free and sleek that she couldn't bring herself to look away and felt a beat of surprise and pleasure as he glanced over his shoulder, almost as if he'd sensed her there. Laughing at herself, she waved out, wanting him to know she was friendly. Whether he did or not was impossible to tell, he simply stood for a while staring at her, seeming to take her in, before continuing on his way.

As the stag disappeared into a gully she turned around to look down at the vision of Hanley Combe appearing Avalon-like through the mist below. She felt the draw of it in her steps as she began heading home, for part of the way a pair of hawks soaring and swooping overhead. When she reached the woods a solitary doe skittered and leapt out of her way, reminding her of the stag and those few special moments when they'd observed one another.

At the stands a couple of the shooters waved, and someone shouted something she didn't catch, but she didn't go over, only smiled and waved back not wanting to break her pace until she reached the house.

An hour later, showered and dressed, she put a sulking Sienna in the car and drove her into Kesterly to make her apologies to Mr Chaudry – and to buy a twenty-five-pound teddy bear, which she duly donated back to him to give to a charity of his choice. By the time they left the shop they were both far more upset than relieved it was over. Apparently Mr Chaudry was constantly being targeted by yobs and drunks who smashed his windows or daubed them with highly offensive graffiti just for being Pakistani, and only last week someone had thrown a firecracker through the door terrifying the life out of his wife, who had cancer.

'Oh God, oh God,' Sienna groaned wretchedly, as they crossed the arcade to Glory Days, the vintage emporium that both she and her mother loved. 'It's making me think of Granny Gerry and how it would have been if someone did that to her when she was sick.'

Thinking the same, Annie said, 'That was a hard way to learn that everyone deserves respect, no matter who they are, and that poor man has enough on his plate coping with racism and his wife's ill health without fools like you . . . '

'Please don't lecture,' Sienna cried desperately. 'I said I'm sorry and I really am. I just wish it could make a difference for his wife. Do you think she's dying?'

'I've no idea, but let's hope not.'

'I'm going to text the others to tell them they have to apologize and contribute to charity as well.'

'That's good,' and pushing open the door to Glory Days Annie decided they could park the issue for the time being, and start focusing on some Christmas shopping while they waited for Max's train to come in.

'I still have to get something for Grandma and Julia,' Sienna said, going straight for the glittering jewellery displays, quite probably with herself in mind. 'What do you think of these?' she asked, holding up a pair of chandelier-style earrings.

Annie glanced up from a rack of evening dresses – now who was shopping for themselves? – and shook her head.

'I meant for me,' Sienna told her, 'but I guess they're a bit out there. So, what sort of thing do you think Julia would like? By the way, has she made up with Dad yet?'

Confused, Annie threw her a look. 'What do you mean?'

Sienna shrugged. 'I heard them rowing last weekend. Or that's what it sounded like.'

'Where were they?'

'In the shop, at the Byre.'

'And it was definitely Dad, not Uncle Henry? They sound very similar.'

'Duh, I think I know the difference between my dad and my uncle. Anyway, I probably got it wrong, so don't let's labour it. This looks like a really cool scarf for Grandma. She likes yellow and I think she lost her other one, unless she's found it by now.'

'I don't think she has, so it's a good suggestion,' Annie responded, happy to go with the change of subject since it was highly likely Sienna had got it wrong about David and Julia. She'd never known them to argue before, or not seriously anyway, just the snappy sort of disagreements that occasionally broke out between siblings, which was more or less what they were. 'What do you think of this cute woolly beret for your aunt?' she suggested, holding it up. 'It would make a change from a riding hat.'

Sienna laughed. 'It sure would, and red is a great colour for her. Look, there's this lovely muffler we could get to go with it. I only wish the grandpas were as easy to buy for.'

As they continued to browse and Sienna filled a basket with all sorts of trinkets and treasures while managing a simultaneous texting session with her friends, Annie fell into conversation with the shop's owner, Leanne. By the time they were ready to leave she'd treated herself to a slinky sandy-gold, low-backed evening gown to wear to the black-tie New Year's Eve ball thrown annually at Fairley Vale Hall.

'Dad's going to totally love you in that,' Sienna informed her. 'But we'll have to get you some sexy Spanx to go under it – or you could go with no undies at all.' She winked at Leanne, who laughed approvingly.

Half an hour later, after collecting Max from the station and locking his luggage into the boot of the car, the three of them battled the wind whipping in from the channel to go to the Seafront Café for lunch.

No sooner had they settled into a window booth and ordered hot drinks than Max declared, 'I can't believe you were arrested *and* put in a cell. That is totally awesome . . . '

'It's nothing of the sort,' Annie protested, 'so don't encourage her.'

'I'm not saying she has to do it again, but . . . '

'Why don't you choose what you're going to eat,' Annie interrupted, shoving a menu his way.

'Burger and chips,' he replied without hesitation.

'Same for me,' Sienna confirmed. 'Are you joining in the Flurry next week?' she asked him.

'Too right, I mean if Dad'll let me. I know it depends how many guns are out. Are you doing it?'

'Of course, and no way am I paying a hundred and thirty quid,' she informed her mother.

Max spluttered on a laugh. 'Are they threatening to charge you?'

'Not yet, but it's a good idea,' Annie responded, smiling sweetly at her daughter. 'I could wish the two of you weren't so keen on guns.'

'It's not our fault we grew up with them,' Max pointed out.

'Or that you've got a thing against them,' Sienna added. 'Which is totally hypocritical, as I keep telling you, given how rich you and Dad have got off the back of them.'

'Hardly rich,' Annie protested, although they were certainly doing well. 'I don't mind you shooting clays, I guess, I just don't like the idea of you killing things.'

'I'll bear that in mind next time Quin raids my bedroom,' Max quipped. 'How is the little man?'

'As adorable as ever,' Annie assured him. 'Just like you, my love.'

'You've always preferred the boys,' Sienna sighed.

'And who can blame her?' Max grinned, and because he seemed to be growing more adorably handsome every time she saw him, Annie's heart tripped as she laughed. She wasn't someone to torment herself with all the bad things that could happen to her children, but she did occasionally fear for how much more difficult life might be for Max, being gay. Still things had changed a lot these past few years, people were far more tolerant, and what was the point in worrying until she had to?

'Oh God, I've got some news,' he suddenly announced. 'It's even more awesome than your arrest,' he told Sienna. 'I can't believe I forgot about it till now. Wait for it, I've only been approached by an agency in London to ask if I'd be interested in modelling.'

Sienna's eyes lit up with envy and awe as Annie's darkened.

'How do they know about you?' Annie asked carefully.

'Through my Instagram account. I guess they trawl everything, you know, on a talent search . . . '

'All the agencies do that,' Sienna informed him, as if she were far more in the know than he was. 'Did they say what sort of modelling? I'll bet it's nude.'

Annie caught the wink so knew she was being wound up, at least she hoped so.

'They say it's sportswear,' Max told them. 'But obvs, because of my age, I have to have parental consent. And if I do go for an audition, you or Dad or one of the grandparents will have to come with me.'

'Is it something you'd like to do?' Annie asked, not entirely sure how she felt about this, but at the moment not great.

'Of course it is,' Sienna jumped in. 'Who wouldn't want to be a model? Especially a brainy one. It would be so cool if you did it. I'd be like, my brother is the next David Gandy, eat your heart out, bitch!'

Annie said, 'Who's David Gandy?'

Sienna was aghast. 'You can't be serious.'

Annie wasn't, but she enjoyed baiting her daughter. 'So how about Max answering for himself?' she suggested.

He shrugged. 'I don't know if it's really my thing,' he confessed. 'What do you reckon Dad'll say?'

Annie gave it some thought. 'I don't suppose we'll know until we ask him,' she replied, realizing she actually had no idea. David could be unpredictable at times, which was partly why she loved him, and partly why he could drive her mad. 'The big issue will be school, obviously,' she continued. 'We're not going to agree to anything that'll get in the way of that.'

Max looked up as a waitress appeared next to their table, but before Annie could speak, he said, 'Mum, will you please order your own chips or, I know you, you'll end up stealing mine.'

With a laugh, Annie added a portion of fries to her avocado with poached egg on toast.

'Has Uncle Henry got many safaris on before Christmas?' Max wondered, glancing up from his mobile.

'A few,' Annie replied. It was almost always Henry who conducted the Exmoor game drives, or Dickie if he was feeling up to it. 'Why?'

'Because I want to go out with him.'

'Really?'

'Well, I thought it would be a good way to show my mate Justin around, if he comes to stay. Would it be all right if he does?'

'Do we know Justin?' she asked.

'He does, which is the point,' Sienna answered.

'He's a friend from school,' Max told her. 'He just started this term. He was living in South Africa before.'

Sienna scoffed a laugh. 'And you're thinking of taking him on a safari *here*?'

Flipping her off, he said to Annie, 'He's a good guy. I

think you'll like him, and he's into shoots so Dad definitely will.'

Annie said, 'OK, I'm sure it'll be fine if he comes. Just let me know when.'

Having three children brought its challenges on many fronts, although on the whole they were good kids who never caused much trouble, apart from when they were stealing teddy bears and getting arrested, of course. But mercifully, that hadn't turned out anywhere near as bad as it might have, thanks to Mr Chaudry not wanting to press charges.

Later that night, after an evening spent entertaining Pam and Rupert Gillycrest who'd dropped in because they were passing and had ended up staying for supper, Annie was massaging David's shoulders before they got into bed. He was as knotted as ever following a day's shoot, especially when they were as challenging as the one he'd just had, mostly thanks to a rogue client who'd apparently done it all before so wasn't keen to follow all the sporting estate's rules, or those laid down by David.

'The silly bastard's going to blow someone's head off if he carries on the way he's going,' David grumbled, dropping his head forward so she could work on his neck. 'What the hell kind of shoot has he been on where they don't insist on breaking the gun? It was BS, of course, because they don't exist. And he definitely doesn't have a way with dogs, does he Cass?'

The dozing Labrador glanced up from her bed in the corner of the room and gave a lethargic tail wag before closing her eyes again. She'd had a busy day too.

'My sentiments exactly,' he told her. 'Let's make sure

we don't take bookings from him again. One accident and we could find ourselves being closed down for good.' Lifting his head up he said, 'I thought Henry was going to deck him at one point and I wasn't really up for stopping him.'

'How many did he bag?' Annie asked, kneading his shoulders again.

'Ha, that was the best bit – he might have a knack with clays but when it comes to the real thing he's all over the damned place.'

'So, the answer's none?'

'Exactly, but the others made up for it, and I'm pretty sure he won't be invited to join their party again.' He was staring at the new dress hanging on the wardrobe door now and murmured admiringly, 'Is that for New Year's Eve?'

'It is,' she confirmed, with a gentle tap on his back to let him know she was done. 'I thought you'd like it.'

'Love it.' He got up to go and take a closer look. 'Is this the front?' he asked, holding it up to show the draped back.

Laughing, she said, 'Maybe, when it's just the two of us.'

His eyes shone as he said, 'I'll look forward to that,' and replacing it on the wardrobe door he began to take off his clothes. 'So, Sienna tells me you got things sorted at the teddy bear shop,' he said, lowering his jeans and tossing them towards the laundry corner. 'Sad about the man's wife.'

'Indeed, and about the racism.' With a sigh she added, 'I detest what's going on in this country. Luckily Sienna and Max do too, so at least we won't have white supremacy or some other vile hate group to be dealing with in the future. However, we do need to discuss Max's modelling.'

'Let's see what comes of it and deal with it then,' he replied, heading into the bathroom. 'To be honest, I don't think he's that taken with it.'

After putting her phone on charge beside the bed, Annie slipped under the duvet and was trying to remember what else she wanted to talk to David about when a text arrived from Sienna's bedroom.

Just to let you know the others are all going into town to apologize to Mr C tomorrow and I'm going with them. Did Dad talk to the police, do you know?

Waiting until David was in bed she passed the phone over for him to read the message and watched him text back, *He did, and def no charges being brought.*

'She'll be glad to have that doubly confirmed,' Annie said, returning the phone to her bedside table. 'I don't think we need to worry about her being a recidivist,' she added wryly.

He laughed and shut down his own phone before turning out the light. 'I hope you don't want sex,' he yawned, 'because I'm done in tonight, which is a shame, because it was the thought of it that kept me going today.'

'It'll be a lovely way to wake up,' she murmured, nestling in behind him.

Moments later she could tell from his breathing that he was already fast asleep, which was good, he was tired and now she'd remembered what else she wanted to mention to him she was glad she hadn't brought it up. There was probably no need to go there at all, for she'd watched him and Julia during the evening, and they'd been as easy with one another as ever. No undercurrent of tension or barbed comments, very little contact at all.

Julia had talked mostly with Pam Gillycrest, an old friend from way back when who often helped out at the horse and donkey refuge, while David had been caught up in the day's shoot with the men. Dickie had clearly enjoyed every minute of it, in spite of the arrogant ass who'd caused David to send Henry to the game cart to cool off, and Dickie now had a couple of braces of pheasants at his place ready to pluck and prepare for anyone who wanted them. As his sons liked to tell him, he was the best pheasant plucker in a plucking pheasant world – and of course they rarely got it out right. The children never did, which was why they enjoyed saying it so much.

So, if there had been some sort of disagreement between David and Julia – and if there had, Annie suspected David had once again refused to persuade Henry that his injured leg wasn't strong enough for several day-long shoots in a week – they'd clearly moved on from it now.

CHAPTER THREE

The next couple of weeks were as hectic as they always were around Christmas with virtually daily shoots, a surprising number of game drives, the Festive Flurry – a tremendous success again – plus all the shopping, baking, wrapping and partying.

Christmas Eve turned out to be as drear as nature could make it with visibility down to a few feet on the higher ground, and giant white sacks of sand and salt appearing at many road junctions, set down by the National Parks Authority for farmers to grit the road when the snow and ice came. In spite of the weather they all dutifully trotted off to church for Midnight Mass, as much to support Annie, her mother and Julia who were singing with the choir, as to celebrate the Christian element of the season.

The next morning was a chaos of present-opening, champagne corks popping, turkey-stuffing, veg-peeling and table-laying. Everyone had a part to play, including Max's friend Justin, who'd joined them for the next few days before flying out to join his parents at his grandparent's home in Cape Town for New Year's. Whether there was an actual relationship going on between them Annie and David couldn't tell, and didn't like to ask, unlike Sienna who apparently received the gentle brotherly response of 'Off you fuck and mind your own business.'

'Which means there is,' she informed her parents, 'and so I think you're presiding over underage sex.'

Deciding it was best not to run with that, Annie and David simply carried on as they often did when she was being a prima donna, or a pain (same thing really), and pointed her in the direction of the nearest cliff edge with an invitation to go and fling herself off.

'I might just do that one of these days,' she warned, snuggling on to a sofa with her grandma. 'What kind of parents tell you to go and top yourself?' she grumbled, raising Harriet's arm so she was inside a hug.

'That's his fourth whisky,' Harriet commented, as Annie's father, Francis, looking very dapper in his purple paper hat and new yellow tie crafted into a bow by Sienna, helped himself to another generous slug of King's Ginger from the cut-crystal decanter someone had put at his elbow, probably him.

'Hey Grandpa, feeling good?' Sienna called out, saluting him with her own glass of wine.

'Never better,' he assured her. 'Where are the boys? I thought we were going to watch a movie together.'

'I'm here,' Quin told him, not even glancing up from his robot. 'Do you want to play with me? I can teach you how, if you like.'

'Wonderful,' he responded cheerily. 'Where's Dickie? Let's get him to play too.'

'I'll send him in,' Annie said on her way out to the kitchen.

When she got there she found Henry and his father in quiet, but what appeared to be heated, conversation over the Christmas pudding. 'Everything all right?' she asked, going to open a window to let out the steam.

'Everything's good,' Henry assured her. 'Wonderful lunch, as usual.' His eyes were slightly blurry (thanks to the wine), but his normally healthy complexion seemed unusually peaky.

She smiled as he came to embrace her, loving it when he was affectionate with her and she hugged him back hard.

'Don't let me interrupt anything,' David commented, coming in from the wine cellar with two more bottles to pop into the fridge. 'Dad, if you put much more brandy on that pudding you'll set the entire place on fire.'

Looking down in surprise, Dickie quickly stepped back from his floating pudding and gestured for his elder son to do the honours.

'Henry, why don't you take your eyebrows off, while I sort the dishwasher?' David suggested.

And as if everything were normal between younger son and father, no angry words, no moment of tension, Henry lit the pudding with a whoosh while Dickie went ahead to announce its arrival.

'What's going on with them?' Annie whispered when she and David were alone.

He glanced over his shoulder to make sure no one was listening. 'Now isn't the time to get into it,' he said softly, 'but Henry's got it into his head that he wants out of the marriage.'

Annie couldn't have been more shocked, or upset. 'But I thought . . . That doesn't . . . Why?'

'To be honest, it's not the first time it's come up,' he admitted. 'I didn't say anything before because he seemed to get over it, and I thought everything was OK again.'

'Why wasn't it OK?'

He shrugged. 'I didn't ask for details. Has Julia said anything to you?'

'No, not a word. I don't suppose it's what you and she were arguing about a couple of weeks ago, in the shop?'

He looked baffled.

'Sienna said she heard you,' she explained.

He was still frowning, clearly trying to recall what Sienna might have been talking about. 'All I can think of,' he said, 'is that she heard me telling Julia to cool it.'

'Why? What . . . '

'She was trying *again* to get me to stop Henry from doing full-day shoots. You know how she worries about him overdoing it, and she thinks it's too long for him to be out. I guess I was too sharp when I told her to back off. That's probably the bit Sienna heard. I apologized after and Julia was her usual forgiving self. Where is she, by the way?'

'She went with the boys to walk the dogs,' Annie replied, feeling for how upset Julia might have been by David's words, while not able to get started on Henry's problems. She stifled a yawn and changed the subject. 'Do you think anyone would notice if we disappeared for an hour?' she said. 'We've been awake since four thirty, thanks to our darling youngest.'

Drying his hands on a dish towel, he said, 'Well, I definitely want to pass on the pudding, at least for now, and as I'm keen to see you in your Christmas present . . .'

Her eyes reflected the teasing light in his. 'I guess there was no self-interest at play when you got me that,' she murmured, referring to the transparent cream silk teddy he'd presented her with before they'd come downstairs to open other gifts.

'None at all,' he promised, kissing her. 'Or maybe just a bit.'

'Oh, no,' Quin groaned from the doorway, 'they're at it again, Sen! Can you please get a room, you two?'

Laughing as much at the source as at the advice that usually came from his sister, David said, 'Exactly what we had in mind. Can we leave you in charge?'

'Sure. As long as you promise to play Twister later. It's a tradition.'

'It is indeed, so you have my word. Just don't go throwing up on it again like you did last year.' It was true, Quin had laughed so hard that his dinner had staged an explosive return, and it was quite probable no one was ever going to let him forget it.

The rest of Christmas Day played out much as it usually did with naps, games, movies and Julia's mother and aunt coming to join them for a couple of enjoyable cocktail hours, unable to spare any longer with so many animals to attend to. The stables and the kennels were full due to the time of year, and as good as their support staff might be, they needed to be close to ensure that everything ran smoothly.

The next day, in keeping with a long-established Crayce family tradition, they joined a large group of friends at Wincanton Races. Henry and Julia weren't present; they preferred to ride with the hunt on Boxing Day, following a previously set trail to comply with the law. Or so they said, and Annie didn't delve into it. She was just glad to know that they were spending the day together, and when Julia rang later to say they were having a quiet evening at home, just the two of them, Annie couldn't have felt more relieved to hear it.

On the twenty-seventh the men gathered at Hanley Combe to play poker, another tradition, while Annie, her mother and Julia met up with ten or twelve female friends – it depended who had visitors for the period – for a long walk in the morning followed by lunch at a pub. It was a treat they felt was richly deserved after all the hard work of Christmas: time to blow away the cobwebs, work off some calories (before taking in more) and a welcome hiatus from worrying about kids, husbands, jobs and most definitely Agas and dishwashers.

This morning's hike was due to take place along the Meanders to Nettleton Manor, passing the Murder House on the way. This was always a source of fascination for the visitors, and Julia never failed to get a kick out of explaining how such an exquisite thatched cottage had come by its inglorious sobriquet. She'd embellished the story shamelessly over the years, so that it was no longer simply about the mysterious dispatch of a mother and her two spinster daughters. It had now acquired all manner of lurid and thrilling detail with which to entertain her audience.

Today, because no one wanted to brave the driving winds and rain, Julia's wicked rewriting of history was put on hold and they went straight to the pub.

Nestled as it was in the quaint village of Monksilver, where thatched roofs and a thirteenth-century church were much cherished and photographed, the Notley Arms was very dear to Annie's heart. It was where she and David had met, almost twenty-four years ago, although at the time it had been nothing like the desirable eatery it was now, catering largely for tourists and sportsmen. Back then it had been more of a pie and a pint sort of place for locals and hikers, and it was while there one evening with her parents, who'd recently purchased a weekend cottage in the village, that Annie, a student aged eighteen and annoyed at having been made to leave her London friends for a couple of days, had looked up to find herself being frankly regarded by a strikingly handsome young man who was in a group at the bar. Although she'd tried to scowl discouragingly, she'd ended up smiling despite herself and then blushed when, to her amazement, he'd come over to introduce himself.

From that very day they might have been inseparable, had David not recently completed his officer training at Sandhurst and been commissioned into the army's elite Parachute Regiment. However, it didn't deter them. They simply made sure they saw one another at every opportunity, spent the entirety of his leave together either in London or on Exmoor, and even when he was deployed overseas they spoke most days. It was only after he'd applied and was selected for the airborne rapid reaction force, the Pathfinders, that communication became more sporadic – it was before mobile phones – and even ceased completely for short periods of time, leaving her with no idea of where in the world he was.

During these early years she'd continued with her English degree at UCL, sharing a house with friends in Balham and preparing to become an army wife. However, David's dream of a lifelong career in the forces turned out to be not what he wanted after all. For all sorts of reasons that he'd never discussed, things hadn't gone as well for him with the Pathfinders as he'd expected. Following his discharge, they'd rented a small flat in Clapham while he took a job in the City working as an analyst at a hedge fund firm that belonged to the uncle of one of the Moor-auders. Within two years, in spite of his wildly unpredictable behaviour and heavy bouts of drinking, he'd made enough to put a down payment on the one hundred acres of farmland that his father was selling, and so had begun his new dream of starting a shooting school on Exmoor.

And now here they were a couple of decades later, early troubles all but forgotten, mortgage paid off long ago, business thriving, marriage stronger than ever, and though it hadn't been Annie's dream back then to spend her life in this remote part of the country, she couldn't imagine ever wanting to be anywhere else. Even her parents who'd sold both the cottage in Monksilver and their Richmond home five years ago to retire to a picturesque manse on Westleigh Heights, much closer to Kesterly-on-Sea, claimed to feel more at home in the area than they had in London.

'Penny for them,' her mother whispered as they found their places at the long table that had been specially set for them in the pub's cosy main bar. With its log fires blazing away in both hearths, colourfully lit Christmas tree, berry-speckled garlands, flickering candles and cheeky sprigs of mistletoe it was the perfect place to be at this time of year. 'Reminiscing, by any chance?'

'Kind of,' Annie smiled, waving to Julia as she came in the door looking extremely fetching in her new red beret and matching muffler. No sign of her mother and aunt, but they often said they were coming and then some crisis or other forced them to back out at the last minute.

'Oh good, Jules is here,' Harriet said, following Annie's greeting. 'She thought she was going down with something yesterday. Are you OK dear?' she asked as Julia joined them.

'Never better,' Julia replied brightly, 'but poor Henry's struggling. I told him to give me a call if the poker gets too much and he needs to go home.'

'I'm sure David or one of the others can take him,' Annie told her.

'Ah, but they won't hang around to care for him when he gets there. OK, I know you're going to get on my case about smothering him, but who really wants to be on their own when they're ill?'

Annie and her mother exchanged glances as they said in unison, 'Me?'

Julia laughed. 'OK, maybe I do too. Anyway, I don't think we three should be sitting together, given how often we see one another.'

She was right, and it was no hardship to split up given what good friends they were amongst. In no time at all, the wine was flowing and hilarious Christmas confidences were under way.

By the time they left more than two hours later Annie felt the same as she did most years after one of their post-Christmas indulgences, the wrong side of tipsy and deeply thankful that she had such a wonderful family. Some of the ghastly stories she'd just heard about hostile in-laws or rude and rebellious children must surely make the period more of a nightmare for some than a celebration.

'It's why we call Hanley Combe the Little House on the Prairie,' Cathy Rowbotham teased her as they went for their coats.

'Please tell me that's not true,' Annie groaned.

'It's not,' Cathy laughed, 'but maybe we should. Who's coming to pick you up?'

'I've no idea, but I've sent a text so hopefully someone will head over this way.'

'I brought my car,' Julia reminded her, 'so I'll drive you back. Just let David know we're on our way.'

'Pam Gillycrest has offered to take me,' Harriet told them. 'It'll give us a chance to talk food banks since I've offered to help out, starting in January.'

After embracing the others, most of whom they'd catch up with again at the New Year's ball, Annie slipped into the passenger seat of Henry's Range Rover and gave a satisfied sigh as Julia started the engine. 'That was fun, wasn't it?' she said, after texting David. 'And no word from Henry, so I guess he's surviving?'

Accepting the tease good-naturedly, Julia said, 'He's either feeling OK, or he's crashed out on one of the sofas at yours. I guess we'll find out soon enough.' With a chuckle she added, 'Listening to some of those stories over lunch made me realize how blessed we are with our family.'

Experiencing a surge of affection for her sister-in-law, Annie turned to look at her and felt a stab of concern to think that Henry might not be as content in his marriage as she'd believed him to be. It would break Julia's dear and very tender heart if he decided to leave her, but Annie wasn't prepared to believe that he would, for she was certain that Henry cared deeply for his unquestionably devoted second wife. The trouble was, there was never any knowing what went on behind closed doors, much less inside a marriage, as she well knew, although she'd never once felt afraid that David might leave her.

Deciding not to broach the subject unless Julia did, she said, 'I noticed you chatting quite a bit to Chrissie Slater. Did she have anything interesting to say?' Although she tried to hide it, Annie had never been overly fond of Chrissie, one of the original Moor-auders, probably because of the way Chrissie looked at her sometimes, as if she knew something Annie didn't, and the something was most likely about David. Annie had even asked David once if she was imagining things, and he'd assured her she was, although she hadn't really expected him to say anything else. If he and Chrissie shared a secret neither of them was likely to admit it if they wanted it to stay that way, and now, rather than give Chrissie the satisfaction of trying to find out what it was she might know, she'd opted to pretend not to notice the smug little smiles and quizzically raised eyebrows.

As Julia accelerated out of the village and up over the hill towards Wind Whistle Lane and Galloping Bottom, handling the large vehicle with her usual ease, she said, 'Interesting? Not especially, but it's always lovely to see her, you know we all go back a very long way. Of course you do, but she is rather fixated on her work.'

'Remind me again what she does?' Annie knew very well, but would rather feign indifference.

'She's something top-notch in a publishing house. I don't know what her actual title is, but she definitely likes to name drop.'

Remembering that from her own brief conversations with Chrissie, Annie reflected on what else she knew about her, but it didn't amount to much more than the fact that she used to spend her summers on Exmoor as a child, when she had become an honorary Moor-auder. Sometime in her thirties she'd inherited her aunt and uncle's place close to the top of Porlock Hill, and after fixing it up she and her husband had become regular visitors for high days and holidays, so were often a part of the social scene during those times. 'What big names did she treat you to this year?' Annie asked with a sigh.

Julia groaned as she rolled her eyes. 'Actually, I hadn't heard of half of them, but I believe there was a politician in the mix and some Hollywood actor. She showed me photographs of herself with them, but I'm afraid I was still none the wiser. Not my thing. Now, if it had been Charlotte Dujardin or Michael Jung, she'd have had me at the first hurdle.'

Annie laughed. 'However, knowing you, you pretended to be impressed anyway.'

Julia didn't deny it and her voice was imbued with mirth as she said, 'Why not? It makes her feel important, and I kind of got the feeling she needed it today. Did you notice that famous sphinxy smile of hers wasn't quite as much in evidence as usual?'

Surprised, Annie said, 'No, I didn't.'

'Well, she definitely wasn't herself. Kind of edgy and distracted.'

Annie's eyebrows rose with interest. 'Did you ask if anything was wrong?'

Slowing up at Ralegh's Cross, Julia indicated right and swung out just in time to avoid a horsebox hurtling along the main road towards them. 'Not exactly, but she told me that her husband's gone back to London already, leaving her here on her own.'

Not much relishing the idea of a lone Chrissie rolling around the moor like a loose cannon, Annie said, 'Did she seem upset about it?'

'I couldn't really tell. She's very . . . Not easy to read.'

'So how much longer is she staying?'

'Apparently until after the New Year's ball. Actually, I was thinking we should invite her to sit at our table if she's going to be on her own and if there's room.'

Seeing no way of objecting to the suggestion, Annie was about to say so, when Julia added, 'I've arranged to have coffee with her in town tomorrow. It turns out we're both going in so I thought, why not?'

Annie shrugged, why not indeed? She started to speak again, but suddenly cried out as they took a left turn too sharply and would have plunged into a ditch had Julia not jerked down hard on the steering wheel to avoid it. After bringing them safely back on to the road she stopped the car, breathing heavily. 'I'm so sorry,' she gasped. 'Oh my God. How could I . . . ? I know that bend is there . . .'

'It's OK,' Annie soothed, her heart still pounding from the shock of such a near miss. 'It comes up so fast . . . Are you all right?'

'Yes, yes I'm fine.' After a moment she added, 'Are you?'

With a wryness she wasn't quite feeling yet, Annie said, 'It sobered me up, that's for sure. Let's just sit a minute and get our breath back.'

'We're blocking the road,' Julia pointed out. 'Don't worry, I'm good to carry on. As long as you still feel safe with me?'

'I do,' Annie promised, 'but let's take it a little slower, just in case.'

They travelled on in silence, each wrestling with how narrowly they'd missed the uncompromising trunk of a giant oak tree, and were almost back at Hanley Combe before Julia said, 'Please don't tell David what happened. Or Henry.'

Annie hid an exasperated smile. Even after all these years of adulthood, there was still something in Julia that continued to need both brothers' approval, or to avoid their censure. Not that they seemed to notice, nor were they especially judgemental of her, although perhaps naturally, as her husband, Henry was more critical and sometimes impatient of her insecurities. 'Of course not,' she said gently, 'but it could have happened to any of us, that bend is notorious.'

Julia nodded, clearly knowing that was true. 'Especially when you're distracted by the headless horseman on his phantom steed,' she said, attempting a laugh.

Annie threw her a look. She really did come out with the strangest things at times.

Julia turned into the lane leading up to the Hanley Combe gates. 'Sorry, just being silly,' she said. 'I wasn't paying proper attention, and you're so precious to David and Henry. I couldn't bear to think of what they'd say if they thought I'd put you at risk.'

Annie reached over to squeeze her arm. 'There's no harm done, and you're just as precious to them, you know that, and you always have been.'

Giving no response, Julia drove on into the estate and brought the car to a stop behind the half-dozen or so others parked outside the house. 'Here's David,' she said as he came out on to the veranda to meet them.

Annie turned to look at her and was surprised to see tears in her eyes. 'Julia, what is it?' she asked worriedly.

Forcing a laugh, Julia said, 'Nothing. You know me, I get emotional so easily and I was just thinking about how David would have blamed me if anything had happened to you.'

'But it didn't, and he'd understand it was an accident. Anyway, you shouldn't put so much store by what he thinks.'

'No, you're right, I shouldn't. I won't any more,' and pushing open the door she jumped down just as David reached the bottom of the steps.

'At last,' he declared, going to Annie's side of the car. 'Henry's about to bet the farm, Jules, so you'd best get down to the games room or you'll end up sleeping with the horses.'

Given the long-established thousand-pound cash ceiling to their poker games – to save them from themselves – they invariably ended up writing promissory notes for their vehicles, property, stocks and shares, livestock and even their wives and children. It formed the source of much teasing and hilarity in the weeks to come, especially when someone threatened to call in a debt.

With a playful roll of her eyes, Julia said, 'He lost it last year, if you remember, so I'm not sure who we're paying rent to these days.'

'That would be me,' David informed her, slipping an arm round Annie as they started back inside, 'except being the good guy that I am I returned it.' To Annie he said, 'Your dad ended up taking the kids to the cinema in town. He'll bring them back after he's fed them.'

'I'll make sure the guest room's ready,' she said drolly, 'as I'm sure the poor thing will be dying for a drink by then. Is Mum back yet? Pam was bringing her.'

'Here they are,' Julia said as a Toyota 4x4 came in through the gates. 'I'll go and find Henry and see if he's ready to be taken home, assuming we still have one to go to.'

Needing to get out of the cold Annie and David hurried after her, and Annie kicked off her boots as David helped her out of her Christmas muffler and padded coat. The men might be downstairs in the games room, but the smell of hard liquor was all over the house – though not on David's breath when he kissed her. He'd have had a beer or two, she felt sure, maybe a glass of wine, but no more than that. Those dark and difficult days after he'd left the army when he'd struggled to control so much of his life, including the nightmares that had plagued him, were only ever brought back by excess alcohol. Nowadays he seldom went beyond a few glasses.

'Did you have a good time?' he asked, catching her as she staggered against him.

'Wonderful,' she assured him, 'and I'm sure you did too. Is there any coffee on?'

'No, but we can make it happen. Hey Harriet, looks like you've been enjoying yourself too. Isn't Pam coming in?'

'She had to get back,' Harriet replied, closing the door and toeing off her own boots. 'I hear Francis drew the short straw to drive the kids around today. Roll on when one of them has passed their test.'

'I'll second that,' Annie told her and wandered through to the kitchen. 'Oh my God, it's a disaster zone . . . '

'Don't worry, I've got it all under control,' David insisted, though he clearly hadn't. 'You just sit there and let yourself be waited on. Your wish shall be my command.'

Annie eyed him suspiciously. 'You've wagered me away to the old goat Connor Fredericks again,' she accused.

David grimaced. 'Henry's trying to win you back. He's got more left to play with than I have . . . '

'So, you've already lost Hanley Combe?'

'Good God no. I have my priorities sorted.'

Flinging a balled-up napkin at him, she slumped down in a chair at the table and put her feet up.

As Harriet sank down on another chair and David set about making a fresh pot of coffee, Julia returned from the games room and declared, wryly, 'He's lost me to Hubert Haverman and the farm to Dickie, but I think he's managed to win you back for David.'

Henry came in behind her, tousle-haired and not quite steady on his feet. 'Don't worry, my darling,' he slurred, putting an arm around her, 'I won't leave here until I've won you back too. Unless you'd rather go home with Hubert, of course. I hear they're into swinging so his wife should be OK with it.'

'You're funny,' she told him, with a playful kiss. 'Although I've heard that about Hubert and Sally. Do you think it's true?' she asked Annie.

Annie shrugged. 'No idea. Henry, I think you need to sit down.'

'I do,' he agreed, staggering towards the table. 'How's the coffee coming along, oh bro of mine?'

'Almost there,' David replied, catching him mid-lurch and guiding him to a chair. 'Blimey, how much did you have? I think we should call it a day now, anyway. I'm an entire grand down and I don't see much chance of winning it back this side of my fifties.' He yawned loudly and began stretching out his muscled limbs until Henry mock-punched his bare midriff. 'Must go for a run in the morning,' he decided, 'try and get myself back into some sort of shape for Sunday. Hell, did you really have to book me a shoot in Yorkshire right before the new year?' he grumbled to Annie.

'Given what good clients they are, and how much they're paying, yes,' she replied sweetly.

'Are you going?' Julia asked Henry.

Henry swallowed a burp. 'Probably,' he answered, 'but don't worry girls, we'll be back in time for the ball.'

'Well, there's a relief,' Harriet quipped, 'we can't have our Cinderellas without their Prince Charmings, now can we?'

'Julia's going to invite Chrissie Slater to join our table,' Annie informed them. 'Apparently her husband's abandoned her and gone back to London.' She was watching David, but turned to Henry as he said sharply to Julia, 'Why would you do that?'

Colouring slightly, she said, 'Annie just explained, Chrissie's on her own. And why shouldn't she sit with us?'

Henry stared at her, eyes swimming with unfocused anger.

'Hey Henry,' David came in lightly, 'we've known Chrissie a long time. She's one of us . . . '

'Not any more she isn't,' Henry argued.

'I think she'd like to be,' Julia said.

'It's only lately, since she got her inheritance, that she's found time to come here again,' Henry practically shouted.

Incredulously David said, 'What's got into you? You've had too much, that's your trouble. You need to take him home, Jules, let him sleep it off.'

'I've lost the farm,' Henry told him, starting to laugh. 'To Dad, so I think you're safe for a place to stay.'

'Ha ha. Well I'm telling you this,' he said to Julia, as she started to help him up, 'I don't want her at our table. If she's there, I *won't* be.'

David looked at Annie. 'Is there something going on that I don't know about?' he asked her.

Annie simply shrugged as Henry pushed his face at Julia, saying, 'Ask *her* what's going on. She's the one with all the answers.'

'Henry, you're not making any sense,' Julia retorted mildly, 'and much as you might want me to, I'm not getting into a pointless fight with you while you're in this state. So let's say our goodbyes and get you home before you start coming out with things that you really will end up regretting.'

After they'd gone no one spoke for a while, still trying to work out exactly what had just happened. In the end, Harriet was the first to break the silence, 'This time of year is never without its dramas,' she reflected, 'and it would appear we've just witnessed one, even if we don't know what the heck it was about.'

Wrinkling her nose, Annie said, 'What I'm asking myself is why would Henry object to Chrissie joining us on New Year's Eve?'

David shrugged. 'I've no idea, but given the state he was in I'll lay money that he'll have forgotten all about it by this time tomorrow.'

Two days later, as scheduled David and Henry took off for Yorkshire in time to spend the night before the shoot at the same hotel as the clients. That way they'd all meet for breakfast before being ferried off to Warter Priory, a prestigious estate with a notable history and generally accepted to be one of the highest quality shoots in the land.

While the men were away Annie and Julia tackled the workload that had piled up over Christmas, while four of their regular freelance coaches came in to take the sessions already booked. With a lot of marketing, website and accounting issues to deal with as well as the regular enquiries, they were so busy that there wasn't much time for Annie to ask about Henry's strange reaction to Chrissie Slater joining them on New Year's Eve.

However, during one lunch break Julia mentioned that her coffee date with Chrissie had gone well, and she was happy to announce that Henry had got over himself and accepted that Chrissie would be at their table for the ball.

'But why did he object in the first place?' Annie wanted to know.

Julia shook her head in fond exasperation. 'Because he was drunk and feeling querulous, as he often does when he's had too much. He didn't remember much about it when he woke up in the morning, although he did say he was sorry if he'd said anything to offend anyone.'

'And you told him that of course he didn't?'

Julia's eyebrows rose in surprise. 'I don't think he did. Did he?'

Accepting that if Julia didn't think so then perhaps she shouldn't either, Annie merely shrugged, and moments later they were once again absorbed in the matters at hand.

The brothers and their dogs returned triumphant on the afternoon of New Year's Eve – the quality and presentation of the high birds at Warter Priory had once again surpassed expectations – and luckily for them they were in plenty of time to get ready for the ball. David was even able to play an Xbox game with Quin before taking him to his friend's house for a sleepover, in spite of Quin's loudly stated insistence that he'd rather stay at home to party with his brother and sister.

'Not happening,' David informed him while ushering

him and his overnight bag out to the car, 'you're too young and you'll have more fun at Godfrey's.'

'Mum!' Quin yelled. 'Tell him!'

'He's right,' Annie shouted back from the kitchen where she, Sienna and Max were preparing toppings for the youngsters to make their own pizzas later.

Finding her brother hunched over his phone, Sienna teased, 'Are you missing Justin?'

Max didn't deny it. 'I just wish he could have stayed for the party tonight,' he grumbled.

He roared a protest as Sienna grabbed him into a boisterous hug and began showering him with noisy kisses. 'Have you heard any more from the modelling agency?' she asked, letting him go.

'No, but it's not what I want to do. Great to be asked though,' he grinned, and earned himself a slap from Sienna.

By the time David returned from dropping Quin off in town Annie had finished in the bathroom, so while he went in, Sienna set to work creating an artful updo for her mother's fine golden hair. She was so pleased with the result that as soon as she'd finished she raced off to try the same with her own thicker and longer tresses, leaving Annie to make a careful slide, unassisted, into an extremely tight body shaper with openings in the right places, followed by her slinky new dress.

Fortunately she was in it by the time Max walked into the bedroom. Glancing up from his phone he pretended to swoon. 'Mum, you look totally amazing,' he told her, apparently meaning it. 'Has Sienna seen you?'

'She was with me when I bought it,' Annie reminded him, and because it seemed to be such a success she turned back to the mirror to take another look. Given how unforgiving silk jersey could be, and how much she'd eaten over the Christmas period, she was lucky to be in it all, never mind without any evidence of overindulgence – she had the body shaper to thank for that, of course. The dress itself fitted so closely along her arms, around the bust and hips, and down to her knees where it swirled softly to the floor, that she had to admit Sienna had been right when she'd declared in the shop that Spanx or no underwear at all would be the best solution. 'And either way,' she'd added later, 'you have to get a Brazilian at least, but a Hollywood would be better.'

Annie had opted for the latter and because she'd managed to get into everything while David was still in the bathroom, she had yet to experience the pleasure of him finding out that she was completely naked in a whole other way than he was used to. For now, she was still slightly breathless from the way he'd dropped kisses down her bare back when he had seen her in it, grazing his knuckles over her nipples to make them stand out far more than she'd have liked them to in public. Or in front of her son.

'I think it's too revealing,' she declared now, not wanting to change, but giving them the chance to say that she should.

'You look like a gen-u-ine movie star,' Max told her warmly. 'Like, you know, from way back. I mean in a good way, not that you're old . . . '

David whispered in her ear, 'It's not coming off until we're back here after midnight, then I'll take it off myself.'

As Annie laughed at the thought of him wrestling with the body shaper, Max said, 'I heard that, but I'll pretend I didn't. I just came to let you know that Grandpa's downstairs, so your carriage awaits.'

After treating her elegant hairstyle to a last-minute check, Annie gave David a final once-over before they left the room. In his black satin-trimmed tux with royal blue cummerbund, matching shirt studs and bow tie, he was every bit as desirable to her as she was to him, and as she leaned in to tell him so she discreetly slipped a hand between his legs.

Catching it, he held it in his and grabbed her purse before leading her out to the landing, where Sienna was waiting to ambush them for Instagram shots.

The journey to Fairley Vale Hall took around twenty minutes through drizzle and swirling mist clouds. As they approached the medieval castle at the heart of its own vast acreage Annie once again found herself agreeing with her children that the place with all its history and randomly bricked-up windows just had to be haunted. The estate had been privately owned for generations by the Diffley family, whose income these days came more from the City than the properties and farms they owned. The current occupants, Grayson and Rosa, had long ago earned their reputation for being the most generous hosts on Exmoor, and the New Year's Eve ball was always the biggest and most glamorous of their events. Everyone with any standing in the area was invited, along with the Diffleys' many friends and acquaintances from London, New York, Singapore and various other financial capitals around the globe. The Crayce brothers had acquired so many new clients through their old friends' annual event that it had become a joke between them that the Diffleys should be on a handsome commission.

Fairley Vale's ballroom was exquisitely dressed with

cascades of shimmering organza floating around the windows and walls as well as tenting the ceiling, while impossibly large and exotic flower displays graced each table along with elaborate place settings and sparkling crystal glasses. The anteroom was already filling up with expensively dressed guests, while uniformed staff passed around fizzing flutes of champagne and succulent bite-sized canapes.

David and Annie soon lost sight of one another as they mingled happily, greeting old friends, meeting new ones and joining in exclamations of how gorgeous and glamorous everyone looked.

'And none so much as you, my stunning sister-in-law,' Henry declared as he swept her into a gentle embrace. 'I won't ask if you're wearing anything under that dress,' he murmured, 'because I'm afraid of what the answer might be.'

With an arch smile meant to scold as much as convey humour, Annie turned to Julia, whose eyes were on stalks. 'That dress is scandalously sensational,' she declared, careful to hold her glass aloft as they air-kissed. 'And I won't ask what Henry just whispered, because I probably don't want to know.'

Annie laughed and linked Julia's arm as Henry moved off to greet someone else and their hostess came to join them. Rosa too showered Annie with compliments, and by the time she moved on Annie admitted to Julia that she was starting to feel slightly more embarrassed than sensational.

'Don't,' Julia chided. 'If you've got the figure, why not flaunt it, is what I always say.'

Annie regarded her in surprise. 'So why don't you?' she

challenged with a glance up and down Julia's silver and grey Empire-line gown, certainly elegant with its soft chiffon folds and sparkling sequins, but the long butterfly sleeves and plain round neckline could hardly have been more modestly cut.

'You know I don't have your confidence,' Julia replied with a self-mocking smile. 'I'd probably want to die if anyone knew I wasn't wearing a bra.'

Wishing for a moment that she was, while knowing that it wasn't in Julia's nature to be bitchy, Annie was saved from responding by Chrissie Slater's arrival.

'Annie, how lovely to see you and how *gorgeous* is that dress?' she said warmly, holding out one of Annie's hands to get a better look at the slinky robe.

'Thank you,' Annie smiled, somehow managing not to grab at Julia as she floated off into the crowd. 'You're looking very glamorous yourself,' she told Chrissie, wishing she didn't mean it. 'Is that a Jenny Packham?'

Chrissie's dark sloe eyes lit with pleasure, and not for the first time Annie was struck by how the quirkily sloppy features that seemed almost too big for her small face weren't quite beautiful but almost. 'How clever you are,' Chrissie cooed from her inferior height, 'but you know I've always thought that about you. Annie is extremely clever, I often say to myself. She's the one who got David Crayce and broke all our hearts.'

Since Annie had heard this before, she simply smiled sweetly and said, 'I believe you're sitting at our table this evening?'

Affecting concern, Chrissie replied, 'If you're sure you don't mind. I don't want to gatecrash or take anyone else's place.'

'It's fine,' Annie assured her. 'We were always one short, so it's as if it was meant for you.'

Chrissie was about to respond when Dickie bustled in to put an arm around her.

'Good to see you, young Chrissie,' he declared, giving her a squeeze, 'looking as delectable as ever. I hear you're joining us this evening. Couldn't be happier.'

'Me neither,' she murmured, and the way she smiled into his eyes made Annie wonder if she was sharing some sort of secret with him, as well as with David.

'I miss you guys so much when I'm not here,' Chrissie was telling Dickie, 'but I'm intending to be around a lot more over the next few months.'

Before Dickie could take up the jarring flirtation, Annie said, 'If you'll excuse me,' and tilting her champagne flute in farewell she slipped into the crowd.

A while later, as she chatted with two of the original Moor-auders, Grayson Diffley and Julia, she looked around for David, and spotting him with a group she didn't know, she was about to go and join them when everyone was called to table.

When she and Julia reached theirs they found Henry already seated next to Chrissie Slater, and as Julia went to take a place the other side of her new best friend – old friend, Annie reminded herself – it soon appeared that all three were on the very best of terms.

Surprised, considering Henry's odd outburst the other night, she greeted her parents who'd apparently been here for some time, and noticing Dickie closing in on them with David close behind she sat down next to Hugo Blum, friend, neighbour and legendary lawyer, whose mop of inky black curls and jaunty moustache, all streaked with silver, made him one of the jolliest-looking distinguished people she knew. His wife, Sukey, another original Moor-auder, floating into the chair the other side of her, provided an enchanting contrast to Hugo's faintly devilish looks, for she was an angelic sort of hippy with silky blonde hair, whimsical ways and flowing kaftans no matter the occasion.

As the three of them started to catch up Annie noticed David had made a beeline for Chrissie, who, as she stood up to embrace him, was smiling so radiantly that Annie actually blinked. There was no mistaking how pleased they were to see one another, and Annie couldn't help thinking that Chrissie's stunning pale blue sequinned gown was quite probably out-dazzling every other dress in the room. For a horrible moment she felt the vintage nature of her fifties creation, as if it might be patched with age and fraying at the seams.

At that low moment David caught her eye and the way he winked told her that he was reading her mind and in his opinion no one could outclass her. However, he continued chatting with Chrissie – flirting, by the look of it – for much longer than Annie considered necessary, so she decided he would pay for it when the dancing began and she took the floor with his old nemesis Bradley Haines.

As the food was served a five-piece band played classic jazz tunes that drifted around the room as effectively and unobtrusively as the wait staff, while a couple of magicians flitted between tables making everyone gasp and laugh with incredulous delight. David, who was seated between Sukey and Harriet, was frequently interrupted by shouts from half-cut acquaintances for his opinion on the quality of certain birds, sporting estates, or shotguns, or by a server wanting to know what he thought of the wine. Since that particular enquiry had come from Grayson Diffley, David saluted his host across the room to signal his approval.

'I think it's bloody undrinkable myself,' Dickie grumbled, loud enough to remind them that his hearing wasn't what it used to be. 'I reckon he gets it cheap from some hypermarket in France.'

'You've poured it in with your water,' David informed him. Getting up, he came to rest his hands on Annie's shoulders for no apparent reason, and as this emphasized their closeness, she found herself treating Chrissie to one of her friendliest smiles. Maybe it was a 'he's mine' sort of look. It might have had some effect if Chrissie had noticed. But she was quite focussed on whatever she was saying to Henry, who appeared to be listening intently until he quite suddenly erupted into laughter. Chrissie turned to Julia and presumably repeated the story – a childhood memory? – because Julia laughed too.

So, there really didn't seem to be any friction between them, although as the evening wore on and Henry danced with Chrissie, almost to the exclusion of every other woman present, Annie could have wished he'd pay more attention to his wife. However, it didn't look as though Julia was having a problem with it; she simply watched from the table with a benevolent smile, or danced with anyone who invited her.

Although Annie was never short of partners, after constant groping from the older male guests whose understanding of Me Too appeared to be that they also got a go at fondling her bottom or making lewd suggestions, she began sitting out more dances than she accepted. So much for making David pay for his brief flirtation with Chrissie.

It didn't matter, she was happy to chat and laugh with Hugo and Sukey, until at last the countdown to midnight began and as David came to find her she spotted her parents and Dickie and grabbed them so they could cheer in the new year together. There was no sign of Henry, Julia or Chrissie, they were lost in the crowd, but it didn't matter, there would be plenty of time later to raise a glass with them.

'Happy New Year,' David murmured against her lips as the first chime of midnight sounded.

'Happy New Year,' she echoed softly.

'Looking forward to it?'

'I think so. How about you?'

He gazed searchingly into her eyes as he said much the same as he did every year at this time. 'Whatever the next twelve months have in store for us, as long as we're together and the kids are safe that's all that matters to me.'

'I love you, David Crayce,' she whispered.

'I love you too, Annabelle Crayce,' and drawing her more tightly into his embrace he kissed her deeply and tenderly as the fireworks began.

CHAPTER FOUR

It was two weeks into the new year and Detective Sergeant Natalie Rundle was at her desk in Kesterly CID reviewing the department's current caseload. The rest of the team was busy working phones and computers as they pressed on with various enquiries and investigations, and making plenty of noise about it. She didn't mind, she quite liked noise and even enjoyed chaos when it was of the right sort – for her this meant intellectual challenges or crimes of an unsolvable nature.

She was an energetic woman, with a mass of crinkly black hair trapped by a slide at the nape of her neck that usually matched her silk shirt of the day, piercing ebony eyes and blood-red lips. In the six weeks since she'd arrived to this outpost of the Dean Valley Force, as their only mixed-race detective, she'd demonstrated to no small effect how her scowl could be as withering as any spoken reprimand, while her smile was often genuinely disarming. She was, she'd informed the team during her introductory address, a no-nonsense sort of person who didn't waste time talking about getting things done, she was all about action.

'I don't encourage slackers,' she'd told them, 'and I

don't value anyone who can't speak truth to power.' She'd flicked a glance towards her superior, DCI Gould, at that point to check he'd got the message – it appeared that he had. 'I'm about getting villains off the streets,' she continued, 'gaining community trust and achieving the right results. I'm also a team player and I consider it fortunate for you lot that I'm on your side.'

It had taken a moment for everyone to realize she'd just cracked a joke; when they did she loudly joined in the laughter.

As yet no one had asked why she'd left the West Mercia force to come here, although she didn't doubt that HR, and probably Gould, had the backstory, but as it no longer reflected negatively on her performance as a detective, it was really neither here nor there. A violent past thanks to a severely damaged husband wasn't something she wanted to discuss with anyone. All that mattered, at least to her, was the blessed relief of finally escaping him and being a very long way from any reminders – and it was no one's business that she'd had to go through a great deal of therapy herself to try and deal with the trauma of living for so long with such a beast of a man. It had just about killed her, mentally if not physically. Now she was deeply grateful for this second chance as a detective sergeant. The fact that she only had one friend in this part of the world, who wasn't even around right now, didn't worry her even if it meant she wasn't going to find much of a social life here, in the back end of beyond as her twenty-three-year-old twin daughters called it. She could live with it, and probably better than they could if their nagging over Christmas was anything to go by.

'Ma'am. Have you opened your emails in the last couple of minutes?'

Natalie looked up from her screen to where DC Leo Johnson was sitting at his desk, directly opposite her. He was studying something on his computer, his pleasant, freckled face creased in a frown. 'What is it?' she asked, wondering if it was a mother or girlfriend who turned him out so immaculately each day. Maybe he did it himself.

'One just came in from DCI Gould,' he answered, and glanced over his shoulder as an explosion of laughter erupted from somewhere behind him.

Natalie ignored it and waited. She had time for this lad, but only so much.

'The lab's been in touch,' he explained, 'and attached a report. It turns out a DNA sample we took following an arrest just before Christmas has gone and found itself a familial match to a cold case.'

Natalie's artfully sculpted eyebrows rose. 'Go on,' she prompted carefully.

'Apparently the sample taken came from a girl who'd been picked up for nicking a teddy bear from Arnie Choudry's shop in the arcade. I'm guessing uniforms only responded because it's well known that the old bloke's going through a rough time, and there probably wasn't much else happening that night. Or not until a punch-up broke out in Paradise Cove, at which point the girl and her mates were let go with no charge in order to free up the cells. They'd be off our radar now, but for the fact this girl has provided us with said familial match to a murder dating back to 1999.'

Natalie's attention was hooked. Cold cases rarely

excited her, but with new evidence of this nature . . . 'Do we know who the victim was?' she asked.

Referring to his computer again, he said, 'Karen Lomax, a seventeen-year-old from the Old Town, here in Kesterly. Her parents owned a wine bar called Cheers. I don't think it's there any more. She disappeared early in August that year and her body was found a month later in an old railway hut on what's now the Embury Vale Estate.' He looked up again. 'No arrests were ever made.'

Natalie was increasingly intrigued. 'Seems like we're about to put that right,' she commented, 'thanks to Miss Teddy Bear Thief,' and calling for everyone's attention, she briefed them on what Leo had told her so far. Looking at each of them in turn she said, 'I'm guessing none of you were involved in the initial investigation – probably weren't even on the force at that time?'

Twenty years ago? No one had been.

'It was during DCI Underwood's time,' Leo Johnson told her.

Having never heard the name, and experiencing little interest in it right now, Natalie said, 'We need to pull up the case . . . '

'I'm on it,' DC Shari Avery piped up, turning to her computer.

'Good. What about the girl who provided the familial DNA? What can you tell us about her, Leo?'

Reading from the screen he said, 'Her name is Sienna Crayce. She lives up on the moor at Hanley Combe . . .'

'One of the rich kids then,' a male voice muttered.

Natalie slanted its owner a look. 'Anything you want to tell us, Detective? Do you know the place, the family?'

A red-faced DC Shields shook his head. 'Just saying, is all.'

She gestured for Johnson to continue.

'The corresponding DNA is male,' he said, 'could be an older brother, but given her age – she's sixteen – and the timeline I'd be more inclined to go for the father who,' he continued drawing out the word, 'contacted us the day after his daughter's arrest to find out if the case was going to be taken any further and if not could the fingerprints, DNA etc please be destroyed?'

Natalie's eyes rounded. 'Did he really? Now why would he be so keen for that to happen?' She looked around the room, not needing an answer, and no one tried to provide one.

For the next hour she read everything that was passed to her about Karen Lomax, focusing on both investigations – when the girl had disappeared, and after she was found – but there was no mention anywhere of David Crayce.

How odd, when he'd obviously had some connection with Karen Lomax, and apparently, given the semen sample taken from the girl's underwear and jeans, an intimate one.

'OK, Shields,' Natalie looked up from her screen, 'start formulating an arrest package . . . '

'Hang on, before we do anything,' a voice called out from the back, 'I've been checking our own files and we have Hanley Combe listed as a shooting school. In other words, guns on the premises.'

Natalie's eyes widened. 'Good to know,' she told the detective. 'Contact the firearms unit while I go talk to DCI Gould. Everyone else, find out what you can about Mr

Crayce – I take it no previous convictions or it would have come up already. So how long's he been in the area, past career, when he got married, extramarital affairs, illnesses, charities, hobbies, anything. There's no rush on it, the man's presumably not going anywhere, nevertheless I'd like to have a chat with him sooner rather than later.'

Three hours later Natalie and Leo Johnson were in a parked, unmarked car at the side of a meandering moor road that led to the turn-off towards Hanley Combe. Though the day was chill and gloomy, visibility was reasonable considering how high they were, although they had no sight on the firearms officers currently spreading like an invisible net around the estate to establish the whereabouts and status of David Crayce. Given the man's profession he'd no doubt be as good a shot as anyone closing in on him, so if he had a weapon in his hands he'd have to be disarmed before he was approached.

For the sake of everyone's safety Natalie and Johnson would stay put until DI George Gavern, head of the firearms unit, radioed the go-ahead for them to enter and make an arrest. If there was a fight back, Gavern would affect the arrest himself.

For now there was only radio silence, leaving Natalie and Leo to picture the stake-out using the map on their tablet screens. They saw acres of rambling woodland, an open heath, a small lake, a stream and the estate's properties, already identified as the shooting school, main house and a cottage. A Google search had revealed that the school was closed on Mondays, but that didn't mean no guns were out, or that it hadn't opened for a special client.

They also didn't know at this time if Crayce was actually there, but they'd find out soon enough.

More minutes ticked by, and feeling her tension increasing Natalie popped a mint. She didn't often get spooked, but there was something about this moor that unsettled her, like it had some hidden force in its stark and rugged landscape that breathed and watched and waited . . . It made her wonder about the people who chose to live up here. She could imagine a lot of inbreeding, swinging, devil worship, even. For one moment she felt swamped by an irrational fear, as if her past was trying to close in on her through the hostile terrain, to persuade her she wasn't up to this, that she was weak, ineffective, incapable . . .

She breathed through it, silently, determinedly. He only had power over her now if she allowed it.

Her eyes went to the radio as Gavern's voice came through. 'Suspect sighted.'

She didn't move. This was simply to let them know that Crayce was on the property and presumably not yet aware that he had company.

'The perfect family,' she muttered almost to herself, 'until you scratch the surface and out come all the bugs.'

Johnson glanced at her, said nothing, but his expression showed how much he'd rather not have that image in his head.

CHAPTER FIVE

Annie yawned loudly as she carried two mugs of tea through to the snug, where David was stretched out on a sofa with one hand resting on Cassie's silky black head and the other still holding the paper he'd been reading before he'd fallen asleep. Given all the back-to-back shoots he'd hosted these past ten days, plus the safaris he'd covered for Henry who'd gone down with flu, he had good reason to be tired. He probably wouldn't have taken a break this afternoon, however, if a group of Germans hadn't cancelled their tour of the moor. As it was she'd persuaded him to leave the Byre for a couple of hours and come over to the house where she was sorting the children's rooms, ready for the decorator to begin freshening them up on Wednesday. She was almost done, partly thanks to her mother and Julia who'd come to lend a hand yesterday while David was over at the Combe Sydenham estate.

They'd had quite an interesting chat, the three of them, mostly about Chrissie Slater and whether her marriage was really breaking up.

'I hope for her sake it isn't,' Julia had stated with feeling, 'and for mine. She's always had a thing about Henry and I'm afraid it might be mutual.'

Puzzled, Annie said, 'I thought it was David she'd always had her sights on.'

Julia nodded. 'Yes, she did, back in the day. As far as I know David was her first, but she was with Henry after that, until he went to uni.'

'I thought you were with Henry then.'

Julia grimaced. 'He kind of played us off one against the other, especially after David went to Sandhurst.'

'That's awful,' Harriet commented, wrinkling her nose.

Julia shrugged. 'We were young and pretty naïve. None of us had been out into the big bad world by then, so those of us who were left kind of clung together, missing David, dreading Henry going too . . . Mummy often says I probably would never have gone to uni myself if Henry and David hadn't, and I sometimes wonder if that would have been such a bad thing. It might have saved me from my miserable marriage, short-lived though it was, thank God. Chrissie didn't rush into anything the way I did, she was almost thirty by the time she got married, and I can tell you she seemed pretty cut up about things when I had coffee with her a couple of weeks ago. And it was her husband she called at midnight on New Year's Eve, although not before she'd managed a quick snog with Henry, I have to say.'

Shocked, Harriet said, 'Don't tell me he kissed her before you?'

'No,' Julia laughed. 'I was first and he was very loving, which isn't always the case with him, as you know.'

Annie did know that, and she'd been relieved to hear that Henry's entire focus hadn't been on Chrissie that night, because it had looked for a while as if it was going that way.

Now, all she really wanted to hear was that Chrissie had taken herself back to London. Not that she didn't trust David, she did implicitly, but she wasn't sure she could say the same for Henry, especially when he'd already told his father and David that he wanted out of his marriage. She still felt sure he didn't mean that, but was ready to believe that Chrissie being around and potentially single was making him restless, as if he could go back to his old ways of stringing both women along.

Smiling at how comfortable David looked lying there asleep on the sofa, she stood watching him until his eyes began to flicker open. 'Hey you,' she said softly.

Closing them again, he smiled and put an arm across his forehead as Cassie's tail gave a thud on the side of the sofa. 'What day is it?' he croaked.

'Monday. You're at home and I'm your wife.'

He cocked a look at her, feigning surprise. 'Lucky me,' he commented, and swinging his legs to the floor he took the tea Annie was offering, while Cassie wolfed down the treat she pulled from her pocket. 'Any word from Henry?' he asked, taking a sip.

'Not yet, but Julia thinks he'll be able to take some stand sessions tomorrow. Thankfully there's no safari booked, I don't think he's up to that, but you're due to take a party of Japanese businessmen over to the Withycombe estate.'

'You're working me to death, woman,' he grumbled.

'And you love every minute of it.'

'Actually, what I really love is the thought of our ski trip at half-term. Please tell me it's happening.'

'It is,' she confirmed.

He looked around at the sound of a car pulling up

outside. 'Are we expecting someone?' he asked, taking another sip of tea.

'I don't think so. It'll probably be your dad or Julia, so I'll wait to talk to you about the call I had earlier from Quin's school. Apparently he got into a fight with one of his classmates about who to vote off *I'm a Celebrity.*'

David spluttered on a laugh. 'I wonder who he wants to sack,' he commented. 'Not that we'd be any the wiser. Anyway, I'll go pick him up today, and have a chat with him on the way home about fighting.'

Knowing he was likely to advise Quin how to throw a good punch rather than explain that it was wrong to lash out, she was just starting to warn him that their eight-year-old was easily influenced, especially by his dad, when someone knocked on the front door.

'Apparently not Dad or Julia,' he remarked, but as he made to get up she pushed him back down and went herself.

'OK, I'm coming,' she called as whoever it was knocked again. 'So impatient.'

Pulling the door open she blinked in surprise as two strangers, standing very close to the threshold, began identifying themselves as . . . Detective Sergeant Rundle and Detective Constable Johnson?

'Mrs Crayce?' the mixed-race woman asked, before Annie could react.

Annie said, 'Don't tell me you've had a complaint from the anti-blood sport . . . '

'We're here for your husband,' the woman interrupted, and to Annie's amazement she was pushed aside as both detectives entered the house followed by *four armed officers* who'd appeared out of nowhere.

'What the hell . . . ?' Annie cried, going after them. 'You can't come crashing in here like this . . . '

David appeared in the doorway of the snug, Cassie beside him, growling.

'Stand the dog down, please,' the female detective instructed.

'It's OK, girl,' David said, putting a hand on Cassie's head while surveying the guns all trained on him. 'What's this about?' he asked, sounding far calmer than Annie felt.

The woman stepped forward. 'David Crayce, I'm arresting you for the murder of Karen Lomax . . . '

Annie's eyes flew open in shock.

'You do not have to say anything, but it may harm your defence . . . '

Annie stared at David, stupefied, waiting for him to protest, to show them out . . .

'Who?' he asked.

'You have the wrong person,' Annie heard herself shout. 'Don't touch him! David!'

David was spun around, his arms wrenched behind him, and the instant handcuffs were clamped around his wrists the guns went down.

'Stop!' Annie seethed, as they marched him towards the door. 'David, for God's sake . . . '

'It's a mistake,' he told her. 'It'll get sorted.'

'At least let him put some shoes on,' she yelled as they reached the front door.

They waited as he dug his feet into his boots, but allowed no time for the laces before manhandling him out onto the veranda.

'Where are you taking him?' Annie cried going after them. 'I need to know . . . *David*!'

Looking back over his shoulder, he said, 'Call Hugo Blum. Tell him what's happened and that I'm at Kesterly police station?' He looked to the arresting officers for confirmation, and received it.

Annie stood with Cassie on the front steps, watching in mounting disbelief as he was shoved into the back of an unmarked car and driven away.

Quickly collecting herself she ran for her phone, scrolled to Hugo Blum's number with shaking hands and pressed to connect. 'I need to speak to him,' she told the female voice that answered. 'It's Annie Crayce, and it's urgent.'

'Mr Blum's in our Bath office today,' she was told, 'but I'll see if I can put you through.'

As she waited, pacing and trembling, she still wasn't able to make any sense of what had just happened. Detectives, armed officers in her house, accusing David . . .

Hugo Blum's voice, deep and authoritative, but friendly, came down the line. 'Annie. What's going on?'

Gasping for air, she said, 'David's just been arrested . . .'

'What for?'

She couldn't make herself say it.

'Annie?'

'For murder,' she blurted. 'It's a mistake, obviously, but they came with armed police . . . '

'Who's the victim?'

She tried to think, but couldn't remember the name. 'It's a female,' she said, certain of that. 'Oh God, Hugo, how soon can you get here? They've taken him to the station in Kesterly.'

'From where I am now it'll be a couple of hours, but I'll leave right away.'

'Thank you. Thank you. What shall I do meantime?'

'Sit tight. I'll be in touch as soon as I have some news.'

As she rang off she looked down at Cassie, who seemed to be waiting for instruction. 'It's going to be all right,' she told the dog, dropping down to hug her, 'it's obviously a mistake, so we need to stay calm and think what's best to do.'

'Annie! Are you in here?'

Leaping up, Annie ran out to the kitchen.

'What's going on?' Julia asked, tearing off her riding hat. 'Was that the police I just saw . . . '

'They've taken David,' Annie told her.

Julia's face paled. 'What do you mean? I don't understand.'

Without thinking about what she was doing, Annie grabbed the keys to David's Defender and went for her coat. 'Would you mind collecting Quin from school?' she asked. 'I need to go to the police station. I'll call as soon as I know what's happening.' At the door she turned back. 'Don't mention anything to Dickie yet. It's all a mistake so he won't need to know,' and running outside with Cassie at her heels, she was in the car and about to drive away when Julia shouted for her to stop.

'You'll need this,' Julia said, holding up her phone.

Stretching past the dog, Annie took it, thanked her and drove off at speed.

CHAPTER SIX

'Have they processed him yet?' DCI Gould asked, his grey-blue eyes fixed on Natalie, although she could tell his mind was leaping ahead to what came next – as was hers.

'They're doing it now,' she replied. 'And his lawyer's on the way.'

Gould's attractive, though weathered features tightened into a frown. He was a well-built man in his early fifties with thinning grey hair and a powerful demeanour that sat well with his senior position and formidable, though slightly flawed, reputation.

'It's Hugo Blum,' she added.

At that his eyes sharpened.

'It's not a name I know,' she admitted, 'but I'm guessing from what I've heard so far that he's a Mr Bigshot.'

Gould nodded. 'His firm is London-based, but he has offices in Bath and Bristol, and if I tell you that even cops say they'd want him onside if they were in trouble you'll get an idea of the man.'

More intrigued than impressed, she said, 'I'll look forward to meeting him.'

'Does Crayce know about the familial DNA?'

'Not yet.'

'OK. If Blum's coming from one of his offices it'll give his client plenty of time in a cell to think about things – and give you just as much time to go back through the original case notes before you start interviewing.'

'Is there anything you can tell me about it, sir? Were you here twenty years ago?'

With a sardonic smile he said, 'I was not, but I can tell you that my predecessor, Underwood – actually there was another DCI between his time and mine – did not preside over Kesterly CID's best years.'

'Care to elaborate?'

'I'm told he liked to talk the talk, but when it came to walking the walk he didn't have much of an appetite for detail, nor did he encourage anyone who tried to bog him down in it. He didn't earn himself a stellar record for convictions or diplomacy – you can read racist into that. They retired him early, but if you want to know where he is now you'll have to go to HR, because I don't have the first idea.'

'Well, if he was as big a dickhead as he sounds I'm not sure he can help us much, but I do find your precis of his character interesting. It tells me that revisiting this case could be long overdue, new DNA notwithstanding.'

Not arguing with that, he said, 'Let me know when you're ready to interview Crayce, I'd like to watch the video feed. Unless his hotshot lawyer instructs him to go the no-comment route. Won't be much to see then if he does.'

Hoping that wouldn't happen, although ready to deal with it if it did, Natalie left Gould's office and returned to her desk where the original case notes were waiting to be gone through again. Before settling down for a more careful scrutiny she strolled to the refs to make herself a coffee, thinking hard and recalling her instincts at the moment she'd first laid eyes on David Crayce. Although she accepted it wasn't possible to get the full measure of a man in such a brief time, what had interested her, a lot, was the fact that he hadn't panicked, hadn't even shown any particular surprise at finding himself surrounded by armed officers. He'd simply cooperated, had said very little apart from telling his wife to call a heavyweight lawyer.

Finding DCs Shari Avery and Noah Shields ahead of her at the coffee machine, she said, 'I take it you're still combing through the Karen Lomax case notes?'

Avery said, 'If you're asking have we managed to dig up a mention of David Crayce yet, the answer is no, but we're still looking.'

Nodding approval, Natalie retrieved her mug from the dishwasher and stood it on the machine.

Noah Shields said, 'I don't know if you've heard about DCI Underwood's reputation . . . '

'I have,' she interrupted. 'At least in part. Where are you going with it?'

'I was thinking of looking into whether he had any connections with the Crayce family back when he was on the force.'

'Do that,' Natalie told him. 'And Shari, the minute they've finished processing our friend downstairs make sure his DNA goes straight to the labs. I know this is a cold case so it's unlikely to get priority, but don't let that stop you trying.'

Annie was seated in the police station's front office with Cassie between her knees and her mobile clutched tightly in one hand. It was fortunate the duty officer had allowed the dog in; she wouldn't have wanted David to hear his best friend howling up a storm the way she had when Annie had tried to leave her in the car. It was as if she'd known that David was nearby and was calling to him. Either that, or she'd sensed that Annie needed her comforting presence.

They'd been here for almost two hours by now, watching the comings and goings, being told nothing about David, or offered any refreshment. She didn't want anything. She simply needed this to be over so she could drive David home, and turn it into the joke it obviously was.

Glancing at her mobile as a text arrived she felt her heart turn over. It was from Hugo. *Just parking up.*

There was another she hadn't noticed until now. From Julia. *Quin home, I'll sort his tea. He's asking where you are so told him you and David at a meeting in town. Any idea what time you'll be back?*

Having no idea at all, Annie could only reply with, *Still waiting for news. Will text soonest. Thanks for taking care of Q.* What a mercy that Sienna and Max were at school; they wouldn't be anywhere near as easy to deal with as their younger brother.

Getting up as she spotted Hugo approaching the glass doors, his large frame as smartly suited as his profession required, his intense manner both reassuring and yet alarming, she felt her heart stumble into a sickening thud. *It's going to be all right,* she told herself fiercely. *Stop thinking the worst,* although she had no words for what that might be and she wasn't going to try to find them.

'Annie,' Hugo said, drawing her into a comforting hug. 'Sorry it took a while. Hey Cass,' he added, patting the dog. 'Has anyone told you anything?' he asked, checking his watch.

'Nothing, apart from to confirm he's here.'

'OK, leave it with me. You should go home now and I'll bring him just as soon as he's out of here.'

Almost unravelling with relief to hear those words, she said, 'How long do you think it'll take?'

'Depends, but I don't want you to worry . . . '

Desperately she said, 'He didn't do anything, Hugo. I know you know that . . . '

'Of course I do.'

'I can't even remember who they said it was . . . '

'I'll find out,' he interrupted gently, and pushing his glasses up his nose he went to introduce himself at the front desk.

Annie watched him, holding Cassie, and trying to process the reality of their dear friend, a criminal lawyer, being buzzed through a security door to go and see David . . . Not even Hugo's departing smile of reassurance did anything to ease the irrational sense of dread she had building inside.

David hadn't denied it, a little voice reminded her. *He just went with the detectives as if some part of him had been expecting them to come.*

Upstairs on the second floor of the police station, Natalie was so engrossed in the background information on Crayce that she barely looked up when her desk phone rang.

'Madely here,' the custody sergeant told her. 'The lawyer's arrived. Do you want me to fill him in?'

'I'll come down,' she replied, and replacing the receiver

she picked up her mobile phone along with the notes she'd prepared for this meeting and started for the lift.

So, just like her ex-husband who'd earned his own special place in hell, Crayce had once been in the armed forces.

Hugo Blum listened with quiet attention as Detective Sergeant Rundle disclosed why she had arrested David Crayce in such a draconian manner, but so far nothing she'd said had particularly impressed him. Quite the reverse, in fact, although he was prepared to concede that her desire to interview his client shouldn't – actually probably couldn't – be denied, so he was willing to let it go ahead. Before they got that far, however, he felt this uppity DS could do with a little bringing-down, so he set about it in an avuncular sort of way that surprisingly didn't appear to get quite as far under her skin as he'd expected.

'Please don't lecture me on familial DNA,' she told him. 'I'm not a rookie and you need to talk to your client. Have the custody sergeant call me when you're ready.'

He didn't have to wait long in a consultation room before David, minus boots, belt and usual gilet was shown through from the cells. He looked shaken, Hugo noted, and . . . wary? He had a talent for reading his clients, but wasn't arrogant enough to claim he was always right – he'd been wrong too often for that. 'Sit down,' he instructed gently. 'Can you bring us some coffee?' he asked the custody sergeant.

The look he received didn't fill him with much hope of refreshment any time soon. It didn't matter, they could manage without.

'So,' he said, fixing David's cautious eyes with his own penetrating gaze, 'I've had a chat with the uncharming DS

Rundle and you did right, my friend, to say nothing before I got here. I know she hasn't given you any details of what led to your arrest, but she obviously told you the victim's name, so let's start there. Who is Karen Lomax?'

David shook his head. 'I've no idea,' he replied and his tone, to Hugo's ears, was entirely convincing. 'Who is she?'

Blum explained how the girl had gone missing twenty years ago at the age of seventeen, and that her body had turned up in an old railway hut a month later.

David shook his head. 'Actually, I do remember vaguely . . . Didn't her parents own a café, or something? But what does it have to do with me?'

'It turns out,' Blum continued, needing to cut to the chase, 'that the police have acquired some DNA with a familial match to that found on Karen Lomax's body.'

David waited, showing no signs of confusion, or anything at all, apart from a need for further explanation.

Blum said, 'The recently acquired DNA, came from your daughter, Sienna.'

David frowned, as if not quite understanding, until he evidently did. 'Are you telling me . . . ? You mean the teddy bear thing? Are they saying . . . ? Jesus Christ, Hugo, this is insane.'

Hugo didn't disagree.

David cried, 'I don't care what their DNA says, I didn't kill anyone, so they've clearly screwed up.'

'Of course,' Blum confirmed, 'but we still need to take a hard look at what a familial match means . . . '

'I know what it means, but it's wrong. I told you, I had no idea who she was until you just explained.'

Blum said, 'Can you say the same for Henry or your father?'

David's jaw dropped as he took in what was being suggested. 'For God's sake, man,' he protested. 'You can't seriously think . . . '

'It doesn't matter what I think,' Blum interrupted. 'The fact is the DNA found on the inside of the victim's underwear comes from semen, and there are only three possible familial matches to Sienna's – five if you include your sons, but obviously no one is.'

David looked aghast, lost for words, and closed his eyes as he shook his head.

'Why me, and not Dad or Henry?' he asked bleakly.

'Good question,' Blum retorted. 'And one we'll certainly be asking. Meanwhile, we're going to spend the next hour running through everything I expect you to be asked in interview, and how you should answer. You might not like some of it, in fact I guarantee you won't, but the point of the exercise is for me to know what you know, and to prepare you for anything that might come at you from left field. If it does, please try not to lose your temper. Just let me handle it.'

David's eyes dropped to his hands bunched on the table. It was impossible for Hugo to know what he was thinking, but he was obviously in turmoil, as any man in his position would be. However, he sounded reasonably calm when finally, he said, 'OK, let's do it.'

As Natalie and Leo Johnson made their way down to the interview room, files and phones clutched to their chests, she was mulling her first meeting with Hugo Blum. He'd accused her of jumping the gun – ha ha, good pun – and acting far too heavy-handedly, considering the various ambiguities of her case. She hadn't argued, since he was right, she probably had gone in too hard and too fast – although the nature of Crayce's business had made the firearms unit a necessity. The point, as far as she was concerned, was that she had her man where she wanted him – right here and under caution, with a charge imminent.

Neither she nor Johnson offered a greeting as they joined Crayce and Blum in the interview room, they simply identified themselves for the voice and video recordings. After their guests had done the same Natalie sat back in her chair, eyes trained on her lead suspect, as Leo Johnson said, 'Mr Crayce, can we begin with you telling us why you were so concerned to have your daughter's DNA expunged from the record? You called the day after her arrest to make the request.'

David's eyebrows rose as he replied, 'Doesn't everyone want to make sure their children's details are removed from police records when no charges have been pressed?'

Johnson said, 'Did you have a particular reason to make sure it happened?'

With an exasperated sigh David simply shook his head. 'No,' he said.

'Were you concerned that a match might be made to your own DNA?'

'No.'

Natalie couldn't help being impressed by how calm he seemed, although she wasn't altogether surprised, given his background. It might have been a long time ago, but he'd have been trained to withstand all manner of interrogation techniques and this was hardly one of the toughest.

'How well did you know Karen Lomax?' Johnson asked.

'I didn't know her.'

'She was last seen alive on 7th August 1999 at her parents' wine bar, Cheers, in Kesterly Old Town. Did you ever frequent that wine bar?'

'I went in a few times, but I was never a regular.'

'Were you there on 7th August 1999?'

David regarded him incredulously. 'I have no idea where I was or what I was doing on that day, but I'd say I probably wasn't there.'

'But you might have been?'

'I *might* have been anywhere.'

'Can you be sure you weren't *there*?'

'No.'

Glancing at a note Natalie passed him, Johnson said, 'Where were you living in 1999?'

David took a moment to work it out. 'We had major construction work going on at Hanley Combe, so we were either staying with my parents at their farm next door, or at my parents-in-laws' cottage in Monksilver.'

'Who's we?'

'My wife and I. Actually, we got married in October of that year.'

'Your wife,' Johnson was consulting his notes, 'is Annabelle Crayce?'

'That's right.'

'And when did you move into your property at Hanley Combe?'

'In January of 2000.'

'Are you sure you can't remember what you were doing or where you were on 7th August?'

'I'm sure.'

'Perhaps, if we give you a little more time to think,' Natalie suggested, 'it might come back to you?'

'I doubt it,' David responded smoothly. 'Can you remember what you were doing on that day?'

'I'm not the one whose DNA was found . . . '

'It's familial DNA,' Blum reminded her.

Natalie moved on. 'From 1993 until the start of 1998 you were in the armed forces.'

David regarded her curiously. 'Is that a question?'

'It is.'

'Since you've asked, you obviously know it's true.'

Glancing at her notes, she said, 'Your record shows that you were with the Parachute Regiment.'

'Yes.'

'Would it be correct to say that you're a trained killer?'

David's eyes widened. 'If you want to put it that way, then yes, I was a trained killer.'

'And that gives you a certain sense of . . . power?'

He regarded her intensely, as though trying to read where this was going. 'At the right time and in the right place,' he admitted.

'Did you feel that sense of power when you were with Karen Lomax?'

'I was never with her, so no.'

Allowing him that for the moment, she said, 'After you left the army you continued to kill?'

'What? No, of course not.'

'I'm thinking of your current occupation?'

His manner was more condescending than outraged. 'You can hardly compare game-shooting with war . . .'

'Are you fond of blood sports?'

'It's what I do.'

'You kill birds, animals . . . People?'

Blum said, 'My client has already told you that he didn't kill Karen Lomax . . . '

'Actually, he hasn't told us that,' Natalie corrected. 'Did you kill her, Mr Crayce?'

'No, I did not.'

'Then how do you account for your semen being found on the gusset of her knickers?'

Blum said forcefully, 'Can I once again remind you that the match is familial? So, until you can eliminate other members of my client's family by taking their DNA for analysis I ask that this interview be terminated.'

Natalie didn't respond, simply let long seconds tick by before finally gesturing for Johnson to stop the recordings. She'd expected the interview to end this way, but she had enough to satisfy her for now, so was prepared to let Blum have his way.

A few minutes later, in the custody area, as David's belongings were being returned to him, she turned to Blum. 'Your client is being released under investigation,' she stated. 'We'll be in touch,' and leaving them to find their own way out she returned to the second floor of the station, where an incident room was in the process of being set up.

Annie hadn't wanted to leave the station when Hugo had told her to, but nor had she wanted Quin to worry – or anyone else, come to that. So, hardly taking in where she was going, or the darkness smothering the moor, she'd driven back to Hanley Combe to be greeted on the veranda by a flustered Julia.

'I'm sorry but everyone's here,' Julia whispered. 'It's just, when your mother rang I felt I had to tell her . . . '

'How much did you tell her?' Annie broke in, before remembering that Julia didn't know what the arrest had been for – or that it had even been an arrest. *Murder! Oh dear God, dear God.* It made her feel sick simply to think of it.

'Only what I saw,' Julia assured her, 'the police driving David away. Then Dickie came over and he knew straight away that something was wrong. After I told him he called Henry and so he's here too. None of us feel right about leaving until we know what's happening . . . '

'It's all right,' Annie said, hoping with all her heart that it would be. *How could it not be?* 'Let's go inside.'

All eyes came to her as she entered the kitchen, though thankfully Quin was downstairs in the games room with his friend Godfrey. She wouldn't have been able to tell them anything if he'd been there, and she wasn't sure what to tell them anyway.

'What was it about?' her father asked sounding every bit the magistrate he'd once been. 'Why were the police . . . ?'

'Let her take her coat off,' Harriet scolded.

'I'll put the kettle on,' Julia offered, going to fill it.

'I think we'll need something stronger than that,' Annie told her. 'Cocktail us up, and make mine a large one.'

Taking a bottle from the fridge Henry opened it, while Dickie set out six glasses and Harriet encouraged Annie to sit down. It was hard to be still when she wanted to pace, or call David, or Hugo, or even the police to make them explain what the hell was going on.

Looking pale following his flu, and even slightly shaky, Henry said, 'So why do the police want to talk to him? Couldn't they have done it here? Jules said they drove him away in the back of a car and there were armed . . .'

'I don't know why there were armed officers,' Annie

broke in quickly, and seized the glass Dickie was passing her. 'But I can tell you he was arrested . . . '

'What for?' her mother demanded indignantly.

Annie's eyes went to her father-in-law, tall and erect, still a handsome man in his seventies, the patriarch of their family who'd once been as strong and admired as his sons. His wife's death had changed him, left him less than he'd been, as if part of him had gone with her – and seeing how baffled and alarmed he looked now Annie wanted to protect him, to protect them all, including herself and David, but how? 'They've got the wrong person,' she assured Dickie. 'There's no doubt about that, but until they sort it out . . . '

'Darling, you need to tell us what it is,' her father said gently.

Steeling herself, she closed her eyes as she told them rather than have to see their shocked expressions.

Julia was the first to speak. 'But that's nonsense,' she protested, distractedly fingering her pearls. 'How can they have made such a stupid mistake?'

Henry said, 'Thank God you called Hugo.'

'David told me to.' Recalling his words and how he'd looked as he said them, she cried, 'It was awful. If you'd been there . . . '

'What did he say when he realized what was happening?' her mother asked. 'Surely he told them they were in the wrong house.'

'They weren't,' Annie shouted. 'They knew his name, they said it . . . ' She couldn't tell them he hadn't seemed shocked, or that she was the one who'd insisted they were making a mistake. He'd said almost nothing, had simply allowed them to take him away . . .

'When they made the arrest,' her father said, 'they must have named the victim.'

Annie tried again to recall what she'd heard. 'It was female,' she said, 'I think Carol, or Karen . . . I can't remember the surname. It wasn't anyone we know, I'm sure of it. Or no one I know, anyway.' What was she saying? She'd just made it sound as though she thought David might know the victim.

'Mum, what's going on?' Quin wanted to know, coming into the kitchen.

'Nothing, sweetheart,' Harriet assured him, 'just a company meeting about accounts and things. Where's Godfrey?'

'Downstairs. Can we have something to eat?'

'I'll find you something,' Annie said, getting to her feet.

'Top!' he cried, as she handed him two packets of crisps, then spinning around he was gone again.

'Maybe we should all have something,' Julia suggested.

'I'm going to call Hugo,' Henry said, taking out his phone, 'see if there's any news.'

They waited, hardly daring to breathe as he made the connection, but he ended up leaving a message asking Hugo to call asap.

One hour turned into two and then three. Godfrey's parents came to collect him, and Harriet took Quin upstairs for a bath. Although Julia and Annie had rustled up omelettes and a salad no one had been able to eat more than a few mouthfuls and no one, Annie realized, was intending to go home until they knew what was happening to David.

She wasn't sure if she was glad they were there, until she realized she'd probably have asked them to come if they weren't. It would have been too difficult to be alone, trying to make everything seem normal for Quin, while nothing could be with David where he was and no understanding of why.

At last, just after seven thirty, her mobile rang and seeing it was David she snatched it up so fast she almost dropped it. 'Where are you?' she cried, aware of the others watching her. 'Are you OK? Shall I come and get you?'

'I'm fine,' he assured her. 'Hugo's driving me . . . Is anyone with you?'

'Everyone,' she replied. 'We've been so worried. What's it about . . . ?'

'I'll tell you when we get there. Ask Dad and Henry to stay . . . ' He broke off as Hugo spoke, and coming back on the line, he said, 'It doesn't matter if everyone's there. They'll find out soon enough anyway, so best they hear it from me.'

CHAPTER SEVEN

Cassie was already on her feet, tail wagging joyously, as David came in through the back door with Hugo. Both men were wet from a quick dash through the rain, and looking strained in spite of the upbeat tone Hugo injected into his voice as he greeted them. Thankfully Quin was in bed by now, and more food had been prepared in case David or Hugo were hungry.

Annie went straight to David and was so relieved to feel his arms around her that she willed him not to let go. She'd never admit to him that she was afraid of what he was about to tell them, that she was so thrown by everything that she had no idea what to think, but she guessed he knew it anyway. She didn't. How could she, when she knew he'd never hurt anyone?

'Can I get you a drink, Hugo?' Henry offered, as Julia pulled out a chair for the lawyer to sit down.

'I'll take a Scotch, if I may,' Hugo replied, and handed his Barbour to Francis, who went to hang it in the cloakroom.

'Help yourself to some game pie, or quiche,' Harriet told him. 'You too David. You must be famished.'

'I'm going to wash my hands,' David responded, and

as he left the kitchen Annie realized he'd barely even looked at anyone – that alone made her so tense she was hardly able to breathe. She wanted to go after to him, to insist he explain what was happening before he told everyone else, but she stayed where she was. She wasn't sure why; perhaps because she didn't want him to try to avoid her, or to confirm her dread that something was horribly wrong.

Of course there was. He'd been arrested, for God's sake, taken away by armed police, and the very fact that he and Hugo hadn't come in declaring that it had all been cleared up could only mean that it hadn't been.

Eventually everyone was seated around the table with the hall door closed in case Quin woke up, and rain battering the windows so hard that they held the silence for a while until the worst of it passed. To Annie it felt like demons trying to force their way in, a terrible fate determined to access their perfect world and smash it to pieces. She tried to push the disturbing thoughts aside and slipped a hand into David's. She wasn't entirely sure whether she was hoping to comfort him, or if it was an attempt to draw on his strength; she only knew that she needed to remind him that she was there, and to feel the solace of their connection.

At last, deciding he'd have no trouble being heard now, Hugo said, 'David and I agreed that I'd explain what this is all about, but David, please jump in whenever you want to.'

David nodded, and downed a neat double Scotch before pushing his glass forward for a refill. As his father obliged, Annie felt the unsteadying memories of David's post-army and City days stirring inside her. She hoped to God the stress of this wasn't going to make him take that sort of refuge again.

Noticing how worried Dickie looked as he passed back the refill, Annie wished there was something she could say to reassure him, but right now all they could do was brace themselves for whatever Hugo was about to tell them.

'We're in a very tricky place,' Hugo began, seeming to feel it as much as anyone present, 'but I'm going to do my best to talk you through the details. I guess you all know by now that David was arrested this afternoon for a murder that was committed twenty years ago.'

Annie's heart skipped beats as she felt her family's shock and confusion like a palpable force. She hadn't known it had happened so long ago, and wondered what effect this would have on the situation.

Suddenly everyone began speaking at once.

'It's crazy . . . '

'They've obviously got the wrong person.'

'I don't believe it.'

'Why did they pick on you?'

Hugo said, 'What led the police to David is going to be difficult to hear for all of you, but most of all for Sienna when the time comes, because it was her DNA that provided a familial match to the DNA found on the underwear of the young girl who was killed.'

Annie's blood ran cold, then unbearably hot, as she took in the fact that Sienna's stupid escapade with a teddy bear had led to *this* . . . To her father being arrested, accused . . .

Realizing she was fixating on the wrong issue, she looked at her own father as he said, 'Can we ask who the victim is?'

'Her name is Karen Lomax,' Hugo replied. He waited a moment for someone to utter some sort of recognition, or even ask a question, but no one did. 'Her parents used to own the Cheers wine bar in Kesterly Old Town back at the time she disappeared.'

Julia said shakily, 'I remember her, now you've put her into context. I mean, I didn't *know* her, but I do remember that the couple in the wine bar had a daughter who went missing.'

'And her body was found some time later?' Harriet asked, clearly struggling to recall the detail. 'Somewhere on a building site?'

Hugo said, 'You're thinking of the right girl. Her body was discovered in early September after she disappeared in August. It had been dumped in an old railway hut on what's now the Embury Vale Estate.'

Harriet was nodding. 'We still had the place in Monksilver at the time,' she reminded her husband. 'It was so sad. I felt desperately for her parents. I didn't know them, but . . . ' Seeming to reconnect with what it was now meaning to her family, she trailed into silence.

Hugo continued. 'I guess we all went to that wine bar from time to time, I know Sukey and I did – we were still dating then – but I have to admit I don't recall much about the girl, only that she was in her teens and kind of out there, if you know what I mean.'

Realizing now that she remembered the girl too, Annie felt terrible to think that she'd been so easily forgotten. At least, by them.

'There's no way in the world my son is responsible for this,' Dickie declared. He was regarding Hugo balefully, as if it were the lawyer doing the accusing rather than the police.

'Absolutely no way,' Julia added, sounding aggrieved that anyone could even suggest it. Her cheeks were flushed, her eyes bright with anger and what seemed to be fear, making Annie wonder if she truly believed what she was saying.

Tightening his hold on Annie's hand, David spoke for the first time. 'I don't know if you missed exactly what Hugo said just now, but it's important – and it's bloody devastating unless . . . you, Dad, can tell us that you've got another son or a brother out there somewhere.'

Dickie frowned in confusion.

David said, 'The DNA match is what they call familial. This means that a male relative of Sienna's is . . . Connected to the murder.' He swallowed and squeezed Annie's hand again as he waited for his words to sink in.

Julia suddenly cried, 'You surely can't be saying that Henry was responsible?'

David didn't answer.

Henry's face was ashen; so was Dickie's.

'This can't be happening,' Harriet muttered, looking at Francis as if he could explain it, or make it go away.

Hugo spoke again, his tone of pragmatism and calm cutting through the building tension, but only for moments. 'The police have already taken David's DNA,' he said. 'They'll be in touch with you, Dickie, and you, Henry, over the next couple of days to collect samples from you and probably to question you as well.'

Julia was having none of it. 'I think they should refuse,' she protested. 'There has to be a mix-up, something has got into the wrong place at the labs, these things happen . . .'

Hugo said, 'Whatever the scenario, and we hope you're right, we still have to comply with the law.'

Annie could almost feel the strain increasing between

David, Dickie and Henry, the disbelief of the position they were in, the horror, the questions they must want to ask, the tangle of so many emotions she could hardly begin to imagine them. How afraid they must be, how desperate to cling to the possibility that there had been a mix-up, for otherwise it meant that one of them had, at the very least, had sexual relations with young Karen Lomax before she died. She swallowed hard as the horror of it rose up like a deafening white noise in her head. Not Dickie surely, he'd been in his fifties by then, more than thirty years Karen's senior although still attractive, and the girl she remembered had flirted with just about anyone who came through the door. Dickie had always had an eye for the girls, could give as good as he got when it came to a tease, but she'd never suspected him of taking things any further than the moment. Henry, on the other hand, had long had a reputation for sleeping around, except he'd been married to Laura by then, no longer even living in the area . . .

Harriet said to Hugo, 'So what happens next?'

The lawyer replied, 'We wait for the results to come back from the labs. We'll know then who the sample found on the victim actually belongs to.'

'How long will that take?' Julia asked. She was fingering her pearls so aggressively now that Annie felt sure they were going to break. For a moment she wished she had pearls to agitate too.

'David's DNA will already have been sent to the labs,' Hugo said. 'Dickie, yours and Henry's will go as soon as they have it, so depending on the backlog it could be a couple of weeks, maybe longer.'

'You mean we have to live with this hanging over us

for all that time,' Julia protested, 'no one trusting anyone, or having any idea who might be lying . . . '

'That's enough,' Henry told her quietly.

Julia shut up.

Annie looked at Henry, half expecting him to admit that it had been him if only to put his brother and father out of their misery, but he said no more.

'Who's that texting you?' Julia snapped, as Henry's phone pinged for the third or fourth time in less than a few minutes. 'Why don't you check?'

Anything to distract them from this nightmare, Annie thought, but Henry said, 'It doesn't matter who it is. Not while this is going on.'

After that a horrible silence fell; no one was able to think of anything to say that would seem right, or appropriate, or in any way reassuring; it had already gone too far for that.

Hugo rose to his feet. 'I should be going,' he said. 'Sukey'll be expecting me.'

David got up too. 'Thanks for being there today,' he said, shaking Hugo's hand, 'and for bringing me home.'

'You got it,' Hugo told him, clapping a supportive hand on his shoulder. To the others he said, 'Any questions, anything you want to get off your chest, you know where I am.'

After he'd gone Henry said to Julia, 'I guess we should be going too. Dad, can we give you a lift to the cottage?'

Dickie looked at David. It seemed he wanted to say something, but in the end he merely got up and went for their coats.

Harriet said to Annie, 'Dad and I can stay if you'd like us to.'

'It's OK,' Annie replied. 'The rain seems to have gone off, so you shouldn't have any trouble getting back.'

Harriet came to hug her, and Annie couldn't have loved her more when she did the same to David. 'It'll get sorted,' she said to him softly. 'Call if you need anything.'

'Thanks,' he murmured, and as he accepted another hug from his father-in-law, Annie knew he hadn't missed the fact that his own father and brother were at the door ready to leave.

Annie looked at Julia, not sure what to say, or even if she should approach her for their usual parting embrace.

Julia stayed where she was, at Henry's side. 'I don't suppose any of us is going to sleep well tonight,' she said, an accusatory note in her voice as she looked at David. 'I know I won't.'

David said nothing, only waited until the door had closed behind them all before heaving a weary sigh. 'That didn't take long, did it?' he commented.

Annie regarded him questioningly.

'For our family to fracture. I guess it's no surprise, we'd have been crazy to expect anything else given these fuck-awful circumstances.' He dashed a hand through his hair and suddenly clenched it in a fist as he growled in frustration.

Going to him, Annie said, 'I'm not making excuses for Julia, but obviously she's upset . . . '

'I don't care about her,' he cut in fiercely, 'it's my brother and father . . . What the f . . . ? It's like they think I did it and now I'm trying to push it off on them.'

Taking his hands in hers, she said, 'Let's try to put that to one side for the moment. Just tell me what the police asked you . . . '

'Not now,' he protested, pulling away. 'I've had about as much as I can take for one day.'

She watched him walk away, feeling desperate for him, and helpless to know what to say or do, but most of all she was thinking of the children and how the heck they were going to explain any of this to them.

CHAPTER EIGHT

Natalie was perched on the edge of a desk in the incident room where there was space enough for five times as many detectives as were currently present. However, it wasn't the size of her team that was occupying her attention. It was one of the photographs of Karen Lomax, pretty, blonde and blue-eyed, sassy-looking, too much make-up, lash extensions, lip augmentation – a child trying to be a woman.

Next to her picture was the mugshot taken yesterday of David Crayce, not quite so handsome here – harder, threatening, as most came across in mugshots.

Seeing a suspect in close proximity with a victim like this could often be unsettling, especially when there was such a discrepancy in size, power and age. It did things to the imagination she'd rather shut down than run with even though it was her job to explore all possibilities. Of course she realized that Crayce now was not the Crayce of almost twenty years ago; back then he might not have appeared quite so lived-in, or self-satisfied, king of all he surveyed. However, he'd not long been out of the forces so he'd no doubt have had the same formidable physique and arresting good looks, a tough, all-pervasive masculinity that had probably appealed to many girls.

Next to their images were two more that had been lifted from the Hanley Combe website, Crayce's father and brother. Both appeared smart and confident, distinguished business- and sportsmen, but few knew better than her how deceiving looks could be, how easily a person could be taken in by charm and flattery, status, background, age and intelligence, only to find out the hard way what a terrible mistake they'd made.

Right now, Leo Johnson was talking the team through dates and other details he'd already written up on the board, and Natalie listened carefully, wanting the information implanted in her mind as indelibly as her own name.

'So, what we know,' he was saying, clearly comfortable with taking the lead she'd offered him, 'is that Karen was reported missing on the morning of 8th August 1999, but it wasn't acted on until much later that day, given her age and habits of staying out all night with friends. Her disappearance is dated 7th August because she was last seen at a bus stop near her home on the Old Moor Road around ten o'clock in the evening of that day. It was a bus driver who pulled over to let her on board, but she waved him on. It's presumed from this that she was waiting for someone to pick her up, but none of her friends could throw any light on who it could have been, and Lucy Aldridge, who she'd told her parents she was going to stay the night with, claims in her statement that they'd had no such arrangement.'

'Shame they didn't have Facebook or Instagram back then,' Shari commented. 'Just thinking about how useful they are now.'

'Indeed,' Johnson replied. 'She had a mobile phone – Nokias were all the rage back then and she had one, apparently, but it was never found.'

'And no such thing as a tracking device,' Noah Shields sighed.

Johnson shook his head and moved them on. 'The lead suspect at the time,' he said, 'was an individual by the name of Timbo Jaks. He was a fairground Traveller who'd been in the area just prior to Karen's disappearance. Her friends say she had a fling with him, but nothing ever turned up to indicate she'd run off with him, and after her body was found and the semen proved not to be his, he was let go.'

'Was she raped?' Shari Avery asked.

Johnson projected the pathologist's report from his laptop to the screen beside the whiteboard. 'Although a degree of deterioration had occurred by the time she was found,' he replied, 'it's not believed to have been violent if intercourse took place. There were no detectable injuries apart from one to the back of her head, which could have been sustained in a fall, or by a blow from a heavy instrument. The pyramidal-shaped depression in the skull suggests a sharp corner either of a step or maybe a table, or it could have been caused by some sort of tool used as a weapon. There's no evidence of where the crime might have taken place, but it's not thought to have happened where the body was found.'

As he turned to the area map covering one half of the whiteboard Natalie was picturing someone – David Crayce? – carrying Karen's fragile and lifeless body to the spot Leo was indicating, marked with a red pin. How had he got her there? There weren't any roads shown in the old photographs, it was wasteland, nothing around for miles. Only a four-wheel drive could have navigated that terrain, the very sort of vehicle Crayce owned now and quite likely had then.

'Given that this is the Embury Vale Estate today,' Leo continued, 'we have to rely on photographs taken by SOCOs and forensics at the time of discovery, along with their reports which luckily are pretty detailed. Apparently she was wearing a pink halter top, white jeans and metallic platform sandals, all of which coincides with what her parents said she'd been wearing when she went out on the evening of 7th August. She also had a fake Louis Vuitton bag with her, which never turned up. Needless to say, the clothes were in a pretty bad state by the time she was found, weather, wildlife . . . It's all detailed in the report. Noah, you have a question?'

Noah Shields dropped his raised hand as he said, 'Were any other premises searched at the time besides the wine bar and Traveller caravan site?'

Leo nodded. 'Her parents' flat was given a thorough going-over, ditto her grandmother's house, and the homes of her friends, but nothing suspicious ever came to light.'

'So the parents were definitively ruled out?' Shari Avery asked.

'They were.'

'Which isn't to say we won't be interviewing them again,' Natalie assured her. To Leo she said, 'Give me an idea of distance between the Crayce part of Exmoor and where Karen's body was found.'

Turning back to the map, he said, 'At a guess it's around fifteen miles, could be a bit more.'

'Do we have anything to say that she ever visited the Crayce farm?'

'No.'

She made a mental note to add that to the questions

she had for the parents, given there was nothing about it in their statements, and nodded for Leo to continue.

'Moving on to David Crayce,' he said, 'and what we know about his situation in August of 1999. Apparently he and his then soon-to-be wife were constructing a house on the land they'd recently purchased next to the Crayce family farm. So, he was around, albeit out there on the moor, ten or more miles from town and even further from where Karen was found, but he admits to visiting the wine bar from time to time. He claimed at first to have no idea who Karen was, but eventually he admitted that he did vaguely remember her.'

Noah Shields said, 'Do we know if his brother and father were also around at the time?'

'I think we can safely say the father was,' Leo replied, 'given that he and his wife lived at the farm, but on the actual dates in question he could have been anywhere. You and Shari can ask him later today when you go to interview him and Henry Crayce. I'll email addresses and map coordinates when this briefing is over. Apparently the father lives in a cottage on the Hanley Combe Estate these days, and the brother's next door at the family farm that's now a stables and animal refuge. I'm sure you know that next door up there can mean miles apart, but in this case the satellite tells me it's no more than three.'

Natalie said, 'Remind me, what age was David Crayce in 1999?'

Indicating the board where he'd written it up, Johnson said, 'He'd have been twenty-six in June of that year.'

'And his brother?'

'We don't have a DOB for him yet, but apparently he's younger. The father would probably have been around the fifty mark, unless he was a lot older than his wife who died three years ago aged sixty-eight.'

'Do we know how she died?'

'Cancer.'

'How do you know all this?' Shari Avery demanded.

'I used Google,' Leo told her simply. 'Most of it's there if you scroll through far enough.'

Miming a shot to her own head, she said, 'Do any of us seriously believe the father, Richard Crayce, might have done it?'

Surprised by the question, Natalie said, 'Do you have a reason why we shouldn't?'

Colouring slightly, Shari said, 'I guess the age and everything, but hey, when did that ever make a difference?'

'He's not being ruled out,' Leo informed her.

Natalie said, 'Tell me about the female members of the Crayce family, I mean those still living. Obviously we know David has a sixteen-year-old daughter who's obligingly kicked all this off, but what do you know about his and Henry's wives?'

'Not much,' Leo admitted. 'I didn't see them as a priority, so . . . '

'They're not, yet,' Natalie assured him, 'I'm just trying to get a better picture of the brothers, but it'll come in good time.' She glanced round as someone came into the room, and seeing it was DCI Gould she and the others got to their feet.

Standing them down, he said, 'I know it's too early for any breakthroughs on this, but I'd appreciate an update on how you're going to handle it, DS Rundle. We're not flush with manpower, and you won't want to hear me banging on about budget cuts again. I'll just say that we need to come up with something convincing pdq to persuade those in charge that we really do have a case.'

'Of course, sir,' Natalie responded. 'I think the DNA surely tells us that . . . '

'It's compelling, but we all know that finding DNA isn't necessarily proof of a crime.'

'I realize that, sir. I'm happy to come to your office to discuss developments before we go to visit Karen Lomax's parents.'

'No, no, you can fill me in when you get back.' He took a long look at the whiteboard and then stepping in closer he said, 'I'm not a shooting man myself, but I know a few who are, so if you're looking for background on the school and those that run it, just let me know.'

'Thank you, sir,' Natalie replied. 'We'll do that. Before you go,' she added quickly, as he started to leave, 'I was thinking of tipping the press off about Crayce's arrest. I understand that it's not a story of national interest – at least not yet – but it could shake a few things up locally, get people remembering stuff they thought they'd forgotten, either about Karen Lomax, or about the Crayces.'

Gould regarded her thoughtfully as he considered this. Bringing in the press could be risky and many pressures and useless leads could result from it, but in the end he nodded. 'OK, do it,' he said, 'but don't use the official channels yet.'

'I didn't intend to,' Natalie assured him. 'I'll ask someone downstairs to put in a call to someone he or she knows on the *Gazette*.'

After Gould had gone, Natalie turned back to her three-person team. 'I'll leave the tip-off to the press to one of you, as you know more about who's who and what's what around these parts. Just make sure no one on our side is persuaded into any statements or interviews until we're ready.' She checked her watch. 'OK, I think we all know what we're about for the rest of the morning, so we'll reconvene here at one. Just don't forget to take the elimination kit with you,' she told Noah, who'd done exactly that on a case before Christmas. 'And as soon as you get back here with those DNA samples,' she said to him and Shari, 'make sure they go straight off to the lab. We need an answer on this as fast as they can turn it around.'

CHAPTER NINE

Annie wasn't sure what made her leave her desk and go to the front window of the byre when she did, but having done so she was in time to see a man and woman she didn't recognize coming out of Dickie's cottage and getting into a car. She watched them drive away and waited to see if her father-in-law came out, but there was no sign of him. She wondered if she ought to go over there, he'd probably just been questioned by the police and had a swab taken, but she had no idea how welcome she'd be or if David would want her to discuss this intolerable situation with anyone but him.

Not that he was opening up about anything himself. He still hadn't told her any details of his interview with the police yesterday, so all she knew was what Hugo had shared with them last night. However, she accepted that David had been exhausted by the time everyone had left, and there had been no opportunity to talk this morning, given his five o'clock departure to host a shoot.

Turning away from the window she looked around the Byre taking in the antlers, the fireplace with fitfully flaming logs, leather chairs and centre table with complimentary copies of specialist magazines for clients. Outside two regular freelance coaches were taking lessons on the stands; she could see one of them through the back windows showing a group of giggling women how to hug the gun and follow the clays. The explosions of the shots that she normally barely registered seemed to be jolting through her like lightning today.

She glanced at her watch as if it might tell her whether it was permissible to text David to make sure he was OK. She sensed it would be the wrong thing to do – he wouldn't appreciate any reminders of his situation while out with important clients. The whole crazy mess would be waiting for him when he got home, and she supposed she should feel thankful that at least Henry wasn't with him today. That would almost certainly have been too much of a strain on them both, so just as well Henry had a safari booked in for this afternoon. He was due to meet a local history group in Porlock at one, and she wondered if the police had managed to catch him for a DNA swab before he'd left. She could call Julia to find out, but didn't feel comfortable about doing so, not after how angry she'd seemed with David last night.

'It's bloody awful,' she told her mother when Harriet rang for the second time that day to find out if there was any more news. 'I don't see how we can keep going like this, we've no idea how long it'll be until those results are back – and what are we supposed to do when Sienna and Max come home at the weekend? They're bound to realize something is wrong, so what do we tell them?'

'You'll have to be truthful with them,' her mother replied soberly, 'and actually it's why I'm calling. It's only a matter of time before it'll find its way onto social media, so if you want me to come and man phones at the Byre while you drive over to the schools . . . You really don't want Sienna finding out from anyone but you or David.'

Of course, her mother was right, and it wasn't as if she hadn't thought of it herself, but now she needed to act on it. 'I'll have to speak to David first,' she said, 'find out if he wants to come with me. If he does, it'll have to wait until this evening. Do you think we're safe until then?'

'It's hard to say, but I agree, you can't go without letting him know what you're doing. Can you call him?'

'I don't know if there's any phone reception where he is today. There usually isn't, but I'll give it a try and get back to you about whether I need you to stand in for me here.'

'OK. Before you go, I'm guessing still no sign of Julia today?'

Annie's heart sank as though it was being drawn into the rift opening up between them all. 'Not yet, and she hasn't called either. I just saw the police leave Dickie's, so I presume they've tried to catch up with Henry too.' She took a breath and let it go heavily. 'You must have picked up last night that Julia's furious with David . . . Oh God, I can hardly believe this is happening. When I think of this time yesterday . . . Actually, there were armed police creeping about all over the place that we didn't see until they were bursting in through the door like they were in *Line of Duty*. One minute your life is completely normal, the next it's like someone's thrown a ticking bomb into it and no one knows when it's going to go off. Maybe it's already happened, and we're just waiting for the fallout.'

'I wish I knew what to tell you,' her mother sighed, 'but you know I'm here if you need me. Just text if you want me to come over and I'll ask Dad to collect Quin from school.'

After ringing off Annie returned to her desk and opened up the week's calendar. Even this close to the end of the season they had wall-to-wall bookings for shoots and lessons, so they needed everyone pulling their weight, but what if Henry decided to stay away from Hanley Combe until this nightmare was resolved? Would he even be with them once it was, if it turned out that he was guilty?

She wondered if she should go warn Hans, in the shop about what was happening, or if the two freelance coaches outside should be told before they left today.

Deciding not to worry about that now, she scrolled to David's number and clicked to connect. As she'd feared, there was no service where he was, so she sent a text on the off-chance it might get through.

We need to talk to Sienna before things hit SM. Thinking of driving over this p.m.. Let me know if you'd rather I wait so you can come with me. Love you, Ax

After she'd sent it she debated whether to follow up with another message letting him know that the police had visited his father, and probably Henry, but in the end she decided not to. He'd find out soon enough, and right now being focused on a shoot was probably a blessed relief for him.

Lucky him. I'll just sit here and worry myself sick over it.

It wasn't you, David, was it? I mean, I know it wasn't, and I hate myself for even thinking it . . .

'Hello,' a tremulous voice said from the door. 'Is it OK to come in?'

Annie looked up and her heart soared with relief to see Julia half in, half out of the Byre. She appeared worried, contrite, oddly lost and clearly not sure of her welcome.

'Of course,' Annie said, putting her phone aside. 'Frankly, I didn't expect to see you today.'

'No, well, I wasn't going to come,' Julia admitted, closing the door, 'but then I decided I had to. I feel so awful about the way I spoke to David last night. I'm sure he doesn't want to talk to me, but at least I can apologize to you.'

Annie sighed and pressed her fingers to her tired eyes. 'I don't blame you for being upset,' she said. 'It was a big shock for us all.'

'You're not kidding. I still can't get my head around it. Henry, David, Dickie . . . And I keep thinking of that poor girl, Karen . . . ' She sat into a chair on the other side of the desk and gazed at nothing as she went on, 'Mummy says she was always a bit too full of herself, asking for trouble, but that's no reason to want to hurt her, is it?'

'No,' Annie answered quietly, because it wasn't. She could imagine how Geraldine would have reacted if she'd found out Dickie had been with a girl more than half his age. It made her think of Sienna and how she'd feel if . . . she quickly shut it down. She just couldn't go there. It was all too awful, too unbearable . . .

Julia said, 'The police came about an hour ago to swab Henry and ask him some questions. I know he called Hugo, but he wouldn't let me be in the room while it was all going on so I don't know what was said – and after they'd gone he wouldn't talk to me about it.' She looked at Annie with teary eyes. 'Has David said anything to you that Henry and I might need to know? Sorry to ask, but I feel if we don't try to stick together as a family . . .'

'He's not talking about it either,' Annie told her.

Julia seemed momentarily alarmed by that, then deflated. 'I honestly don't think that Henry would have hurt that girl,' she said, 'but I get that you don't believe David would either. So that leaves us with Dickie, and where the heck do we go with that?'

Having no sensible answer to offer, Annie got up to fill two mugs with coffee and handed one to her sister-in-law before sitting down again.

'I hate to say this,' Julia said, 'but you've probably noticed anyway how . . . off-key Henry's been acting lately.'

Annie waited for her to go on.

Julia shrugged. 'It's got nothing to do with this. It started a while ago . . . ' Her voice fractured as she said, 'I'm pretty sure he's been seeing Chrissie, it might even be why her husband went back before New Year, and now, if Henry could get me out of the way I'm sure nothing would make him happier.'

'Oh God, Jules,' Annie murmured, not sure whether to get up and comfort her, or simply to pass her a tissue. Opting for the latter, she said, 'I don't think . . . '

'He never really wanted to marry me,' Julia said bleakly. 'I know that, and I think you do too.'

Annie shook her head because she didn't know it at all.

'Back when we were young,' Julia went on, 'I know he was always more interested in her than he was in me, and she was nuts about him . . . ' She gave a dry, shaky laugh, 'First David, then him. I wonder if Henry ever knew he was second choice. He wasn't really, it's just that David was older and kind of more serious, and Henry was . . .

Well, it doesn't matter what he was. It's all so long ago, I don't know why I'm even bringing it up, except she knows she'll never get David now, but she probably doesn't think that about Henry.'

Feeling as caught between the past and the present as Julia clearly was, Annie said, 'I thought she was upset about her husband.'

'It's what she says, but who knows if it's true?'

'But I've seen you with her,' Annie protested, thinking back to New Year's Eve, and wondering if she was properly following this. 'You seem so friendly with her and . . .'

'Because I thought if we became close again, the way we used to be, that she'd feel guilty about what she was doing and leave him alone. I mean it's different now, isn't it? We're older and Henry and I are *married*. It doesn't seem to be working, though. She's still here and whatever's going on with her husband, she surely ought to be back at work by now.'

Not disagreeing with that, Annie said, 'Have you asked Henry about it?'

'Yes, and he denies it, but he would, just like he's denied hurting poor Karen Lomax.'

Annie was caught by a jolt of shock. 'Does that mean you think he did hurt . . . '

'No, no, that's not what I'm saying. What I mean is that anyone can say anything, can't they, and you've got no way of knowing if it's the truth.'

Annie stared at her, thinking of how depressingly true that was.

'I still reckon there's been a mix-up with the DNA,' Julia stated. 'I'm sure that's happened, aren't you?'

Annie so desperately wanted to say yes that she almost

did, but it seemed naive, delusional even to grasp at such an unlikely straw when she only had to think of the way David was handling things, Henry and Dickie too, to feel that there was more to this than anyone was admitting.

Julia's eyes came to hers. 'You don't believe it?' she asked, looking slightly panicked. 'Oh God, has David told you something?'

Annie looked at her mobile as it jingled out Sienna's ringtone. After holding the phone up for Julia to see who was calling, she clicked on.

'Mum! What the f—?'

'Sienna, I'm coming over to the school.'

'*What!* Why would you do that? Just tell me it's not true.'

'It's . . . complicated,' Annie said lamely as Julia buried her face in her hands.

'How can that be? It's either true or it isn't, and why am I finding out on effing Instagram?'

'I'm sorry . . . You shouldn't . . . ' Annie quickly asserted, 'Listen, I want you to go to your housemistress – you know how much you like her – tell her what's happening and ask if you can stay with her until I get there. It'll only take me an hour . . . '

'All right, I'll do that, but Mum, I'm scared. Like *really* scared.'

'I understand, but please try to stay off social media until I've had a chance to talk to you.'

'Where's Dad? Is he in prison?'

'Of course not! He's on a shoot. If I can get hold of him I expect he'll come with me.'

'No! You can't bring him here. Everyone knows . . . '

'OK, I'll come alone. Actually, I think I need to bring you home for the night. I'll get hold of Max and pick him up at the same time.' How fortunate that their schools were right next to each other.

'Yeah, you have to do that, because if he doesn't know already it'll only be because he's on the rugby field.'

Suspecting that was the case, Annie said, 'Do as I say now and go see Mrs Jackson. I'll call to let her know I'm on my way.' As she rang off she saw that Julia was frantically sending a text.

'I'm letting Henry know where I am,' she explained, 'and that I'll be here holding the fort until you get back from the school. I'll text Matilda now to ask if she can stay on at the stables until I can get there.'

Annie was about to call the school when a message arrived from David.

We need to talk to her together.

Though relieved by that – at least he wasn't shying away from it – Annie couldn't help noticing the absence of his usual *Love you*. Putting it aside, she quickly messaged back.

Things have moved on. Going to get her and Max now. We'll see you at home later.

She considered ending it there, but told herself it was petty and added *love you, x*

'Thanks for staying,' she said to Julia as she went for her coat and car keys. 'I'll call Mum from the car to let her know what's happening. Hopefully she'll keep Quin at hers tonight while we deal with Sienna and Max.'

Julia glanced over her shoulder as Hans came through from the shop with a customer and sat him down in front of the fire to try on some boots. Keeping her voice low she said to Annie, 'What shall I do if the police get in touch?'

Annie stared at her. 'Why would they?'

'I don't know, but if they do?'

'They won't,' Annie stated, and before Julia could unload any more insecurities she continued on out of the door.

CHAPTER TEN

Natalie was in DCI Gould's office updating him on the morning's progress, while just along the corridor the rest of CID – those not involved in the Karen Lomax investigation – were tackling their own workloads in the open-plan area. By the sound of it as she'd passed they had a lot going on, and she knew it was all current and pressing, but so was her case given the familial DNA match. So there was no need for her to feel anxious or inadequate, her demonstration of strength and capability was holding up well, and seemed to be convincing everyone to the point that it was convincing her too. She'd always been a good detective, one of the best, and there was nothing or no one, but herself, to stop her being one again.

'Shields and Avery collected samples from the other two Crayces this morning,' she was telling Gould. 'Apparently they both called Hugo Blum before answering any questions, so whichever way this falls it looks like the hotshot lawyer has himself a client.'

'I'm guessing from that there wasn't a confession,' Gould remarked, glancing at his computer screen as an email dropped in.

'No, but we weren't really expecting one, and frankly

my money's still on David. That's based as much on gut instinct as it is on the fact that Henry was living in London at the time Karen went missing. Which isn't to say he wasn't visiting these parts; he's doing some checking to see if he can be specific about his movements. Same goes for the father, Richard, although he was definitely living at the farm and says it's very likely that he was around.'

'Did the father ever visit the wine bar?'

'Apparently yes, a few times with his wife, and with other members of the family, and he remembers Karen as being a "bit of a lass", not that he ever spoke to her much.' Her look was as cynical as her tone. 'Henry says his memory of her is vague, he'd left the area a few years before she disappeared, but what he remembers from the odd occasions he went to the bar was that she had a loud laugh and seemed to enjoy being the centre of attention.'

Gould nodded thoughtfully, but she could see he was distracted by whatever was happening on his screen.

'The swabs have already gone off to the labs,' she informed him. 'I'm hoping to hear something within a fortnight.'

He took a moment to bash out a few words on his keyboard, apparently clicked send, and said, 'How did you get on with the victim's parents? The Lomaxes? Where are they living now?'

'On the Fairweather estate in a very nice detached place not far from the coast. However, as luck would have it, they took off yesterday for Cape Verde where a neighbour kindly informed us they have an apartment. According to the same neighbour they're not expected back until the end of March.'

Gould frowned a warning. 'I hope you're not angling

to go out there and talk to them,' he told her. 'If you are, it's not going to happen.'

She smiled sweetly. 'And there I was thinking you might like to come with me.'

To her surprise he looked amused, or not offended anyway, while she was rather pleased with her little show of temerity. 'Have you spoken to them by phone?' he asked. 'Do they know yet that the case is back on the front burner?'

'They were out when Leo called earlier,' she replied. 'He left a message, so we're hoping to speak to them some time this afternoon.'

'OK, so your next move is?'

'We're currently going over every statement taken during the initial investigation and where it seems worthwhile we'll interview the witnesses again. Some might be dead by now, others will have moved away, but some are sure to still be around. What we're really looking for is someone who might have seen Karen with either of the Crayces, preferably on August 7th, but any other time will do if it establishes a connection.'

'OK, anything else?'

'We've had some responses following the leak to the *Gazette*, none have proved fruitful so far. Shari Avery's on it, she's also monitoring social media. You never know, now the Crayce name has been added to the mix it might jog a few memories, or get people thinking in a different way.'

'Sure. Anything else?'

'Actually, I'm quite interested to talk to David Crayce's wife, find out what she remembers about that time. Unfortunately, we can't do the same with Henry's or Richard's wives as both are dead, but Henry's married again and apparently she's an Exmoor girl, so there's a chance she was around back then.'

'Expect Hugo Blum to be all over that,' Gould advised, but he was looking at his screen again and she could see that something was pleasing him.

'Good news?' she ventured.

He chuckled., 'I guess you could say that. I've got myself a date.'

Astonished, as much by the admission as the event itself, she couldn't think what to say.

'Have you ever used the online matchmaking thing?' he asked, getting up from his desk to head for the door, apparently her cue to leave. 'If not, you should try it some time.'

'Do I take it you're a veteran?' she dared to enquire.

He chuckled again. 'No this'll be my first time, so to speak, but I can tell already that she's someone with a GSOH.'

She frowned, then connecting with *good sense of humour,* she said, 'A very important quality, sir. I hope it goes well.'

As she left his office and started back to the incident room, she realized his delight at the prospect of a date was making her feel slightly down about her own lack of a love life. She didn't need her daughters to remind her she was lonely – although they would if she ever confessed to feeling low – because she knew she needed to get out more, especially if she was serious about starting a new life. The trouble was, when she wasn't in someone's face being a cop, she was worried about making the same mistake as she had with her marriage. One bullying misogynist who'd nearly dragged her down with him was enough for this lifetime thank you very much.

So, the slight pang she was feeling that she wasn't DCI Gould's date with a GSOH could just be quelled like the pathetic little delusion that it was. Much better that she waited for her one friend in the area to get in touch, which she would when she got back from her travels, Natalie was sure of that, and when she did it would mark the beginning of a natural return to a wholesome and uncomplicated social life.

Better still right now would be to focus her mind on getting justice for Karen Lomax.

CHAPTER ELEVEN

The south-westerlies were tearing wildly across the moor, moulding the landscape with their relentless might as Annie drove towards Hanley Combe with Sienna and Max in the car. Julia had called before she'd picked them up to let her know that someone had been in touch from the local press wanting an interview, but fortunately she'd managed to get rid of him. As far as Annie could tell, as they went in through the gates, no one was hanging around, and she wondered if Dickie was in his cottage aware of them passing and if he'd been on his own all day. He had few others to talk to, apart from her parents, and she knew he hadn't been in touch with them. There were Julia's mother and aunt, of course, he was close to them, but they were always so busy, and maybe they would be feeling more of an allegiance to Henry. He had other long-time acquaintances in the vicinity, some he'd known since he was a lad, but she couldn't imagine him opening up to any of them. These days his rock, his everything came from his sons, and from her and Julia, so in spite of how David might feel about it, she would go see him soon.

Right now though, getting through the next few hours with the children had to be her priority, and she could only feel thankful that they'd heeded her advice to stay offline during the journey home. They'd already seen enough to alarm them, and she could sense how nervous they were as she brought the Range Rover to a halt at the back of the house, next to their father's Defender.

No one spoke as they jumped out of the car and battled the ferocious winds to the veranda and in through the back door, nor did they think to take their overnight bags. She'd leave them for now and come back for them later.

David was in the boot room feeding Cassie, and as both children went to him, pressing hard into his embrace, she could see how much it meant to him that they hadn't yet turned against him. She gave a small shake of her head as his eyes found hers, letting him know she'd told them nothing yet about the familial DNA. He'd have guessed it anyway from the way Sienna teenage-raged, 'This is so mean, Dad. Why are they saying such evil things about you?'

'We know you didn't do anything,' Max told him, just as passionately.

'I'm sorry you're having to go through this,' David said, still holding them tight. 'Sometimes crazy things happen . . . '

'Who's it supposed to be?' Max demanded. 'Was it something that happened on a shoot?'

David's eyes returned to Annie as he said, 'No, nothing like that.'

Annie took off her coat and, aware that she hadn't embraced David herself, went to take pizzas from the freezer. She was in no mood to cook tonight and guessed he probably wasn't either. Just thank goodness they weren't going to have to explain this to Quin yet, but they would at some point and sooner rather than later.

David took a bottle of chilled white wine from the fridge. 'Shall I open it?' he asked, holding it up.

She nodded, and took down two glasses, expecting he'd have one too.

He did, and to her surprise he poured a couple of inches each for Sienna and Max.

Deciding this might not be good for them on empty stomachs, Annie filled a bowl with Pringles and set it on the table as the three of them sat down, while she retreated to lean against a worktop next to the Aga. She wanted to observe more than participate, at least for now – after all, this was David's situation to explain, not hers, and maybe she was finally going to learn something about his interview with the police.

'Whatever you're going to tell us,' Sienna said, in the bossy tone that often irritated Annie, 'I want you to know that we're on your side.'

'Totally,' Max confirmed. 'I'm guessing it's a mistake, or someone's got it in for you, put you in the frame, set you up . . . '

David glanced at Annie, and she felt a pang of guilt for not having been so vociferous – or blind – in her own support of him. However, they didn't know the full story yet, and she really didn't want to imagine how they were going to react when they found out that the victim was a girl close to Sienna's age who their father might have had sex with before she was killed. She wondered fleetingly how she'd feel if it were *her* father, but couldn't go any further with it without feeling sick.

For the next few minutes she listened, saying nothing, as David ran through what had happened the previous day when he'd been arrested, and that he'd been so shocked by the suddenness of it that he hadn't fully taken in what was happening.

Did that account for why he'd said almost nothing before they'd taken him away?

He went on to tell them how Hugo, whom they knew well, had come to the police station to help sort things out, but in the end it hadn't turned out to be as straightforward as an actual mistake.

'But why did they even think it was you?' Sienna wanted to know, her stroppy tone condemning all police officers as idiots.

'And who's dead?' Max added, an equally relevant question.

With another glance at Annie, David began to explain about Karen Lomax, saying that she was someone who used to live in the Old Town, but that he hadn't really known her so couldn't tell them much about her. 'She disappeared a long time ago,' he continued, 'before either of you were born. She was found dead about a month later and they've never caught who did it.'

'I still don't get what this has to do with you,' Sienna protested.

Realizing how hard it was going to be for him to continue from here, Annie slipped into a chair beside him and put a hand over his as she said, 'DNA was taken from the girl's underwear at the time her body was found that they had no match for until quite recently.'

Max's eyes widened as he looked at his father. 'Are you saying it was yours?' he demanded, starting to look scared.

David shook his head and Annie said, 'There's something called familial DNA, which means . . . '

'Hang on,' Sienna interrupted, clearly muddled, 'why would they come and talk to Dad if they've had the DNA for so long?'

Annie said, 'There's no easy way of telling you this, sweetheart . . . The reason they wanted to talk to Dad is because a match was made from your DNA to the DNA that was found on the underwear.'

Sienna looked perplexed. 'That's insane. Obviously it wasn't me . . . '

'The way it works,' David told her, 'is after they took yours when you were arrested at Christmas, they carried out a routine check with everything else on the database and came up with what's called a familial match.'

The blood was draining from Sienna's face.

'So, it could be like any of us?' Max said.

'Not really,' David replied. 'It was definitely male, but obviously it can't be you or Quin . . . '

'Too right it wasn't me,' he blurted.

David said, 'No, it can only be me, Uncle Henry or Grandpa.'

Annie watched Sienna take this in, and saw the moment when the horror of her part in it truly hit her. She winced as Sienna suddenly shouted, 'Well it has to be Uncle Henry, doesn't it? I mean we know it wasn't you, and it obviously wouldn't be Grandpa . . . Did they arrest them too?'

'No,' David said calmly, 'but the police have taken samples from them to send to the labs. We should know in a couple of weeks who . . . What the outcome is.'

Annie watched the three of them as they fell silent and felt herself breaking apart inside. She wanted with all her heart to believe that the match wouldn't be made to David, and right now she realized that she did believe it. She even wondered how she could have doubted him, and hated herself for it.

Going to stand behind him, she slipped her arms around his neck and rested her head on his.

Holding on to her, he said to Sienna, 'I understand why you think it can only be Uncle Henry, but please don't say it again. This is a very difficult time for the family, especially Grandpa . . . '

'It definitely couldn't be him,' Max protested, echoing his sister.

'So that only leaves Uncle Henry,' Sienna pointed out, 'but don't worry Dad, I get why you don't want us to say anything. But what are me and Max supposed to do when we go back to school? No way am I going to let everyone go on saying terrible things about you.'

Not correcting the grammar for once, David said, 'I wish we could keep you at home until it's all cleared up, but that's not the answer . . . '

'Because it's never going to be cleared up,' Max put in furiously. 'One way or another we've got a killer in the family, so basically our futures are fucked.'

As if only picking up on this now, Sienna wailed, 'And it's all my fault. I'm destroying my family . . . If I hadn't done that stupid thing . . . I didn't even want to . . . '

'Ssh,' David soothed, pulling her to him. 'You can't go blaming yourself for this . . . '

'I'm never going to be able to look at Grandpa or Uncle Henry again,' she sobbed.

'Then there's one good reason why you should go back to school tomorrow.'

She didn't argue with that, only clung to him while Max stared blindly at the wine he hadn't touched as though caught in the grip of a nightmare, which of course he was. Going to him, Annie tried pulling him to her, but instead of yielding he continued to sit stiffly in his chair, unable to move.

In the end, he snapped at Sienna, 'Why don't you stop crying? Oh, that's right, because everything has to be about you . . . '

'Shut up,' she yelled savagely.

'You're selfish and thoughtless and yes, you are to blame for this . . . '

'Stop!' Annie and David cried together.

David said, 'Getting angry and sounding off is understandable, but it's not going to get us anywhere.'

'Tell him to apologize,' Sienna demanded.

'No fucking way,' Max spat, and slamming back his chair he stormed out of the room.

'Mum,' Sienna said plaintively, 'he doesn't get how bad it is to be in my position.'

'I think you're probably right,' Annie agreed. 'I'll have a chat with him later. We'll give him some time to calm down for now.'

Seeming satisfied with that, Sienna took the square of kitchen roll Annie offered and said to David, 'Do you know it was Uncle Henry? I mean deep down, you have to.'

Smoothing her hair, he said, 'No, I don't. Now I think we should probably leave it there for tonight, don't you?'

Much later, after Sienna had cried a lot more and Max had shouted at her to drop dead when she'd knocked on his door, Annie stood outside her son's room for a while, wondering if tonight was the right time to try and talk to him. Or should she leave it until tomorrow?

In the end she tapped the door gently, and to her surprise and relief he said, 'If that's you, Mum, you can come in. Everyone else, stay away.'

Glad David hadn't heard that, she pushed open the door and found the room in semi-darkness, the only light coming from the screen where some sort of video game was in progress. She went to sit beside him on the bed and watched his face in the changing strobes, fierce, intense and ghostly pale.

'It's you I feel sorry for,' he stated, not taking his eyes from the screen. 'You didn't ask for any of this . . .'

'None of us did,' she came in softly.

'But it's still Sienna's fault. If she hadn't . . .'

'You know she had no idea it would come to this, and being angry with her isn't going to help you to deal with it. You two need to pull together, we all do, and we will.'

Still not looking at her he carried on playing. Annie sensed the pent-up emotion inside him, desperate for release.

She made to stroke his hair, but he jerked away. 'You think he did it, don't you?' he growled.

Shocked, Annie said, 'No, I don't. What makes you say that?'

He shrugged.

'Max, he's your father, the best dad in the world, you know he couldn't do anything like that.'

'I'm not saying he did, but you . . . I don't want you to think it either.'

'I don't,' she assured him. 'Max, look at me . . . '

At last his eyes came to her, and seeing they were full of tears she took the remote from his hands and pulled him into her arms. 'I don't know what to do,' he sobbed into her shoulder. 'All the stuff they're saying about him and it's only just started . . . It's like I can't believe it's my dad they're talking about . . . I can't face going back to school, but I know you'll say I have to.'

Aware that Sienna felt the same way, Annie tried to decide how best to handle it, but she could see no alternative. They had to go back, if not tomorrow then certainly the day after, and what kind of hell was it going to be for them? 'We'll talk to Dad again in the morning,' she said, stroking his hair and wanting to keep him safe in her arms forever. 'He doesn't have a shoot so he'll be here . . .'

'He'll say we have to go back, you know he will.'

'Because you do, sweetheart. You can't hide out here until we know the results, it's at least two weeks away and missing that much school isn't an option.'

'But it's OK to have my dad branded a murderer and all the other crap they're saying about him, and you and us . . .'

'What are they saying?'

He shook his head. 'I'm not repeating it. They're just trolls, sickos, but everyone else is reading it.'

'Have you been online since you came up here?' she asked gently.

He nodded. 'Not for long, I just wanted to see if it was still happening, and it is.'

Feeling as upset and frustrated as he was, she said, 'Try not to go on again. If need be close your accounts and if you'd like me to have a word with someone at school, ask them to keep an eye out . . . '

'No, don't do that. It'll only make things worse.' Sitting back, he let his head fall against the wall as he steadied his breathing. 'Justin said he'll be there for me,' he told her, 'so I guess that helps.'

'He's a good friend, and remember he's someone who knows Dad – actually a lot of your friends do, so I expect you'll find there's more support for you than you realize.'

To her relief he didn't argue with that, if anything it seemed to lift him a little, for when he brought his eyes back to hers he attempted a smile. 'I guess having us around will make things more complicated for you guys,' he said, and added quickly, 'Don't worry, I'm not having a go, just saying, is all.'

Pressing a kiss to his forehead, she handed him back the remote and got to her feet. 'Don't stay up too late,' she cautioned, 'and if you feel upset in the night come and find me.'

He waited until she was at the door before he said, 'Sienna's right, it has to be Uncle Henry, but that's nearly as bad because I don't want it to be him either. Or Grandpa. It can't be Grandpa, can it? She was only a kid.'

Unable to do any more than shake her head, Annie told him to try and stop tormenting himself, and closed the door quietly behind her.

She found David in their room still dressed and sitting on the edge of the bed, elbows on his knees, hands clasped between them as he stared down at the floor. He seemed so shattered, defeated even that all she could think to do was massage his shoulders.

'Is he OK?' he asked.

'He will be. Did you talk to Sienna again?'

'Not much. She keeps going back to blaming herself, and nothing I say seems to be making a difference.'

'She's in shock and I guess she's finding her part in it

all easier to understand, hard as it is to deal with. It's very touching how much they believe in you, don't you think? They're not doubting you at all.'

His eyes came up to hers. 'Unlike you,' he challenged softly.

A stab of guilt hit her as she said, 'It's not that I doubt you, I just don't understand why you didn't say anything when they took you away.'

'Do you now?'

'I know that it shocked us both, terrified us even, and I guess we just reacted differently. You stayed silent while I became hysterical.'

Pulling her onto his lap, he held her close as he said, 'There's no right or wrong way to deal with something like that, it's just what happened, but if it helps: I didn't say much because I could hardly take in what was happening, and by the time I did I realized I might need some help. That's when I told you to call Hugo.'

She nodded, and rested her head against his. 'It was a nightmare,' she murmured. 'I can still hardly believe it happened.'

'It's the same for me, but I want you to know that I didn't do anything to that girl. I barely remember her, apart from the fact that she went missing and then they found the body. It was so long ago.'

Annie said, 'I recall seeing her a few times when I was in the wine bar, but I've no idea if you were with me. I could have been with Mum and Dad, or your parents, or friends down from London. I mean, we didn't always go together, did we? Just like we don't always go to the Notley Arms together now. So just because I remember her doesn't mean that you do too.'

With an ironic sort of smile, he said, 'It's starting to sound as though you're trying to convince yourself of my innocence, and I'd rather you just believed in it.'

'I do,' she assured him softly. 'I know you'd never hurt anyone, least of all a defenceless young girl like that.'

As she gazed into his eyes seeing the only man she'd ever loved and wanted to be with forever, she wouldn't let herself think about the dark days when he'd cheated on her. These 'episodes' had happened such a very long time ago, while they were still in London, when he'd been unable to control his drinking, or the nightmares, or the urge to escape in ways that were as self-destructive as they were irrational. His one-night stands had never meant anything, she'd known that even then, although she'd hated it and him for what he was doing to himself and to their relationship. Mercifully he'd had a far better grip on things by the time they'd come here. He'd been much calmer, was over the worst of whatever had bedevilled him since leaving the army, and was energized by the new house, new business, and so in love with her.

She'd never doubted him since then, and she didn't now, but there was no getting away from the fact that waiting for the results was going to be a nightmare for them all, although she suspected it would be worse for Henry and Dickie. Neither one of them had been as faithful in their marriages as they'd wanted their wives to think, especially back when they were younger and seemed to feel free to respond to any pretty girl who looked their way.

CHAPTER TWELVE

31st July 1999

'Mum! Mum! What do you think?'

Jess Lomax looked up from the rail of jean cut-offs she was browsing to where her crazy, lovely daughter Karen was outside a changing room modelling a zebra print mini dress with plunging halter neck and playful black silk ruffle hem. The shameless garment clung so lovingly to her curves and left so little to the imagination that in Jess's honest opinion it was beyond tarty. However, she could see from the sparkle in Karen's eyes that she considered it the coolest thing ever. Maybe she was being too old-fashioned.

'It's a good fit,' Jess smiled, raising amused eyebrows at the gushing praise flowing in Karen's direction from other shoppers, mostly girls her own age, and a couple of sales assistants.

'God, that's totally awesome on you,' a dark-haired teenager with plaits and braces cooed enviously.

'I'd die for legs like that,' another sighed, staring at Karen's smooth bare limbs – not long, but certainly taut and shapely – as though she'd never be able to tear her eyes away.

The pleasure her girl was taking from her reflection was so immodest yet infectious that Jess couldn't help a surge of pride – and she was actually ready to admit that Karen did look good in the dress. If only it were a tad longer and not quite so low cut.

'So, do you like it?' Karen asked over one shoulder.

Feeling many eyes coming to her, challenging her to declare it anything but amazing, Jess said, 'It's gorgeous. Let's get it.'

Breaking into a whoop of delight, Karen threw her arms around her mother. Her father wasn't going to like this much, in fact not at all, although it was unlikely he'd protest too loudly since he'd long ago accepted his role as someone who knew absolutely nothing about fashion.

'When will you wear it?' Jess asked after she'd paid and they were heading out of the air-conditioned shop into a sticky, slightly overcast day to weave through clusters of tourists meandering to and from the beach.

Karen shrugged. 'I guess when we go clubbing. It's a kind of disco thing and it'll go really well with the platforms we got last week in Shoes for Yous.'

Agreeing that it would, if you were into that sort of look, Jess smiled as Karen tucked an arm into hers and gave it a squeeze. 'I know you don't really like it,' she whispered, 'but it did look good on me, didn't it?'

Knowing that in spite of her showy confidence and natural gregariousness Karen's need of her mother's approval was as ingrained now as it had ever been, Jess said, 'It did, and it's not that I don't like it, it's just a bit . . . revealing, is all. I worry someone will think you're giving out the wrong sort of signals.'

Karen laughed. 'And what sort of signals would be wrong?' she teased. 'It's OK, you don't have to answer that. I get what you're saying, but everything's cool, and it's not like you didn't wear revealing stuff when you were my age. I've seen the photos, remember?'

Wryly, Jess said, 'They were private, between me and Dad, you weren't supposed to see them.'

'Then you shouldn't have left them out for me to find. You looked really hot, by the way, and Dad obviously thought so. I reckon half of them are blurred because his hands were shaking when he took them.'

Unable to suppress a laugh, Jess said, 'You could be right there, but I didn't wear that stuff to go out.'

With a sigh, Karen said, 'No, you were all padded shoulders and pouffy permed hair back then. Never a good look. You're much better now. Now tell me, have you decided yet if you're going to come see Westlife with us? Lucy's mum is definitely up for it.'

'Provided we can get cover at the wine bar I'll be there,' Jess assured her, already looking forward to it. The band was one of her favourites, and how she loved the way Karen was always so eager for her to go to concerts with her. In the past year alone they'd seen Bryan Adams, Simply Red and Robbie Williams – although the standout for Jess, which had happened only last month, was when they'd gone to Wembley as a family, plus a dozen or more friends, to see The Rolling Stones.

What an experience that had been, one that she and Eddie would never forget, and would treasure along with many other high points in their lives such as their wedding day, Karen's birth, her first tooth, first steps and the first time she'd come top of her class. This had happened many times since in all sorts of subjects for she was a bright girl. Her teachers predicted a promising future for her, provided she got the grades to study media and communications at the University of the West of England as she hoped. She might be a little wild right now, but that was normal for a girl her age and Jess didn't doubt that when it came time for exams Karen would apply herself with every ounce of determination she possessed in order to achieve her goal.

She was like that, as single-minded as her father could be at times, and as impossibly romantic as him too. Jess couldn't love them more if she tried, or feel more grateful that one of her babies had come to full term and survived – and had turned out to be as special and headstrong and healthy as Karen. Their girl meant everything to them, so much so that she was a little over-indulged, maybe more than that, but being at the centre of her parents' world hadn't made her in any way selfish or entitled or unfeeling towards others. To the contrary, for she was naturally generous and kind and so inclusive of her friends that many of them almost felt like family.

'Dad's already here,' Karen stated cheerily as they entered Brasserie Michel to find her father at the bar, chatting with Michel and his younger brother Anton, the restaurant's flamboyantly French owners.

'Oh lá, lá, if it is not my favourite ladies,' Michel cried delightedly, coming to greet Jess and Karen with outstretched arms. 'My 'eart he is joyful to see you. Karen, I sink you are even more beautiful than when I last see you three days ago.'

Laughing, she kissed him on both cheeks and did the same with Anton before going to embrace her father. 'Who did you leave in charge of the wine bar?' she asked Eddie.

'Mike's there,' he replied, referring to their full-time manager, 'and Ruthie doesn't need my help in the kitchen, so I'm free until two. I have to get back after that for a meeting with a new supplier.' His deep brown eyes softened as they met his wife's. 'Am I bankrupt after all the shopping?' he teased.

'Almost,' she smiled, touching her lips to his. He might be starting to go bald, and was even growing a little paunch, but he was as handsome and desirable to her now as he'd been the day they'd met more than two decades ago.

By the time they were settled at a table on the shady terrace more customers were beginning to pour in, most of them known to Eddie and Jess, so there was a lot of chat and boisterous laughter before they were finally able to order. By then, to Jess's dismay, Karen was exchanging some rather flirtatious smiles with Anton who, though old enough to be her father, possessed the kind of Gallic charm that appealed to females of any age. Not that Jess minded really, she trusted Anton implicitly, even if he was a bit of a rogue; he'd never lay a finger on their daughter and in truth she couldn't imagine Karen was interested really. She was just having fun practising her flirting skills – Jess had done the same when she was that age.

'Lucy always calls him a letch,' Karen whispered, flicking her long brown hair over one shoulder while still smiling Anton's way, 'but he's kind of cute, in a sad old bloke sort of way, don't you think?'

Sighing dejectedly, Eddie said, 'I expect that's how your friends talk about me.'

'Mm, I expect so,' she agreed, and after a moment they burst into laughter.

'So, I have news,' he informed them once their drinks had arrived. 'I popped in to see Millie, the travel agent, on my way here and if anyone's up for it we can have flights and hotel in the Canaries for the autumn half-term break.'

Jess's eyes lit up. They were always in sore need of a holiday by the time the summer rush was over and though she and Eddie might have preferred to go further afield such as Mauritius or the Seychelles, they had to think of Karen's schooling.

Karen said, 'Sounds totally brilliant, Dad, but why don't you guys go somewhere just the two of you? I'm seventeen now, I can take care of myself and you know you don't want me along really.'

'Not true,' he protested. 'We always want you with us, but I get that you're of an age now that you might not want to come. But what if we invited one of your friends? Lucy, for instance. You'd have company to go to the pool and beach . . . '

'Nightclubs more like,' Jess put in.

'Them too. And Mum and I can do our own thing. We wouldn't have to meet up unless you wanted to.'

'That's just weird,' Karen told him. 'Course we'd want to meet up with you, and course I want to come, I just didn't want to be third wheel, but if Luce is up for it, and I know she will be, sure, let's do it. Can't wait.'

Beaming, Eddie said, 'I'll give Millie a call as soon as we've got confirmation from Lucy.'

Taking out the new Nokia she'd received for her birthday, Karen was about to scroll to Lucy's number when she noticed a new string of texts and squealed with delight. 'It is so cool being able to text people,' she declared. 'I'm still rubbish at it, but hey . . . ' She frowned as she saw who they were from.

'A problem?' Jess ventured.

Eddie was getting to his feet to greet arriving acquaintances.

'Not really,' Karen replied. 'It's Timbo. You know, the guy from the fair I told you about.'

'Oh, yes.' Jess had never been wholly approving of that little liaison, had hoped he might have moved on by now. 'Is he all right?'

'Yeah, I guess so. He wants to meet up again, but it's kind of over for me. I don't want to hurt his feelings though.'

'Well you can't see him out of pity. That wouldn't be right.'

'No, I know. He's kind of sweet though, not like you'd imagine from the way he looks. He writes songs, did I tell you that?'

Jess shook her head. 'What sort of songs?'

'They're mostly about dreams and heartbreak, you know, slow dance stuff, but they're really good some of them.' She sighed and put down her phone. 'I'll give him a call later, try and work something out. Look who Dad's talking to now.'

Turning to check, Jess broke into a smile. 'Dickie and Geraldine Crayce.'

'Mm,' Karen replied, smiling too, although she wasn't as fixed on the older couple as she was on one of their sons who'd come in with them. Jess wasn't sure whether it was Henry or David, she didn't know them well enough for that, only that they were both mid-twenties and one of them was married. She watched as this one caught Karen's eye and now Karen was blushing as delightedly as if she'd just been spotted by Robbie Williams.

To Jess's relief the Crayce family were seated at the other end of the terrace – she didn't enjoy the way Karen sometimes played up to men, especially in front of her father. However it was unlikely she'd have done so today, for two younger women had just joined The Crayce's table. The son's wife, she thought, and one of the moor set whose name was escaping her for the moment. Carrie? Katie? Something like that.

'I'll call Lucy,' Karen declared as Eddie sat down again.

'You haven't done that already?' he teased.

Minutes later they were laughing as Lucy could be heard shouting 'Yes, yes yes!' down the phone.

So apparently they were off to the Canaries in October. A lovely treat to look forward to, a rest, some fun, lots of sun and probably too many cocktails next to the pool. The thought of it would keep them going during what was left of this summer, the wine bar's busiest period by far, and by the time it came around they were going to be more than ready to kick back, lie low and forget all about the rest of the world.

CHAPTER THIRTEEN

Before returning to school Sienna and Max insisted on going to see Grandpa Dickie, so Annie took them over. Seeing how overjoyed and relieved he was by the visit persuaded her to invite him to the main house for supper that night. He accepted, not immediately, but she could see that his reluctance was more about what David might think than wanting to stay away. She quickly texted David and got him to call his father to tell him he was welcome.

Annie's parents came too, and although Annie invited Henry and Julia to join them, she received a message back saying that they'd already arranged to go to Chrissie Slater's that night with a few other friends.

'They're definitely avoiding us,' Annie commented after showing the text to David. They were the only ones in the Byre at the time, Hans having left the shop in their care while he went into town for a dental appointment. Henry and Julia had simply not shown up in spite of their admin and coaching commitments.

David shrugged at the text, and carried on rearranging a display of gun slips. As she watched him, his hands steady, his concentration seeming overly intense, she wondered, as she did almost constantly now, what he was thinking. If it was about this nightmarish wait – and how could it not be – he never admitted it.

'Do you know,' she said after a while, 'that Julia suspects Henry of seeing Chrissie, I mean in a romantic way? I don't know how she can go there if she thinks that. Theirs is an odd friendship, it always has been.'

Crossing to a pile of boxes that had recently been delivered, David broke open the top one and began to unpack a new consignment of cartridges. 'It's possible Julia's right,' he stated.

Turning to look at him, Annie said, 'Why? Has he said something?'

'He doesn't have to. When I saw them together on New Year's Eve . . . You know they go way back, he always had quite a thing for her. I even wondered a couple of times if he was unfaithful to Laura with Chrissie.'

Feeling oddly betrayed on Laura's behalf, Annie said, 'Fidelity has never really been a thing for him.'

David merely shrugged. 'I don't think it means he thought any the less of Laura. He loved her, I'm sure of that, but he and Chrissie . . . It's like they can't be together, but they can't help getting it on when they do see one another.' He paused what he was doing, frowning as he thought. 'Julia will remember the way they were, which makes it odd, as you said, that she agreed to go to Chrissie's for dinner if she thinks they're sleeping together.'

'She told me she was trying to befriend Chrissie in order to make her feel guilty about getting involved with Henry.'

David blinked. 'How does that work?'

Wryly Annie said, 'I don't know if it does, but I guess I can see where she's coming from. I'm just not convinced it'll help her, and if it doesn't she'll end up being even more hurt should Henry decide to leave her.'

With a dark irony in his tone, he said, 'The way things are it might not be for another woman, but let's not get into that until we have to.'

Over the following few days, although they had a couple of cancellations for clay pigeon shoots it was easy to put them down to the weather, for heavy snow had come to the moor, smothering the landscape in a dazzling white crust and closing off many of the roads. Perhaps, Annie thought, it was sparing them from unwelcome stalking by the *Gazette* reporter, who'd tried several times and in several ways to be in touch. So far they'd managed to put him off either by not responding to messages, or telling him if he did get hold of them that they had nothing to say. Whether he'd managed to contact Henry or Julia they had no idea, for they hadn't seen them since the day Julia had come to apologize, but Dickie had assured them that he wasn't being bothered, at least not yet.

Glancing out of the window and thinking they'd need one of the Range Rovers to get from the Byre to the house later, Annie picked up her mobile as it rang. She had no chance to speak before Julia's panicked voice came down the line.

'Have you heard from the police?' she cried. 'Did they get in touch with you too?'

With a pang of unease, Annie said, 'No. Are you . . . ?'

'They just rang to ask if they could come and have a chat with me. I told them it wasn't convenient. I mean, why would they want to talk to me?'

It was a good question, although it would be about the case, obviously. 'Is Henry there?' Annie asked.

'No, he went out while I was over at the stables and I can't get hold of him. Do you know where he is?'

Thinking immediately of Chrissie, Annie said, 'He hasn't been here.'

'He'll be with her,' Julia stated flatly. 'He'll lie about it later, but that's where he'll be, and I expect they'll be conveniently snowed in together now. Oh God, oh God!' Annie could almost see her fretting her pearls in anguish. 'Do you think I did the right thing telling the police I wasn't free?' she asked.

Not sure whether she had or not, Annie noticed another call coming in and having an uneasy feeling about who it was she said, 'Let me call you back.' Clicking to the other line she said, 'Hanley Combe Shooting School, can I help you?'

'Mrs Crayce? Annabelle Crayce?' an unfamiliar female voice asked. 'It's DS Natalie Rundle here from Kesterly CID. I'm wondering if we could come and have a chat with you, maybe later today, or tomorrow morning?'

As Annie's mouth turned dry she glanced at the window, to see that the snow was falling more thickly than ever. 'I think you'd find it hard to get here today,' she replied calmly. 'I haven't been out there, but with so much snow I'll be surprised if the roads are passable.'

There was a moment before Rundle said, 'There's no snow here, Mrs Crayce.'

'Well there is here, lots of it, so perhaps we could speak next week? The conditions might be better by then.'

Again a pause before Rundle said, 'I'll get back to you,' and as the line went dead Annie realized she must be going to check the weather on the moor, which meant she couldn't be local or she'd know that rain in town could easily be snow on the higher ground at this time of year.

Clicking off at her end, she went to the gun store where David was cleaning his own and Henry's Perazzis. Hauling Cassie away from the threshold she closed the door so no one who might venture into the shop could hear, and said, 'The police want to talk to me.'

He looked up, frowning. 'Why?'

'They didn't say, but they've also been in touch with Julia. She rang a few minutes ago sounding worried and upset. It seems Henry's done a disappearing act, just to make things worse for her. Anyway, I told the police that we're quite probably already snowed in up here, so it might have to be next week.'

Although they both knew the Defender could get her into town if asked to go, neither of them mentioned it as David put the guns and cleaning rods aside, and took out his phone.

'What are you doing?' she asked.

'Calling Hugo. We need to get his take on this.' Once he'd made the connection he put the call on speaker and said, 'Hugo, are you on the moor by any chance?'

'No, I'm in Bath,' came the reply. 'Is everything all right?'

'The police want to interview Annabelle and Julia, so what do you advise?' His eyes went to Annie's as they waited for an answer.

'They're trying to build a case,' Hugo explained, 'so they'll want to find out whatever they can about your movements at the time of Karen Lomax's disappearance. Does Annie know what she was doing?'

She shrugged helplessly. 'We were working on this place, but as for where we were on any given day . . .'

'Don't worry,' Hugo interrupted. 'I'm sure it's the same

for Julia, but as she wasn't married to Henry back then I can't see what they're hoping to gain from her. I'll give her a call after this. Annie, I think I ought to be there when they question you.'

Startled, she said, 'Really? Why?'

'If nothing else it'll give me an idea of what they do and don't know, which could be helpful going forward. Now, Sukey tells me it's snowing hard with you, so it's not likely I'll get back this weekend, but I'll be on the end of the phone if you need me. Sorry to rush, but I've just stepped out of a meeting.'

After he'd rung off, David was about to speak when his phone rang. 'Euan MacCauley,' he told her and clicked on. 'Hey, Mac, how're things?'

Leaving him to chat with one of the local gamekeepers Annie returned to her desk, going over in her mind the kinds of questions she imagined the police might ask when they did catch up with her. Most seemed fairly obvious, but before she could get a handle on any Sienna rang for the third time that day.

Knowing she'd never forgive herself if she let it go to messages, much as she wanted to, she clicked on.

'Mum, I can't stand it,' Sienna sobbed wretchedly. 'Everyone's being so mean . . . '

'Everyone?' Annie asked, feeling increasingly helpless each time Sienna or Max called or messaged.

'Almost everyone. They won't shut up about it. They're calling me the killer's kid and they pretend to be scared if I even look at them. I spoke to Max just now and you'll never guess what someone said to him – that it's lucky for the girls he's gay, he won't be leaving any sperm on their dead bodies.'

'Oh, God,' Annie groaned, dropping her head into one hand. It was monstrous what they were having to deal with, and though she'd called both schools more than once she knew that trying to rein in this sort of abuse was a losing battle. 'It's almost time to leave for the weekend,' she said, thankful for the truth of it. 'Grandma and Grandpa are coming for you. Have they been in touch?'

'Yeah, Grandma texted when they left the house so they should be here soon. We're staying with them because it looks like you're going to be snowed in?'

'That's right, but if you'd rather come home, Dad'll drive down in the Defender to get you.'

'It's OK.' There was a moment's silence. 'Mum, please don't tell Dad I said this, but it might be easier not to see him while all this is going on. I mean, it's not like I think he did anything, it's just . . . it's doing my head in and I feel so responsible . . . '

'Sen, how many times do we have to tell you it's not your fault?'

It was her fault, if she hadn't got involved in that ludicrous teddy bear prank . . .

'I know, I know,' Sienna wailed, 'it's just really hard to deal with. It's the same for Max. He still hates me, but he's kind of glad we're going to Grandma and Grandpa's this weekend. Don't feel offended, OK? We love you both more than anything, but we . . . Have I upset you, Mum?'

'No,' Annie lied, 'I understand what you're saying, and Dad will too. Call me when you get to Grandma's so I'll know you're safely home.'

* * *

The following afternoon, with David hosting a shoot for five hardy souls over at Fairley Vale and the children with her parents, Annie tried to call Dickie to make sure he was warm and not too lonely over at the cottage, but there was no reply. She looked out of the window, half-expecting him to be making his way through the drifts over to the house, but there was no sign of him. Everything was pristine and white; even David's and Cassie's footprints and the Defender's tracks on the drive had disappeared under the fresh snow that had fallen about an hour ago.

She wondered if Henry, like her, had been worried about his father and so had come to take him to the farm, or perhaps Dickie had gone with David, although David hadn't mentioned taking his father today. She tried Dickie's number again, and after leaving a message for him to call if he needed anything, she conceded that she had no more excuses now not to take the opportunity of being alone in the house to climb up into the attic. She was aware that she should have done it days ago; the only reason she hadn't was because she was afraid of what she was going to find. She still was, and as soon as she was up there a very strong part of her was ready to climb back down, close the hatch and pretend the search was over and had yielded nothing.

She wouldn't do it, her conscience wouldn't allow her to, but as she stood a moment looking around the crowded rafters lit by two bare bulbs and strung with gluey cobwebs she felt momentarily defeated. Apart from the recently returned Christmas decorations neatly packed into various containers, there was so much stuff – boxes, bags, suitcases, abandoned toys, forgotten baby paraphernalia, sports equipment, an entire bric-a-brac shop of family flotsam. She could be up here all day and still not find a medium sized red leather trunk with brass hinges that had once belonged to her paternal grandmother. She was sure at least some of her old diaries were stored in it – not journals, she'd never been one to write down her innermost thoughts. These small notebooks were simply handy week-to-a-page reminder logs that she'd used before switching to the calendar on her phone.

It was clear even before she was properly under way that a thousand memory lanes were tempting her and she could only feel thankful that most of their photos of the children were stored digitally or she'd likely be up here forever.

She'd been going for about an hour when a message pinged into her phone and expecting it to be Dickie, or one of the children, she brushed loose strands of hair from her face and sat back to read it.

It was from Julia.

Hello sweetie, just wondering how you are. This is so awful, isn't it, and I really miss you. Sorry I haven't been over much, issues here ☹ I've been checking the school's shooting messages through the website and can't believe how sick some people are. Hope you haven't seen them, wish I hadn't. I've deleted them, but in case I didn't get to them before you please try to ignore them. I haven't told Henry about them, it'll only make things worse, and they're bad enough already.

I'm guessing the children are having a difficult time of it with social media trolls – oh God, Annie, how is this happening? I hardly know what to say to Henry, not only about this, but about the Chrissie thing. I feel as though I'm losing my mind; the only time anything seems normal is when I'm galloping like the wind over the moor on Moondance, but I dare not risk it in the snow. Don't want her going lame. Sorry if this seems like I'm dumping my problems on you, not my intention, it's just that now I've started this message it's making me think of how much I miss talking to you and being at the Byre. I'm not coming because I'm afraid of saying the wrong thing again and I don't want to upset you, but I hope you've noticed that I'm keeping a check on the website and regularly entering the updates you send me.

Have you decided what to do about the police yet? Hugo says it's OK for me to talk to them because I don't really have anything to say, but that he's going to be there for you. That's good (secretly I wish he'd be there for me too, but didn't like to make a fuss). I don't really remember much about that time, do you? It's so long ago, but I do remember Karen and how pretty she was in her over-the-top way. Horrible to think of anyone hurting her – devastating to think it was someone we love.

Have I said too much? I should probably end now.

Sending love, J x

PS: Any time you want me to cocktail you up just let me know. We could probably both do with one.

With a heavy sigh Annie lowered her phone and turned to gaze at the small dormer window, piled up with snow. If she had her bearings right it faced in the direction of the Crayce family farm and having picked up on her sister-in-law's loneliness she felt tempted to try and get over there to offer some comfort. A cocktail would be welcome, or even a hot chocolate, but she couldn't go now. She'd set herself this task and she needed to carry on with it, at least for the next hour or so – or until she became so cold she couldn't take anymore.

Messaging back, she said,

I miss you too and yes it's awful what's happening. Like you I can't remember much about that time, but trying to find diaries to help remind me before I speak to the police. If you want Hugo to be with you, you should ask him, I'm sure he'll say yes.

She stopped, thinking that over and feeling her heart twist as she wondered what was behind Hugo's decision to be there for her. Maybe David had secretly confessed and Hugo was embarking on some kind of elaborate defence strategy to get him off.

Realizing she was letting paranoia get the better of her, she closed her mind to it, knowing how destructive it could be if unchecked. She didn't believe David had done anything to Karen Lomax, least of all murder her, she needed to think no further than that for now.

Continuing her message to Julia, she said,

We're both victims of our own imaginations as much as the circumstances we find ourselves in, so we have to do our best to stay in the moment and try not to second guess where this will end.

She wanted to tell Julia she was wrong about Henry's relationship with Chrissie, but decided to leave the subject alone for now.

Thanks for all you're doing re the website, and for deleting the horrible messages – no I didn't see them, thank God. There have been some pretty ghastly emails as well, but not as many as I'd feared might turn up, and so far no cancellations attributed to anything but the weather. Given we're dependent on the Defenders to get around at the moment, and David has his with him – guessing Henry does too if he's out – the cocktails might have to wait. Or we can make them for ourselves later and chat on the phone.

Sending love, Ax

Hoping her words might make Julia feel slightly less alone, she then sent brief messages to all three children saying she was missing them, and another to David that simply contained a row of love hearts. To her surprise one came back only minutes later containing a row for her.

She'd been in the attic for almost two hours by the time she located the red leather chest, and it took only a few minutes to dig out the relevant diary. As soon as she saw the year 1999 embossed on the front cover she wanted suddenly to destroy it, to pretend it hadn't turned up, except she'd never do that when there was a chance it might provide an alibi for David that would stop the investigation in its tracks, at least for him.

Unable to bear the cold any longer she tucked the small book into the back pocket of her jeans, closed up the red chest and turned out the lights before descending the mechanical ladder to the upstairs landing.

Fifteen minutes later she was warming herself at the Aga, a fortifying glass of wine in one hand and the diary in the other, open to the week Karen Lomax had disappeared. There was no ambiguity in what was written there; she knew now where she'd been over that crucial time – having been reminded she remembered it well. However, it wasn't going to help David. In fact, unless she lied to the police, this wasn't going to help him at all.

CHAPTER FOURTEEN

August 7th 1999

The bar was so crowded Jess could hardly hear herself think. The Backstreet Boys were making the walls vibrate and the raucous revelry from so many tourists and locals was a pulsing, shrieking cacophony of its own. It wasn't easy to move either, trying to whisk trays of drinks and food overhead to tables both inside and out in the garden. It was a miracle, she thought, that nothing had been dropped – yet.

Spotting Karen pushing her way to the bar, she leaned in to hear what she was saying.

'Just going to Lucy's,' Karen shouted, staggering slightly as someone barged into her. 'I'll stay over, so see you tomorrow.'

Jess might have asked why she was all made up and dressed to kill in her shimmery top and skinny white jeans just to go to her friend's, but the noise was deafening and Karen was already turning away. 'How are you getting there?' she called after her.

'. . . a lift . . . don't worry . . . ' came the reply. 'Love you.'

With a smile Jess said, 'Love you too,' but Karen had already disappeared into the crowd and the rowdy bunch at table eighteen had started to sing 'why are we waiting'.

'I'll take it,' Eddie said, grabbing the tray she'd prepared.

'Bottle of French Sauvignon and five glasses for table six outside.'

'Got it.'

'Where's Karen off to?'

'Lucy's.'

'We should have got them to work tonight. We could do with the extra hands,' and weaving expertly through the crush of drinkers he began cheering along with the cheeky lasses at table eighteen as he delivered their fourth bottle of Prosecco and third selection of tapas.

The partying and high-summer excess continued non-stop until they finally closed the doors at midnight, allowed themselves a breath, and another, before Jess and four bar staff started on the clearing up while Eddie dealt with the evening's takings.

It was almost two in the morning by the time they finally sank into bed, feet sore, heads throbbing and exhaustion already shutting them down.

'Any word from Karen?' Eddie yawned as he turned out the light.

'I haven't checked,' Jess replied, 'but I shouldn't think so. She was only going to Lucy's. They're probably all tucked up and fast asleep by now.'

'Mm,' he responded sleepily, and finding her hand he brought it to his lips. 'Crazy night,' he murmured. 'If it's the same tomorrow we'll ask her and whoever else she can find to muck in. They'll be glad of the money and we might avoid the regular staff walking out through overwork.'

Jess closed her eyes as she smiled, but as tired as she was she knew she wasn't going to rest until she'd checked her phone just in case Karen had tried to get hold of her.

She hadn't. So sending a quick text saying, *Nite nite,*

call if u wnt picking up tmrw. Love you. Mum she dropped her phone on the floor and should have fallen straight to sleep, but for some reason she didn't. She kept thinking about Karen, wondering about her, worrying even without really knowing why. Had she really been going to Lucy's, all dressed up like that? They must have arranged to go clubbing or to a party or something, although it wasn't like Karen not to say so. She was usually quite upfront about her plans, even if less so about the detail of her nights out. It was OK: as her mum, Jess didn't need to know everything, it wouldn't be normal if she did – and obviously the reason Karen hadn't said much about where she and Lucy were going tonight was because she'd been unable to make herself heard over the noise in the bar.

So why was she lying here fretting over where Karen might be, when she didn't usually, especially not when Karen had told her she was staying at Lucy's? It was too late to call, and she'd already sent a text so the best thing she could do now was accept this strange agitation was no more than tiredness and get herself some sleep.

She woke early in the morning, just after seven, and as she slowly came to she felt another wave of edginess descending. Reaching for her phone she checked to see if Karen had been in touch, but she hadn't. She sent another text:

Hey babe, just making sure you're OK. Call when you can. Mum xxx

By midday there was still no word, and they knew now that Karen hadn't been with Lucy last night.

Eddie didn't want to wait any longer, nor did she. Instead of opening the bar, they called the police.

CHAPTER FIFTEEN

It was late on Saturday afternoon and Natalie was alone in the incident room having stood her team down for the weekend. The reason she'd come in was to replay the video call they'd recorded yesterday of her chat with Karen Lomax's parents, Jess and Eddie.

When they'd come onto the screen she'd noted right away that the couple, in their early sixties now, seemed to have aged well considering what they'd been through. Smart, small-business professionals – they ran a deli these days – they wore no outward signs of their loss. Those sorts of scars were rarely visible on the outside, the effects of the devastation being buried so deep in the heart and psyche that they only became apparent through a complicated prism of behaviour, thought and speech.

The shock of learning there were new developments in Karen's case had clearly shaken them both, the reverberations of grief and loss coming down the years to the present day. Once again they were immersed in the pain and tragedy of it all.

Natalie had offered to give them some time to assimilate, but they'd insisted on proceeding with the video call, so she had begun gently, asking questions they had already answered earlier, a simple way of putting them at their ease.

Jess had done most of the talking, her West Country

burr as endearing as it was melodic, though she'd frequently glanced at her husband to be sure he agreed with what she was saying. They hadn't contradicted anything they'd said in their previous statements, at least not in a material way, but when Natalie began to ask about the Crayce family they'd seemed less certain of themselves. This was why Natalie had come in today; she'd wanted to listen to the call again, make notes and sort things out in her head before giving instructions to the team on Monday.

Once the recording was lined up to where she wanted to begin she hit play and sat back in her chair, coffee in one hand, pen poised in the other.

Her voice was first to be heard.

'. . . So you're saying you did know the Crayce family?'

Jess: 'Not well. They used to come into the wine bar from time to time. I'm not sure I can remember all their names now . . . '

Eddie: 'The father was called Dickie, as I recall, and his wife was Geraldine. They were a nice couple. Friendlier than some from up on the moor, although none of them ever gave us any trouble.'

Jess: 'She brought us eggs a couple of times from their farm.'

Natalie: 'Did they usually come in together?'

Jess: 'No, I wouldn't necessarily say that. Sometimes he'd stop by with his sons, or other farmers I suppose they were, and she'd turn up with a group of her friends after bell ringing practice, or for someone's birthday. To be honest, months would go by and we'd never see them.'

Natalie: 'Do you remember any of them talking to Karen?'

Jess: 'Not specifically, but I'm sure they did. They weren't the type to ignore people or be rude in any way, and Karen was always very sociable with the customers. Actually, I expect you already know that she was a bit well, over-friendly at times. She had her ways, our girl. She liked the limelight, and she was always something of a . . . romantic.'

Natalie had felt saddened by the euphemism when she'd first heard it, and did again now. All these years on and they were still trying to defend their daughter's reputation from all those who blamed Karen's promiscuity for what had happened to her.

Eddie: 'She'd go from one crush to another to another. We could hardly keep up with her. And she was mad about the boy bands, always going to concerts and the like. Jess would go too, sometimes, wouldn't you, love? And me, but not so often. If they were staying overnight they'd take tents and picnics and all the essentials. I was usually the one to go and pick them up the next day. I had one of those people-carriers back then and I never minded being called on. At least I'd know they were all home safe, even if they were a bit worse for wear.'

Jess: 'I expect you already know that she went on the pill at fifteen. Eddie didn't know at the time, but obviously it all came out later. When she asked . . . Well, it seemed the sensible thing to do. I couldn't stop her being sexually active, so I thought it was better for her to be safe. Some of her friends' mothers put their girls on when they were still only fourteen. I don't expect that shocks someone like you, but I can tell you it shocked us when we found out. It's not what you want, is it, as parents? Your child out there doing things they ought not to be doing at that age, but you can't pretend it's not happening if it is, so you have to do what you can to protect them.'

Eddie: 'I don't want you to think she was a bad girl, Detective. She was a lovely girl really, you know, in her heart, and she was doing well at school . . . It's just the way things were back then with teenagers, I guess they still are now, maybe they're worse . . . You hear about what they get up to. We never wanted to believe it of our Karen . . . It was a terrible shock for us when it all came out. We've blamed ourselves for not realizing, for being too busy with the business . . . Maybe it was the wrong sort of environment to bring a girl up in with all that booze around. Not that we ever let her drink in the bar. She was underage, so of course we didn't, but I'm sorry to say she used to steal from us sometimes. A bottle of wine here, another of spirits there. She always denied it, but we knew none of the staff would have taken it so it had to be her.'

Jess: 'It wasn't the way she was brought up to behave. She was always such a good girl growing up, wouldn't have dreamt of stealing from anyone least of all us. I suppose you could say we turned a blind eye to her faults, told ourselves it was all a part of being the age she was, spreading her wings, pushing boundaries the way kids do.'

Natalie: 'As a parent of two daughters myself, you have my sympathy.'

Jess: 'How old are yours?'

Natalie: 'Twenty-four. They're twins.'

Jess: 'Oh, that's nice. Are they married?'

Natalie: 'No, but they both have live-in partners – and the jury's still out on one of them. What about Karen, did she have a boyfriend at the time she disappeared? Anyone special?'

Jess: 'Not that we knew of, and none of her friends said there was anyone.'

Natalie: 'Did you ever see her with anyone from the Crayce family?'

Jess: 'Why are you asking about them? Are you saying you think they might have had an involvement in what happened to her?'

Natalie: 'If you don't mind just answering the question.'

Jess: 'Well, I suppose she talked to them in the wine bar when they were in. She was always very sociable with the customers – and those brothers, they were older than her of course, probably had about ten years on her, but they were good lookers, the pair of them. You'd see girls' heads turn when they came in the door.'

Natalie: 'What about the father?'

Jess: (a laugh) 'I won't repeat what some of my female friends used to say about him, but he was a looker too, so I expect you can work it out for yourself.'

Natalie: 'Did you ever see him respond to your friends' interest?'

Jess: 'Well, he enjoyed a bit of a flirt, I suppose, blokes like that often do, don't they? They like to see themselves as players, if you know what I mean, especially when they're starting to get on in years.'

Eddie: 'Rumour didn't always paint him in the purest of lights, but whether any of it was true . . . Things get exaggerated, don't they? We thought that about the things people said about Karen.'

Natalie: 'Do you recall either of the Crayces being in the wine bar the day she disappeared? Or on any of the days leading up to it?'

Jess: 'As far as I remember they were in on that Saturday. There was a group of about eight or ten of them. They used to call themselves the Moorauders, not that they ever caused any trouble.'

Natalie: 'Can you remember what time they came in?'

Jess: 'I'm sure it'll be in my statement, but I think it was the middle of the afternoon, around three o'clock.'

Natalie paused the tape, and sat for a moment staring at the frozen image of Jess Lomax looking entirely earnest about the Crayces coming into the bar that day – and yet there was no mention of it in either her or her husband's original statements.

She hit play and Jess continued.

'There was a group of them, blokes and girls. They were all in their country gear, you know, tweeds, flat caps, gilets, like a uniform it is – or it was for them. I know both brothers were there.'

Eddie: 'David's the older one, right?'

Natalie: 'He is.'

Eddie: 'The one who started a shooting school up on the moor?'

Natalie: 'That's him.'

Jess: 'Their dad came in after them, but only about ten minutes or so.'

Natalie: 'Did you see Karen talking to any of them at any point?'

Jess: 'It's hard to remember now, but I expect she had a bit of a laugh with them, the way she did with everyone. We were rushed off our feet that day. It was summer and sunny, lots of customers in the garden – the place was pretty packed for most of the day right up until closing.'

Natalie: 'Can you remember what time the group left?'

Jess: 'I wasn't checking, but I'd say it was around four, half past, something like that.'

Natalie: 'Did they all leave together?'

Jess (to Eddie): 'I don't think we can be sure about that, but I expect so.'

Eddie nodded agreement.

Jess: 'Detective, please tell us, are you saying that one of *them* did this to our girl?'

Natalie fast-forwarded through her explanation of the DNA match and stopped at the point where Jess, visibly upset, said, 'I don't believe it. Not them. That's . . . Oh God, that's terrible. Why did no one . . . ? Oh God, Eddie . . .'

As she buried her face in her hands Natalie let the recording run watching Eddie put his arms around her and feeling glad for her that she had such a supportive husband.

Eddie: 'When will you know which one it is?'

Natalie: 'We're hoping to get the results in the next week or two. Do you mind if I continue to ask a few more questions?'

Eddie (after consulting his wife): 'That's OK. We want to help you all we can.'

Natalie: 'Do you recall any of them hanging back after the others had left, or returning later in the day?'

Jess: 'Not that I saw. What about you?'

Eddie: 'No, but like we already said, we were run off our feet. People were coming and going faster than we could bring the drinks.'

Natalie: 'OK. Now let me get this straight, you're sure, when the police interviewed you during the search for Karen, that you mentioned the Crayces had been in the bar that day?'

Jess: 'Oh, yes. We gave them the names of all the customers we could remember from that day and the days before, and I'm absolutely certain we told them about the Moor-auders.'

Natalie: 'Can you remember any other names from that group?'

Jess: 'Oh gosh, it's been so long . . . What about you, pet?'

Eddie: 'There was one of the Diffley family, you know from Fairley Vale Hall. The Granger boy, Frank, I think his name is. Rupert Gillycrest. Sukey Blake-Forster, I think she's married now so she might be called something else these days.'

Jess: 'I'm trying to remember if Julia Barnes was there? She was generally with them . . . I'm sure Chrissie Smart was, wasn't she?'

Eddie: 'You mean Tillie Smart's niece, yes I think she was there. She's married now, I think, so that might not be her name anymore. You'll have all this on record, Miss . . . Um . . . '

Natalie: 'Rundle, but please call me Natalie.'

'Happy to,' a voice said behind her and, startled, she swung round to find DCI Gould standing in the doorway.

'Sir,' she said, stopping the video and getting to her feet. 'I thought I had the place to myself today.'

'So, did I,' he said wryly. 'What's that you're listening to?'

'I spoke to Karen Lomax's parents yesterday. They're flying back, by the way, should be here tomorrow or the next day.'

'Anything interesting?'

'If you call a failure to question potential suspects or record parts of statements interesting, then yes.'

'Go on.'

'The Lomaxes seem pretty certain they told the original investigating officers that the Crayces, along with a group of friends, had been in the wine bar on the day Karen went missing. It's possible some of them were questioned, I've still to check, but so far nothing has come to light about the Crayces.'

'OK, that's interesting, and it's sounding as though you'll have to track down the old dog Underwood. Let's just hope he still has all his marbles.'

'Leo's already arranged the pleasure,' and shutting down the computer she tucked away her pen and notebook. 'So, what brings you in at this time on a Saturday?' she asked chattily.

Going with the change of subject, he said, 'Secure access for classified stuff.' He glanced at his watch.

'And now you're in a hurry to be gone. Another hot date, may I ask?'

He almost visibly deflated.

'I see.' She tried not to feel pleased. 'GSOH not up to much?'

He grimaced. 'Let's say more S & M.'

Her eyebrows shot up.

'As in sad and morose,' he hastily clarified. 'Her husband's not long left her for a younger model, and now I'm feeling terrible because I'm giving up on her too and I don't even have an alternative model as an excuse. Maybe this internet dating thing isn't all it's cracked up to be.'

Still managing not to smile, Natalie gathered up her belongings and joined him in the corridor outside as she closed and locked the door. 'So where are you rushing off to now?' she dared to ask.

'Oh, dinner with friends,' he replied. He was still sounding less than thrilled. 'They've no doubt got some poor unsuspecting female lined up for me – that's usually the way these things go for the newly minted single bloke, I'm finding. Even one of the vintage variety.'

Taking that in, she said, 'Am I allowed to ask what happened to Mrs Gould?'

'You are, but I don't like speaking ill of the still living so you won't get an answer. What are your plans for the evening?'

'Me? I'm going to pick up a Chinese, open a nice bottle of wine and carry on prepping for my next date with the

Crayces.' *And if you can't resist that on a Saturday night,* she was thinking as she peeled off in a different direction, *you're even sadder than I am.*

CHAPTER SIXTEEN

Annie was doing her best not to worry, and failing spectacularly. It was after ten o'clock, pitch dark, blowing a gale, and there was still no word from David. The last communication had been the row of hearts he'd sent around two o'clock when he was on the shoot. He'd have finished by five at the very latest given the failing light, and though it was quite usual for him to join clients for drinks when it was all over, especially at Fairley Vale where Grayson Diffley would have insisted on it, David almost never stayed any later than seven.

'No darling, he left right after they brought the clients here,' Rosa Diffley had informed her when she'd called around eight-thirty. 'Grayson tried to persuade him to come in, but he said he needed to get off before the weather got any worse.'

The snowstorm had been over by then, leaving rain and winds in its wake so conditions on the road were improving, not getting worse. However, that hardly ruled out the possibility of an accident, so Annie had immediately rung the nearest hospital and police station to find out if anything had been reported.

Apparently all was quiet up on the moor.

Afraid he might have swerved to avoid a stag or taken a bend too fast and ended up rolling into a ravine, she'd called Henry, needing him to use his Defender to go out and look.

'He's not here,' Julia told her. 'I haven't heard from him all day. Do you think they could be together somewhere?'

Hearing the desperate hope in her voice, *please let Henry be with anyone other than Chrissie*, Annie said, 'I guess it's possible,' but David hadn't mentioned that Henry would be on the shoot, or that he'd arranged to see him later, and given how awkward things were between them . . .

'Maybe I should try Chrissie to see if Henry's there,' Julia suggested stoically. 'If he is, I'm sure I can persuade him to go out and search for his brother.'

Feeling wretched for her, Annie said, 'Why don't you give me the number and I'll call?'

'It's OK, I'll do it,' and the line went dead.

Hardly more than a minute passed before Julia rang back.

'Apparently he's not at Chrissie's. She says she hasn't seen him all day, but I don't know whether to believe her.'

Not sure whether to either, Annie said, 'It's funny that neither of them are answering their phones. Dickie isn't either, or maybe you've spoken to him?'

'No, I haven't heard from him since the day before yesterday. What's going on, Annie? Where can they be?'

Having no idea, Annie was about to promise she'd call as soon as she had some news, when Julia said, 'How did your diary search go?'

Almost groaning out loud, Annie said, 'Apparently Laura and I were at a friend's baby shower in London that weekend, so nowhere near Kesterly, and if memory serves me right Henry was here giving David a hand with the renovations.'

What she didn't recount was her memory of how angry and worried she and Laura had become when they hadn't been able to get hold of either brother for over twenty-four hours. Mobile phones were next to useless on the moor in those days, but there had been no reply from the land-line at the farmhouse either. Not so unusual if it were during the day when Dickie and Geraldine could have been outside in the barns or rounding up livestock, but through the night? David and Henry were supposed to be staying with their parents – she and David were practically living with them during the build and renovations, so he really should have been there. It wasn't until much later the next day that her mother-in-law had finally answered the phone, and it was clear she wasn't happy. Apparently a crowd of the usual suspects had crashed at the farmhouse overnight, and Geraldine had come back from her mother's to find bodies still slumped on sofas, floors and in spare bedrooms and enough alcohol fumes in the air to get them drunk all over again.

'I know you warned David,' she'd said, her voice shaking with worry and anger, 'that if anything like this happened again, him getting out of his mind on booze, you'd call the wedding off. It's what he deserves, the bloody fool, but I'm begging you not to do it, Annie. Please wait until you've calmed down before you speak to him, and remember that everything's been good for over a year, no hiccups or backslides of any kind, and at least his father and Henry were with him this time – not that they're off the hook, believe me. They're all going to be sorrier than they've ever been when they sober up, I can promise you that, I just don't want you to say or do something now that you'll end up regretting.'

So Annie hadn't spoken to David that day, instead she'd taken Geraldine's advice and had waited until she was back at Hanley Combe before tackling him about the state he'd got into, but all the fury and fear had gone out of her by then. And he'd been so sheepish and apologetic, so obviously scared that she was going to call everything off (she'd found out later that his mother had warned him it was about to happen), that she'd ended up letting it go. After all, as Geraldine had said, at least he'd been with his father and brother (who should have known better but apparently hadn't), so someone had been there to make sure he'd got home in one piece.

Now, Julia was saying, 'Henry used to do that quite a lot when he was married to Laura and living in London. He'd come to Exmoor for the weekend to give David a hand with all the work and there was a vast amount to do. I guess we all mucked in in our way, labouring where it was needed, driving stuff about, conjuring up refreshments.'

Recalling those joyful and challenging days of building their dream, of truly believing David's worst days were behind them, Annie said, 'It seems so long ago now and yet sometimes it feels like it was only yesterday.'

'I know what you mean. But now here we are, your business an amazing success, three lovely children, I'm married to Henry, he's having an affair with Chrissie – some things never bloody change . . .'

'Oh, Julia . . . '

'I'm sorry. Forget I said that. I'm becoming obsessed with it and there are much more important things to deal with right now. Like where are they tonight?'

Having no answer to offer as rage and fear struggled inside her, Annie said, 'Let's keep trying them, we're sure to get through sooner or later.'

Another twenty minutes passed with Annie working through a list of the pubs on the moor, starting with those closest to Fairley Vale, and getting as far as Exford before the sound of the Defender pulling up outside made her drop the phone and run out onto the veranda ready to explode.

Cassie leapt from the vehicle first, but with the headlights still on Annie couldn't see who was at the wheel, she only knew it wasn't David because he was getting out of the passenger side and thanking the driver. It turned out to be Simon, landlord of the Notley Arms, who'd apparently taken David's and Henry's car keys when, together with their father, they'd started on a second bottle of Scotch. In the end he'd decided to use David's Defender to deliver the men home – Dickie was already at his cottage, and Henry, who was half-passed out on the back seat, would soon be despatched to the farm.

'Come and pick the car up any time you like tomorrow,' Simon told her as he made a circle and started through the slush back along the drive.

'I'm fine, I'm fine and I'm sorry,' David told her as he stumbled into the kitchen and almost fell over Cassie. 'Sorry, girl . . .'

'Has she eaten?' Annie snapped.

'Course she has. Simon and Caroline always have something for the dogs, you know that.'

'I don't suppose you've had anything yourself apart from a skinful. For God's sake, David, I've been going out of my mind . . .'

'I know, and I'm sorry. I should have rung. I meant to, but . . . It's just with all that's going on . . .'

'How did you end up with your dad and Henry?'

'They came on the shoot, so we've been together all day.' He tried to embrace her, but she pushed him away.

'Don't do that,' she growled. 'I'm so angry with you I can hardly bear to look at you.'

Clearly dismayed and chastened, he said, 'I'm not as drunk as you think . . .'

'You reek of it . . .'

'OK, I'll stop breathing over you and make some coffee.'

He got no further than lifting the jug before she whisked it away.

'I'll make it,' she told him. 'Sit down before you fall down, and get ready to tell me what the hell is going on, because neither of us is leaving this room until you do.'

A few minutes later with hot coffees in front of them, and Cassie snoring softly at David's feet, she sat staring at him, waiting for him to begin while almost not wanting him to. *What's the matter with me,* she asked herself angrily. *Since when did I become afraid of hearing the truth? This isn't you, Annie. You're stronger than this.*

Abruptly she said, 'How did your father and Henry come to be on the shoot today?'

Circling his hands around his mug, he said, 'I stopped by Dad's this morning to see if he wanted to come; when he said yes I texted Henry and he met us there.'

Setting the surprise of that aside she said, 'So why didn't Rosa say anything about them being with you when I rang to find out if you were there?'

He shrugged. 'I guess she didn't know. We didn't go

into the Hall. We just took off for the Royal Oak and then went on to the Notley.'

'And you could have called at any point, but didn't. Instead you decided to ignore the fact that Julia and I might be worried, that conditions out there . . .'

'The Defenders are equipped.'

'But they don't make you invulnerable.' Deciding there was nothing to be gained from pursuing that line, she said, 'So, did the three of you discuss the situation you're in?'

'We were a bunch of blokes on a shoot . . . '

'I mean later, while you were at the pub getting off your face? Did you talk about it then?'

He shook his head. 'What were we going to say? "Was it you? Or you?"'

Incredulous, she cried, 'I don't believe you! How could you not mention it?'

He simply shrugged, and realizing she'd never understand the way men could bury their heads in the sand while the world was crashing around them, she suddenly felt tears burn her eyes. Furious with herself, she forced them away. She might be frustrated and afraid, and unable to comprehend why he didn't feel the same, but she was damned if she'd let herself cry.

In the end, she said, 'Why did you have a drink? What were you . . . ?'

'Annie, this isn't easy,' he cut in harshly. 'My father and brother . . . ' He shook his head. 'Don't make me say it. Just please try to understand what it's like. The not knowing . . . This effing waiting . . .'

She started to speak, but he cut her off again.

'It's getting to us all, and OK, I let go tonight. I know

I shouldn't have, and I wish I hadn't, but it's too late to take it back.' His eyes came to hers and seeing how angry he was with himself she decided there was no point going any further with this – at least not now.

'I guess we better brace ourselves for the nightmares,' she said, feeling angrier about it than she sounded. He hadn't had one in so long that she could barely remember how bad they were, only that they were invariably brought on by excess alcohol and were sometimes so violent they scared her.

'I can always sleep in Max's bed,' he said.

Though a part of her was tempted to tell him to do that, she decided she probably ought to be there if he did go to the dark places so she could gently bring him out of them. 'Lucky the children aren't here,' she said crisply, 'because you're going to have a hell of hangover in the morning.'

'No less than I deserve,' he admitted. 'None of this is what you deserve.'

She shrugged and got up from the table. Now wasn't the time to try asking him about the lost hours one weekend almost twenty years ago when a young girl had disappeared at the same time as he, Henry and their father, had been on such a wild bender that even his mother, the most tolerant of souls, had been furious when she'd come home the next day. Even if he did recall it, and realized the coincidence, she didn't imagine for one minute that he was going to say oh yes, that's right, it was the weekend I helped Henry, or Dad, cover up what they did to the girl from the wine bar.

And that, she was thinking as she took herself off to bed, *is what's making this so bloody intolerable.* Because even if the DNA didn't end up belonging to David, and she truly believed it didn't, there was a very high probability that he was either already covering up for Henry or his dad, or he was preparing to do so.

And love them all as she did, if it turned out that any one of them had been involved in that young girl's murder, and thought their own freedom mattered more, she simply wouldn't be able to live with it – or them.

CHAPTER SEVENTEEN

The following morning Annie was up earlier than normal for a Sunday, but with so much spinning around in her head she knew it was pointless trying to lie in, especially when she'd hardly slept anyway. So, raising herself quietly from the bed, she took care not to wake David – she really didn't want to make love this morning, the way they often did on Sundays, although after last night's session he probably wouldn't be in much of a fit state for it anyway.

After showering and dressing she went downstairs to make coffee and call Julia. She should have told her sister-in-law last night what she'd found in her diary, and wasn't sure now why she hadn't, but whatever the reason Julia and Henry needed to know.

She'd just rung off, feeling regretful that she hadn't driven over to the farm to break it to Julia in person, when David appeared in the kitchen doorway. To her surprise he was dressed in old jeans, a dark navy sweater with denim collar, and he'd clearly shaved and showered. In fact, he wasn't looking anywhere near as hungover as she'd expected.

As he passed her to go and let Cassie out she caught the familiar scent of his shampoo and soap and suddenly wished everything could be normal, that she could put her arms around him, inhale more of him and be as affectionate as they usually were when alone in the house together.

'Are you OK?' he asked, closing the door.

She watched him go to take Cassie's bowl from the drainer, fill it with kibble and take it into the boot room. When he came back she decided to stop stalling and deal with this head-on. 'If you don't remember what you were doing the night Karen Lomax disappeared,' she said, 'I can tell you.'

He looked up in confusion, almost as if he wasn't sure what she was talking about, but of course he knew. 'Go on,' he prompted.

'I found one of my diaries from that time,' she explained. 'I was in London at a baby shower that weekend, and if memory serves me correctly I'm pretty sure Henry was here, with you, helping out with the build.'

His face darkened as he took this in, and she had a sense of old memories struggling to emerge from where they'd presumably been buried for the past twenty years.

'It was the same weekend,' she continued, 'that you and several of the gang, Dickie included, went on a bender. You might remember I couldn't get hold of you . . .'

'Just a minute,' he interrupted, his eyes suddenly hardening, 'are you leading up to saying that because you couldn't get hold of me for a few hours during some random weekend back whenever, you think I was somewhere murdering a girl I didn't even know? Jesus Christ, Annie!'

'That's not what I'm saying. I'm just telling you that it was the weekend she disappeared and . . . If the police ask me . . . '

'If they ask you what *I* was doing then you tell them. Simple as that. It proves nothing, apart from in your head, apparently.'

Angry with him for being so antagonistic, she said, tartly, 'You're putting words in my mouth. It's not what I think, at all, I'm simply saying that when, if, they ask you again what you were doing that weekend, well, now you know, except you probably don't know because you'd have been too drunk to remember.'

His face had turned rigid and pale. She could see, almost feel his temper, and as thoughts she had no way of reading crashed about in his head she watched him helplessly, unable to tell what he might be hiding, even concocting, although it surely had to be something.

'Why won't you speak to me?' she demanded furiously. 'What are you keeping back? We should be discussing this, working out how best I can support you, but you're not letting me in.'

His voice was cold as he said, 'You're getting this out of perspective . . . '

'Out of perspective?' she yelled. 'You've been accused of murder . . . Semen was found . . . '

'Just stop, Annie, please. It's bad enough it's happening at all without us fighting over it.'

'We wouldn't be if you'd just open up.'

'Open up to what? To admitting I did it? Is that what you want?'

'Don't be ridiculous, I just get the feeling you're not telling me everything . . . '

'Well, I'm sorry if that's how you feel. I don't know why, or what I can do about it, but I have nothing else to say. I got drunk that weekend, as did everyone else, and there's no reason not to tell the police that. Does Henry know which weekend it was?'

'I called Julia just before you came down. She said she was going to tell him.'

'And Dad?'

'I haven't mentioned it to him yet, but I think I should.'

He turned to stare out of the window, once again seeming deep in thoughts she couldn't penetrate. She wanted to bang her fists against him, to shake his secrets out of him, make him tell her something, anything, she could hold onto to help ease the mounting dread inside her.

'It's such a long time ago,' he said finally. His tone was calmer, although it seemed distant and tight. 'I haven't thought about that weekend in years . . . ' He broke off, took a breath and pushed a hand through his hair. 'Not my finest hours that's for sure,' he admitted, 'but now it's come up I do remember a couple of the gang being questioned when the girl disappeared. We'd been in the wine bar that day – I think half the world was there . . . '

Shocked, she cried, 'So you did see Karen Lomax that day?'

'No!' he snapped irritably. 'I mean maybe, if she was there, but if I did, I don't remember it. We didn't stay that long, an hour, maybe less. The place was heaving, the way it always was in summer. We decided to carry things on up here on the moor . . . ' He sighed, looked exasperated as if he still regretted it, as he bloody well should have given the situation he was in now. 'You already know what kind of state we got into,' he continued, 'so I'd be amazed if *any* of us can remember anything, but that's not going to help our case much, is it?'

She shook her head *He'd been at the wine bar that day. They all had. What was she supposed to think now?*

Seeming to realize she needed more, he said, 'What can I tell you that you don't already know? We went on a pub crawl, it wasn't planned, just a spur of the moment thing on a hot day. Frank and Chrissie came by to find out if Henry and I were up for hitting the coast, we decided we were, and thought Dad would be too so we gave him a call. He decided to drive himself so we arranged to meet at Cheers and on the way we stopped by Fairley Vale to pick up Grayson. Sukey, Pam and Rupert were at the hall so they came too. We were in two or three cars by then . . . I honestly can't remember who else came, it's too long ago, but I do recall the wine bar being rammed when we got there, so we didn't end up staying for long. I don't know who had the idea of visiting all the pubs on the moor, but at some point that was our goal . . . I'm pretty sure we didn't make it to every one before we decided it was time to get off the roads, so we hit the farmhouse where we carried on drinking and playing poker until after midnight. By then, as far as I remember, we'd cleaned out Dad's whisky reserves, all the beer in the fridge and probably most of the wine cellar. It was a bad one, I'm not going to deny that. Everyone crashed out more or less where they were, too drunk to make it upstairs, although I guess some of us did, because it's where I was when Mum stormed in on me the next day telling me I could forget all about my wedding because you knew what state I was in, and you were as disgusted with me as she was.' With a sigh, he went, 'She scared the hell out of me, obviously her intention – and I guess it scared her too coming in and finding us the way we were.' His eyes came to hers, holding them as he said, 'Too drunk to remember is hardly a defence, is it, when we're looking at the kind of evidence we're being presented with. Someone was obviously with Karen Lomax that night, or maybe it was the next night, who knows? Do we know the exact day or time of death?'

Annie could only shake her head. No, she didn't know, and wasn't entirely sure if it made a difference. She said, 'Do the police know you went to the wine bar that day?'

'I've no idea. They asked if I'd ever been there and I didn't deny it, but at the time I had no way of knowing if I'd been in that day.'

'Why didn't they know you had if Dickie and Henry were questioned?'

'I've no idea.'

'Are you going to tell the police?'

'If I have to, yes, but I imagine Hugo will advise me not to do their jobs for them.'

Realizing he was probably right about that, and that Hugo would no doubt give her the same instruction, she stood looking at him, wondering how they'd got here, and how on earth they were ever going to surmount it.

Reaching for her hand, he said, 'Listen, I'm the one who should speak to Dad, remind him of what we were doing that weekend. You shouldn't have to do it.'

Worried about being cut out of the discussion, maybe enabling them to carry on trying to cover for one another, she said, 'It's OK, I think it might be easier for him if it's me.'

To her surprise and relief he didn't argue, simply went to let Cassie back in before coming to help prepare their breakfast. When his phone rang he showed her the screen and clicked on. 'Henry,' he said, 'I guess . . . sure, we were just talking about it. No, Annie's going to speak to Dad. Was Jules with us that night?'

Although Annie didn't hear the answer, she knew from her call to Julia earlier that Julia didn't think she had been. She was going to check her journals from that time – it was so typical of Julia to keep one – they might be in the boxes she'd brought from her mother's, she'd said, so she'd get back to Annie as soon as she had anything to tell her.

'What was it about?' David asked Henry.

Annie looked at him quizzically, and putting a hand over the phone he said, 'He's had a message from the police . . . ' He listened again and after saying, 'OK, I'll speak to you later,' he hung up. 'They want him and Dad to go in for questioning tomorrow,' he said. 'Isn't that when you and Julia are going?'

'In the morning, yes. Not something I'm looking forward to. Julia's dreading it.'

'Well, if she wasn't there she doesn't have anything to worry about, does she?'

'No, but you know what she's like. Did Henry just tell you she wasn't there?'

'No, but apparently she doesn't think she was. She's checking. Like you, it seems she's always kept a diary.'

'Although in her case,' Annie said wryly, 'there's probably a lot more than a date and time involved, there could be pages.'

A flicker of wary humour showed in his eyes. 'Well, if they help clear up this mess let's bring them on, but I don't think I'll be holding my breath for that.'

'Was she still married then, do you remember?'

He shrugged. 'I've no idea, but if she was she'd have been living in Devon, so presumably she'd know already where she was – or that she wasn't on the moor, anyway.'

'Do you remember if Henry was with Chrissie that weekend?'

He shook his head. 'All I can tell you is that she was with us. Did she end up spending the night at the farmhouse? I should think so, since no one was in a fit state to drive. Pam and Rupert stayed over, so did Frank and the girl he was with back then, her name escapes me. I can't remember if Sukey stayed, or Grayson, actually I know he did because he's who Mum fell over when she came in . . . '

'And you're sure you didn't pick up anyone along the way?'

His eyes flashed. 'You mean like Karen Lomax? Well, thanks for that. It's good to know what you're really thinking, but frankly I've had enough of it,' and calling Cassie after him he grabbed his coat and left the house.

There was still no sign of him by the time Annie walked over to Dickie's cottage an hour later, not at all sure she wanted to do this, while knowing she had to. She wondered why the police had asked her and Julia to go to the station tomorrow before calling in two of their main suspects. Surely Dickie and Henry were of more interest. They'd been questioned when officers had come to take swabs, so maybe it was simply about making their statements official.

Knocking as she opened Dickie's front door, she called out to let him know she was there, but received no reply. Going through to the sitting room. she found him staring blankly at a morbid metaphor of the situation he was in – a jigsaw puzzle he'd hardly begun to piece together. Beside him was a cup of cold tea, and the radio was on so low she couldn't even determine the station. Finding herself drawn to the photograph of Geraldine on the mantlepiece, lively eyes full of fun and vitality, her all-nonsense curls, as she used to call them, tousled by the wind, she could only feel thankful that her mother-in-law wasn't here to witness any of this.

Or had she died knowing more than she'd ever told?

Discomfited by the thought, she looked down at her father-in-law again and wondered what was going around in his mind, what was happening to his conscience, his heart, to make him seem as lost as he did. 'Dickie?' she said softly.

His head came up and he seemed surprised to see her there, and embarrassed to be found unshaven and probably unwashed, for he always took pride in his appearance.

'When did you last eat?' she asked, deciding to keep things simple for the moment.

'Not all that hungry,' he replied, his voice roughened and low, presumably the first time he'd spoken today. He cleared his throat and pressed his fingers to his blood-shot eyes.

'Do you have any food in?'

'Some, I think. There are a couple of pheasants out there in need of plucking.' He made an attempt to brighten, as if only now remembering his manners. 'How's everything? Sorry we stayed out so long last night and came back . . . a little worse for wear. Was David OK?'

'He was fine. No nightmares, thank God, but I expect he has a bit of a sore head even if he'd deny it.'

Dickie nodded. 'That's good about the nightmares. Very good, considering the situation we're in. I was afraid they'd come back.'

So why did you encourage him to drink?

Why had he felt the need to?

Why did any of you?

Dickie gazed down at his jigsaw, everything about him seeming even more diminished than he'd been at the time of his wife's passing. Annie had often wondered if he'd only realized after Geraldine had gone just how much she'd meant to him, how deeply he'd needed her, depended on her, truly loved her – and how bitterly did he still regret the times he hadn't been as true to his marriage as he should have been?

'How are the children?' he asked quietly. 'I hear they're with Harriet and Francis for the weekend.'

'Yes, they are, and they send their love.' They hadn't said that, but Annie felt sure they would have if they'd known she was coming here. It was strange and extremely hard, she thought, how she, Julia, her parents, the children, were like a jury at a trial, the readers of a book, the watchers of a film, gripped by what was happening, appalled by it with no idea of what might come next, only fearing that someone they loved had done something so terrible they were probably going to end up in prison for life.

Shying away from the horror of that she said, 'I'll make you a fresh cup of tea,' and taking his mug through to the kitchen she put the kettle on and set about clearing up the few dishes he'd used and not bothered to wash.

'I can tell,' he said, when she took a steaming mug of strong brew through to him, 'that you've come here for a reason, and it's probably to do with this mess we're in, so let's get on with it, shall we?'

Appreciating his instinct and bravado, she sat down on a comfy chair with her own cup of tea and told him how her diary had reminded her of what he, David and Henry had been doing on that fateful weekend over twenty years ago.

His face was haggard by the time she'd finished, and she could see his hands had started to shake. 'Well, that's not a very happy coincidence, is it?' he said hoarsely. 'The three of us on a bender and everyone else too, so how are we supposed to remember anything?'

'David said you went to the wine bar that day, the one Karen Lomax's parents owned.'

He nodded slowly. 'Yes, we did,' he agreed, 'but we weren't there for long. It was busy, I recall, difficult to get a drink . . . '

'Did you see Karen while you were there?'

He shrugged. 'Not that I can remember, but I suppose it's possible.'

'You don't have any memory of talking to her?'

He looked incredulous. 'After all this time? It would be a bit of a miracle if I did, especially after all we had to drink that day.'

Since that was a reasonable answer, if unsatisfactory, she said, 'David tells me you all piled back to the farm that night after a pub crawl and played poker before crashing out.'

He nodded distractedly, apparently still taking time to connect with such a distant part of his past. It probably had very little sense of reality for him now, much less clarity, presuming, that was, nothing had happened to make it a night that none of them had ever truly forgotten. In the end he said, 'I remember Geraldine not being too happy about it all when she came back from her mother's the next day. It was afternoon by then, and there were still bodies all over the place, not to mention bottles, glasses, ashtrays . . . She never liked smoking.'

While picturing the scene, Annie steeled herself as she said, 'Were David and Henry there all night?'

Dickie glanced at her briefly and away again. 'If you're asking can I swear to them being there the entire night . . . It would be hard, given the state we were all in, but I'd do it if I thought it would help them.'

It was far from the answer she'd hoped for – perhaps she should have expected it – even so, it terrified her to think he might be trying to cover up a murder for one of his sons. She couldn't help wondering if David and Henry were ready to swear that their father had been in the farmhouse all night, if asked. Was that what the three of them had been discussing when they'd gone to the Notley Arms without telling anyone where they were? Had they been working out how to alibi one another for a weekend they did remember and had hoped never to speak of again? But even if that were true, would they have done it in such public place? It seemed so unlikely, reckless even, and yet there was no escaping the fact that one of them had got themselves involved with a girl young enough to be Dickie's granddaughter and that girl had ended up dead.

After leaving Dickie's, Annie returned to the house to find David on his way out.

'Eli's just called,' he told her, referring to their groundsman, 'apparently a couple of branches came down in the night so he needs help moving them. How was Dad?'

Fussing Cassie, she said, 'He might look worse than he feels after last night, but I'm not sure about that.'

Henry grimaced. 'What did he say when you told him where we all were that weekend?'

'That it was an unfortunate coincidence.' She'd already decided not to tell him that his father had said he was prepared to lie to protect his sons, it wasn't something she wanted to get into, at least not now.

'Julia,' she announced, holding up her mobile as it rang.

'I'll leave you to it,' he said, and brushing a kiss to her cheek he unhooked his keys and whistled for Cassie to follow.

'Hey,' she said into the phone as she shrugged off her coat. 'Everything OK with you?'

Sounding agitated and slightly breathless, Julia said, 'I'm not sure. I mean, I am, but . . . Can Henry and I come over?'

'Of course. David's just gone out, but I can ask him to come back if you . . . '

'David's gone out,' Julia told Henry.

Annie heard Henry say, 'Where?'

After relaying the answer to Henry, Julia said to Annie, 'Henry's going to find David and Eli so I'll come on my own.'

Twenty minutes later, hands cupped around a mug of coffee, riding hat and jacket still on as she paced up and down the kitchen, Julia said, 'I wasn't there that night. I found my journal . . . I wasn't there. I really wanted to be of some help to Henry, to be a kind of alibi if I could, but I was eventing in Wiltshire. It's why I can't remember anything about it.'

Annie said, 'It's not your fault if you weren't there, so there's no need to be so upset about it.'

Julia was barely listening. 'I'd already left Roger by then,' she said. 'I was living back at home so I probably would have been with the gang if it had been any other weekend.'

Pointing her to a chair, Annie said, 'If you ask me you're best out of it . . . '

'That's exactly what Henry said, and I know he's right, but . . . Oh, Annie, this is going to sound so stupid, but it made me really angry when Henry told me *Chrissie* was there. OK, I'm sorry, I know it's not important, that it's like I'm trying to make it about me, and I understand perfectly that it's not. I need to focus on that poor girl and what happened to her . . . Actually, I don't even know what did, do you? Has anyone told you how she actually died?' Her eyes were big and anxious, as if she really wanted to know, or was afraid to know.

Feeling the same, Annie shook her head.

'Or where it happened even?'

'I've no idea what they do and don't know.'

'No, of course you haven't. How could you? How could any of us? Henry says I'm getting myself too worked up about it, but it's hard not to when you consider what he could be facing. What any of them could. Is it too early to cocktail us up?'

'Probably,' Annie smiled, but going to the fridge she took out a bottle of wine and poured them both a glass. 'What time are you due at the police station tomorrow?' she asked.

Shuddering, Julia said, 'Nine thirty. What about you?'

'Eleven.'

'So why am I first? Do you think that means anything?'

'I don't expect so. One of us had to be. Is Hugo meeting you?'

'Yes, he said he would, thank goodness. I don't think I'd want to do it alone.'

'Well, you don't have anything to worry about so . . .'

'I wonder if they've asked Chrissie to go in? They're bound to have, don't you think?'

'Probably. And the others. Actually, David said Sukey was there that day, which might be a problem for Hugo, given she's his wife.'

'But they weren't together at the time.'

'I don't know if that makes a difference. We'll have to let them sort it out.'

'Of course. Do you know who else was there?'

'Pam and Rupert, apparently. Grayson, Frank, I'm not sure who else. I think what matters for us is that we weren't.'

Julia nodded and after gulping down her wine she finally managed a smile. 'That's better,' she declared, blinking rapidly with relief, 'and sorry again.'

'You don't have anything to be sorry for. We're all wound up right now, how can we not be? I only wish I could say we'll feel better after we've spoken to the police, but I can't really see that happening, can you?'

CHAPTER EIGHTEEN

Natalie hadn't been expecting great things of ex-DCI Carl Underwood, but discovering that he wasn't even half the size of the chip on his shoulder was surprising. She'd had him down for a strapping sort of Wexford type, all heft and attitude, and while he definitely had the latter, the rest of him was pure elfish Columbo without the shabby raincoat and hair. And as for expecting him to be holed up half-drunk in a stuffy little cottage at the back end of nowhere, well here he was on the south coast of Devon in a top floor apartment with concierge, all mod-cons and panoramic sea views.

All this on a police pension?

'I'm not sure we ever made Sunday visits back in my day,' he said, gesturing for her and Leo to make themselves comfortable on one of his plush damask sofas, 'but it's good of you to fit in around me. I'm part of a golfing tournament this coming week, been looking forward to it, and I don't want to let them down.'

Smiling sweetly to cover her instinctive dislike, Natalie confirmed why they were there. 'As we said on the phone, we'd like to talk to you about the Karen Lomax murder.'

'OK,' he said, drawing out the word as if it were a game he might be a little rusty at, but he'd pick it up again as they went along. Another way of describing his manner, Natalie thought, was cagey, maybe even arsey, which she could kind of understand as he couldn't be feeling good about having left the force with a murder unresolved. Especially if he was part of the reason for it. 'How can I help?' he asked.

She glanced at Leo, his cue to take over. She wanted to observe the ex-DCI's demeanour to see what subtext she could pick up from what he said.

'We talked to the Lomaxes at the end of last week,' Leo began, taking up a half-mast mansplaining position, 'Jess and Eddie. I expect you remember them?'

Underwood's eyes narrowed as they darted between his interrogators. 'Of course. How could I forget the parents of a child who was murdered? Stuff like that imprints itself on a person's brain.'

'And you're aware that we now have a familial DNA match to . . . '

'Yes, yes, you told me on the phone. So, whose is it?'

Sidestepping the question, Leo said, 'Karen's parents provided us with the names of several individuals whom they remembered being in the wine bar during the day before Karen was reported missing. The familial match belongs to one of them, although we still haven't established which one . . . The point is, in spite of the Lomaxes being certain they named all three men in their statements there's no record of any of them being questioned.'

Underwood's hackles were rising; he clearly had a fair idea of where this was going now and he wasn't liking it a bit.

'Just as concerning,' Leo continued, 'is that the names don't appear in the Lomaxes' statements either, and as I mentioned, they are quite certain that . . . '

'Who are we talking about?' Underwood cut in sharply. 'Who's this familial match supposed to belong to?'

'Either Richard Crayce or one of his sons, David and Henry.'

Underwood's upper lip curled. 'Are you serious? The Crayces? There's no way it was any of them . . . '

'And yet the DNA is saying otherwise,' Natalie reminded him, and arched her eyebrows at the scathing look that came her way. Wow, this man didn't like women, or maybe it was mixed-race he had a problem with – more likely both. 'So why didn't you interview the Crayces when you knew they'd been at the wine bar that day?' she asked mildly.

'Because,' he said tightly, 'they'd long gone before she disappeared. People saw her after, talked to her even, right up until nine or ten o'clock that night if I recall correctly. Maybe later. It was a waste of police time going after them.'

Frowning to show she didn't quite follow that, she said, 'Or was it because they were shooting buddies that you decided not to bother them? People you didn't want to upset, or offend in any way?'

Fit to burst, he spat, 'What the hell are you talking about? I couldn't care less about offending them or anyone else. I'm just telling you that they'd long gone and it was a waste of time . . . '

'But it wouldn't have been a waste of time, because we now know that the semen taken from Karen's underwear when her body was found belongs to one of them.

You have to admit that there was a good chance of this being discovered at the time if you'd interviewed them.'

Unable to argue with that he simply glared at her.

'Can we assume,' Natalie continued, 'that you were responsible for removing the Crayces from the Lomaxes' statements? Or that you gave instructions for that to happen?'

To Leo he said, 'You didn't tell me on the phone I was going to need a lawyer for this.'

Ignoring the comment, Natalie said, 'I believe that other names were also removed. I'm talking about Frank Granger, Grayson Diffley, Christina Edmonds . . . '

'They were a clique,' he blustered, 'the bloody Moorauders they used to call themselves. They were always together, eight or ten of them, so yeah, those you've just mentioned were probably in the wine bar too, and a bunch of others who *did* get interviewed. I can't remember their names now, but they all said the same thing, that they'd left the bar around four, never went back and spent the rest of the day and night boozing it up in pubs on the moor before crashing out somewhere. I forget where now, but I do know there was no point going after them *all* when there had been hundreds of people in and out of that bar that day. Everyone, including the Lomaxes, agreed that the moor set had left some time in the afternoon, and no one ever said that any of them went back again.'

'Which isn't the same as not going back. Maybe one of them set up a rendezvous with Karen that she told no one about. Didn't that occur to you?'

'No, it didn't, but I'll admit, now that circumstances

have changed, I made the wrong call about interviewing them all.'

As if it were as simple as forgetting to hang up a coat. 'And what about removing their names from the Lomaxes' statements?' she pressed again.

'They signed those statements. If there was no mention of the Crayces it's because the Lomaxes were happy for there not to be.'

'Well, they're not so happy now, and you and I both know that there's a good chance they were so distressed at the time that they probably didn't notice certain names were missing amongst so many.'

He fixed her with a fierceness she guessed was meant to be intimidating, but she'd dealt with far worse; he was a clown by comparison.

'If you'd followed up the way you should have,' she stated, 'you might have saved Karen's life.'

'How the hell do you work that out?' he demanded angrily.

'We don't know if she was held somewhere for a period of time – say a day or two – before she was killed. If she was, and you had conducted a full and proper investigation, you might have found her in time.'

His face was turning puce, and his fists were bunching and twisting into one another as if he were trying to stop himself taking a swing. 'You don't know that,' he growled.

'No, I don't, but you have to admit, it's a possibility.'

'If you're trying to suggest I covered up a murder . . .'

'Actually, that's not what I'm suggesting, although I did wonder before we came here. Now I think you were negligent to the point of botching the investigation when she went missing, and again after she was found. I'm sure there'll be an inquiry following this meeting today. Thank you for your time,' and with a nod towards Leo she led the way out into a welcome waft of fresh air.

CHAPTER NINETEEN

It was becoming very hard for Annie to keep a sense of reality about what was happening to her life, to her family, most of all to her marriage. The seriousness of it was at once threatening and terrifying, as though a small part of the past had opened up and was sucking them all back into an unfathomable place of clouded memories and even lies – yet at the same time they were going about their business as if everything were normal.

However, today definitely wasn't normal, couldn't even begin to be described as such. She was at the police station about to be questioned concerning the murder of Karen Lomax, a young girl she'd hardly known and yet was now at the very centre of her world. She was bewildered by the shock of it, couldn't think how to deal with her conscience or her emotions as they flew about unchecked, unreachable even. Clearly she wasn't going to lie to the police, and yet maybe she should if it proved necessary. David was her husband, she loved him with all her heart, trusted him, couldn't believe he'd be capable of committing this act, and she needed to protect her family . . .

But how could she protect them from something that was already done, that there could never be any going back from, that one of them at least had clearly been involved in? And what about Karen's parents? Didn't they deserve the truth, whatever it was? They were as blameless in this as their daughter had been – their daughter who was barely older than Sienna at the time of her murder.

Murder. Annie felt sick to her stomach, torn by horror as she considered how she would feel if they lost Sienna in the same way.

Looking up as Julia and Hugo came through from the station's inner sanctum, she got to her feet.

'Don't worry, it wasn't too bad,' Julia assured her, clutching her hands. 'You just have to tell them you weren't around at the time, which you weren't, and provided your story checks out, which it will, they'll let you go.'

Annie looked at Hugo.

'It'll be fine,' he said gently. 'Remember you're here voluntarily. You're not under arrest, you're not even under caution. If you want to, you can leave at any time.'

'I just want to get it over with,' she told him, glancing at Julia's phone as a text arrived.

'It's Henry,' Julia announced, flushing slightly. 'He's outside, waiting to take me home. He has to come back himself later, but he wanted to make sure I was OK. Honestly, he's being so sweet about this, really supportive . . . I know it should be the other way round, but I'm going to make sure it is from now on. Hugo, thanks so much for being there for me,' she said, embracing him. 'Please send Sukey my love,' and after hugging Annie she all but ran out of the door.

'What about Sukey?' Annie asked Hugo. 'Is she being questioned?'

'She will be,' he replied. 'And I have a colleague standing

by for when it happens, but from what she tells me she ducked out of the pub crawl long before everyone repaired to the farmhouse.'

'So is that where it's supposed to have happened?' Annie asked, sickened by the very idea of it.

'If you mean is it where Karen Lomax was killed . . .'

'Or taken for sex,' Annie interrupted, as if that were somehow better, which obviously it wasn't – or maybe it was, what the hell did she know apart from everything being so appalling she had no words for it?

'Either way, I don't think the police are certain. That's the trouble with cold cases, trying to gather evidence so long after the event can be like trying to gather thin air. But that's not for you to worry about. All you need to focus on now is keeping your answers as brief as possible, offer no information unless asked, and if there's anything you're unsure about we can call things to a halt until you're ready to go on.'

'Easy then,' she quipped drily.

He smiled. 'I'll be there, and I promise you if it goes anything like Julia's interview, and there's no reason why it shouldn't, you'll be in and out in no time at all.'

Minutes later they were in a consultation room with four padded leatherette chairs each side of a Formica table, glass-brick windows that allowed in light, but offered no view of the outside, and a noticeboard full of helpful leaflets from various organizations. One that caught her eye was a guide to filing a complaint if someone felt they had been wrongly treated by the police.

The door opened and the female detective who'd burst into the house to arrest David in what was starting to seem like another life swept in. 'Mrs Crayce, thank you for coming,' she said, managing to sound both business-like and friendly as she put her things down on the table. 'I'm DS Natalie Rundle, and this is DC Leo Johnson.'

Annie looked at the younger detective. He was the one who'd put the handcuffs on David, freckly-faced, fiery red hair, bright blue eyes that bizarrely made her want to like him . . . She'd probably end up hating them both by the end of today, and maybe she did already, she'd just failed to connect with it yet.

She and Hugo took seats opposite the detectives, and after everything about the process had been explained and identified for the recording, DS Rundle kicked things off with a predictable set of questions that Annie had no difficulties with. How long had she and David been married? How many children did they have? Were they both involved in the shooting school? Did she engage in blood sports herself? She wasn't even thrown when Rundle veered off into trickier territory by asking if David had always been faithful, because given the circumstances she'd have been a fool not to see it coming.

'Yes, he has,' she replied, holding the detective's eyes. What was the woman expecting her to say, that he was a serial adulterer? Some kind of predator? He wasn't and had never been anything of the sort. He'd just had issues that he'd sorted out a long time ago.

Rundle was arching an eyebrow, a not very subtle reminder of the DNA checks still in process. So, had he really always been faithful?

Annie's gaze didn't falter. In the true sense of the meaning she was in no doubt that he had.

Apparently letting that go, Rundle said, 'Is it possible

that unlike the rest of your family you remember what you were doing on the weekend of 7th and 8th August 1999?'

'I was in London at a baby shower.' She reached into her bag and drew out an envelope containing her old friend's details. 'This is in case you'd like to check.'

Taking the envelope Rundle passed it to Johnson as she said, 'Thank you. And do you recall where your husband was that weekend?'

'He was at Hanley Combe, working on the house.'

'But you weren't around to know for certain that was what he was doing?'

Since she'd already said she wasn't, all she could reply was, 'No.'

Rundle consulted her notes, and her next question was so out of left field that it took Annie a moment to adjust. 'I believe your husband left the armed forces at the start of 1998?'

Annie was guarded as she said, 'Yes, that's right.' Had David been questioned about this? Hugo hadn't mentioned it. What was she supposed to say if she was asked questions she had no answers for?

'Can you recall his state of mind during the period following his discharge?'

Feeling heat rising through her, Annie said, 'He was . . . It was a difficult time for him.'

Rundle nodded sympathetically, almost as if she'd expected the answer. 'In what way?' she asked.

Hugo said, 'If you want information about David Crayce's time in the Army you'll need to put your request through the proper channels.'

Unfazed, Rundle said, 'Thank you for that, Mr Blum.'

To Annie she said, 'Did your husband exhibit any mental health issues when he returned to civilian life?'

Feeling trapped, Annie said, 'Not really. I mean, he had some episodes when things got on top of him, but they didn't happen often.'

'Were these *episodes* ever violent, or abusive in any way?'

Annie's heartbeat was picking up. 'That isn't how I would characterize them,' she replied. Was that true? It didn't feel like a lie, but it wasn't exactly honest either given the ferocity of his nightmares.

'Then how would you characterize them?'

'Detective,' Hugo interrupted, 'Mrs Crayce isn't in a position to offer professional insight . . . '

'I appreciate that, Mr Blum, but she was in a relationship with David Crayce at the time, so perhaps she can describe the nature of the episodes she witnessed.'

Realizing if she didn't answer she'd make things worse, Annie said, 'He had bad dreams.'

Rundle nodded, again as if expecting the answer. 'Did he, or does he become aggressive in these dreams?'

'I don't know what they are so I've no way of knowing . . .'

'I mean does he become aggressive in a physical way outside of the dream?'

'Well, he would thrash about quite a bit, if that's what you mean, but it doesn't happen anymore. It hasn't for years.'

'Did he ever seek help in dealing with his episodes?'

'No, not that I'm aware of.'

'So, they went away of their own accord?'

'I suppose so.'

Rundle looked sceptical, clearly not quite believing it. 'In my experience,' she said, 'someone who has the kind of issues your husband . . . ' She stopped, looked down at her notepad, and by the time she looked up again she'd apparently thought better of sharing her thought. 'Has he ever been diagnosed with post-traumatic stress disorder?' she asked.

Annie shook her head. 'No.' He hadn't, but she'd often felt certain it was behind his problems, had once even tried to get him to seek help, but he'd flatly refused.

'Dissociative disorder?' Rundle suggested.

'I don't know what that is.'

'It's when someone experiences a disconnect between thoughts and actions, sometimes leaving them with no memory of what they've done. Has your husband ever experienced anything like that?'

Sensing her unease mounting and even showing, Annie said, 'No, not that I'm aware of.' She'd just lied, at least she thought she had, she couldn't be sure.

'But it's possible he could have? Perhaps you weren't with him when it happened.'

'Then I wouldn't know, if I wasn't there.'

'No, I don't suppose you would.'

Annie said nothing.

Rundle made some notes on her pad and moved on. 'Did you ever go to the Cheers wine bar with your husband in the year 1999?'

Feeling slightly sick now, Anne took a moment to assimilate, to grasp the fact that the police must know David had been to the bar that day, or why mention it? 'I can't be sure about dates, but yes, we did go once or twice. We'd moved to Exmoor by then, and it wasn't unusual for us to pop into town for a drink or night out.' *She was saying too much, needed to keep it short.*

'Do you remember Karen Lomax from your visits?'

Her heart clenched as she said, 'Yes, vaguely.'

'What do you remember about her?'

'Um, that she was the owners' daughter. Quite pretty and vivacious.'

'Anything else?'

'Not really.'

'Did you ever see your husband talking to her?'

'No.'

'Did he ever go to the wine bar without you?'

'Sometimes.'

'So he could have spoken to her then and you wouldn't have known?'

Annie stayed silent.

'Are you aware that he was at the bar on the day Karen disappeared?'

Annie swallowed dryly. 'I – I knew he was out with friends that day,' she said lamely.

'Do you know *who* he was out with?'

'His brother and father, various friends . . . I can't say for certain, I just know that a group of them got together.'

'Male and female?'

'I believe so.'

'Do you know where else they went, other than the Cheers wine bar?'

'Not really.'

'Do you know where your husband spent the night?'

'Yes, at the farmhouse.'

'How do you know that?'

Realizing she didn't for certain, she said, 'I – I spoke to his mother the next day and she told me he was there.'

'I see. That was Sunday, so you don't actually know where he spent the Saturday night?'

Wishing Hugo would stop this now, she said, 'I've no reason to believe he was anywhere else.'

Rundle jotted something down and was still looking at the page as she said, 'Is it possible your husband got very drunk that weekend?' Her eyes came up and bored into Annie's.

Holding the stare, Annie said, 'Yes, it's possible.'

'Would it be typical for him to do things while drunk that he doesn't remember the next day?'

'It's not typical for him to get drunk.'

'But when he does?'

'I think most of us have a problem remembering everything the next day if we've had too much the night before.'

Rundle nodded, but it didn't seem like agreement, more like realization that the question was being avoided. 'Do you think he could have experienced one of his *episodes* that night?' she asked.

'I – um, I don't know. They consisted of nightmares . . .'

'Does he ever engage in games of a sexual nature when he's under the influence of alcohol?'

'No!'

'As far as you're aware?'

'I'd know if he did, and he doesn't.'

'You'd also know if he'd sexually assaulted and murdered Karen Lomax?'

As Annie blanched Hugo said, 'Are you accusing Mrs Crayce of something, Detective, because if you are . . . '

'It's merely a question,' Rundle interrupted. 'Would you *know* for certain whether or not your husband committed this crime?'

Annie said, 'My husband is not capable of hurting anyone . . . '

'But he is a trained killer.'

Turning hot as she bit out the words, Annie said, 'That has nothing to do with anything, and it was a long time ago.'

'But not all that long before Karen Lomax disappeared, when he was apparently experiencing some mental health disturbances, and when those killer instincts might have been . . . '

Annie cried, 'He was trained to kill in combat, not to go around harming innocent young girls . . . '

'Or innocent wildlife? He's into blood sports, as we know, and there's a lot of evidence to suggest that someone suffering from PTSD . . . '

Hugo said, 'I think this has gone far enough, Detective. Mrs Crayce has willingly answered your questions, so if you don't have anything further to ask that's relevant to your case I'm going to take her home.'

Rundle didn't object, simply nodded to Johnson to stop the recording. As everyone got to their feet she said to Annie, 'I appreciate you coming in. If anything else comes to mind that you think might be helpful with our inquiries here's my card.'

As Annie took it she was thinking about David. If he really had been suffering from PTSD or this dissociative disorder, should she tell him it had come up in her interview?

'Don't worry,' Hugo reassured her when they got outside, 'it's my job to report back to David, and it's been an extremely useful exercise for me. You did great, by the way. I know it might have seemed tough in places, but you sailed it. Can I give you a lift somewhere now?'

'No, thanks. I'm meeting my mother for a late lunch.'

'OK. Say hi from me, and keep this in mind: they've got nothing, apart from the DNA, and *whoever* it belongs to, it is not proof of who killed her, only of who was with her at some point before she died.'

And that was supposed to be a comfort, Annie was thinking as she walked towards the seafront promenade. It certainly didn't feel like it. In fact, everything about it was making her feel sick to her very soul.

CHAPTER TWENTY

'Well I didn't enjoy that very much,' Natalie commented as she and Leo took the lift to the second floor.

'How so?' he asked, seeming genuinely perplexed.

Still battling the reminders of her own experiences with an ex-soldier suffering from PTSD and the terrible toll it had eventually taken on her, she said, 'What we had there was a decent woman doing her best for her husband and not actually knowing what the best is.'

'Do you mean you think she lied?'

'I know she did, although probably more by omission or obfuscation than design.' She shrugged. 'She's loyal, and no one can blame her for that, it's a good quality in anyone even if it is sometimes misplaced. Anyway, it's very likely that she has no real idea of what happened back then, although she'll have her suspicions, anyone would in her shoes, she just doesn't know where the hell to go with them – and why would she when the dice are still rolling?'

Letting her step out of the lift first, Leo said, 'Did you get the impression Julia Crayce also had suspicions when we spoke to her?'

Natalie almost laughed. 'That poor woman was so strung out I thought she was going to end up throttling herself with her own pearls. But to answer your question, I think she's more terrified it was her husband than suspicious it was him, which is interesting in itself, wouldn't you say?'

He frowned uncertainly, not following the thinking.

'If she's terrified it was him,' Natalie explained, 'then at least a part of her must suspect that it is.'

'Oh, I get it,' he said. 'By the way, Shari's checking out her claim that she was eventing in Wiltshire that day.'

'Good, but even if she wasn't a part of the pub crawl or the poker game, there's still a chance she knows more than she's saying. Both wives could. We'll talk to them again when the time's right. Meanwhile, it's going to be interesting to find out what Chrissie Edmonds has to say when she comes in. What time are we expecting her?'

'Her name's Slater now, and she's due at two. Henry Crayce at three, his father at four.'

'OK, I'm sure they won't mind waiting if we run over. How many of the other Moor-auders from that day have we managed to track down so far?'

'Quite a few, but half of them don't live in these parts any more, and out of those that do they're not all currently available for interview.'

'Let me guess: Caribbean holidays, North American ski trips, African safaris?'

'All of the above, plus an Alaskan cruise. That's the Diffleys, who took off yesterday. How the other half live, eh? No British winter for them, but we'll get to them, no worries, even those in far-off parts.'

'We will indeed,' and leading the way into the incident room she sat down to listen to Noah Shields's update on his and Shari's progress that morning.

'Turns out the bus driver who saw Karen that night is dead,' he said bleakly, 'still trying to track down his wife just in case he might have said something to her that isn't in his statement. For the most part we've been focusing on the customers we could find who were at the wine bar during the day. A few remembered seeing the Crayces with their usual set, but no one could say for certain what time they were there, although a couple said they were sure it wasn't any later than four, which corresponds with the statement given by Frank Granger, one of the Moor-auders who was interviewed during the initial investigation, and with the time Mrs Lomax said they left.'

Natalie said, 'Did anyone see them talking to Karen while they were there?'

'There was one woman – Jackie Bright – who said she's sure she noticed Dickie Crayce coming in on his own, after the others, and that he spoke to Karen as he passed her in the garden. She didn't hear what was said, but apparently Karen was her usual jokey self and they both laughed at something one or other of them said.'

Natalie nodded thoughtfully. 'Could he have been making plans to see her later?' she asked.

'There's no way of knowing, but I didn't get the impression from Jackie Bright that the encounter was very long. More a tease in passing than an actual chat.'

Natalie inhaled, disappointed, but far from defeated. 'OK, I guess it's something,' she said, 'but there's still a way to go, plenty more people to talk to. If you haven't had lunch yet, now's the time to pop out for sandwiches – mine's a BLT – then we'll review what we've pulled together this morning before getting to work on Chrissie Whatever-her-name-is-these-days. She interests me because we know already that she was there that day. And then we have the pleasure of the two remaining Crayces, who interest me even more.'

'Are we allowed to ask,' Shari put in carefully, 'if you're still convinced David Crayce is our man?'

Natalie's head tilted to one side as she considered her answer, but she didn't need long to form it. 'Given his history,' she replied, 'the suggestion of mental health issues around the time we're looking at, and what I know of how men like him operate – also how women, wives in particular, cover up for them – he has to be the obvious choice.'

'But?' Leo Johnson prompted.

'There are a few,' Natalie conceded, 'and the further into this we go the more they come up, because lately I've started to get a very bad feeling about the father. A bit of a Don Juan in his day, it seems . . . '

'What's that?' Shari asked.

Natalie rolled her eyes. 'And the brother is too much of a dark horse for my liking,' she continued. 'His wife's nerviness; the fact that he happened to be around that weekend when he lived in London, giving him the opportunity to play away; the hostile manner you say he adopted when you took a swab . . . ' She gave a sigh as she continued to think it through. 'You know, it must be pretty hellish being a part of that family right now,' she commented, 'because whichever of those men is guilty, and we know at least one of them is, then provided we do our jobs properly they've got to be aware that it's not going to turn out well for any of them.'

CHAPTER TWENTY-ONE

'It threw me badly when they started talking about PTSD and David's behaviour after he left the army,' Annie was saying to her mother over lunch at the Seafront Café. 'It was like the detective already knew he'd suffered from it, or some other condition that sounded just as bad if not worse . . . Dissociative disorder?'

'Mm, I've heard of it,' Harriet responded grimly. 'But how are you supposed to know when nothing was ever diagnosed?'

'I don't think I was supposed to know, only to provide the possibility it might have been the case. And if he did have blackouts . . . Well, I know he did, of sorts, but only when he'd been drinking and like I told her, that happens to everyone.'

Harriet didn't disagree, although she was looking dubious.

'What?' Annie prompted without actually wanting to know.

'Think of it this way,' Harriet said, 'if he was as drunk as we heard he was that night then how on earth would he have even been capable of having sex with the girl?'

Annie flinched, but her mother didn't seem to notice.

'I guess the same goes for Dickie and Henry,' Harriet said flatly, 'because they were apparently legless too.'

Feeling her appetite fading, Annie put down her fork and turned to stare out through the steamy window where sluggish traffic was coming and going along the promenade and a heaving metallic sea was blending with a far horizon. It was painfully clear to her that the police believed it was David who'd had sex with Karen Lomax and then killed her, maybe to keep her quiet, or perhaps accidentally, while not in full control of his senses. It could be that Henry and Dickie, once they found out what had happened, had taken charge of the situation and disposed of the body . . .

'What are you thinking?' Harriet asked gently.

Annie turned back, having no intention of sharing her nightmarish suspicions, not even with her mother. 'I was thinking,' she said, trying to turn things around, 'that when I picture the three of them in my mind's eye it just doesn't seem possible that any of them could have done it.'

Harriet nodded forlornly. 'Maybe that's because you're seeing them as they are now,' she suggested. 'They were much younger men back then, at the top of their games, and they've always been very attractive . . . ' Realizing she wasn't helping one bit, she broke off and regarded Annie regretfully.

Needing to get away from the moment Annie took out her mobile. 'A text I had from Sienna this morning,' she said, handing the phone over.

Hey Mum, just to say thinking of you. Sorry if I've been a pain lately making out like I can't cope. I get that it's a lot worse for you than it is for me. I'm ignoring the trolls and some of my friends are being great, especially Grant. None of them think it's Dad, which is lovely of them. I don't get into anything about Grandpa or Uncle Henry because I don't think they know. It hasn't made it onto Insta yet, thank God. Doing my head in really, and Max's. Don't worry about us though. We're fine. Love you, here to chat any time. Sxxx

Passing the phone back, Harriet said, 'She's just like you at heart, always supportive. It's funny though, isn't it, how it made it into the press about David, but not Dickie and Henry. Has anyone been in touch with you again trying to get some insight?'

Annie shook her head. 'Actually, there have been some calls, but we just ignore them, and I guess until the DNA results are back no one's really interested anyway, not with everything else that's going on in the world right now.'

Harriet nodded slowly her thoughts apparently flitting away to the possibility of a pandemic before coming back again. 'Does Sienna know you were seeing the police today?' she asked.

'No, there was no reason to tell her.'

'Has she been in touch with David?'

'He hasn't mentioned it if she has. She and Max are finding it difficult to know what to say to him, which you can hardly blame them for, I'm not finding it easy myself. I tried calling him while I was waiting for you, but he's either out on the stands or his phone's turned off.' *Or he's avoiding me*. 'I'll be interested to see how much he asks me about the interview when I get home. I know he'll have discussed it with Hugo by then, but with me it's like he doesn't want to go there at all, and I've no idea whether it's because he's in some sort of denial or . . . ' She snapped off the words, picked up her glass, but didn't drink. Where did suspicion of her husband and loyalty to him begin and end? How was she even supposed to know? 'Apparently Henry's been a lot nicer to Julia since she told him the police wanted to talk to her,' she said, moving things out of her own danger zone. 'I guess we can read all sorts into that.'

'Do you know what happened during her interview this morning?' Harriet asked.

'No, not in any detail, but she seemed quite upbeat when I saw her. I don't suppose she could have told them much, because apparently she was eventing over in Wiltshire that weekend.'

Harriet sighed and refilled their glasses with sparkling water.

'Sorry, am I interrupting?'

Annie and Harriet looked up to find Chrissie Slater next to their table holding a take-out coffee in one hand and mobile phone in the other.

'I saw you here,' she explained, 'and I didn't feel I could just go past without saying hello.'

Suppressing a wish that she had, Annie replied, 'It's good to see you,' and out of politeness she slid along the bench seat saying, 'please join us, if you have time.'

Taking the place, Chrissie said, 'Thanks, I have a few minutes.' Annie couldn't help noticing how drawn she looked in spite of the make-up. She was still striking though with her neat dark hair, slanting green eyes and the unusual features that made her something like beautiful.

'I'm surprised you're still here,' Harriet remarked. 'I thought you'd be back in London by now.'

Chrissie's smile was small, and slightly pursed. 'I would

be if I hadn't lost my job,' she replied. 'Cutbacks, you know, and turns out I wasn't as indispensable as I thought I was.'

'Oh, I'm sorry to hear that,' Annie said, meaning it for all the wrong reasons. 'I know how much you enjoyed being in publishing.'

'Do you have something else lined up?' Harriet asked. 'With all your contacts and experience I can imagine a lot of companies coming after you.'

'That's so sweet of you, and would that it were true. Alas, it hasn't happened yet, and I'm afraid my misfortune doesn't end there, because my husband and I have decided on a permanent separation of ways. So, I've been thinking I'll take some time off and spend it here while I work on setting myself up as a freelance editor.'

While worried about how Julia would take this news, Annie managed to sound sympathetic as she said, 'Gosh, you really are having a hard time of it.'

Chrissie's shrug was stoical. 'But with all that's going on in your world,' she said, and met Annie's eyes with her own show of sympathy. 'How's David?' she asked. 'I've called him a couple of times, but he hasn't got back to me.'

Glad to hear that, Annie said, 'He's doing OK, considering.'

'Yes, I'm sure he is. He's not the type to let things get to him, is he? He never was.'

And there went another reminder that she'd known David the longest.

'When I look back over the years,' Chrissie said with a sigh, 'who'd ever have thought we'd end up where we are today? A little innocent fun one night, well perhaps a bit more than that – I take it you already know I was there?'

Annie nodded, wondering now if this chance meeting was as coincidental as it had seemed.

'Actually, I'm on my way to the police station,' Chrissie told them. 'They've asked me to come in and answer some questions, which I don't mind, obviously, but I can tell you right now that I don't remember much about that night. We all got smashed, passed out at the farmhouse and I'm sure our heads were extremely sore the next day, but thankfully I've forgotten that part of it.'

'When did you find out Karen Lomax was missing?' Annie asked, trying to sound nothing more than interested, but managing something akin to snappy.

Showing no sign of noticing, Chrissie said, 'I guess a day or two later. I can't remember exactly, but probably when I heard that Frank and a couple of the others had been questioned about it, because we'd been in the bar that day. Then it turned out the poor girl had been seen by umpteen people after we left, so I just assumed we were no longer of interest.' Her eyes went to Annie's, and filled with more fake sorrow. 'Sorry, it's awful that this is happening, isn't it? I can hardly believe it, but I'm sure it's going to get sorted out somehow.'

Annie said, 'So you didn't see Karen that night, at any of the pubs, or at the farmhouse?'

Chrissie blinked with surprise. 'God no. She was just a kid, we didn't even know her, apart from to say hello to at the wine bar, so there's no way she'd have been hanging out with us.' She shook her head as if dismissing the very notion of it. 'I can tell you this though,' she continued, apparently coming down from her little show of indignation, 'she had a big old crush on David. She told me so herself, not that day, ages before, she even seemed to think she stood a chance with him. I told her straight out that she didn't, but you probably remember what she was like. She'd put it out for anyone, at least that's what they said about her and she wasn't one to give up easily. Anyway, the next thing I knew she was after Henry – poor him, he's always come second best to David, hasn't he, although I don't think he'd have minded in Karen's case. She wouldn't have been his type at all.'

Harriet said, 'And he was married, of course.'

Chrissie grimaced. 'I'm not sure that ever stopped Henry.' She leaned in conspiratorially. 'I've never told Julia this . . . Actually, it wasn't anything to do with her at the time, but she wouldn't want to hear it anyway. Henry and I were still seeing one another, on and off, right up until Laura died.'

So the entire time he was married, Annie thought in disgust.

'Everything changed between us then,' Chrissie continued, 'but it was only recently that Henry told me what he and Laura had been rowing about when the accident happened.'

Annie's blood was running cold. 'You?' she asked, already knowing the answer.

Chrissie's eyes went down. 'I'm afraid so. Oh God, life is so strange, isn't it? First I was mad about David, then it was Henry, just like Julia – and Karen, if you come to think of it. Actually, there were plenty of others, before you, of course, Annie, I swear those boys had it all worked out. But the thing with Henry and me, we never really did let go – it was like one day we couldn't get enough of each other, and the next it didn't seem like such a good idea. It was just spur of the moment stuff. He was never going to leave Laura, I knew that. I didn't even want him to.'

'Are you involved with him again now?' Harriet asked stiffly.

Chrissie looked down at her untouched coffee as she said, 'We're close, yes, but it's different now. We're older, life has moved on . . . I don't want to cause problems in his marriage, I really don't, but now all this has come up I'm afraid that when Julia finds out I stayed in his room that night at the farmhouse she isn't going to like it very much.'

Annie said, 'But you've already made the point that she wasn't with Henry then, so it had nothing to do with her.'

Chrissie simply smiled. 'Get Julia to see it that way,' she responded. 'You know what she's like with all her insecurities, but actually I'm sure he's far more committed to her than she seems to think. OK, he has a funny way of showing it sometimes, but that's Henry. He's never really known how to treat a woman right.'

Not sure what to say to that Annie looked at her mother, but Harriet was clearly at a similar loss.

Chrissie said, 'I want you to know that given the choice I wouldn't be telling anyone that I'd slept with Henry that night, but now it turns out I'm a good alibi for him it would be very remiss of me not to come clean, wouldn't it? Actually, everyone who was there is an alibi for everyone else, because I'm damned sure no one came or went from the house after we bowled up and broke open more bottles.'

Suddenly disliking her more intensely than she ever had, Annie said, 'What time are you due at the police station?'

Chrissie checked her watch. 'In about fifteen minutes, so I ought to go. Please send my love to David, and tell him if I could swear I'd slept with him that night it would have been my pleasure.'

After she'd gone Annie and Harriet sat quietly absorbing what had been said, and only looked up again when the café's owner, Fliss, loudly greeted someone she knew as they came in the door.

'Do you believe her?' Harriet asked in the end.

'About sleeping with Henry that night? Why? Don't you?'

Harriet shrugged, 'Does it make a difference to anything?'

Annie shook her head despairingly. 'I've no idea, but I get the impression she thinks it does.'

'Which leads us where?'

Having no answer for that, Annie said, 'Mum, like you, I don't know what went on back then, or what the heck's going on now, but I think we both have a very strong feeling that something is. And frankly I'm becoming increasingly afraid to find out who's at the centre of it.'

CHAPTER TWENTY-TWO

'So, what did you make of that?' Natalie asked Leo after a uniformed officer had come to escort Christina Slater out of the station.

'Honestly?' he replied. 'I couldn't read her. I mean, she seemed genuine enough but at the same time there was something . . . I dunno, I can't put my finger on it. How about you? You're better at reading people than I am.'

'Don't be so sure of it,' she commented, aware of how easy it was for anyone, including her, to bring personal grievances or bias to bear on character judgements, 'but I agree there was something about her – and it's making me wonder if one of the Crayces has got to her in some way. The obvious choice for that is Henry, given her readiness to set up an alibi of sorts for him.'

'Which begs the question, why would he need one?'

'Indeed. And, if the DNA match turns out to be his, claiming to be in the same room with Chrissie Slater all night with the door shut tight isn't going to help him much – or her, come to that. Did he say anything about spending the night with Ms Slater, or Edmonds as she was then, when Shari and Noah first spoke to him?'

'Not that I recall, but we can check.'

'Let's do that before we talk to him. If he didn't bring it up before it'll be reasonable to assume that the two of them have got together at some point during the past few days to discuss their stories. In fact, it's highly likely the whole lot of them are in touch about it, reminding one another of the tale they concocted at the time to make sure they stick to it.'

'Which will involve them all in a cover up, making every one of them complicit in the crime.'

Nodding agreement, Natalie said, 'We need to try harder to get hold of Frank Granger, the one who was actually interviewed at the time, to see if his version of events today matches the one he gave all those years ago. He and his wife are somewhere in Australia for the next month, is that right?'

'We've left messages, but he hasn't got back to us yet.'

'Probably because he wants to speak to the others first.' Tapping a pen against her notepad as she thought, she said, 'I don't know about you, but I'm becoming increasingly certain Karen Lomax was at the farmhouse that night.'

'I've always been convinced of it; trouble is we haven't found anyone who remembers seeing her at any of the pubs during the bender. Of course, it would have been helpful if inquiries at the time had been properly carried out, but even so, finding everyone who was working or drinking in those places that night is next to impossible.'

'She doesn't have to have been on the bender, someone could have gone to pick her up and taken her straight to the farmhouse. I guess, it's even possible she was there without everyone knowing, tucked away in a bedroom somewhere before they all piled in, given we've no idea if they all arrived at the same time. It's how they're making it sound, but has that question been asked?'

'Not as far as I know. We can put that right when we talk to Crayce senior and second son.' After noting it down, Leo said, 'Something we're still no closer to answering is *how* she got there. We know she was at the bus stop in town just after ten o'clock, but not waiting for a bus, so it's reasonable to suppose she was waiting for someone to pick her up. Trouble is it's a quiet road, and there are no witnesses to her getting into a car. Plus her mobile phone records from that time, such as they are, show no calls or messages from her number to anyone other than her friends.'

'And none of them claim to have been expecting to see her that night, even though she told her parents she was going to Lucy Aldridge's. Have we got hold of Lucy yet?'

'Still trying, as far as I'm aware.'

Natalie glanced up as an officer came in to let them know that Richard Crayce was waiting. After thanking him she said, 'At the moment we have zero evidence to say she *was* at the farmhouse, so we'd never get a warrant to search it, even if it was worthwhile all these years later and that's highly doubtful. So, we still have no crime scene, or weapon. In fact, all we know for certain is that one of the Crayces had sex with her, either that night, or maybe the next day, the science isn't giving us clarity on that, nor is it able to tell us if it's the person who ended her life.'

'You don't think they're one and the same?'

'That's the more likely scenario, but my mind remains open to all sorts of others, none of which are actually holding together at the moment. However, with any luck that might have changed by the end of the day.'

Johnson's eyebrows arched. 'Cue Dickie Crayce,' he said, getting to his feet, 'the only one of them, *so far*, who was seen actually speaking to Karen that day.'

CHAPTER TWENTY-THREE

Annie was quiet, only listening, as she served chicken and feta tortillas to everyone around the table while they helped themselves to salad and filled their glasses with beer or wine. She wasn't sure whose idea it had been for everyone to get together this evening, only that David had called her at the Byre to say his father, Henry and Julia were coming over to discuss what had happened during the day. Since her parents had collected Quin from school and brought him home they were here too, although her mother was presently upstairs putting her grandson to bed.

'It's a shame Hugo had to rush off,' Francis commented, spooning guacamole onto his plate, 'we could do with his input right now.'

'When I spoke to him,' David responded, 'he didn't sound unduly worried about anything, said it had all gone much the way he'd expected, they're still groping around in the dark for ways to build the case.'

But not to prove someone's semen was found on the girl's clothes, Annie was thinking.

'I'm glad he thought that,' Dickie grunted, 'because sitting here now I can tell you I'm convinced they think those test results are going to be mine.'

Are they? Annie couldn't help wondering as she looked at him. *Do you know already that they will be yours? If you do, why are you putting your sons through this?*

'They kept banging on about the fact that I was seen speaking to her,' he continued, 'wanted to know what it was about, had I arranged to meet her later in the day.'

Did you? Annie asked him silently, hating herself for it, but unable to stop it.

'They seemed to think I picked her up, took her to the farmhouse and . . . Well, I don't want to go into detail about the rest, not with ladies present.' His face was ashen, haggard, showing how hard he'd found the interview, which apparently had been a lot tougher than when the detectives had come to his home to take a swab. 'Then they started asking if I'd brought some sort of influence to bear on Underwood, who was leading the investigation back then, like we were old buddies, part of a network of some sort, so he'd agreed to protect me.'

'Did you know him?' Francis asked.

'No! I mean, I knew who he was, and we were on the same shoot a couple of times, but I hardly even spoke to the guy.'

'It's absurd,' Julia stated crossly. 'If you ask me, they're making it up as they go along.'

David said, 'You could be right about that, Jules, because according to Hugo they still don't know where any of it was supposed to have taken place.'

But one of you does, Annie thought dolefully.

'Were you asked if you picked her up from the bus stop?' David asked Henry.

Henry nodded, and glanced up to thank Annie as she put a tortilla in front of him. 'They managed to make me feel guilty about everything,' he declared. 'I even started doubting myself before I remembered I *didn't* pick her up, or take her to the farmhouse, or anywhere else, come to that.'

You sound so certain, Annie reflected, *I could almost believe you, and why would you lie if you know the results are yours? Why would any of you?*

'Has anyone spoken to Chrissie since she was interviewed?' Francis asked, taking the wine from David to refill his glass.

Annie noticed all eyes going to Henry, including Julia's whose hand tightened on his as he shook his head.

Was that true? No contact at all with Chrissie today? How could anyone possibly know apart from Chrissie and Henry?

Coming into the kitchen, Harriet said, 'Did Annie tell you we saw Chrissie at the café on her way to the police station?'

Everyone looked at Annie, and in an effort to prevent her mother blurting out the fact that Chrissie and Henry had spent that fateful night together in front of Julia, she said, 'She doesn't seem to remember much more about things than the rest of you,' *unless she's holding something back of course, but any of you – all of you – could be doing that.*

'Well, it was a long time ago,' Harriet stated, sitting down next to Dickie and helping herself to salad.

'You still haven't told us much about your interview, Jules,' David remarked, his eyes on Annie as she returned to the Aga for more of the savoury tortilla filling.

Julia shrugged dismissively. 'There's not much to tell,' she replied. 'Once they realized I wasn't around that weekend they seemed to lose interest in me. I thought it would have been the same for you, Annie, but then I remembered of course you and David were together at the time, unlike me and Henry, so they'd naturally have more to ask you.'

Annie swallowed dryly. She knew Hugo had already talked to David about her interview, but they hadn't discussed it yet and she wasn't sure that they would.

Turning around she found his eyes on her and for a moment she wished everyone would leave, that they could put their arms around one another and be who they really were, not the strangers they were becoming. She wanted him to swear to her that he'd had nothing to do with it, that the test results were not going to be his, that they couldn't possibly be because he remembered everything about that night and he'd been nowhere near Karen Lomax.

'Aren't you going to eat?' he asked her curiously.

Bringing a bowl to the table, she sat down between him and her father and smiled at Julia as she filled her glass with wine.

Dickie said, 'I had a call from Frank Granger before I came over. He's still in Australia, but the police have left messages for him to get in touch with them.'

Why did he call you and not David or Henry?

'What else did he say?' Henry asked.

'Just that he's going to call them tomorrow. He asked if there was anything he should know in advance. I said he should stick to the statement he gave before, if he can remember it. Nothing's changed.'

Apart from the case being reopened, and Crayce DNA being found on the victim's underwear, that bit's changed.

Days passed with suspicions, fears, memories and emotions scattering over Annie's mind like fallen leaves blowing across the humped peaks of the moor. Business continued, although it was the end of the season so games shoots had come to an end, only clays now, and safaris, and maintenance. There was no more contact from the police, although Hugo was keeping them up to date as far as he could. Sukey's interview sounded as though it had been much the same as Julia's; once they'd ascertained that Sukey's mother (still alive and memory as sharp as ever) had collected her from the Bridge Inn that night, they accepted she hadn't been at the farmhouse.

The farmhouse. It kept coming back to the old family home, in spite of no one knowing for certain if Karen had ever been there.

Apparently Pam Gillycrest rang the police from her luxury hotel in the Caribbean to share what she remembered about that night. Grayson Diffley also called from his cruise ship in Alaska. Both had spoken to Hugo before getting back to the police and again after, so the lawyer was able to report that neither's recall was any different to David's, Henry's or Dickie's.

It was Sunday now – where had the days gone, and how was it possible for pockets of time to seem normal, as though nothing unusual or threatening was happening at all? It was as if everything beyond Hanley Combe was part of another world, one that could only be drawn into their existence by thoughts or discussions so it was best to put it out of their minds and not mention it at all. It would catch up with them when the results came back, so why torment themselves with it now? Nevertheless, Annie couldn't prevent herself from constantly returning to what was hanging over them all. She and David continued to clash over it, and though neither of them said so, not even in their most heated exchanges, she knew he was as afraid as she was that he'd had some sort of black out that night.

But even if he had surely he'd remember something, such as picking the girl up, or, God help them, disposing of the body. He'd never blanked for more than a couple of hours, so why would it have been any different that night – if he'd even blanked at all. Considering how long ago it was he still seemed to remember most of what happened, and as far as she knew he'd never once hurt anyone while he was in an inebriated state. He'd get angry, yes, furious even; he'd punch walls, kick furniture, growl and seethe in terrible frustration, but he'd never hit out at anyone else, much less tried to kill them.

However this turned out, and she prayed night and day that it wouldn't be for the worst, she couldn't imagine ever not loving him. Her feelings for him were too much a part of her, too deep in her heart, in her psyche, in her everything, simply to disappear as if all the years they'd spent together no longer mattered – as if they could be wiped away by some sort of psychotic episode that had struck him such a long time ago. Everything they'd shared as a couple, as a family, still had value and substance, and it was what would hold them together if the unthinkable did come to pass and they were torn apart.

On Friday Sienna and Max had arrived home for the weekend, and it had gladdened Annie's heart to see how warmly they'd greeted their father when they'd come through the door. However difficult they were finding all this, they clearly didn't want him to feel they'd stopped trusting in him, even if secretly they must be terrified of what was going to happen. Please God it would turn out that their father wasn't responsible, but there would still be a monumental ordeal for them to get through when it became clear that their uncle or grandfather had done this terrible thing.

Today she was determined not to think about it at all. She was clearing her mind, emptying her heart of misgivings and dread in order to make at least one day in the children's lives seem normal. David was doing the same, which was why they were here, on the moor, just the six of them, including Cassie, trekking and nature-spotting and sharing stories from the past school week.

After a while Annie found herself falling back, walking more slowly so she could enjoy watching them and feeling how very much she loved every one of them. Sienna was hanging onto David's arm, hair cascading over her shoulders, bobble bobbling about on her hat. Quin was riding on his father's back, probably half-throttling him, while, Max close to his side, was almost matching him these days in height. To watch them they were simply a normal family lapping up their father's attention, laughing together and throwing sticks for the dog. It made her feel proud and hopelessly emotional to realize how strong the children were being, and how unswervingly determined to believe in their dad. Last night was the closest they'd come to talking about the situation with David. Annie was still impressed by the way Sienna had sat him down at the kitchen table and told him in her very bossy way, 'I know you want us all to carry on like this isn't happening, and we're OK with that, and I'm not going to get into how it's all my fault, because I know someone will accuse me of trying to make it all about me.' She shot a glare at Max. 'What I want to say,' she continued, 'is that all three of us need you to know that we're here for you, we love you and we support you. Same goes for you, Mum. We're not interested in the crap people are saying on social media, or anywhere else, they don't know us, and most of all they don't know you.'

'We know you, Dad,' Quin added seriously, and the way he blinked as though for emphasis must have turned David's heart inside out, for Annie hadn't missed the tears that briefly shone in his eyes as he swept their youngest onto his lap.

'Come here, you,' David had growled, pressing his face into Quin's neck. 'I want you in striking distance for when I'm ready to eat you all up.'

'Oh no!' Quin cried, struggling to get away.

Going to them Sienna had wrapped her arms around them, and then Max was piling in too, and as Annie joined in, David said, 'You don't have anything to worry about, OK? I know this is a difficult time, but we're going to get through it, I promise.'

Knowing each of the children were hanging onto the fact that he didn't make promises he couldn't keep, Annie had taken heart from it too, and as she watched him now she felt his centrality to their lives, holding them together in ways he might not even be aware of himself. He was truly the beating heart of their family, a good man, not without flaws, God knew he had plenty, but he was as decent and honourable as anyone she'd ever known. As she thought this, and felt it, she continued watching him, as at home here in this harsh and unforgiving landscape as he was in the calm and comfort of Hanley Combe. He took strength from the moor, pulled it in as if the snow-patched terrain, dramatic ravines, waterfalls, frozen streams, forests and endless stormy skies were a god-given elixir, and she guessed for him they were. He never seemed fazed by how dangerous and unpredictable the terrain could be, or how cleverly it could disguise itself with tricks of shadow and light. He saw beauty in all its forms, rugged, severe, gentle, persuasive, dramatic, hostile, bigger, bolder, stronger – as he'd told her once, he felt the rhythm of its soul, and she understood that, because she did too.

'Mum! Look!' Quin cried excitedly, spinning round on his father's back and almost toppling them both over. He was pointing towards Dunkery Beacon, the highest point of the moor, several miles distant. It was so clear today that there was no mistaking the landmark, or South Wales in the opposite direction (the Dark Side, as many locals called it), or the heavy churning of the sea. However, what had captured everyone's attention was an enormous stag standing proud on a rocky outcrop, its antlers intricate and stately against the milky sky, its sleek, muscular body showing its power of strength and speed.

'Isn't he something?' David murmured as she joined them.

'He's king of the world,' Quin declared.

Sienna quickly positioned them to capture a shot with the magnificent beast in the background, but by the time she was ready it had disappeared.

Annie felt suddenly desperately afraid, and a moment later, foolish for the way she'd just allowed herself to see the animal as a symbol of their happiness: beautiful and steady one minute, the next simply gone.

It was just before seven that evening, late lunch over and everyone, apart from Annie, down in the games room, when the kitchen door opened and Henry and Julia ran in out of the wind, laughing and apologizing for not calling ahead, although they never did normally.

'We've just dropped Dad off,' Henry explained, helping Julia out of her coat and giving her a quick peck on the cheek before hanging it with his in the cloakroom. He really was being sweet these days, Annie found herself reflecting. 'He was going to come too, but then decided he was tired. Where is everyone? I thought the children were home.'

'They're downstairs,' Annie told him, as Julia opened the fridge to take out a bottle of wine. 'Time to cocktail up,' Julia declared, unscrewing the bottle top. 'After a day with the mother and aunt, we need it. They send their love, by the way. Would you like one?' she asked Annie.

Amazed by how they were able to carry on as if this interminable wait wasn't happening, Annie took down three glasses and decided that the best course for now was simply to be pleased to see them.

'How was your walk today?' Henry asked, running a hand into Julia's hair as she poured.

So affectionate, so tactile in a way I haven't seen in a while. What does it mean?

'Cold, windy,' Annie replied, 'but wonderful. How were Celine and Ruth?' she asked Julia.

'Same as ever. They always enjoy seeing Dickie; he's like their tour guide down memory lane, if only they didn't keep getting lost.'

Easily able to imagine the two women ambling off on tangents and squabbling over dates and detail, Annie smiled and picked up her own glass of wine.

'To us, and all who sail in us,' Henry toasted. 'Or something like that.' After they'd clinked and sipped, he said, 'Are they watching a movie?'

'They were in the middle of a table-tennis tournament when I came up,' Annie told him, 'but things could have moved on since then.'

'I'll go find out,' and treating Julia to another quick peck he took the back stairs down to the games room, where they heard him being greeted with a chorus of cheers and, 'You have to be on my team,' 'No mine.'

Even the children seem to be doing a better job of pretending everything's normal than I am.

She watched Julia sit down at the table and raise her glass again. She seemed about to make another toast, but said nothing, simply held Annie's eyes as she took a sip of her drink.

'What is it?' Annie asked, coming to sit down too.

Julia shrugged. 'Nothing and everything. How are things with you?'

'OK. As good as they can be given where we are.'

Julia's smile became distant and sad. 'Given where we are,' she echoed, her gaze drifting away on a tide of her own thoughts, 'and where exactly is that, I wonder.' She looked up. 'Oh, don't worry, I'm not expecting an answer, I'm just . . . ' She shrugged. 'Actually, I don't want to talk about what's happening, but I sure as hell can't stop thinking about it. Can you?'

'Not really,' Annie admitted.

Julia sipped her wine and frowned as she said, 'Henry . . . You must have noticed he's being so much nicer to me . . . Not that I'm complaining, would I ever, but I have to admit it's confusing me.'

Annie had no problem believing this, knowing how difficult Henry could be. 'Has he said anything?' she asked. 'I mean, something to explain? Or . . . ' She wished she hadn't started this now, because she wasn't sure how to phrase her question.

Julia's fingers went to her pearls as she said, 'He's apologized for being off these past few weeks, says he needs to wise to up to how lucky he is to have me, and that he realizes he has to do something about his moods . . . We're a bit like newlyweds, if you get my meaning. Strange, isn't it? Especially when I heard the other day that Chrissie's marriage has broken up.' Her eyes came to Annie. 'Did you know about that?'

'I found out last Monday,' Annie admitted, 'when Mum and I ran into her at the Seafront Café. She told us then.'

Julia nodded. 'Of course, you know she was at the farmhouse that fateful Saturday night?' She sipped more wine and stared down at the glass as she said, 'I can't help wondering if she was with Henry, but he was married to Laura then, so . . . ' She broke into an unsteady laugh. 'Why am I doing this to myself? I have no idea, but I wish I could stop everything going around and around in my head until it's impossible to make sense of anything anymore.'

Understanding her turmoil, Annie said, 'It's this waiting that's driving you nuts. It's doing the same to us all.'

Julia smiled gratefully and got up to go and take more wine from the fridge. 'You'll never guess what I did today?' she said, looking sheepish.

'Tell me.'

'We all went out for a ride this afternoon, Dickie included, and I made sure we went near Chrissie's place. I wanted her to see Henry *en famille* . . . ' She banged a fist to her forehead. 'Now if that wasn't childish or unsubtle I don't know what it was, but I'm sure Henry was aware of what I was doing. Not that he said anything, but how could he not be?'

Unable even to guess what might have been going through Henry's mind, while understanding what had been in Julia's, Annie still found herself struggling for something to say.

'You know,' Julia said, sitting down again, 'it would just about kill me if I lost Henry too.'

Frowning, Annie said, 'Who else did you lose?' before remembering and wishing she could take it back.

Julia was already looking at her in surprise. 'My father,' she said, sounding slightly embarrassed. 'OK, I know you're going to say it was a long time ago, but take it from me, that sort of thing stays with you. And when stuff like this is going on . . . I keep wishing I had him to turn to . . . Oh God, I'm going to cry'

'It's OK,' Annie told her gently. 'Talk about him if you want to. I know he was special to you.'

'I suppose like yours is to you. The trouble is, him going off like that when I was fifteen, deserting us for another woman and never being in touch, it felt like such a horrible rejection . . . And why wouldn't it, because that's what it was, not only of Mummy, but of me. He abandoned us both, the bastard, and when you're that age your mind twists things around. And I can feel myself doing it again over all this, tying myself up in knots, going to all the dark and unhappy places. I did it when my marriage came to an end too, and I couldn't stand by Roger then.' She shuddered. 'What a horrible mistake that was, but I guess we all make them.'

'We do,' Annie agreed gently.

'Geraldine was wonderful, of course. I think I've told

you that before, but she was. She had a way of listening and understanding that Mummy's never quite managed – not that I don't love Mummy, obviously I do, madly, but you know how special Geraldine was. She was so happy when Henry and I got married. It was like both of our dreams coming true, she always wanted me to be part of the family, and it was what I wanted too. And now this is happening I can't stop thinking about her . . . ' She shook her head in self-mocking despair. 'You're right, Annie, the waiting is definitely driving me nuts. It's been two weeks now, and they said it might be longer, but I'm not sure I can deal with longer.'

Having every sympathy, Annie wanted to ask what she thought she might do if the DNA was matched to Henry, but as she'd barely even broached that herself should it turn out to be David's, she decided it probably wasn't a good route to go down.

In a whisper, Julia said, 'Do you think it could have been Dickie?' Hurriedly she added, 'I only say that because Mummy and Ruth . . . They remember better than any of us what he used to be like, you know when he was younger. I think they know things about him that they're glad not to be asked about.'

Having no idea how to respond to that, only how wretched it was making her feel, Annie said, 'How about we stop the speculation and suspicion and wait until we know more?'

CHAPTER TWENTY-FOUR

After a gruelling week of tracking people down, going over old interviews, statements and evidence, and talking to people whose memories were about as useful as old tea bags, Natalie had been more than ready for a break at the weekend. Just a few hours of not obsessing about the Crayces was going to do her the power of good, and maybe sharpen up her mind ready for when those results came in.

She wasn't wrong.

It might be Tuesday by now, but she was still feeling the uplift of having spent an enjoyable Sunday with both daughters, who'd driven down from London to sweep her off to lunch at a delightful pub on the edge of town called the Mermaid. How proud she was of her twins, so much so that simply thinking about them could warm her with the reminder that she was human, a mother, a still fairly young and reasonably attractive woman, not just a detective. Although she was usually the listener at their family get-togethers, on this occasion she'd allowed herself to be drawn an inch or two on her love life. Not that there had been anything to tell, nothing at all really. However, both girls had returned to London happy in the knowledge that their lonely mother had found someone to fancy who wasn't married, a murderer, a wife-beater or a molester. In other words, the kind of bloke she usually met in her world.

'Ah, there you are,' Gould said from the doorway of the incident room.

To Natalie's horror she felt herself blush as she tried to quip, 'Yep, here I am.'

'Did I see you on Sunday, driving out of the Mermaid?' he asked, remaining in the doorway.

'Yes, that could have been me. I went there with my daughters, for lunch.'

'A good pub. Did you enjoy it?'

'Yes, we did, thanks. It was my first time. I mean at that pub.' *Jesus, Natalie, what's wrong with you?*

He laughed and she only blushed again as her stupid heart turned over. Those girls, they'd got her all worked up over something that was nothing, and now it was like she was actually buying into it.

Surprising her, for she felt sure the conversation would end there, he said, 'So what did you want to see me about?'

Quickly pulling herself together she said, 'Richard Crayce's connection to DCI Underwood. You said you knew people in that world. I'd like to find out how close they were, and if Crayce might have leaned on Underwood, or called in some sort of favour to keep the investigation clear of him and his sons.'

'OK, I'll ask around. Is it going to make a difference to this investigation if he did?'

'Not that I can see right now, but we're exploring all possibilities. Is there going to be some sort of hearing about Underwood's handling of the case?'

'It's certainly looking that way.' He stood to one side, allowing Shari Avery to enter the room.

'Morning, sir,' she said chirpily. 'Morning ma'am.'

Wanting to tell her to turn around and come back in five, Natalie said, 'Is that coffee for me? You're an angel.'

'Of course it's for you,' Shari lied, handing it over, 'but that's not all I have. I checked my emails on the way in and I've heard back from Lucy Aldridge, Karen Lomax's bestie from way back then.'

'I'll leave you to it,' Gould said, and off he went.

'Does she have anything significant to tell us?' Natalie asked, sipping her coffee and knowing she'd spend some time later thinking about the past couple of minutes with Gould.

'I've only scanned it so far,' Shari replied, 'but basically she's saying she's read through her original statement and there's nothing she wants to add or change, blah blah. However, and this is where it gets interesting, she told me that Karen had a bit of a thing for the Crayces, used to wonder what it would be like to have all three at the same time.'

Natalie's eyebrows shot up. 'Not that this hadn't occurred to me,' she stated, because it certainly had, although not in a particularly realistic way. 'She was some girl, our Karen,' she remarked. 'Did it ever happen?'

'Not that Lucy knew of, she thinks it was just something Karen used to say, although she reckons Karen would have gone for it given the chance.'

'So now we wonder, did it come along the night Karen told her parents she was staying at Lucy's?'

'Only one lot of DNA,' Shari pointed out.

'The others might have used condoms, or it could have been oral, or a couple of them couldn't get it up considering how much drink we're told was involved.'

'Ma'am,' Leo said coming into the room with Noah. 'Have you looked at your emails in the past few minutes?'

'No, why?' Natalie asked, sensing from his tone and the look on Noah's face that something important was there.

'The results are back,' Leo told her. 'We have a definitive match.'

Natalie felt a rush of adrenalin kick in, and quickly opened her emails. It took only seconds to find what she was looking for. 'OK,' she barked, taking out her phone. 'Leo, get onto the Crown Prosecution Service. Noah, start drawing up the paperwork said prosecutor's going need. Shari, let the custody sergeant know what's happening – and while you're all doing that, I'll call the Billy Big Bollocks lawyer to tell him which one of his clients he needs to bring in.'

CHAPTER TWENTY-FIVE

'Dad?' David said, touching a hand gently to his father's arm. 'Are you with us?'

Dickie's tired eyes left the flames in the hearth and made a slow journey up to his son's half-smiling, half-concerned face. 'I wasn't asleep,' he said gruffly.

Henry said, 'And you weren't snoring either.'

Dickie managed a smile and watched his sons sit down on the leather sofas in front of the fire with him.

From where she was at the other end of the Byre's main hall, Annie wasn't able to make out what they were saying, although it was apparently something teasing because Dickie's responding tone was chiding and Henry play-acted being wounded. David got up to put more logs on the fire, and Hans came through from the shop, but left again when he'd got an answer to whatever he'd asked.

Returning to the calendar on her computer screen, she set about highlighting the clay-pigeon shoots for the weeks leading up to their ski trip – *would that really go ahead? Shouldn't she have cancelled by now* – and added a couple of meetings with estate managers and game-keepers, before downloading a proposed menu from the caterer for an Easter flurry.

An Easter flurry. They were carrying on as if the world wasn't about to collapse in on them at any moment, as if there was nothing more to worry about than the usual day to day issues, but as the alternative was simply to freeze like deer in the headlights it seemed the only sensible thing to do.

'Ah, I was just about to ask if you'd received that yet,' Julia said, reading over her shoulder. 'I've drafted an invitation, so once we're agreed on it I can send it out.'

'That'll be great,' Annie responded, thinking of how awful it was going to be when they were forced to cancel. Everyone would know why, would probably have had no intention of coming anyway. The whole family would be ostracized, the business would fail, their futures would be in chaos . . .

Aware of a car pulling up outside and guessing it was someone coming to the shop, she continued her conversation with Julia, her words moving smoothly past the fear she felt which could easily choke her. 'We need to decide numbers, and how much to charge,' she said. 'I'll make a note to bring it up at the meeting later. We should also start discussing whether or not we're going to get involved in grouse shooting again this year.' *This was insane and they both knew it, there was no way it could happen with this hanging over them, even if it was still months away.*

'I think Henry's up for it if David is,' Julia said, going to pour herself a coffee, 'which means we'll have to call on Trevor Beach to take over the safaris again. He said he enjoyed it last summer, so I'll . . . '

Taking a moment to realize she'd stopped speaking, Annie glanced over her shoulder to find out why. To her surprise Julia was standing very still, mug in hand, staring at something. Annie turned around and seeing Hugo at the door she felt everything in her freeze into a state of abject dread. She knew from his expression why he was here, that the day had come, answers were about to be revealed, but something in her was refusing to accept it – was suddenly making her smile and blather on about how lovely it was to see him. If she was nice to him, kept it jokey, maybe he'd tell her not to worry, that she was reading it all wrong.

She wasn't and she knew it, and as her words ran out she watched David and Henry get to their feet, their expressions telling her that they too understood why Hugo was here, and as he approached them she found herself unable to move or breathe. Her heart was pounding too hard to hear what was being said. She felt Julia stand close to her, registered Dickie still sitting, not even trying to stand. Then she realized Hugo was talking to David, saw the blood drain from her husband's face and Hugo move aside as though to clear the way.

'No,' Annie said hoarsely. 'No, it can't . . . David?' she called out.

He didn't answer and she almost fell over as she scrambled around the desk, needing to get to him.

'David! Hugo?'

'I'm sorry,' Hugo said softly.

Her eyes darted to David. This couldn't be happening. *It just couldn't. Worst nightmares didn't come true.* 'David?' she choked out.

He said nothing, simply put on his coat and pulled her to him, holding her as though he'd never let go. Then suddenly he did, and he was walking to the door with Hugo.

'No!' she shouted. 'This is wrong. Hugo, you have to

tell them . . . ' Someone put hands on her arms, gently but firmly and seeing it was Henry she shrugged him off. 'Did you know?' she yelled at him. 'Were you expecting this?'

'No,' he answered.

'Did you?' she yelled at Dickie.

He shook his head; tears were on his cheeks.

She raced to the door. 'David!' she cried. 'You have to tell them they're wrong.'

Catching her as she threw herself at him he held her again. 'I will,' he promised. 'I'll tell them,' and pressing a kiss hard to her forehead he gazed into her eyes for a moment and then he was getting into Hugo's car.

She stood watching them drive away, oblivious to the sleet and cold, seeing and feeling nothing, hardly able to function past the horror, the brutal, inescapable fear that he wouldn't be coming back. It was closing around her like a cloak, a black screen of finality. She needed to stop it from becoming reality, to keep the darkness, the truth of what it meant at bay.

Feeling something against her leg she looked down and found Cassie's soulful brown eyes gazing up at her. Choking back a sob she sank down to bury her face in the Lab's silky black coat and clung to her, inhaled her earthy scent and slowly made herself understand the need to calm down, to clear her mind and decide what had to be done.

Julia appeared beside her. 'Come in,' she said softly.

Annie stood up, allowed Julia to put a coat around her and walked back to the Byre.

Inside the fire was still lit, the air was warm and smelling of leather and wood smoke. It was the same as before, and yet entirely different, because David wasn't there. She saw Hans pouring brandy into tumblers; Henry was kneeling beside his father, who was crying. When Henry looked up she registered his white face, saw how shaken he was too, and yet how could he be if he'd known it wasn't him? Maybe he'd thought it was Dickie, but had anyone ever really believed it could be?

'I've called your parents,' Julia said, taking a glass from Hans and passing it to Annie.

Realizing her hands were shaking, Annie didn't take it. She didn't know what to say to them, what to do, where to go . . . Her mind was with David in the car travelling across the moor, heading down to the coast . . .

Going to her desk she picked up her phone and called Hugo's number. It went to voicemail and half-suspecting he was avoiding her she left a message. 'I need to know what to do,' she told him. 'Please tell me what's happening, and what I should do.' After ringing off she said to Julia, 'I have to contact the children before this gets out.'

'Of course,' Julia replied. 'Would you like me to drive over and get them?'

'I'm not sure. I can't think. What's the best thing to do?'

'You should bring them home,' Henry said.

Accepting he was right she connected to Sienna's school, but before anyone answered she rang off. 'I need to go over there,' she said. 'I can't let someone else tell them.' As she went for a set of Range Rover keys, she scrolled to her mother's number.

'Darling,' Harriet gasped, 'Julia told us. We're on our way.'

'Can you pick Quin up first?' Annie said. 'I'm going to collect the others.'

'Are you sure? Maybe Dad should go. You've had a

dreadful shock. I don't think you should drive, and you never know David or Hugo might need you to go to the station.'

Having no idea if her mother was right, but wanting to be around in case she was, Annie said, 'OK. If Dad doesn't mind . . . '

'Of course he doesn't. He'll leave now. Both our phones will be on, call if you need to.'

After ringing off Annie stood for a moment, trying again to collect herself. She still wasn't ready to take on what this really meant, to deal with the sickening truth that began with the death of a young girl twenty years ago and ended with where they were now.

But it hadn't begun with the death. There was only one way his DNA could have got to where it had been found, and she was afraid someone would say it. If they did she might strike them.

No one did. Henry and Dickie simply sat staring at nothing, as though trying to deal with the shock, to decide what needed to be done, but she had no idea what was really in their minds. She only knew, with complete and utter conviction, that there was a lot more to come out about that night at the farmhouse, and no matter how much Dickie and Henry tried to fight her, or how terrible the answers might be, she had no choice now but to support David the best she could while bracing herself and the children to deal with whatever was coming next.

CHAPTER TWENTY-SIX

'We're betting on a prepared statement,' Natalie told Gould when he came through to find out if David Crayce was still closeted with his lawyer.

'Doesn't sound like it's going to be a quick read then,' he said drily, 'considering how long they've been in there.'

'Three hours and counting,' she sighed, trying to sound phlegmatic when she was actually becoming quite pissed off. 'Did you get any feedback on his army career?' she asked, not very hopefully. 'Or anything about an old moor boy's network involving funny handshakes or weird clothes, that make nutters swear allegiance for life?'

Grimacing, as he glanced at the others, he said, 'On the latter, I'm not sure it exists, but no reason to stop looking. The former: officer training at Sandhurst, moved on to the Paras, aka the Red Berets, in '95. Left in in '98, nothing yet on where he was during that time, or if he stayed with the same regiment throughout. There's a chance he changed, but I'm waiting to hear back on that.'

Working this through in her mind, she said, 'Does the timeline coincide with the Balkan conflict?'

He frowned as he thought. 'I'm pretty sure that started at the beginning of the nineties, so was it still going on then?'

'That's got to be an easy Google,' Leo Johnson piped up, turning to his keyboard.

'This is only going to be relevant,' Gould pointed out, 'if he tries playing the PTSD card.'

'Of course,' Natalie agreed, 'but no harm being prepared, and based on what we've learned so far, I've got a strong feeling he will. There's something else that's a possible – he or his lawyer might try to claim that his semen was harvested while he was under the influence and smeared inside Karen's underwear.'

Gould's eyebrows shot up.

'It couldn't have been obtained orally,' she continued as if this might actually be a reasonable scenario, 'or we'd have three sets of DNA. Karen's, Crayce's and the harvester, unless Karen did it, but that's got to be a stretch in anyone's book. I mean, why would she? That leaves us with a condom as a receptacle, if we're thinking someone did help themselves to a dose of his semen.'

Gould was incredulous. 'You mean someone might have masturbated Crayce into a rubber, then emptied it into her knickers, which she then put on . . . '

'Or someone put on her.'

'It would have to be someone who was deliberately setting him up.'

Natalie shrugged. It was possible.

Gould didn't appear to be buying it – at least for the moment. Nor was she really, she just felt it had to be said.

Gould said drily, 'Well, good luck to his lawyer trying to make that stand up in court,' and the others sniggered at the pun. 'Anyone arrived from the Crown Prosecution Service yet?' he asked, checking his watch.

'Yes, Geoffrey Reynolds,' she replied. 'He's downstairs. Do you know him?'

'Not well, but he's one of the senior guys, as you'd expect for something like this. I take it he's fully up to speed with the case?'

'We've kept them informed all along, so yes, he's on it.'

'And ready to sign off on the charge?'

'Depending on what we get from the interview.'

'Indeed. Right, we've got some sort of riot kicking off on the Temple Fields Estate so I'm out of here. Call if you need to,' and he left.

Natalie sat quietly going over everything in her mind, until reading from his screen, Leo Johnson said, 'The Dayton Agreement was signed in 1995 bringing hostilities to an end, but war broke out again in '98 between ethnic Albanians and Serb armed forces. It ended in 1999 after a massive NATO bombing campaign. We're part of NATO so there's a chance our guy was part of an advance mission?'

Natalie sat forward to give her temples a soothing massage. What a bitter irony that life had kicked this particular case her way before she'd properly found her feet in her new job. It was as if someone up there was having a joke at her expense, or was setting her some sort of test, or God only knew what the hell it was about. But even if Crayce had been in that part of the world during his army career, it was long after her ex had served his time over there and come out a changed and deeply damaged human being. And since he had no relevance to this, and had been something of a beast even before he'd gone in, she forcefully ejected him from her mind. This was all about Crayce and Karen Lomax, nothing at all to do with ghosts from her past, or the fear that it would somehow interfere with her judgement as the case unfolded.

Leo's mobile buzzed and he said, 'OK, we're on.'

'Good luck,' Noah and Shari offered as Natalie and Leo headed for the door.

'Thanks,' Natalie responded. 'You guys carry on here, because as good a breakthrough as this is, there's nothing illegal about him having sex with her, it's the how, when, where and even why he killed her that we need to focus on now.'

By the time they reached the custody area with its bulletproof screens and high-security paraphernalia, she realized she was feeling faintly nauseous; nerves of course, and she silently scolded herself. Wanting to impress Gould was figuring too large in the equation, but in truth she was always apprehensive going into something this big. And being up against Hugo Big Bollocks on the one hand, and the Crown Prosecution Service on the other, was just the beginning. But hell, she was going to do it, and no one, absolutely no living soul, would ever know that she'd doubted herself for a single minute.

Hugo Blum and his client were already in the interview room, as expected, when she and Leo entered. The lawyer was sitting, Crayce standing with his back turned until he heard the door open. She was struck again by the man's good looks in spite of the pasty complexion and bloodshot eyes, but looks had long since failed to hold any sway with her.

'Sit down please, Mr Crayce,' she said, taking a chair herself.

Crayce did as instructed, and sat staring at his loosely bunched hands as Leo started the recording and cautioned him. His manner was much as it had been before, not arrogant, or hostile, more respectful, maybe slightly questioning – much as anyone would expect of someone who'd once been in a crack Parachute Regiment.

When Leo had finished Blum thanked him and drew out a single-page document. 'A prepared statement,' he said, 'which I will read out for the record.'

Natalie sat back to listen, knowing already she wasn't going to like this, but it had to be got through.

Blum read, '*I, David Crayce, admit to being at the Cheers wine bar on August 7th 1999, but I have no recollection of seeing or speaking to Karen Lomax on that day. She was someone I only ever spoke to in passing, usually in a friendly way, or if I ordered food. My friends and I didn't eat there that day, we had a couple of drinks and left at around 4 p.m.. We continued drinking at the Royal Oak in Winsford, the Ralegh's Cross Inn on Brendon Hill and the White Horse, Exford, before returning to Crayce Farm where we spent the rest of the night. Below I've listed the names of everyone I can remember who was there that night. I have no knowledge of anyone adding to our numbers at any time.*'

Natalie was barely disguising her frustration and contempt. *Three and a half hours, and this is all they can come up with.* A repeat of everything he'd said before, like she was some halfwit who needed it spelled out, or re-emphasized for clarity.

On the other hand, it was pretty certain that Crayce had used the time to confide a fuller story to his brief and said brief, on receiving the clearer picture, had advised Crayce to exercise his right to remain silent.

Interesting.

Blum continued: '*On August 8th 1999 I was still at the farmhouse. I slept in my own bed, alone, and because of how much I'd had to drink I was still there when my mother came in around 2 p.m.. I didn't go out again that day, which both my father and brother can attest to. I left on August 8th when Annabelle Dawns, now Annabelle Crayce, my wife, returned from London. I was with her that entire day, which she will confirm. I became aware of Karen Lomax's disappearance through the news some time that week, but I'm unable to say which day.*'

As Blum put the single sheet of paper down and slid it towards her, Natalie looked at it and the portable printer he'd produced it from, knowing very well how things were going to progress from here and somehow suppressing a sigh. However, she'd had plenty of experience of offenders popping out from behind prepared statements when the right buttons were pressed, so now that Blum's recital was over she prepared herself to be bombarded with a barrage of no comments. If that happened, her questions would still be important, for they'd help shape the case going forward.

'Mr Crayce,' she said, looking up from her tablet and dispensing with any sort of preamble, 'is it actually true that you didn't speak to Karen Lomax that day?'

Crayce met her gaze as he said, 'No comment.'

'Did you, or any of your party, arrange to see her later in the day?'

'No comment.'

'Did you, or any of your party, pick her up from the bus stop on Old Moor Road in Kesterly, some time around 10 p.m. on August 7th? 1999?'

'No comment.'

'Was she taken straight to the farmhouse?'

'No comment.'

'You say you slept alone in your room that night, can anyone confirm that?'

'No comment.'

'Is it possible you were too drunk to know if anyone had come into the room?'

'No comment.'

'Were you actually drunk or just pretending to be?'

'No comment.'

'Did you have sex with Karen Lomax that night, or at any time before her disappearance was reported?'

'No comment.'

'Were you the *only* one to engage in a sexual act with her that night, or at any time before her disappearance was reported?'

'No comment.'

'Were you aware that she harboured a fantasy of engaging in a multiple-sex act with you, your father and your brother?'

'No comment.'

Natalie had to hand it to him he was good, no emotion, no shake in the voice, no sign of tension at all, although this had to be child's play for someone with his training even if it had been over twenty years ago. 'Did you intend to kill her?' she asked. 'Or was it an accident?'

'No comment.'

'Was it a sex-game that went wrong?'

'No comment.'

'Did she die at the farmhouse?'

'No comment.'

'Was it you who dumped her body in an old railway hut in the middle of what's now the Embury Vale Estate?'

'No comment.'

'How did you get her there?'

'No comment.'

'Did someone help you?'

'No comment.'

She paused, glanced down at her notes, then fixed him with steely eyes, keen to find out how he was going to deal with the curveball heading his way. 'Had you ever raped anyone before that night?' she asked.

Betraying no reaction at all, he said, 'No comment.'

'Have you ever joined in acts of gang rape?'

'No comment.'

'Have you ever killed anyone in the line of combat?'

'No comment.'

'Why did you leave the army?'

'No comment.'

'Have you ever been diagnosed with post-traumatic stress disorder?'

'No comment.'

'Have you ever been diagnosed with any other kind of mental disorder?'

'No comment.'

'Do you have a problem with alcohol?'

'No comment.'

In the end, accepting that there was no point continuing, she signalled to Leo to stop the recordings and got to her feet. It wasn't her job to warn Crayce, or his lawyer – who surely had to know anyway – that prosecutors, courts of law and juries were allowed to infer guilt from a refusal to answer questions, so she said no more and left the room.

'What was that about a gang rape?' Leo Johnson asked after closing the door behind him.

'A shot in the dark,' she admitted. 'Members of the Parachute Regiment were found guilty of gang rape just after the Falklands War ended, but that was long before his time. Just prodding around to see if it hit a nerve because it might have happened again, and a lot did in that Kosovo conflict.'

Falling in beside her as she walked on he said, 'So what's next?'

'We talk to our trusty Crown Prosecutor,' she replied, 'put a couple of my theories his way to add to what he already has, and after that . . . ' She checked her watch. 'I estimate David Crayce will be charged with murder by the end of today, and remanded into the custody of Her Majesty's Prison Service by this time tomorrow.'

CHAPTER TWENTY-SEVEN

Annie, all three children, her parents, Henry, Julia and Dickie were gathered in the sitting room waiting for news. Over the past few hours since the children had arrived home many tears had been shed, fears shared, panic suppressed. It was hard for Annie to comfort them, or to explain things, when the situation could hardly have been worse: David, their father, when a much younger man had apparently had sex with a girl who'd died, been killed, shortly after, and the police obviously thought he was the one who'd killed her. She kept telling herself that he couldn't, wouldn't have done anything so monstrous – and yet the way he'd been back then, disturbed, angry, not always in control . . . It might not have been deliberate, it wouldn't have been; maybe he didn't remember it, but would he really forget killing someone? She veered chaotically between a complete inability to believe he'd done it, to the way he'd failed to speak up for himself when he'd been arrested, and again today when Hugo had come for him . . .

And there was no getting away from the DNA match.

She looked up as Julia broke the awful silence to ask if she could get anyone anything.

There was a general murmuring of no thanks, and for one wildly ridiculous moment Annie wanted her to offer to cocktail them up as though it could bring everything back to normal.

Feeling Sienna move even closer to her, she kept an aching arm around her daughter and let her head fall onto Max's shoulder. Quin was on her father's lap, mercifully asleep for now. She wasn't sure how much he understood, if he'd cried because the others had, or because he was afraid for his dad. Probably both and more, because she was afraid for David too, for all of them.

She must try not to let her mind fly beyond this room, to torment her with scenarios of what might happen next, where this was going to end for them all, not just for David. But even here, in the moment, her thoughts were making her head pound as they became tangled in questions she had no answers for, in fears that as yet had no real foundations. She kept trying to imagine where David might be, what was happening to him, how he was feeling, but it wasn't possible when she had no idea of the process he was going through.

She thought back again to that weekend in 1999. So much of it was hazed now by the passage of time, distorted even, but not for a minute had she suspected that he'd betrayed her that night. She'd remember something like that, she'd been through it often enough during those dark days, and there had been nothing about him when she'd got back from London that had seemed guilty or evasive, only apologetic and hung over. She'd detected none of the usual tell-tale signs that he'd had nightmares or an episode of violent frustration: no shadowed eyes, no glazed expression, no sense of his self-abhorrence.

She could ask Henry about it. He'd been there, but did she really want answers from him right now? She still wasn't sure if he was covering for his brother in some way. Or if Dickie was trying to protect his son. She hated thinking like this when they both looked shattered, bewildered, even traumatized, but they would, wouldn't they, if the past had just caught up with them?

Her phone vibrated, but the only call she intended to take was from Hugo – or David – and it wasn't either of them. Surely they'd be in touch soon . . .

Suddenly Henry got to his feet. 'I'm going to drive down there,' he declared.

'I'll come with you,' Max said, standing up too.

'What are you going to do when you get there?' Francis asked, settling Quin more comfortably on his lap.

Henry shrugged. 'I guess try to find Hugo. We can't just carry on sitting here like this. We need to know what's happening.'

Annie glanced at her phone as it vibrated again, and seeing who it was she felt her insides turn to liquid. 'It's Hugo,' she told Henry.

Seeming both relieved and alarmed, he said, 'Do you want me to answer?'

She did, but shook her head and took the phone out to the kitchen.

'What's happening?' she asked, before Hugo could speak.

Sounding tired, he said, 'He's just been charged.'

Her world turned upside down, seemed to slip away in a kind of intangible vacuum. 'With what?' she asked, as if she didn't know, as if something might have happened to change things from a few hours ago.

'Do you want me to say it?'

'Yes! No, oh God, Hugo . . . '

'Listen, Annabelle, I want you to hang in there, OK . . .'

'Just tell me where he is, what I can do.'

'He's here at the police station where he'll stay tonight. In the morning he'll appear in front of a magistrate . . .'

'Can I be there?'

'No, he doesn't want you to come.'

'What? Why? Someone has to tell them he didn't do this.'

'I'll be there for that and I fully expect that once this has been properly assessed I'll be bringing him home.'

She grasped those words and hung onto them, shared them with the others and allowed them to carry her through the night.

But that wasn't what happened.

The following morning, after an interminable and torturous wait, Hugo rang again to let them know that the magistrate had remanded David in custody.

Annie thought she was going to pass out. *He was being sent to prison*. She couldn't get her mind around it. It was as though she was at the start of a slow-motion collapse of everything she knew and loved. The very ground seemed to be shifting beneath her. She had no idea what to hold onto, how to keep her children safe, how to see her husband in her future.

'I'll be there in about an hour,' Hugo told her. 'There are things we have to discuss.'

Before she could ask what he'd rung off, and putting her phone aside she turned to find Max standing in the doorway. He looked as frightened as he clearly felt, but she could tell he was trying to be strong for her. 'He's been remanded in custody,' she managed to tell him.

Though he shook, he drew her into his arms as she started to sob. 'It's OK, Mum,' he soothed. 'We'll be all right. We'll get through it. It's what Dad would want, that we pull together.' He was still talking about him as if he was the father he'd always known and loved, not the man who'd done something so terrible that none of them had yet put it into actual words. It would change, she realized; when the shock wore off and the hideous reality of it began to set in, they might turn against him.

'What's happened?' Sienna cried as she came into the kitchen.

Max said, 'Dad's in custody.'

Sienna gasped in anguish and Max pulled her into his embrace too, much as his father always did when there was a family upset, to demonstrate their support for one another.

And now he was the very cause of the upset, the reason they were standing here in the home he'd built for them, holding one another and not knowing which way to turn, how to comfort or reassure, how to face what lay ahead.

By the time Hugo arrived an hour later everyone was in the sitting room. Annie had Sienna and Max either side of her on the sofa and Quin on her lap, though she'd have preferred that her eight-year-old didn't have to hear what was about to be said. However, they'd decided that shutting him out was only going to aggravate his fear further, if that was possible. At least this way, whatever his questions might be, they'd have a good chance of understanding where they were coming from and be better able to deal with them.

To her surprise, when Julia led Hugo into the sitting room a smartly dressed red-headed woman came in too.

'This is Helen Hall,' Hugo announced. 'She's a colleague of mine and I thought it would be a good idea to introduce her to you.'

Helen Hall's smile was friendly, she looked a nice woman, but even so Annie felt annoyed with Hugo for bringing her here now. They didn't need any more people, or complications, or distractions.

'I'm sorry we're getting to meet like this,' Helen Hall said, 'but I'll let Hugo explain. Thanks,' she smiled as Julia handed her a coffee.

'Please sit down,' Francis said, the first to remember his manners as he indicated an empty armchair beside the lit fire, the one they'd been saving for Hugo.

As Helen sat down, Hugo, the first-class lawyer and dear, dear friend, went to stand with his back to the fire, tall, almost comical-looking with his curly black hair and thick round glasses.

Sienna said, 'Where's Dad now?'

'That's a brave question,' he told her kindly, 'and it won't be easy to hear the answer, but I want to be truthful with you. He was picked up from the magistrates' court just before I left, so he'll probably be at Sellybrook by now.'

'Is that a prison?' Quin asked shakily. So he was taking things in, and understanding in a way Annie wished wasn't necessary.

Hugo nodded. 'I'm afraid so, son, but I don't want you to think we're giving up on getting him out of there, because we've already set wheels in motion to make it happen.'

'What sort of wheels?' Henry asked, clearly eager to know.

'To keep it simple,' Hugo replied, 'we're in the process of going to a higher authority within the Crown Prosecution

Service to request a review of their decision to charge. There are many reasons why this case should not be going forward the way it is, not the least of which is that the police have not, in my opinion, made a good enough case for a successful prosecution.'

Clearly the CPS thought they had, Annie wanted to point out, nor was this the same as saying a mistake had been made, or David was innocent. And who was Helen Hall? Why was she here? Hugo still hadn't told them, apart from saying she was a colleague.

'I had a long chat with David before I left,' Hugo continued. 'I explained to him, as I'm now about to explain to you, why I have to hand his case over to Helen – and please believe me it's not only because I have a big trial starting in London the week after next. I truly believe that Helen is the right person for this. She's not only good at what she does – outstanding, in fact – she's also local. This means she'll be here on the ground, giving you easy access to her as events unfold and her contacts in the area are far superior to mine. She has the kind of resources ready to go that would take me, a London-based chap, some time to set up. I should also add that she has an excellent track record of getting the right results for her clients.'

Annie had no idea what to think about that, simply looked at Helen Hall as, with a certain wryness, the substitute lawyer said, 'An extremely generous introduction, Hugo, thank you, but seriously, all of you, after reading the case notes and speaking with Hugo, I agree that having someone on the ground is going to be more helpful to you – and to David – than trying to rely on Hugo when he's very soon going to be involved in a major fraud trial.'

Annie was still taking this in as Max asked, 'Have you met Dad yet?'

'No, but I'm expecting to in the next few days.'

Annie glanced at her phone as it vibrated. Seeing a number she didn't recognize she declined it and said to Helen Hall, 'That might have been someone from the press. Do you, as a local, have any suggestions about how we handle them?' She hadn't meant to sound sarcastic, or had she?

'For now,' the lawyer replied, 'the best course will be to refuse their calls or go the "no comment" route. I'll put out a statement when the time is right, with your approval of course, but that won't be yet.'

Henry said, 'Is it possible to see him?'

Addressing both him and Annie as she replied, Helen Hall said, 'You need to ring the prison, or go online to find out times and book yourself in. He's currently allowed three one-hour visits a week.'

Annie felt the words spinning her off into yet another realm of unreality. *Three hours over an entire week*. David was part of her daily life: she couldn't imagine him not coming in the door with Cassie, or sitting down to eat, or lying beside her in bed. She almost asked if he could refuse to see them, but thought better of it in front of the children. She said, 'Can we take anything for him when we go?'

'Extra clothing, footwear, toiletries, books, towels, anything you think he might need or appreciate.'

Already imagining getting it together, while recoiling from the mere thought of taking it to a prison, Annie heard her mother ask,

'Will he be able to call us?'

'Yes, so whoever goes to see him should take some cash to buy phone cards. I think Hugo gave him some before . . .'

'He already had some,' Hugo told her.

'So, he might call today?' Sienna put in hopefully. *Why didn't the children hate him yet? Thank God they didn't. She wouldn't be able to cope with that.*

'He might,' Helen confirmed. When no one said anything else she looked around at them all and said, 'Is there anything more you'd like to ask me?'

As everyone searched for more questions, Annie held back what was in her mind. She didn't want the others hearing it, and hadn't yet formulated how to say it.

Hugo said, 'I want you to know that I'll be in touch with Helen regularly, and with all of you, of course, and if you want to speak to me for any reason just pick up the phone. If I can't answer right away, I'll get back to you the minute I can.'

'Thank you,' Dickie said, seeming to feel this was some sort of lifeline – but he'd known Hugo a long time. Helen Hall was a stranger, an as yet unknown quantity.

When the time came Annie got up to walk out with Hugo and David's new lawyer, slipping into her coat to protect herself from the icy wind outside.

'I'd like to set up a meeting with you.' Helen Hall had to shout to make herself heard.

Annie said, 'Of course, Just let me know when, and where to find your office.'

Helen handed over a card. 'There's visitor parking on the forecourt,' she said. 'I'll make sure a space is saved for you. If, when, you speak to your husband please try to persuade him to start opening up about what really happened that night.'

Hugo shouted, 'Let's get into the car for a moment.'

Once they were cocooned from the howling gale, Hugo turned around from the driver's seat and said, 'All David will say is that there are reasons he can't tell me everything. The problem is, if he doesn't, it's going to be very difficult to help him.'

Reasons? What reasons?

'The police will continue building their case,' Helen Hall resumed, 'and we need to do the same so we're prepared for whatever they might find. With that in mind, there's someone I'd like you to meet. I've worked with her a lot, and she has even better contacts than I do in the area. She also has superior investigative skills, which come from being an ex-detective.'

'So, she's a private investigator?' Annie said, not sure how she felt about that.

'Well, yes I suppose you could call her that, but she doesn't do it for money. She uses her experience, expertise, whatever we want to call it, to get to the truth. I'll introduce you to her when you come in and you can tell me after if you're comfortable with her taking the case on – presuming she's willing, of course, but I think she will be.'

'You might know her,' Hugo said. 'I don't personally, but I've heard a lot of good things about her. Her name's Andee Lawrence.'

Annie frowned. 'The name rings a bell,' she said, 'but I don't know why.'

'She's quite well known around town,' Helen said, squeezing her arm, 'and I have to say if I were in David's shoes, or yours, Andee is certainly someone I'd want on my side.'

CHAPTER TWENTY-EIGHT

Jess Lomax was standing at her bedroom window staring down into the garden of the house she and Eddie had lived in for the past eighteen years. They'd abandoned their holiday the day after they'd spoken to DS Rundle by video link; it simply hadn't been possible to stay. Instinctively, they'd needed to be here, close to hand. It hadn't felt right to be so far away when there was a chance the killer was about to be named.

They had him now. David Crayce. He hadn't only been arrested this time, the way he had a couple of weeks ago, and then let go, he'd also been charged.

It didn't seem real; Jess was still trying to process it, but right now all she could feel was glad that his mother, Geraldine, wasn't having to live through the shame and heartbreak of what her son had done. No mother deserved that. It was easier, Jess found, to think about that than to try to deal with how it was affecting her and Eddie.

So many years had gone by, they'd known so much suffering, loss, untameable grief – and then there was the missing of Karen that came to them every day in all kinds of ways. Perhaps worst of all were the wakeful hours when she couldn't stop herself picturing what might have taken place before her daughter's death. That was its own kind of torment, when she saw Karen terrified, being hurt, beaten, trying to run, shouting for her daddy, and all the therapy she and Eddie had received during the early years hadn't been able to fully suppress the unspeakable horror of it.

She wondered now, as she had all along, how anyone could have just dumped Karen's beautiful young body in that derelict railway hut as though it were of no more value than a sack of old clothes. How could Crayce have done that? What sort of man was he? Why hadn't he called someone, even anonymously, to tell them where to find her? He must have known what would be happening to her, the slow, terrible decay, the gnawing, scratching, feeding . . . The tearing grief of her parents, the desperate need for answers.

All these years he'd kept it to himself, had continued to live his life, build a business, have children of his own . . . Apparently his daughter was sixteen, almost the same age Karen had been when everything had ended for her. Did he ever think of Karen when he looked at his own teenage girl? Was he ever haunted by what he'd done? As a parent, how deep was his guilt and shame? Did it even exist? Had he somehow managed to shut it all out?

For Jess there was no shutting it out. She thought about Karen constantly. She even talked to her as if she were still there, and sometimes she heard her answer. Right now she could see her down there in the garden as if no time had passed, flitting between the wine bar's bench tables and blue striped parasols, joking with the customers, taking their orders, serving up their food. Her laugh was too loud, her backchat sometimes too raucous, her love of life always infectious. She had a fleeting memory of

Karen making eye contact with one of the Crayce brothers at Brasserie Michel; Jess hadn't known which one it was.

She blinked visualizing the wintry garden below as it should be today with a trampoline for her grandchildren, a slide maybe and a swing. Karen would be almost thirty-eight by now, probably married, a mother, a successful businesswoman maybe. She'd have had a lovely wedding, Jess and Eddie would have seen to that, and they'd have been close at hand when the children came. They'd have spent every Christmas with Karen and her family, even if they'd gone to live overseas in Australia or Canada. Jess and Eddie would probably have moved there too, so they could see the grandchildren grow up and still be a part of their precious girl's life.

All these things should have happened, were meant to have happened, and because Jess believed that in a parallel world they really had, she often allowed herself to go there in her mind. It helped to bring her back from acknowledging just how empty their lives were without their girl.

Hearing the bedroom door open she turned to see Eddie coming in, and her heart turned over with pity and love. To anyone else he might look like an older version of the man he'd once been, the handsome, humorous and always sociable wine bar owner, but she knew how much he'd changed inside. The verve and light had gone out of him, his easy trust of the world had disappeared, along with what had always seemed an unfailing belief in himself. Over the years he'd begun suffering from occasional nervous attacks, his blood pressure was high and he was still unable to fully accept that he wasn't to blame for what had happened. He believed he should have taken better care of Karen, that he'd failed as a parent, and Jess understood because she felt it too.

They had a deli now, two streets away, at the end of a parade with a hairdresser's next door and a tattooist upstairs. They'd made new friends since moving to this estate, and were still in touch with some of the old ones, but they weren't as gregarious now as they used to be.

Coming to take her in his arms, he said, 'Mel's arrived.' He was referring to the Family Liaison Officer the police had appointed for them during this time, a kindly, bright-eyed woman in her early forties who never really felt like an intruder, although inevitably she was.

'Is there any news?' she asked.

'Not really. She just wanted to find out if we need anything.'

Gazing into his eyes, she forgot the question for a moment, until it came back to her and she said, 'Do we?'

'No, I don't suppose so, not today anyway.'

She turned to check herself in the mirror. 'We should make her a cup of tea,' she said, wiping her fingers under her eyes. 'I could do with one myself.'

'I'll do the honours. Come down when you're ready.'

Later, after Mel had left and the sun had set, Eddie fixed them a gin and tonic each and carried the tray into the sitting room. 'How are you feeling?' he asked as they clinked glasses.

Jess frowned as she thought. 'Kind of disconnected,' she said, half surprised to realize it was true. 'As if this is happening to someone else, or more like someone we used to know.'

He nodded, as if saying it was the same for him.

'I keep thinking I should be angry,' she said, 'and

maybe I am, deep down. Do you remember, before, it was a long time before we got mad? Much good it did us when we did.'

With a smile he said, 'You gave me a black eye, as I recall.'

Smiling too, she said, 'By accident. I felt terrible after.'

They sat quietly sipping their drinks, feeling their closeness, the unbreakable bond of their grief as if it were everything now, what held them together in a way even their love might fail to do. Or maybe it was all about love, and grief was the tightening force. 'I'm surprised it turned out to be him,' she said in the end. 'For some reason I thought it was going to be the other brother.'

Sighing, Eddie said, 'Me too, although I don't know why. It's not like we really knew either of them to be able to say one way or the other.'

That was true. 'Was it Mel who told us the younger brother lost his first wife and son in a car accident some years back?' she asked.

'Yes, it was.'

'That must have been hard. I suppose it makes me glad it wasn't him who hurt Karen, although I can't feel glad it was anyone. What do you suppose it's like for that family, with all this going on?'

When he didn't answer she looked up and saw that he was sunk inside himself, a single tear hovering on a lower lash, a tremor in his cheek as he tried to deal with all the emotions this had stirred up for him.

Deciding they probably ought to consider some further grief counselling soon, she went to sit beside him and put a hand on his. She wanted him to know that she'd always be there for him, just as she hoped he always would be for her.

He'd never let her down yet.

She didn't doubt him.

'I wonder if they're sparing many thoughts for us and how we're coping?' There was a break in his voice.

Trying to imagine the family up there on the moor, the residences she only knew from press and police photographs, the people they had next to no familiarity with, the fact that even the world at large was making it all about the Crayces, hardly about Karen, she said, 'The mother would care, Geraldine, if she were still around. We don't know the others well enough to say whether or not it matters to them, but I don't suppose it's easy for them.'

She hadn't really considered that very much before, but now it was in her mind she found herself worrying about the children and feeling sorry for David Crayce's wife. Annabelle, Annie, that was her name. Jess remembered her vaguely: tall, blonde, very pretty. From news reports she was still an attractive woman. She wasn't to blame for what had happened, presumably hadn't known anything about it until now, and one way or another it was going to affect the rest of her and her children's lives in the most awful way imaginable.

They didn't deserve that. Only he deserved the punishment that was coming his way, the loss of everything – absolutely everything – that he cared about. It would be its own kind of death, and maybe the worst part would be knowing how his family was suffering for what he had done.

If he was the kind of person who would have cared, and maybe he wasn't.

CHAPTER TWENTY-NINE

'Why doesn't he ring!' Annie cried in a burst of near violent frustration. 'He has to know how worried I am, how desperate to speak to him and he's let over thirty-six hours go by without picking up the phone. I don't understand it. Hugo said he has money. He can buy a card. *So why doesn't he ring?'*

Her mother looked at her helplessly and Annie turned abruptly away still needing to rant, but knowing she had to rein her anger in somehow. 'I can't even get through to book a visit,' she growled, 'but even if I get one will he just refuse to see me? He didn't . . . '

'That's not going to happen,' her father said firmly. 'We've just got to try and be patient. I know it's hard, but he'll call, I'm sure of it.'

Annie might have been certain too if so much time hadn't passed since David had been taken into custody, leaving her to spend an almost sleepless night tormenting herself with what could be happening to him, whether he was safe, if he'd been injured by other inmates . . . How afraid was he? How sickened by his guilt, if it was real, and in spite of the evidence she still couldn't make herself believe it was. Then she could, and it would come over her in such horrific waves that she was barely able to stop herself from screaming as she foresaw the loss of everything: their home, their business, the children's schooling and futures . . .

What *reasons* did he have for holding back even from Hugo?

Around three that morning she'd heard the thump of Cassie's tail in the corner and for one wild moment she'd thought David was about to come into the room. It was Quin with a giraffe he hadn't cuddled in a long while, and as he'd crept quietly into bed with her he'd said, 'Daddy promised it'd be all right, so it will.' It was as though he was trying to comfort her, and her heart had just about broken at such blind faith in his father, and such blessed naiveté.

By the time she and Quin had come downstairs for breakfast Sienna and Max were already up with toast and eggs on the go. They'd even beaten her parents out of bed, although her father came in halfway through Sienna explaining why it wasn't possible for her and Max to go back to school. Annie didn't argue for the simple reason she had no idea what to do for the best.

Her father said, 'I don't think we have to make a decision this week. I'll call both headteachers to explain.' Sienna had GCSEs this year; she'd have to go back at some point and sooner rather than later, but her grandfather was right, perhaps not this week.

The morning dragged on, with everyone constantly checking their phones in the hope of hearing from David. Dickie and Henry had closed the estate gates the night before, and had gone out first thing to make sure no one came through apart from the freelance instructors and those booked in for a clay-pigeon shoot. It wouldn't be easy to keep the press out if they really wanted to get in since there was no fence around the land, but fortunately it didn't seem as though anyone had tried so far.

By the time Julia came in at lunchtime having spent the morning at the Byre taking care of bookings and other business, she was able to report that no one had failed to show up for their session, and nor had she received any cancellations for later. The fact that most of the clients this week were tourists from other parts of the country, or even abroad, meant that they probably hadn't made the connection. It was in the news and online, but Annie wasn't engaging with any of it yet. She simply couldn't face it, and certainly not before she'd spoken to David.

It was almost five o'clock now, and Julia had just returned from the Byre again having left Dickie and Henry to deal with the sophisticated security system. The children were downstairs with their grandfather watching videos in the games room, or texting, or even trawling social media for all Annie knew, though she'd warned them not to and she was sure Francis would be keeping an eye on it. In spite of no calls from David her phone had been busy most of the day as friends and neighbours got in touch to say how shocked and sorry they were, and please let her know if there was anything they could do. Considering the horrific nature of the situation, she couldn't help being touched by their kindness and understanding. Julia's mother had said

Darling, just say the word and I'll be there to man phones, make tea, sweep floors, anything you need. We love David very much, of course we do, but you

didn't ask for any of this and we want to support you and the children in any way we can. Celine and Ruth.

Chrissie had texted

I'm totally shocked by what's happened. I can't think about anything else.

(Who cared what she was thinking about?)

You know I was there that night, but I swear I didn't see Karen Lomax. I can't think how David could have gone to get her, he'd had too much to drink, he went to bed before the rest of us. I keep asking myself, could it have happened the next day, or somewhere else. All very confusing and upsetting. Please send David my love. I'm here if you need me. C x

'There you go,' Harriet said, putting a cup of tea on the table in front of Annie.

Annie stared at it. 'I think it's time to cocktail us up,' she said, so savagely that it made Julia flinch.

As Harriet went for the wine, Annie turned away and stared out of the window, seeing only her reflection as night began settling over the moor. David was out there somewhere, thirty or more miles away in a place she could hardly begin to imagine, thinking thoughts she had no way of connecting with . . .

'Is there any sign of Henry yet?' Julia asked.

Unable to stop herself, Annie rounded on her. 'Is that all you care about, where Henry is, when you know damned well he's locking up at the Byre? I guess you're pleased about this; it must have been such a relief for you when you found out . . . '

'Annie, stop,' her mother barked. 'Taking things out on Julia isn't going to help.'

'I'm sorry,' Julia said, as if she were the one who'd just exploded. 'I swear I'm not pleased about David. I mean, of course I'm relieved about Henry . . . '

'It's OK,' Harriet told her, 'you don't have to explain. It's not your fault this is happening.'

'No, it's David's,' Annie raged, 'and I'm the one who's sorry, Julia. I shouldn't have said that. I'm not thinking straight . . . '

'Have you spoken to the lawyer, Helen Hall?' Julia asked. 'Maybe she can tell you something.'

'I'm seeing her tomorrow,' Annie replied. 'Let's hope we've heard from him by then or I won't know what to say to her.'

'Will this Andee Lawrence be there?' Julia wondered. 'Aunt Ruth says she knows her, not well, but she's met her a few times.'

'Actually, I know her mother,' Harriet said. 'She belongs to my book club. A lovely woman. I didn't mention it before,' she explained to Annie. 'It didn't seem very relevant.'

Since it probably wasn't, Annie sighed and slumped down at the table. 'I googled her today,' she admitted. 'She's not at all how I'd imagined her. Much younger, well, around my age, but I'd envisioned someone in their fifties, even sixties and a bit drab, I don't know why. She looks a lot like the actress Andie MacDowell, funny they have the same name.'

'She works as an interior designer with her partner

Graeme Ogilvy who's a property developer,' Harriet told them.

'I think he also owns the antique shop in town,' Julia said, 'but I haven't been in there for a while. Maybe he's sold it by now.'

'It's still called Ogilvy Antiques,' Harriet chatted on, 'so he probably still has an interest. It's run by another man now – his name will come to me . . . Anyway, he's a neighbour of Maureen's.'

'Who's Maureen?' Annie snapped, failing to hide her irritation.

'Andee Lawrence's mother. Sorry, I can tell we're getting on your nerves.'

Annie shook her head, meaning to apologize, but her phone rang at that moment and her heart leapt to see No Caller ID. 'Hello?' she said cautiously, hopefully, her eyes going to her mother.

'It's me,' David said.

Fighting an onrush of tears and fury, Annie took a moment to say, 'At last. How are you?'

'I'm OK. Worried about you and the children.'

'We're worried about you. David, please tell me what's really going on . . . '

'Did Hugo come to see you?'

'Yes, he brought Helen Hall. Have you spoken to her?'

'Not yet. I don't know if it'll do any good . . . '

'David, you have to talk to her. Please . . . She's trying to help you. We all are.'

'OK, don't let's argue.'

Unaware they were doing that, she said, 'Why won't you explain things to Hugo?'

'Let's not discuss this on the phone.'

'OK. If I can book a visit will you see me?'

'Of course. It's killing me not being with you.'

Feeling the wrenching ache of it too, she said, 'I keep trying to get a slot. I'll go online again as soon as this call is over. Is there anything you'd like me to bring? I have a list here extra clothes, shoes, towels, toiletries . . .'

'That all sounds good. A few books would be welcome, and maybe the usual magazines.'

A short, nightmarish silence followed as she tried to think what else to say. There was so much, but it was stuck somewhere inside her, blocked by the growing dread of answers to questions she had to ask, for his sake as well as her own, but not now.

'I love you,' he murmured.

'I love you too,' she said, tears distorting her voice.

'Don't cry. Just book that visit.'

'I will.'

As the line went dead she covered her face with her hands and tried not to sob, but she couldn't help it. This was so confusing and devastating that she hardly knew what was right or wrong to feel any more. But she loved him so much, every bit of her yearned for him, and right now she couldn't imagine getting through even one more night without him, so how the hell was she going to get through the rest?

CHAPTER THIRTY

Annie recognized Andee Lawrence from her online profile as soon as she was shown into Helen Hall's office, although in person Andee seemed to exude a more captivating quality than the internet allowed. Her hair was dark, naturally wavy it seemed, almost tamed into a bob, and there was an aura about her that lowered Annie's defences in a way she hadn't expected.

Why was she even feeling defensive? These women were trying to help her, it was why she was here. She needed to trust them and stop being so afraid.

After making the introductions Helen took Annie's coat and indicated the comfy sofas in front of a large marble fireplace as her assistant, Tamsin, brought in a tray of coffee and pastries. As Helen poured, Annie said, 'My brother-in-law, Henry, and father-in-law, Dickie have been summoned back to the police station today for further questioning.'

Helen said, 'Actually, Henry called me after he was contacted so one of my team is meeting him and his father there. Oscar will be present for both interviews so we'll know what was said and if there's anything we need to be concerned about. Do you think there is?' she asked Annie.

'I've no idea,' Annie replied. 'As a family we're hardly

discussing it, so I can't tell you what they might say.' Did her anger and resentment of that show? She didn't care if it did.

'OK, we'll park that for the moment,' Helen declared, 'and come back to it when we know more. Meantime, I have a visit booked at the prison for tomorrow afternoon. Have you managed to arrange one for yourself yet?'

Annie's heart twisted jealously to think of anyone seeing David before she did, even if it was his lawyer. 'The line is constantly busy,' she said, 'and apparently it takes three days for website applications to be confirmed, so I might not get there until next week at this rate.' Tears were shaking her voice as she added, 'David might not know that, so please will you tell him when you see him, just in case he doesn't ring tonight and ends up thinking I'm deliberately staying away?'

'Of course,' Helen assured her. 'And if you're wondering, official visits are in a different category, so I won't have used up his allocated social hours. Now before we continue I need to be sure that you feel comfortable about talking in front of Andee.'

Annie looked at the other woman and gave a faint smile as she nodded.

'If you decide at the end of this,' Andee said, her voice as smooth and cultured as her aqua blue eyes were arresting and friendly, 'that you'd rather I wasn't involved, I'll step back.'

'I'm sure I won't,' Annie told her. Released from her own defences she now wanted everyone as involved as possible, especially someone whose investigative skills had been so highly praised. Annie might not like what Andee turned up, but whatever it was it had to be faced.

'Have you actually spoken to David yet?' Helen asked.

'He called last night, not for long, but I told him he must talk to you so that you can help him.'

'Good. What did he say?'

Annie's face flushed hot as she said, 'That he wasn't sure it would do any good.' Did he realize how guilty that made him sound?

Andee said, 'But it wasn't a no, so we'll take that as a positive, especially as he's agreed to the visit.' She glanced at Helen, who nodded agreement.

Helen said, 'In case this wasn't made clear when Hugo and I came to the house, it's our opinion that the police and Crown Prosecution Service acted too hastily. They don't have sufficient grounds to charge your husband with murder, so that's why Hugo is taking it to a higher level. If he's successful David could be released until they can build a viable case – if indeed they can.'

Annie sat with that, trying to take in how it was going to feel to have him at home with this hanging over them, how they were going to deal with it, what it was going to mean for the children, for everything, in the future.

She'd far rather he was at Hanley Combe than where he was now.

'Whatever happens,' Andee said, 'the police will continue their investigations, so it would help us a lot if we can try to get ahead of the game and find out what David isn't telling his lawyers – or you – because we know there's something.' In a gentler tone she added, 'Do you have any idea what it might be?'

Annie regarded her helplessly. 'I don't understand it,' she admitted. 'Why keep anything back if he's done nothing wrong – unless he did it and doesn't remember . . . '

'Why wouldn't he remember?'

'Because he used to have . . . *lapses* at that time. He'd get drunk, I mean horribly so. He was fighting things going on his head . . . '

'I take it this was around August 1999?'

'Before. He was a lot better by then. He'd virtually stopped drinking and the demons, or whatever they were, had practically gone away.'

Andee consulted her iPad for several moments and when she looked up again said, 'Hugo's left us with some very comprehensive notes on the police interviews with you and David, so we know that you were both asked about his time in the military, or more specifically about his frame of mind after he left. Can you tell us any more about it?'

Annie shook her head. 'It's all so long ago, but there was a period when he . . . He struggled with stress and bouts of . . . not depression, exactly, more frustration, you could even call it fear. The police asked me if he'd ever been diagnosed with PTSD or some other disorder, but the only doctor he saw at the time was our GP who gave him something to help him sleep. We'd already worked out by then that alcohol acted as a trigger for his nightmares . . .'

'Did he ever tell you what the nightmares were about?'

'No, and before you ask he didn't talk in his sleep either, so I can't give you any names, or suggestions of what was going on in his mind. Obviously I guessed something had happened while he was on active service that had got to him, and he didn't deny it, but all he'd say if I asked was, let's not go there.'

'And when he was having the nightmares did he become violent, or sleepwalk? Shout? Cry?'

'All of the above, apart from sleepwalk. He'd kind of growl in rage, you know, like through his teeth, and he'd grab a pillow so hard he'd sometimes tear it. When he woke up he'd lie really still, breathing heavily, whispering, but I could never make out what he was saying.'

'Did you ever get a sense of what it might be?'

'All I can tell you is that he said once that he'd done something he shouldn't have, and he didn't know if he could trust people not to go back on their word.'

'So he was hiding some sort of . . . crime?'

'I asked him that, but he just told me to forget about it.'

Andee checked her list of questions. 'Have you ever spoken to anyone who was in the army with him?'

Annie shook her head, and suddenly finding this all very difficult, she turned to gaze out of the window, hating herself for feeling so thrown by the way the past was rising up to take over the present as if it had more significance, as if today had ceased to matter. It was so destabilizing and frightening that she couldn't be sure what she really remembered and what had been distorted or even rewritten by time.

Apparently understanding how she was feeling, Andee said, 'Maybe we should leave it there for today. You've been extremely helpful. We know a lot more now than we did before you came, and it's given us something to work with when we see David tomorrow.'

Annie felt suddenly anxious, edgy in a way she didn't quite understand.

'Don't worry,' Andee told her, seeming once again to pick up on how she was feeling, 'sometimes these things can become overwhelming, but we'll get through it, I promise. We'll find the truth, whatever it is.'

'I think that's what frightens me the most,' Annie confessed, 'but I need to know what happened that night at the farmhouse, how he came to have sex with . . . '

'Stop,' Andee said, putting up a hand. 'We don't know that it went any further than that, in fact there's a lot we still don't know, so let's not get ahead of ourselves.' She turned to Helen. 'Have we heard back from Oscar yet about the police interviews?'

'I'll go and check.'

As Helen left the office Andee took out her card. 'If you remember anything, or if you just want to chat, please feel free to call me any time, day or night .'

Taking it, Annie said, 'Thank you,' then added, 'I can't help feeling that my brother-in-law and father-in-law know more than they're telling, so maybe you should speak to them as well.'

CHAPTER THIRTY-ONE

Natalie was regarding Henry Crayce with a semi-affable gaze as she listened to him describing his brother's mindset during the time between leaving the army and Karen's Lomax's disappearance. Apparently he'd had a pretty hard time of it. He started to drink in a way he never had before, something seemingly getting to him, but he'd never say what it was. 'To be honest,' Crayce stated, 'I think he was ordered not to.'

That got Natalie's attention, and she noticed that his lawyer, Oscar Radcliffe, had sharpened up too. 'What makes you say that?' she asked carefully.

Crayce shrugged. 'It's just something Mum, Dad and I had a feeling about.'

'That he'd been ordered to keep silent? By whom?'

Crayce shook his head. 'The powers that be. Those at the top. I don't know, it was just guesswork on our part.'

'But you were concerned about his frame of mind?'

'Of course, and so was Annie. He hadn't been a hard drinker before he signed up – I'm not saying he really was after, but sometimes it was like he was trying to . . .' He shrugged. 'I'm not sure really . . . '

'To escape something?'

'Your words, not mine.'

'So, did you think something happened to him while he was in the army – or that maybe he did something that he wasn't coping with back in civilian life?'

His eyes moved away as he said, 'Either, both, or none of it. I can't tell you anything, because it was never up for discussion.'

Not entirely sure whether she was buying his lack of knowledge, Natalie said, 'Did he remain in contact with anyone from his army days after he left?'

'Not that I'm aware of.'

'Why did he sign up in the first place? You're not a military family, as far as I'm aware.'

He shrugged again. 'It was something he'd talked about since he was a child, going to Sandhurst, joining the Paras.'

'And while he was in the forces did he ever discuss any deployments with you? What, or where they might have been?'

'No, but I don't think they're allowed to, are they?'

Knowing it depended on the deployment, she said, 'Is there anything that stands out for you?'

He gave it some thought. 'There was a period when he was involved in some pretty intensive training, above and beyond the normal exercises.'

'Was it for a particular assignment?'

'If so, he never talked about it.'

Making a mental note to ask Gould to try again with the MOD, she said, 'What do you know about the circumstances of your brother's departure from the army?'

He gave a slight shake of his head. 'Only that it happened earlier than it was supposed to.'

'And you don't know why?'

'No, because if anyone asked he'd just shut it down.'

'But you must have wondered.'

'Of course, we all did, but we also respected the fact that he didn't want to discuss it. It was his business, his world, and he wanted to deal with it his way.'

'Which involved heavy drinking, memory lapses, night-mares – and seeking refuge with women he wouldn't have to see again?'

His expression was stony as he stared at her.

'Would Karen Lomax have been one of those women?'

'I was never aware that he got together with her.'

'But we know that he did.'

He stayed silent.

'Was he still experiencing mental health issues at the time of Karen's disappearance?'

'You make it sound as though . . . He just went off the rails for a while, and by the time she disappeared he was pretty much back together. He'd more or less stopped drinking . . .'

'But not that weekend?'

'It was a one-off.'

'Or maybe he wasn't as drunk as the rest of you?'

'I was with him the whole time, we had the same amount, and it was a lot – whether that makes things better or worse for him, only you know, but it's the truth.'

'What about your father? He also had a great deal to drink.'

'Yes.'

Tearing her eyes from him, she scrolled through her tablet, searching for something Chrissie Slater had claimed during her interview. Finding it, she said, 'Is it true that your brother told everyone not to answer the phone that night in case his fiancée rang?'

Henry's eyes narrowed. 'I . . . he might have. I don't recall it.'

'Apparently he said it was because she'd be able to tell he was drunk, which sounds reasonable, but there again it begs the question, was it because he was planning to go out again and wanted to be sure that none of you told her he wasn't there?'

With no hesitation, he said, 'He'd never have been able to drive. None of us would.'

'Which leaves me asking, how did Karen get there?'

'I've already told you, she wasn't there.'

Sitting back in her chair Natalie regarded him steadily, knowing she wasn't getting to the truth of matters yet, and not sure she was even close. However, deciding to take a punt, she said, 'Do you know what I think happened that night? I think your brother got it on with Karen Lomax, something went wrong and you and your father helped clear up the mess.'

His face darkened. 'You can think whatever you like, but that is not what happened. Karen Lomax was *not* there . . . '

'Then where was she? We have the DNA results now, so . . . '

'All I can tell you is she wasn't in the farmhouse.'

'But if you were closeted with Christina Slater, with the door shut, how would you know?'

His expression remained tight, hostile in a way that was hard to pin down to self-preservation or brotherly loyalty.

'Perhaps you weren't with Christina Slater,' she

suggested. 'Perhaps she knows that you or David went to pick Karen up from the bus stop and she's a part of the cover-up.'

Throwing out his hands, Henry turned to his lawyer as he cried, 'This is crazy. I don't know where she's getting this from, but I can tell you that no one picked Karen Lomax up from the bus stop that night, or any other night. She wasn't with us . . . '

'But she was with your brother,' Natalie jumped in. 'You can't deny that, Mr Crayce.'

Since he couldn't he fell silent and glared at her as if he'd like to shove the table at her and walk out. Before he did, she decided to leave him to stew for a while and instructed Leo to end the recordings.

CHAPTER THIRTY-TWO

'How did it go?' Sienna asked as Annie walked in the door, to be enveloped in the welcome warmth of the Aga and her daughter's evident anxiety. 'Apparently if you've got Andee Lawrence on your side you're going to win.'

More fractious than she realized, Annie said, 'And what does winning actually mean? Can you tell me that, because right now I can't see anything that looks like it might fit that particular bill.'

'Oh Mum,' Sienna groaned, 'I'm trying to find something to be positive about. Didn't it go so well at the lawyer's office?'

Taking off her coat, Annie stooped to hug Cassie as she said, 'I guess it was OK. Where is everyone?'

'Gone to the supermarket and Julia's at the Byre. She said to let her know when you're back.'

'Have there been any more cancellations today?'

'If there have she didn't mention it. Grandpa and Uncle Henry aren't back from the police station yet.'

Feeling suddenly exhausted and out of her depth Annie went to pour herself a coffee but Sienna got there first, filled a mug and handed it to her.

'Thanks,' Annie said, as Sienna gestured for her to sit down. 'Have you been in touch with anyone at school?'

'Only those I know I can trust, not that I've told them anything, but I didn't want to cut myself off completely. It'll make it even harder to go back if I do, and I guess I'll have to at some point.'

'You will,' Annie confirmed, and deciding they'd deal with how awful that was going to be when the time came she said, 'Is Max keeping in touch with some friends too?'

'As far as I know. Don't worry, we're not engaging in any of the usual sites or chats, we know it's bad so we don't have to read it.'

Reaching for her hand Annie watched their fingers entwining, her own long and slim and losing their elasticity now, Sienna's young and smooth, prettily manicured and somehow innocent.

Watching their fingers too, Sienna said, 'There were people at the gates from the media earlier, but I guess they'd gone by the time you came through?'

'Fortunately, yes, but I'm sure they'll be back. Are you getting any calls?'

'No, but I think Julia's pretty inundated over at the Byre.'

Feeling sure she was, Annie knew she ought to go and lend a hand, but right now she didn't want to move from her chair, not even to check her own phone which had been filling up with text and voice messages as fast as she could erase them.

'Do you think we'll have to cancel our ski trip?' Sienna asked. 'I don't mean just over this, but with what's happening in Italy now.'

Knowing she was referring to the spread of a virus,

Annie felt herself moving closer to the edge as she said, 'I don't know. It's not something I can think about now.'

They sat quietly for a while, listening to the wind outside and the gentle snuffle of Cassie breathing at their feet, until finally, Sienna said 'Tell me honestly, Mum, do you think Dad really did kill that girl? I know his . . . '

'I don't know what to believe,' Annie interrupted, not wanting to hear those words from her daughter. 'I wish I did, but all I can tell you is to try and keep an open mind, which I admit would be a whole lot easier if he'd just open up and talk to someone.'

'Why won't he?'

'I wish I could answer that, Sen, but I can't.'

'You know, if it turns out he did kill her, I don't think I'll ever be able to forgive him.' A tear dropped onto her cheek. 'I'll hate not having him as my dad anymore, but if he's some kind of monster . . . '

'He's not,' Annie said, clasping her hand tightly between her own, 'and you know in your heart that he isn't.'

Sienna's face crumpled. 'It's all so horrible, Mum.' She began to sob and Annie pulled her into her arms. In an effort to comfort them both she said, 'Remember what Hugo told us, there's a chance the murder charge will be thrown out, or overturned, postponed, I'm not sure how they term it.'

Sienna's voice was thick with tears. 'Does that mean he could be coming home?'

'I'm not sure, but even if he does the police will continue to investigate until they've built a case that won't be thrown out.'

'Or until they find out he didn't do it.'

Relieved to hear the optimism, while wishing with all

her heart that she could feel it too, Annie was aware that even if she did, within less than five minutes she'd be thinking the worst again. Back and forth, back and forth, how the heck was she supposed to know anything anymore? 'I need to pack some things for him,' she said. 'Helen Hall's going to take them in tomorrow.'

Reaching for her phone, Sienna said, 'I'll send Julia a quick text to let her know you're back, then I'll come up and help.'

'OK, maybe she'll have some news about Grandpa and Uncle Henry.'

Natalie was back in the incident room after spending three excruciating hours interrogating Richard and Henry Crayce, and she was starting to fear they might never make a breakthrough the way things were at present.

'What are we missing?' she growled to no one in particular. 'Tell me how the hell that girl got to the farmhouse.'

Shari Avery said, 'We still don't know if it happened there.'

Aware of that, and irritated by it, Natalie watched Gould pass the office appearing engrossed in whatever was being said to him by the uniformed officer alongside him, but she didn't miss the quick glance he stole in her direction. Pleased by that, she said to Shari, 'Have we tracked down the bus driver's wife yet, in case she knows something?'

'Apparently she lives with her sister in Spain these days. We're still trying to get hold of her.'

'OK.' To Leo she said, 'Let's have a watch of Richard Crayce talking about his son's behaviour after said son left the armed forces.'

Minutes later Leo had a freeze frame of Dickie Crayce filling the screen ready to go.

'Before we start, ma'am,' Shari said, 'I just want to try and get something clear in my head. Why is it so important to find out about the cause of David Crayce's mental issues? I mean, if he really had them and they pushed him to do what he did, I get that, but why do we need to know exactly what triggered them?'

'It's all a part of building a case,' Natalie explained, wondering why she needed to. Shouldn't this be obvious even to a newly qualified detective? 'There could be parallels that we need to be aware of, something that clears the picture in a way we're not managing right now. Whatever the trigger was, you can be sure the defence will use it to their advantage if they can, and if they do we don't want to come out looking incompetent and uninformed, which we would if we're not on top of his background.'

Shari nodded, apparently understanding. 'So we need to be sure that all the stories about him being drunk and not fully in charge of himself, having no memory and the like, aren't part of an elaborate cover-up by the family?'

Natalie nodded, smiled and gave Leo the go ahead to hit play.

Richard Crayce's interview didn't differ in any material way from the one Henry Crayce had given, or David Crayce, come to that. They seemed to have their stories so tightly bound up that they could almost be believed, were it not for the DNA connecting David Crayce to Karen Lomax.

Reaching out to pause the video, Natalie said, 'Does anyone here actually think the semen might have been harvested?'

Everyone exchanged incredulous glances before shaking their heads.

'If it was,' Shields pointed out, 'Crayce would have known, wouldn't he? I mean, it's not like you can just help yourself while a chap's not looking.'

'It's probable he had memory lapses,' Natalie reminded him.

Shields shrugged, clearly still not convinced. 'OK. So, who do you think would have taken it?' he asked.

'Christina Slater?' Shari suggested. 'She's been giving me a bad vibe from the start.'

Natalie mulled it over. 'Let's talk to her again,' she said, and a moment later they were focused back on the video.

When they reached the end of Richard Crayce reacting to Natalie's theory about him and Henry clearing up his eldest son's mess, she hit stop and replayed it.

Crayce: 'That's an extraordinary thing to suggest. Outrageous even.'

Natalie: 'No one's saying this crime wasn't extraordinary or outrageous. And there are plenty of parents who'd do anything to help their children, no matter what kind of trouble they're in. So, did you, Mr Crayce, work together with your son Henry to cover up David's . . . '

Crayce: 'I don't have to listen to this.'

Natalie: 'I'm afraid you do. A young girl lost her life that weekend and your son's DNA links him to the body. You were with him at the wine bar, during the pub crawl and when you carried on drinking and playing poker at the farmhouse. After that we're told

David spent the night in his room and it's my guess it was with Karen Lomax . . . '

Crayce: 'I've no idea how you've come to these conclusions, Detective . . . '

Natalie: 'Who went to pick her up? Was it you? Did you arrange it when you spoke to her at the wine bar? Maybe it was her suggestion to join you all later?'

Crayce: 'I've already told you, I have no recollection of speaking to her that day, but even if I did I can assure you it had nothing to do with picking her up at any other time.'

Natalie: 'She told her friends that she'd be quite keen to have sex with you and your sons. Was that the plan? You'd all take a turn?'

Crayce: 'For crying out loud! I've got no idea what goes on in young girls' minds, or yours for that matter, but I can assure you that is not something either I, or my sons, would ever have entertained. It's preposterous even to suggest it.'

Natalie: 'Why? She was an attractive young girl, up for it, by all accounts, but perhaps it was just your sons, and you weren't a part of it.'

Crayce: 'No! Henry . . . Henry was . . . ' He pressed a hand to his chest; his face was turning deathly pale.

Natalie: 'Mr Crayce, are you ill?'

Natalie stopped the recording and sat back in her chair staring intently at the freeze-frame. 'Now we know his little performance there didn't turn out to be a full-blown heart attack or stroke,' she said, 'we'll have to get him back in. For now, what do we think he was on the point of saying about Henry?'

'That Henry was married,' Noah suggested, clearly thinking it was as lame as it sounded.

'That Henry was with Christina Slater,' Shari offered.

Leo shrugged, having nothing to add.

Since she didn't either, Natalie took the next few minutes to assimilate. 'On the one hand,' she began, 'we have an ex-soldier probably suffering from PTSD and/or dissociative disorder, and on the other we have a dead seventeen-year-old girl with his sperm all over her undies. That's as substantial a link between the two as we're ever going to get. However, we don't have any witnesses to them being together over the weekend of August 7th/8th 1999, so we need to go back to the pathologist and ask if death could have occurred later than in his report.'

'I'll get onto that,' Noah told her, making a note.

'If it did happen later,' Leo put in, 'then she must have been held somewhere before the sex and death occurred.'

Natalie nodded. 'Until we're told otherwise,' she said, 'I'm still favouring the weekend, because I'm convinced we're not getting the truth from anyone about what happened at that farmhouse. All we know for pretty damned certain is that David Crayce had sex with Karen at some point, but was it him who actually killed her?'

'I thought we were presuming he did,' Shari piped up.

'We are, but when it comes to trial we'll have to prove it, and right now we still can't.'

CHAPTER THIRTY-THREE

Annie was watching from the kitchen window as Andee, who'd called ahead, was waved through the gates of Hanley Combe by a local gamekeeper acting as security, and directed over to the main house. There didn't appear to be anyone from the press around at the moment, but a few had been hanging about earlier, and there was never any knowing when they might turn up again.

By the time Andee came to park her SUV beside David's Defender, Annie was already on the veranda waiting to greet her.

'I thought it would be best if I came in person,' Andee said, mounting the steps and appearing to appreciate Cassie's enthusiastic welcome. 'I hope you don't mind.'

'No, it's fine,' Annie assured her, although since Andee's call her nerves had been shredded by all the reasons why she might feel a personal visit to be necessary after seeing David. 'Please come in. My mother's here, and my son, Max, but if you'd rather we spoke alone?'

'We probably should,' Andee replied, and gave a murmur of pleasure as she followed Annie inside. 'It's so lovely and warm in here, and what a wonderful kitchen.'

'Thank you,' Annie said, fleetingly recalling from

Andee's website her connection to interior design. She watched as Max introduced himself and took Andee's coat, pleased with his good manners.

'I'm Harriet,' Harriet said, holding out a hand to shake. 'Can I get you a tea, or maybe something a little stronger?'

'I'm fine, thanks,' Andee assured her.

'Shall we go through to the snug?' Annie suggested, unable to wait any longer.

Andee followed her into the hall and over to what Annie always considered David's room, since it was where he tended to work when he was at home, with music playing in the background and Cassie at his feet. It smelled of him, which was why she liked being in here, and also why she couldn't bear it. 'Do I need to brace myself?' she asked as she let the dog in before closing the door and directing Andee to one of the battered leather sofas.

'Not really,' Andee replied, sitting down. 'I'm afraid when we got there, we were told he didn't want to see us.'

Annie's heart contracted as she stared at Andee, too stunned to know what to say.

'Have you heard from him?' Andee asked.

'He called last night. I told him I'd seen you the previous day . . . He didn't give me any indication he'd . . . I'm sorry you had a wasted journey . . . I don't understand . . .' She wanted to bang her fists against something in frustration, better still scream, but that was hardly going to help.

'Have you managed to arrange a visit for yourself yet?' Andee asked gently.

'I still can't get through on the damned phone, and I haven't had a response to my online request. Why wouldn't he see you?'

'It's a good question, and you're probably the only one who can get us an answer. Will you try asking if he calls tonight? Or when you go to see him?'

'Of course, unless he refuses to see me too.'

'He's calling,' Andee reminded her, 'so that will be your first best opportunity. And I was wondering, when you do get a visit, if I could come too. Obviously I'm not asking you to spring me on him in some sort of ambush, but if you tell him how keen you are for him to speak to me, it might sway him.'

Annie swallowed dryly as she nodded, taking the words in, but not quite connecting with them as she tried to understand what was going on in David's mind. 'I can't believe he's doing this,' she said. 'Why won't he help himself? Or let you and Helen help him?' Her eyes returned to Andee. 'Sorry,' she said, 'useless questions . . . Have you had any news from Hugo about the charge being dropped?'

'Not yet, but I'll be sure to let you know as soon as he gets in touch. What I can tell you is what Oscar reported back after your brother-in-law and father-in-law were questioned today. Is your father-in-law all right, by the way?'

Over that particular shock now, Annie said, 'Yes, I think so. We're urging him to see a doctor for a check-up, but he's insisting it was just a dizzy spell, nothing serious.'

'Let's hope that's all it was. Have you spoken to him or Henry about their interviews?'

'Only insofar as they said there wasn't much to tell, apart from the fact that the police seem to be grabbing at straws. According to them they don't have anything to go on apart from the DNA match – as if that's nothing, for God's sake. What's wrong with them? Do they really not understand how much that matters?'

Andee said, 'Have either of them ever offered an explanation for how it came to be where it was? Apart from the obvious, of course.'

Annie shook her head. 'They're just parroting Hugo and Helen – and you – that it isn't proof he killed her, only that he was with her, as if that's in some way acceptable when obviously it isn't.'

'Did either of them mention the police theory that David killed her and his father and Henry "sorted things out"?'

Annie's eyes closed as her heart turned over. 'No, they didn't mention that,' she said quietly, terrified that it might be true. 'Is that what you believe?'

'It's a possibility,' Andee conceded, 'but there are others.'

'Such as?'

'We're still working on them, but something else we learned from Oscar about the interviews today is that there is still much interest in your husband's time with the military and his behaviour after. Did his father or brother mention that?'

'They said they were asked about it, but none of us know very much about what happened when he was in . . .' She shrugged, at a loss where to go from there.

'OK, it's obvious the police think that on the night Karen Lomax disappeared and possibly died David was suffering from some sort of mental breakdown, blackout, impairment, call it what you will, probably exacerbated by alcohol. Their big problem is going to be proving it.'

Annie pressed a hand to her mouth as though to keep in a need to cry out. It was becoming too much, too overwhelming . . . It had happened so long ago, and now she had no idea what to say, or even to think, that wouldn't end up condemning him.

In a gentle tone, Andee said, 'If you're willing I'd like to spend some time with you over the next day or two, talking through everything you remember from when he was in the armed forces and the eighteen months that followed – up to the August weekend and after. Everything could be relevant, and maybe nothing, but it's important for you to keep in mind that whatever you tell me will go no further. We – Helen, Hugo and I – are acting for David. We have only his, and your interests at heart.'

Aware of how tightly every one of her muscles was clenched, Annie said, 'And if it turns out he did it? Won't you have to tell the police?'

'No. It's their job to prove it, not ours.'

Feeling swamped by the sheer awfulness of that, Annie gave herself a few moments before she said, 'OK, I'll do whatever you want me to, I just don't know how helpful it's going to be.'

'We'll decide that as we talk, and if you can get David to tell you more when he calls all the better.'

It was less than fifteen minutes after Andee had driven off into the darkening afternoon that David rang. Annie had returned to the snug with Cassie, and seeing the No Caller ID on her screen she immediately clicked to accept. 'Why?' she cried, before he could speak. 'Your lawyer and investigator came to see you today. They're trying to help you, but you wouldn't see them. What the hell is going on, David?'

'Annie, listen . . . '

'No, you listen. We're scared out of our minds here. We're trying to believe in you, but you are making it so damned hard that I don't know what to say to our children any more.'

'I know and I understand that – and I'm sorry. I'm just trying to work out the best way to handle this . . . '

'What the hell are you talking about? There's only one way, David, and that's to tell the truth. It's time to do that or you're going to bring us all down, and none of us . . .'

'Annie, please will you listen to what I'm saying? I didn't want to see the lawyers today because I need to talk to you first. Have you arranged a visit yet?'

'I'm still trying, but I can't get through on the bloody phone.'

'Keep at it. Have you tried online?'

'Of course. I'm waiting for confirmation. If I get it, it won't be until next Tuesday, that was the only option they gave me, and I don't know if I can last until then.'

'You can, and so can I, if we have to. I need you, Annie, more now than I ever have.' There was a moment before he said, 'I'm not going to ask if you still love me, I'm just going to say it's never been in any doubt for me,' and a moment later he'd gone.

CHAPTER THIRTY-FOUR

As Natalie made her way from the incident room to Gould's office, weaving around the desks of her colleagues in CID, she was running through all the possible reasons he might have for summoning her, and pausing a while on one or two that were quite pleasing. Not that she seriously expected he was about to suggest a drink after work one evening, or even dinner, but fantasizing about it for a few minutes was a welcome break from banging her head against a wall with the Karen Lomax case.

'Ah, there you are,' he said, looking up from his computer as she came in. 'Close the door, will you. It's probably best if no one else hears this.'

Startled, and starting to worry, she did as told and went to take the chair on the other side of his desk.

After a moment he fixed her with steady, inscrutable eyes, very definitely a part of his attraction, although right now they were making her feel more uneasy than intrigued. 'I'm not good with personal stuff,' he began, seeming more awkward than in-charge, 'and feel free to tell me to mind my own business if you want to, but I'm aware that your ex-husband was in the military, and that there were . . .

er, problems after, so if this case is causing you any personal difficulties . . .'

'It's not,' she cut in quickly, heat rising over her neck and face, right up into her hairline. She hated to be seen as a victim, had always despised herself for being one, even more for letting the abuse go on as long as it had. It remained her secret shame, her Achilles heel, in spite of all the therapy she'd been through. Now, to have him, of all people, bring it up as if it were still a problem that she might not be coping with, or that might be skewing her judgement in some way . . . She was struggling for words, assurances, something to assert her competence and confidence . . .

As though sensing it, he moved on swiftly. 'Just as long as everything's fine. That's good. Sorry to mention it. I've just listened to some of the interviews and you seem to be focusing on Crayce's army career . . . '

'Because I feel it might be relevant,' she cut in stiffly. 'If you'd rather I left it alone?'

'No, that's not what I'm saying. I just wanted you to know . . . Human Resources and all that . . . ' He cut himself off and started again. 'So where are you at with the case?'

Relieved to have been given such a quick out, she collected herself, only wishing she had a more positive response to offer. 'We're hoping to speak to the bus driver's wife later today,' she said. 'She's lived in Spain with her sister since her husband died four years ago; there's a chance he told her something that didn't make it to his statement.'

He grimaced, as did she. It was lame, there was no denying it.

'And I was hoping,' she continued briskly, 'provided I'm allowed to mention it, that this meeting was to tell me that you've made some headway with the MOD on the reasons for Crayce's early discharge.'

He sighed, as though having expected the question, and sitting back in his chair he said, 'I'm afraid I'm still waiting on answers. You understand I'm not in a position to pull strings myself, I have no contacts, so I'm relying on more senior officers to do what they can, but if you really think it's relevant I'll do some chasing.'

'Thanks, but I won't be able to say if it's relevant until I know what it is. There's always a chance that no actual event occurred to cause his trauma, and if it didn't then it's possible we're being lied to on an epic scale.'

'Which in itself tells us there's a cover-up.'

'Indeed, but unless we can get to the heart of it, all we'll end up with is him having sex with a seventeen-year-old girl, which isn't a crime. Damning, yes, but it doesn't come close to proving he killed her. However, if it turns out he was mentally challenged at the time for very specific reasons, then we're as capable of making it work for us as his defence team is of making it work for them.'

His eyes remained on hers as he took this in. 'OK, I understand what you're saying, and frankly it's looking likely you're going to need that information even more than you realize. You might need to brace yourself for this.'

Tensing as her mind shot in myriad directions, she waited for him to go on.

'I've received a call from Geoffrey Reynolds at the CPS. He's not certain yet, but he wanted to warn us that there's a chance the charge against Crayce is going to be dropped.'

Natalie stared at him, dumbfounded.

'They're not confident they can get a guilty verdict as it stands,' Gould explained, 'and apparently your friend Billy Big Bollocks Blum has been talking to some pretty powerful people. I'm not saying it's going to happen; I just wanted to let you know.'

'But they signed off on it,' she cried furiously. 'We all agreed there was sufficient evidence as it stood to press ahead with building a case. For Christ's sake, Crayce's DNA was all over her undies and jeans, what more does anyone want?'

Looking pained, Gould said, 'You just said yourself that having sex with a seventeen-year-old isn't a crime, and a good lawyer, which he has, will argue rings around it in court. As Mr Blum is already doing at the DPP's office.'

'We'll get more,' Natalie vowed. 'Just please do what you can to help us access the information we need, because I'm telling you, Crayce is our man.'

'I'm not doubting it, but you have to know the Ministry of Defence can't be relied on to give us what we want. So, try to come up with something else, like how he got her to wherever it was they had sex, or how he disposed of the body, or I'm afraid, it's looking quite possible that he'll walk.'

CHAPTER THIRTY-FIVE

Seeing signs directing them to the prison was bad enough – how had she got here in her life, how had David? – but when the actual place came into view through the drear of the day with its barbed wire topped fences, sinister surveillance cameras and gothic grey stone façade Annie had to close her eyes as though it might remove her from this awful reality into a dream.

'You'll be fine,' Andee reassured her as they were cleared to enter the visitor's car park. 'I know it's tough, especially the first time you come.'

'It's tougher for him,' Annie replied, flashing on the kind of violence David might be experiencing, and whether his combat training of so many years ago was helping him to defend himself. She shuddered, and swallowed down a rise of choking anxiety.

'I'll wait here,' Andee said after steering them into a space between a pick-up truck and expensive looking motor-bike. 'Getting through security is straightforward, there'll be someone to tell you what to do, and the visiting room isn't as gloomy as you might imagine. They've revamped it recently, so it's a little more civilized than before, and there's a designated area for prisoners on remand.'

Annie was staring at the moss-speckled red-brick wall in front of them, readying herself to move from her seat. 'Thanks for bringing me,' she said. 'I'm sorry he won't see you.'

'It's OK. What's important is that he wants to see you.'

'Unless I get in there and find he's changed his mind.'

'That's not going to happen.'

Spurred by the confidence, Annie almost smiled as she said, 'I don't know whether I'm more angry or nervous or . . . I don't know what the hell I am.'

Andee squeezed her hand and came around to the passenger door to give her a hug before watching her fall in with the other visitors already making their way to the authorized entrance.

As she walked Annie kept her eyes lowered and hands clenched tightly in her pockets, trying not to think too much about how it was going to feel to see David in this place, or about what the next hour would bring. Instead, as she was checked in, searched, screened and told to wait in some sort of anteroom with too few chairs, she focused her mind on Max and Sienna and how they were coping with being back at school. It was difficult, they'd admitted when they'd rung last night, even worse than they'd expected, but after they'd spoken to their father on the phone on Sunday evening they'd seemed more resigned to the fact that it had to happen.

'Do it for your mother,' he'd told them. 'She needs to think that something is normal for you, and I need you to be as strong for her as she is for you.'

Relieved to find that his encouragement still carried weight with them, she'd driven them back the following day and had sat in the car for a long time after they'd disappeared into their respective schools, finding it almost impossible to leave. Absurdly, it had felt as though she was losing them too, that if she drove away she might not see them again. It was only when Julia had called to check on her that she'd finally turned around and headed home.

Andee had helped her through the next couple of days more than she'd realized, until she'd begun thinking about it on the way here to the prison. Talking to her, exploring the past with her as a guide, finding new memories, discussing theories, had proved a kind of therapy in its way. A particular chat had stayed with her and was presenting itself again now as she waited to go through the next stage of security.

'Tell me more,' Andee had said during a blustery walk on the moor with Cassie, 'about David's fear of someone not keeping to their word. Do you have any idea who he might have been referring to?'

Annie shook her head. 'I wish I'd asked at the time he said it. Maybe I did and I've forgotten. It was so long ago, and they weren't the best years of our relationship.'

'Could it have anything to do with the reason he left the army?'

'I guess so, but it's impossible to say for certain.'

'Was he still with the Paras at that time?'

'No, he'd joined another unit about a year before he was discharged. He had to do a lot of really tough training in order to get in . . . I'm trying to remember . . . It was a special airborne, or assault brigade . . . The details are escaping me.'

'Not to worry, I'll look it up. Did he stay in touch with anyone after he left?'

'Not that I'm aware of.'

'Can you recall anyone turning up, or calling out of the blue, who might have done or said something to upset him in some way?'

Annie had no memory of anything like it, although she wished she did, for she'd realized what was happening during that chat – Andee and Helen were trying to find out if someone from David's past had suddenly reappeared while he was working on Hanley Combe and had . . . Had what? Threatened him in some way? Frightened him to the point that he'd . . . Abducted, raped and murdered a young girl? That didn't make sense – unless this person, whoever it was, had been involved somehow. 'If anyone, especially a stranger,' she said, 'had been around that weekend the others would have noticed, and as far as I'm aware they've never said anyone else was there.'

'I'm only throwing out suggestions,' Andee explained, 'just to see if anything sticks.'

Now, Annie looked up as a door opened on the far side of the room, and began moving along with everyone else as they were ushered into the corridor beyond. It led to another scanner. Once through that, she realized she was in the visitor's area.

Andee had been right, it wasn't as gloomy as Annie had imagined it, in fact it was high-ceilinged, smelled vaguely of paint mixed with something less savoury, and was quite bright, although that was due to overhead lights rather than wintry sunlight streaming through the windows.

A security guard directed her to a zone that appeared to have more space between the tables and colourful chairs. She saw David right away; he was one of only two men in that area already seated. As he spotted her coming he got to his feet and her heart felt as though it was being squeezed too hard for her to breathe. Thank God there were no visible signs of him being attacked; even so he looked different – he'd lost weight already and the familiar lines on his face had deepened. What hadn't changed was the profound tenderness in his eyes as they met hers, or the physical strength of him that had always seemed to wrap itself around her even if he wasn't touching her.

He took her hands as they sat down at the table, eyes continuing to feast on each other. *It was him, really him, and they were really here, in this terrible place*. She couldn't be sure in that moment if she'd ever loved him more, or if she no longer loved him at all. 'God, I miss you,' he whispered.

'I miss you too,' she said, meaning it. 'We all do.'

'How did you get here? Did Henry bring you?'

'No, Andee Lawrence, the investigator I told you about. She's waiting outside.'

His eyes went down as he took this in, but instead of running with it, he looked at her again and said, 'Tell me about Max and Sienna. How's it working out for them back at school?'

'It's not easy, but I think they're coping. Quin's been made captain of the junior rugby team. I'm pretty sure Mr Knowles, the sports teacher, made it happen to try and distract the others from what's being said about his dad in the papers.'

David's eyes were bleak, guilt and shame shadowing their depths. 'That's good of him,' he said. 'I expect Quin's pleased.'

'He wants to tell you himself when you call, so don't forget to act surprised.'

'Of course.' They sat quietly for a moment, the buzz

of other conversations going on around them, neither of them coming to the point, both avoiding what needed to be said while knowing they had to broach it eventually or this visit, his promise to talk to her, would mean nothing. 'And how are things with the business?' he asked.

Exasperated and relieved, she said, 'Bookings for next season are down in comparison to this time last year, but at least we've had some. Julia's being fantastic about running things on her own, although Henry and your dad help out, obviously, and I've been over there a couple of times. I just can't keep my mind on what I'm supposed to be doing, so I think I'm more of a hindrance than a help.'

Tightening the hold on her hands, he said, 'Is Dad OK after his turn?'

Knowing he blamed himself for that, she wished she could ease his conscience, but all she could say was, 'He seems to be.' *What does Dickie know?* she wanted to ask. *What are you all hiding from me?* She was about to speak, when he said, 'I'm sorry.'

Not doubting it, she looked into his eyes, aware of all the questions she needed to ask, those Andee had given her and her own, right there between them. She needed to lay them out for him to answer, but for some reason she was holding back. *Come on, Annie, you can do better than this.*

In the end she said, 'On the phone, you told me you wanted to talk to me first.'

He continued to look at her, saying nothing, and she wasn't sure if she wanted to slam her hands into him or not touch him at all. 'David,' she urged angrily, 'you have to . . . '

'It's important for you to know,' he cut in, 'that there's a chance I'm going to be in here for a very long time.'

Panic surged through her like a terrible heat. 'Why?' she cried, gripping his hands savagely.

His expression was one of sorrow, pain and even slight disbelief as he said, 'Annie, you and I both know it's possible that I did it.'

She stared at him, horrified, not wanting to take in what he'd said, or to add any truth to it by agreeing, because yes, she did know . . . 'No! I don't know that,' she protested.

'Yes, you do. You remember what I was like back then, the drinking, the stress, the incidents of memory loss, or blackouts . . . '

'They didn't last long enough for you to have done anything like that. You'd remember . . . '

'I have no recollection of sleeping with that girl,' he reminded her, 'and yet we know I did. So, you see, I can't account for everything that weekend. I'd had too much . . . Oh God, Annie, don't do that, please,' he groaned as she snatched her hands away.

She didn't put them back, only stared at him, feeling as though she no longer knew him, or herself, or even what she should do, or believe.

'There's going to be a lot about this that you won't want to hear,' he told her, 'and if you don't I'm not going to force it. I just want you to understand why I haven't wanted to talk to anyone, why I've needed to try and figure things out before I start saying . . . ' He stopped, shaking his head and seeming to retreat into himself in spite of his promise to talk.

'David, don't do this,' she implored. 'We're trying to help you . . . '

'I'm waiting for answers,' he said. 'I don't know if I'll get them, but if I do . . . '

'Answers to what? Who's going to give them to you? David, does it have something to do with your time in the army? That's what the police think.'

'I know, and I'm not going to disabuse them . . . '

'So instead you're going to let me carry on thinking that at the very least you screwed a teenage girl who . . .'

'Don't do that,' he growled. 'Stop painting pictures neither of us want to see, or live with . . . Just please try to understand that being in here these past eight days has allowed me to think in a way I couldn't at home.'

'And this is where you'll stay if you don't let the lawyers help you.'

'I've already told you it's possible I will.'

'And is that what you want for yourself, for us, for our children? You need to get a grip on this, David, because I don't think you have one at all right now.'

He didn't argue, he simply looked down at his empty hands as though on some level he thought he'd already lost everything, and Annie felt suddenly overwhelmed by the fear that he had.

'He thinks there's a chance he did it,' she told Andee as she got back into the car. She was breathless, head spinning, fury and confusion still burning a chaos inside her. 'I don't mean the sex, we know that already, I mean the . . . the murder.'

Andee turned to her with eyebrows raised. 'Did he tell you how and why he might have done it?' she asked, not sounding as surprised as Annie had expected, which made everything seem so much worse.

'Oh, nothing so straightforward. Apparently he's waiting for answers . . . I've no idea to what, or from whom, and frankly if he carries on being this cryptic I'll . . . I don't know what I'll do, but I'll tell you this, something has to give or I'm going to lose my mind.'

'Actually,' Andee said, starting the engine, 'I received a call while you were in there and it would appear that something is about to give.'

Annie closed her eyes not sure how much more she could take today. 'Will I want to hear this?' she asked.

'I think so, although it won't clear anything up exactly, but apparently Hugo has had some success with the Crown Prosecution Service.'

Annie stopped breathing.

'I'm told that the charge is about to be thrown out, so as soon as all the proper legal channels have been gone through and the paperwork's in order, your husband will be coming home.'

A great rush of relief was threaded through the damning thought: *My husband, whose infidelity twenty years ago could so easily be forgiven if the girl in question hadn't ended up dead.*

This was so much more than the past coming back to haunt them; it was apparently coming back to destroy them.

CHAPTER THIRTY-SIX

'Already!' Natalie cried furiously. 'I thought you were going to try and stop it.'

Meeting her anger with an edge of his own, Gould said, 'You needed to bring me more . . . '

'And I was supposed to do that in less than eight days? The CPS agreed he was the prime suspect . . . '

'No one's arguing with what you have so far, but a decision's been taken that it's not enough to keep him where he is. There are too many questions still unanswered, holes the defence team will drive a truck through, and I have to ask, is it really credible that everyone there that night is complicit in some sort of cover-up?'

'I don't know about everyone, but his father and brother know something, I'm convinced of that, but right now I don't have anything else to throw at them to justify calling them back for questioning.'

'Have you tried?'

'Of course. The lawyers are not having it.'

'What about Richard Crayce? Have you discovered what he didn't manage to get out at the end of his last interview?'

'Apparently he was about to say that Henry was with Christina Slater that night. So, nothing revelatory, and certainly nothing to persuade me that my theory of them cleaning up after David is wrong. More likely that she was involved too.'

Not arguing with that, he said, 'Did the bus driver's wife add anything?'

'No, not at all. What we need is to get some answers out of the MOD that . . . '

'As a matter of fact,' he interrupted, 'I've been instructed to leave it alone.'

She gaped at him, incredulously.

'I'm told,' he continued, 'that it isn't relevant to our inquiries so . . . '

'Jesus Christ, what's wrong with you?'

His face darkened as he uttered her name like a warning.

Remembering where they were – in the incident room with everyone watching the show – she somehow swallowed the next explosion, and said, 'Exactly what do you propose I tell the Lomaxes?'

He looked as awkward as she'd hoped. 'I realize what a difficult position you're in . . . '

'I'm not talking about me. I'm talking about them. Don't you think they've been through enough? All these years, and finally we have the man who killed their daughter, but sorry Jess and Eddie, we're letting him go. How on earth are they supposed to understand that? They are seriously good and decent people who've already been badly served by this force. They don't deserve this.'

'I hear you,' he retorted, 'and you're right, they really don't, but it's out of my hands. Perhaps their Family Liaison Officer . . . '

'I can't push this off onto Mel. I'll need to speak to them myself. So, please tell me he's at least going to have some serious bail conditions slapped on him.'

'That's for the lawyers to work out. We'll be informed when, if, they've been set, but be prepared for the charge to be thrown out until we have enough solid evidence to put him back in custody, and keep him there.'

Natalie turned aside, as much to hide her frustration as to stop it erupting again.

Leo Johnson said, 'Do we know yet when he's being released?'

Gould sighed, a release of his own tension. 'No, but as soon as I know you will.'

Expecting him to leave then, Natalie was readying herself to let rip with a whole string of expletives, but it turned out, to her horror, there was more. 'I'm afraid,' he said, 'that we have to scale down the investigation . . . '

'No!' she cried, almost ready to hit him. 'What the hell is going on here?'

'DS Rundle . . . '

'Who the hell do the Crayces know that can make this happen? Aren't you asking the same questions? Doesn't that innocent girl's life matter? Don't her parents?'

'Yes, to everything apart from who the Crayces know, because frankly I don't have a clue, but I can tell you this: his lawyer has used *his* contacts to outsmart us and the local CPS, so make sure he doesn't do it again. You can keep DC Johnson, but DCs Avery and Shields need to be available for other investigations where necessary,' and before she could argue any further, he left.

'And just like that,' she raged when she was sure he was no longer within earshot, 'a guilty man is being allowed to go free.'

* * *

Jess and Eddie Lomax were staring uncomprehendingly at DS Rundle. She'd arrived a few minutes ago saying that she was sorry, she had news she'd really rather not be delivering, so they'd braced themselves while knowing that whatever it was it couldn't be as bad as when they'd been told about Karen. That was the thing about the position they were in, the very worst had already happened, nothing could ever affect them like that again, so whatever DS Rundle had to say they could handle it.

So they'd listened quietly, calmly, as the detective told them why she was there, and though Jess knew they'd heard right, that David Crayce was going to be released, she was so shocked and bewildered that it hadn't yet occurred to her to be angry.

'You need to explain this,' Eddie said tightly. 'I thought he'd been charged. Are you saying now that he didn't do it?'

'No,' Rundle replied carefully, 'that isn't what I'm saying. We still firmly believe that we have the right man, but the belief now is that if we were to go to court at this time we couldn't be confident of proving his guilt.'

'But we're not going at this time. Isn't the point of the wait so you can build the case against him?'

'It is, but his lawyers have persuaded the Prosecution Service that there are enough anomalies as things stand to warrant his release while we gather more evidence.'

'But you've got the DNA,' Jess cried. 'You know it was him.'

'That's true, but all the DNA actually tells us is that he was with Karen sometime before she died. It isn't proof that he killed her.'

'What more proof do you need?' Eddie growled angrily.

Jess clasped her hands to her face, unable to take much more of this.

'Who the hell else do they think did it?' Eddie demanded, his voice shaking with shock and barely suppressed outrage.

'We're not looking at anyone else, but Crayce's defence team are making the point that he could have dropped Karen off somewhere after they'd been together – and that someone else, anyone else could have picked her up and . . . And so was the last one to see her alive.'

'Who's this mystery person supposed to be?' Eddie snapped.

Rundle regarded him helplessly.

'There's no other DNA,' Jess pointed out.

'There doesn't have to be. As I said, that sort of evidence doesn't prove who killed her, only who was with her in . . .'

Eddie turned away, fists clenched, shoulders hunched making it clear he didn't want to hear any more.

Putting a steadying hand on his back, Jess said, 'What are we supposed to do now, Detective? Where does this actually leave us?'

Her eyes glowing dark with sympathy, Rundle said, 'I promise you I'm not letting it go. No one is. We will continue to do everything in our power to get Crayce back in custody where he belongs.'

'But how if you don't have the evidence?' Eddie spun round, his eyes bright with unshed tears, his cheeks deeply flushed with frustration.

'We'll find it,' she assured him. 'Someone knows what really happened, and I give you my word I will not rest until I know who that someone is and what they're hiding.' She turned as the hall door opened and Mel, the FLO, put her head round.

'Sorry to interrupt,' she said, 'but I thought you'd want to know that the press seem to have got wind of the imminent release. They're starting to gather outside.'

Jess's eyes closed in dismay as Eddie said to Rundle, 'Maybe we should talk to them, see if there's something they can do to help us get to the bottom of it.'

'At this time,' Rundle replied, 'it's doubtful they'll do anything more than sensationalize the situation, but of course I can't stop you if you feel it's a step you need to take.'

He swallowed, clearly uncertain and looked at his wife.

'I don't know,' Jess said, actually dreading the prospect of their names and faces being spread all over the media again, as if there hadn't been enough of it already, back then and of late. However, if it was going to help Karen . . . Except nothing could help her now. She was gone, none of this was going to bring her back, not even a conviction. It all felt so desperate, so wrong and cruelly out of their control.

'There's someone outside who's quite well known to us,' Mel said gently. 'Her name's Wilkie Emmett. She's a local activist, and she's asking if you guys are happy for her and others to mount a campaign to seek justice for Karen.'

Jess turned to Eddie as he said, 'It's really not taking long for the news to get out, is it?'

As Rundle apologized Jess asked, 'When is he due to be released?'

'It has to go through the court,' Rundle replied, 'but I would expect it to be within the next couple of days.'

Reaching for Eddie's hand, Jess squeezed it tightly as she said, 'We need some time to think about things.'

Rundle nodded. Her regret and empathy were so plain

to see that Jess wished she could find some words of comfort for her – her case was being taken apart through no fault of her own – but she couldn't, not right now.

'You have my number,' the detective said, 'please call any time. Would you like Mel to stay with you a while?'

'No, thanks. You were very kind to come, but . . . I don't want to be rude . . . '

'Don't worry, we'll see ourselves out.'

Moments later Jess and Eddie were alone in the kitchen the echo of the last few minutes seeming as real, as audible, as the robin chirruping outside. This wasn't what they'd expected, nothing like it in fact. To have waited so long, to have come this far only for everything to start falling away from them again . . .

Jess lowered her head to rest it on Eddie's chest and felt the comfort of his hands on her shoulders as he held them. Sometimes she wondered if she loved him more because he was Karen's father, the only living link to her girl now, or because he was such a special man. They were so lucky that this hadn't driven a wedge between them; they knew it had happened to many couples in a similar situation, but thank God they had been each other's strength throughout, and they would continue to be so.

They let the phone ring, and didn't answer the door. Neither of them moved; it was as if they were trapped in a bizarre sort of time warp with the tragedy of long-ago stealing into today, making it seem as though they were back there, had never left those terrible days, and were in danger of being consumed by them all over again. They couldn't, wouldn't let it happen. Somehow they'd find a way to cope, to put the right perspective on unfolding events.

Eventually Eddie went to fill the kettle and as Jess watched she tried to connect mentally to where they were now, but everything felt elusive, caught somewhere beyond her reach. All she seemed able to focus on was how much better it might have been if David Crayce had never been found.

'You don't mean that,' Eddie said when she voiced it.

'No, I don't suppose I do,' she replied, 'but I just couldn't bear it if we ended up being cheated of the truth now, after all this time.'

CHAPTER THIRTY-SEVEN

'. . . *just receiving word that David Crayce left the court by a back door about twenty minutes ago. It's expected that he'll come straight here to the school on Exmoor, where he lives with his family in the main house. Multiple Calls to his lawyer have not yet been returned, although we're told a statement will be issued later today. Meanwhile, a spokesperson for the CPS has confirmed that the evidence supporting a murder charge was not sufficient to bring about a conviction. We've yet to hear from the police about whether the investigation continues, but a source assures me that it will. Here at the house a local pressure group has set up camp demanding justice for Karen and their numbers are growing.*'

Annie wasn't sure why she'd put the TV on in the kitchen this morning, it had just seemed to happen, and now she'd heard that the pressure group was still there and increasing she really wished she hadn't.

Shutting down the bulletin, she took the coffee her mother was handing her and glanced at the time. He shouldn't be long now. She'd offered to go and pick him up herself, but Hugo had told her last night that he would bring him. Then Julia had turned up an hour ago, saying that Henry had gone to collect him. So they could talk privately, Annie had immediately suspected. What was there to say? What were they hiding from everyone, including the lawyers?

Now, as she waited with her parents, Dickie and Julia for the big arrival, her mind went to Sienna and Max who were no doubt anxiously watching the time too, wondering if everything had gone smoothly in court and their father really was being allowed to come home. They were planning to ring during their next break to find out what was happening, and would no doubt want to speak to him if he was there. Quin would be excited about coming home from school – one of her parents would collect him, and she must remind them to take David's Defender or one of the Range Rovers if they wanted to avoid bringing him in through the gates.

Ending her call to Henry, Julia said, 'They're crossing the farm now, so they should be here any minute.'

Annie's heart clenched and twisted with nerves. Not knowing what else to do, she tried to distract herself by checking her phone for new messages. The last one she'd received was from Andee saying, *I won't come today. You'll need time to talk. Text or call any time.*

The message before that was from Sukey, Hugo's wife, saying they were welcome to stay with her and Hugo if things got too much at Hanley Combe. Of course Sukey would know that the media was camped at the gates, along with a concerned and impassioned group of vigilantes demanding justice for an innocent young girl. Annie wondered if Karen's parents were amongst them, if they'd been interviewed for TV or a newspaper since all this had happened. She tried to imagine how they must be feeling today, and apart from understanding their devastation, she detested herself for not having thought of this sooner. Naturally, her loyalties were with David and her children, they had to be, but that didn't mean she had no feelings where Karen's family was concerned. They were probably even stronger than she wanted to acknowledge, but she simply couldn't deal with them right now.

She scrolled back further into her message log and found one she'd received from Chrissie a few days ago. With all the turmoil since she'd forgotten about it, wasn't even sure she'd properly read it, but as she took it in now she felt herself start to stiffen.

So sorry for what David's going through. I promise I didn't tell them any more than they already knew. Call if you need to chat or just fancy getting out.

What did she mean, *any more than they already knew*?

She was about to forward it to Andee when Julia said, 'They're here.'

Putting her phone down, Annie went to stand with her father at the window and felt his arm go around her as they watched Henry bring the Range Rover across the back meadow, around the edge of the woods, past Quin's trampoline and up over the lawn to the hardstanding that surrounded the house. She could see David in the front passenger seat, but he wasn't looking her way, he was saying something to Henry that seemed to go on for some time before they finally got out of the car.

As Julia opened the back door Cassie rushed past her and let rip with such a joyful howl that Annie couldn't help but smile. How that dog loved David, and how he loved her in return. Such an uncomplicated and devoted relationship, that Annie could almost envy. She wasn't able to see them on the veranda from where she was, but she could hear David fussing her and knew he'd be on his knees, hands cupping her sleek black head as she wagged her tail so hard that it lifted her whole rear end off the ground.

Henry came in, his expression grim as he met her eyes, but she had no idea what he was trying to say to her, if anything. As he put an arm around Julia and spoke to her quietly Dickie went outside to greet his son, while Harriet and Francis stood awkwardly to one side as though waiting for a lead from their daughter.

Annie stayed where she was, watching Dickie come back inside, Cassie close on his heels. Then David was in the doorway, filling it up the way he always did not only physically, but with his presence, his ownership, his right to be in his home. His eyes found hers right away, held them, seemed almost to penetrate them, but neither of them moved.

You and I both know it's possible I did it.

An image of Karen's young face flashed in her mind.

Not wanting to rebuff him in front of the family, she let him take her in his arms. It felt good, and right, and in spite of everything she didn't want him to let go.

'Have you spoken to the children this morning?' he asked softly.

'They're going to call. They want to talk to you.'

'Good. I want to talk to them. And to you.'

She wished they were already alone, that they didn't have to go through meeting with Hugo and Helen Hall when they arrived, or even feel obliged to talk to their family.

In the end, it wasn't until the middle of the afternoon that they were finally able to disappear to their room, leaving Henry and Hugo to go and deal with the crowd at the gates, while her parents took the Defender into town to pick up Quin. Julia went to the Byre to find out how Hans was faring with the shop, although he had no customers today, since no one had been able to get in.

Annie sat down on the edge of the bed and watched David as he started to pace. She could sense his pent-up tension, the nightmare he was in, the frustration of not being able to unload whatever was tormenting him.

'David, talk to me,' she implored.

When he turned to her she saw in a way she hadn't earlier just how tired he was, as if he might not have slept all the time he'd been gone. 'Did you know that Henry feels you don't trust him?' he asked.

Thrown slightly, she said, 'I'm not sure I do. He seems so . . . secretive. He never talks to me about what's happening, none of you do, so it's hard to trust anyone when I feel – when I *know* – you're holding something back from me.'

He stood looking at her yet seemed oddly distant, as if only part of his mind was on what she'd said. 'Henry doesn't know any more than you do,' he told her. 'I think the reason he and Dad find it difficult to talk to you is because they don't know what to say. Neither of them is great with words, or emotions, but I know they want to help you, support you, they're just not sure how to do it.'

'Maybe they know things they're not telling *you*,' she suggested, feeling her nerve ends prickle.

He stared at her hard, as if not fully understanding her

meaning, but in the end he didn't reply, merely began pacing again.

Leaving her suspicions there for now, she said, 'What about the answers you're waiting for? Have you received them yet?'

'No, but it should be easier to get them now I'm no longer in custody.'

'Who's going to provide them?'

'It's – complicated.'

'You need to explain it to me, David.'

'I know and I will, but right now I can't tell you anything that will . . . ' He broke off and pressed clenched fists to his head.

'David! Don't do this,' she cried.

'What if we find out I killed her?' he shouted. 'That I'm as guilty as those people out there think I am?'

'Do you believe that?'

'Do you?'

'I don't want to, but when you doubt yourself what am I supposed to think? What are the children supposed to think? You're making everything impossible for us, David. If you carry on like this you're going to end up losing us all. Is that what you want?'

'You know it isn't.'

'Then tell me how you're going to stop it.'

'OK.' He nodded slowly, deliberately, taking his time to gather the words he needed. Finally, he said, 'There are things I'm going to share with you, that I've been bound, for my own sake, never to share with anyone, but before I can do that I have to get clearance from a military judge, only I've recently discovered he's no longer alive. That means I have to get through to someone who's in a position to make a decision now.'

'And if you do, how does it relate to what happened to Karen Lomax?'

'It will explain the way I was, my mindset, my behaviour, after I left the army, which you know is what Hugo and Helen want to use in my defence should I be arrested again. The trouble is, it will mean revealing details of an operation I was involved in that went horribly, catastrophically wrong. And if I do that without proper permission I don't even want to think about what the consequences might be.'

CHAPTER THIRTY-EIGHT

'I have some news,' Gould announced as Natalie came into his office, closing the door behind her.

Remembering only too well how one blow had come fast after another the last time they'd spoken, she replied, 'Should I duck?'

With a tilted eyebrow, he said, 'I guess that's going to depend on which way you look at it. First tell me, have you made any headway since Crayce's release?'

Her eyes darkened with annoyance. 'If you're asking, have Leo and I been able to solve it on our own in the past five days I'm afraid the answer is no, but we're still doing our best.'

'Glad to hear it. By the way, a good, robust statement you gave to the press the other day. We want Crayce – and the public – to think we're still as engaged in this as we ought to be, but with our dwindling resources and all the dead ends you're coming up against . . .'

'Am I allowed to say, once again, that his military career . . .'

'We're not going to get anything from that quarter, and certainly not until you can prove that it's relevant. OK, I realize that puts you in a Catch-22 situation, and if I had a way to get you out of it, believe me I would.'

'Thank you,' she said drily. 'And the *good* news is?'

With a sardonic smile he said, 'I'm not sure that's how I'd describe it, but it might help to move things along.'

She glanced round as someone knocked on the door.

'Great timing,' he commented. 'Come in!'

Natalie watched as a willowy, dark-haired woman with a dazzling smile lighting up her lovely face entered the room. Recognizing her immediately she broke into a smile of her own. 'If it isn't the legendary Andee Lawrence,' she declared, sweeping Andee into a warm embrace.

Hugging her back, Andee said, 'And if it isn't the detective who taught me everything I know.'

Natalie laughed at that, since they'd never actually worked together, but a very healthy respect existed between them as well as a lot of history and affection. 'When did you get back?' she asked. 'I was told you were in the Southern Hemisphere for the foreseeable, otherwise I'd have been in touch. God, it's good to see you.'

'Good to see you too,' Andee told her, 'and I apologize for not having rung you before now, but we'll make up for it, don't you worry. There's so much to catch up on, not least of all you moving here and working with this old monster . . . Hello, sir. How are you?'

Gould's eyes narrowed, but Natalie could see how easy relations were between them; she even wondered if, at some point, there might have been something more. However, she knew from Christmas and birthday cards that there was someone called Graeme in Andee's life now.

'I didn't realize,' Gould commented, 'that you two knew each other quite so well, but the fact that you appear to get along is definitely a bonus considering what Andee does these days, and why she's here,' Gould put in.

Looking from him to Andee and back again, Natalie said, 'OK, I'm catching on now, you're carrying out an investigation for the defence team and you've dropped in to find out how much we're prepared to share with you?'

Andee beamed.

Shaking her head in fond despair, Natalie said, 'You realize it will have to be a two-way street?'

'Well, I'm sure we'll both do our best with that,' Andee countered.

Laughing again, and feeling ridiculously happy to see the only friend she had in the area, Natalie pulled her into another hug.

'Sorry to break up the reunion,' Gould said, 'but I've got a meeting about to start so I need you to clear out of here.'

Andee glanced at her watch and grimaced. 'And I'm due to meet your chief suspect and his wife at their home in just under an hour, which doesn't give us anything like the time we're going to need to chat right now. So shall we say my place tomorrow at a time that suits you?'

'Ten o'clock?' Natalie suggested.

'Great. You have the address?'

'I do.'

'I'll make sure the coffee's hot and hospitality warm. I can't promise Graeme will be there, but best to meet him on a more social occasion.'

After she'd gone Natalie turned back to Gould, not sure what to say, but feeling she should make some comment.

'She's a wily one, as I'm sure you know,' he stated, 'but I have no doubt you'll find a way to make this work to your advantage.'

CHAPTER THIRTY-NINE

Annie was watching Andee's car inching through the gates, surrounded by protesters and press, everyone wanting to know who she was, or if their quarry might be in the car. None of them ever entered the property; maybe knowing it was full of guns was a deterrent, although David's licence had been revoked the day he was charged. Such strange things the authorities did, as if losing a firearm licence would deter someone from using one of the hundred or more weapons they had in their keeping if they wanted to. Surely it would have made more sense to confiscate the lot, but what did she know?

So far the press had caught no sightings of David, mostly because the only time he'd left the house was to go to the Byre, and he was able to circle round through the woods and across the stands to get there without being seen. Annie did the same, but someone's long lens, had managed to capture her and Sienna at the weekend, keeping their heads down as they got into the Defender. One of the following day's headlines over the blurred image had been 'The Torture of a Killer's Family'.

Apparently the local paper had begun adopting a slightly softer approach since Andee had come on board – she was good friends with the editor and owners, so had cautioned them to row back from the Take Him Down stand many of the tabloids were splashing over their front pages. Even so, they remained fully supportive of the Justice for Karen movement, as did Annie in her way, for she was every bit as keen for answers as the Lomaxes, although she realised they could bring disaster in their wake. Maybe this limbo was a better place to be than the worst-case scenario of David being sent to prison for life.

'Hi,' Andee said, coming in the door and taking off her coat. 'How are you?'

Wryly, Annie said, 'You probably don't want an answer to that. What are they saying out there?'

Andee shrugged. 'Just the usual, nothing to get worked up about – although I see an anti-blood sports group has set up their own little side-show since I was last here.'

Annie swallowed her dismay and frustration; there was nothing she could do with these negative emotions, they just brought her down or wound her up, and in the grand scheme of things a few people who objected to game shooting were hardly an issue to focus on now.

'Are you still coming and going via the farm?' Andee asked as Annie passed her a coffee.

'More or less, but they've worked it out so there's press over there too. That has David and me shut up here, or at the Byre, and Quin gets down on the floor when my parents drive him through. We told him to do that because his preferred course was to give them a rude sign and I don't think that's going to do anyone any favours.'

Andee smiled. 'There's an eight-year-old for you. How are the other two?'

'Upset on several counts: we cancelled our skiing holiday

at the weekend, probably necessary given what's going on in Northern Italy, but David's afraid he's going to be arrested again so he wouldn't be able to go anyway, and the children won't go without him. Same with Snowdrop Valley yesterday. We take a drive over there every year, it's always been special for us, but someone was sure to have recognized him and people can say the most terrible things even with children around.' Sighing, she added, 'After all the disappointment and tensions of the weekend I thought Max and Sienna might be relieved when my parents took them back to school, but they wanted to stay with their father, which makes me think they're afraid he might not be here for much longer.'

Catching the tremor in her voice, Andee put a hand on her arm. 'You're lucky to have such supportive kids,' she said. 'Being the ages they are – the two older ones – they could be kicking off badly by now, and that's something you really don't need.'

With her fingers tightly crossed, Annie said, 'They're being great, but I think they've got it into their heads that if they don't act up everything will be all right.' She sighed shakily. 'If only it could be so straightforward, so easy to resolve.'

Andee said, 'One day at a time, remember?'

Annie smiled. 'One day at a time,' she repeated.

'Now, has there been any news?'

'Some, but I'll let David tell you. He's in the snug Googling hypnotists, in the hope of finding someone who can help him to remember more details of what happened that night at the farmhouse.'

To Annie's surprise Andee didn't dismiss it, simply said, 'Whatever works,' and though Annie guessed she knew there was no conjuring memories from alcohol-induced amnesia, she appreciated her not saying so. In truth, she'd wondered if David was doing this to try and convince her that he was serious about wanting to fill in the missing spaces – if there even were missing spaces – but she hadn't said that to him. And nor did she like the way she was doubting him, suspecting his online searches were about more than he was saying. Wasn't a wife who loved her husband as much as she did supposed to believe in him come what may?

Anyone can tell you anything, but you have no way of knowing if it's the truth.

She couldn't recall who'd said that, maybe it was something she'd read, or made up herself as she'd tried to find her way through this.

'Darling,' she said, going into the snug.

He looked up, and seeing Andee he set aside the laptop the police had returned following his release and got to his feet. 'Hi,' he said, shaking Andee's hand. 'Sorry we haven't met before now. I think Annie explained . . . '

'That you were waiting to hear from a military judge, yes she did. And have you?'

'I had a call,' he said, gesturing for Andee to sit down. 'I don't know who it was, the number was withheld and he didn't give his name, he just reminded me of my oath of allegiance.'

Annie turned to Andee expecting her to look shocked, or even slightly outraged, which was how she'd felt when David had told her about the call, but Andee was hard to read. She simply said, 'Well, that was subtle. Anything else?'

'I was directed to the line "I . . . will observe and obey all orders . . . "'

'I see, so someone thinks there's a risk you won't?'

'It looks that way.'

'Are they right?'

As his eyes dropped to his clenched hands Annie could feel the tension and conflict building to a peak inside him, and wished with all her heart that he'd just let go and speak. What harm could it do? How could it cause him to be in any worse a position than he was already in?

Andee said, 'Do you suppose the caller knows about your current circumstances?'

'I'd be surprised if he didn't. He'll just be a mouthpiece, of course. Someone carrying out orders.'

'So, it seems they've worked out that you could use your state of mind at the time of Karen's death as part of your defence? Should it come to trial.'

'Why else would they deliver a reminder of my oath?'

Andee appeared to be thinking hard about that, but Annie could see that she too was finding it difficult to know how to press ahead. In the end, putting it aside for the moment, she said, 'Do you really think you might have killed Karen?'

Annie tensed as she watched David seem to retreat from the question, to put up barriers, and she felt sure he wouldn't answer, but after a while he said, 'If I did it wouldn't have been deliberate.' He stopped, and with a jolt Annie realized that he was far more focused on her now than he was on Andee, and the look in his eyes was unnerving her. Finally, he said, 'We all know I had sex with Karen Lomax. I can't tell you how it came about, or how she died, but the truth is I think I do remember her being at the farmhouse.'

Annie stared at him, trying to tell herself she hadn't heard right.

'At the time I thought it was you,' he told her. 'I was drunk, hardly conscious even . . . I've got no memory of what happened, but in the morning, when I woke up, I remember thinking you must already have got up because you weren't in the bed. I guess I crashed out again, because the next thing I knew my mother was shouting at me . . . Then you rang from London, meaning you couldn't have been there in the night, so I swear to God I thought I must have dreamt it, or hallucinated or something.'

'Why on earth haven't you told us this before?' she cried in frustration.

'I would have if the others had said she was there, but no one did, so I told myself it must have been a dream.'

'Is there a chance you could have been drugged that night?' Andee asked.

Shaking his head, he said, 'It was never our thing. None of us were into it, but we know alcohol has a very bad effect on me and I drank a lot that day.'

'OK, so what we're saying now is that you might have a memory of Karen Lomax being there. Do you know how she got there?'

He shook his head. 'I'm sorry, I'd give anything to be able to remember everything as it happened, but I couldn't then, and I sure as hell can't now.'

'What do you think?' Annie asked when she and Andee were alone in the kitchen.

'I'm going to need some time to work it through,' Andee replied, 'so let's keep it to ourselves for now. The mystery phone call is intriguing me. Someone in the MOD is clearly nervous about him revealing details of something they don't want in the public domain.'

Annie said quietly, 'He was involved in an operation that, to quote him, "went horribly, catastrophically wrong".'

Andee's eyebrows rose with interest. 'Which they've kept covered up, and now if he talks about it to explain why he was the way he was after he left, they're threatening to . . . What? Do you know?'

Annie shook her head.

Slipping her tablet back into her bag Andee said, 'Keep trying to get him to talk, and in the meantime, ask yourself this: If David *didn't* kill Karen, and frankly I'm not convinced that he did, then who else could it have been, and why would they have done it?'

David lifted his head from his hands as Annie came back into the room. He looked exhausted, drained of all understanding and rationale. 'I swear, I never meant to cheat on you,' he said, 'and I swear I have no real memory of it . . . '

'Leave that for now,' she said, going to sit with him, 'it was a long time ago and we have so many bigger issues to deal with.'

'I know, I know,' he sighed. 'And it's surely only a matter of time before the police manage to come up with something more definitive, a way of making sure the charge sticks. And if they do that, my only defence will be diminished responsibility.'

She was about to respond when he said, 'You know, to hell with the consequences, I need to start putting you and the children first, not some oath I swore over twenty-five years ago that could end up costing us everything now.' He turned to look at her. 'Maybe it won't. I don't know, it's what they said, that if I talked . . . '

'Do it, please,' she begged, 'for me, for the children, for us.'

He nodded. 'It's a terrible story,' he warned, 'and it'll put images into your head that you'll never be able to get rid of. Are you sure you want that?'

Holding his gaze, she said, 'What I really want is for there to be no more secrets between us.'

CHAPTER FORTY

It was bang on ten when Natalie parked outside Andee's elegant Georgian home in Kesterly's Garden District and was almost hurled across the pavement by a vicious gust of wind.

'Come in, come in,' Andee urged as she opened the door. 'Coffee's on, but Graeme's already gone, I'm afraid. He had an early meeting in Bristol.'

'Wow!' Natalie murmured as she followed her old friend across a blissfully warm hall to the kitchen, 'I heard you were into interior design these days, so I guess it follows that this place is quite something.'

Andee smiled and took her coat. 'I've set us up at the table by the window,' she said. 'Not much to look at in the garden at this time of year, not much of a garden actually, but there's plenty of light. How do you take your coffee?'

'Straight up black,' Natalie replied, and wandering over to the small round table that fitted neatly into its nook of cushioned seats, she put her phone next to her tablet as she sat down.

'Pastries are just out of the oven,' Andee told her, 'help yourself.'

Selecting a tasty looking Danish, Natalie was about to ask how long Andee had been in the house when Andee said, 'So, how's it going with Gould? He's a kind of Marmite guy, don't you think?'

Natalie's eyes narrowed slightly. 'He's . . . interesting,' she replied, and immediately wished she hadn't, for she saw right away that Andee had read into that one neutral observation everything Natalie would have preferred her not to know. At least not yet.

'Don't worry,' Andee told her, 'your secret's safe with me.'

Had it been anyone else Natalie would have slapped them down with a few choice words, as it was Andee she simply laughed and took charge of the coffee.

Coming to the point of their meeting, Andee said, 'Thanks for sending the pathology and toxicology reports. I read through them last night.'

'And did they tell you anything you don't already know?'

'Not really. The blow that caused the pyramidal skull fracture could have been deliberate, as in someone hit her with a blunt instrument, or an accident. Maybe she fell and banged her head on something.'

Natalie said, 'Dead is dead, and let's not forget that the body was dumped in an old railway hut. Why even move it if it was an accident?'

'Good question.' Andee scrolled through her tablet and stopped at a photo of the fatal injury, staring at it so hard that Natalie began to wonder, worriedly, if she was seeing something she'd missed. Andee made no comment, simply scrolled again and this time when she stopped she turned the tablet for Natalie to see what it was. A screenshot of David Crayce's prepared statement.

'Ah yes, a man of few words,' Natalie commented drily.

Andee smiled and putting aside her tablet, she said, 'I'm going to be really frank with you now, Nat. I don't want you to hate me for it, but is it possible . . . '

'I know what you're going to say and the answer is no, I do not have it in for David Crayce because he has a similar history to my ex. There, have I got it right?'

Andee smiled sheepishly. 'You know I had to ask.'

'Of course, no offence taken. And if it helps you to believe I'm not solely fixated on David Crayce then I don't mind telling you that I think there's a good chance the father and brother were involved.'

Andee's eyes widened with interest. 'How so?'

Natalie smiled. 'I'm sure you can come up with your own theories on that.'

Andee nodded, but in a way that made Natalie feel faintly disadvantaged, even uncomfortable.

'There's something you're not telling me,' she accused.

Andee laughed. 'And of course there's plenty you're not telling me, but that's OK. There's still some way to go with this, and I know we both want the right result even if we have different opinions of what that should be.'

'The right result will be naming the killer – or killers.'

'Agreed.'

'And I know you're not going to share any information that might be damning for your client.'

'Would you expect me to?'

'No, but please don't lose sight of that girl's parents and their right to the truth.'

'I never would,' Andee assured her. 'I just don't want to see someone going to prison for a crime they didn't commit.'

'Meaning you don't think David Crayce did it?'

'Meaning I don't think it's as straightforward as any

of us would like it to be. He wasn't in a good frame of mind back then, we know that, we also know that no one can tell you who picked Karen Lomax up from the bus stop or where they took her.'

'It could have been David Crayce who picked her up, and maybe he took her to the building site that's now his home?'

Andee sighed, and Natalie understood why, for if she was right about that it would mean Annabelle Crayce and her children were living on a murder site.

'As I said,' Andee smiled, 'there's still some way to go, but I will share something with you. Karen Lomax was not taken to Hanley Combe that night by David Crayce.'

Natalie stared at her, too startled for a moment to respond. 'Are you going to tell me how you know that?' she challenged.

'No, but if there comes a time when I can I promise I will.' As her phone rang they both glanced at it, and Natalie wasn't surprised when Andee excused herself to go and speak to Annie Crayce in another room.

She wasn't gone long, but apparently something had come up that meant she had to go out.

'It's been really good to see you, Nat,' she said, as they left the house together, 'and please let's do it again, socially, I mean.'

'You can count on it,' Natalie assured her.

Half an hour later Natalie was back at the station saying to Leo, 'She was your boss once, wasn't she, Andee Lawrence?'

'That's right.'

'So you know how her mind works?'

He pulled a face. 'I'm not sure about that.'

'Work on it. Meanwhile, we are going right back to the beginning of this. We need to reread every statement, every transcript, every scientific report, every possible lead no matter where it ended up. Check everyone's alibi, double-check and check again. You know how it goes, good old-fashioned grunt work, and don't forget to keep thinking outside the box, because that's often where the best treasure is hiding. Take nothing for granted, or at face value. *We* – you and I, Leo – are going to find out who killed that girl, and the next time we make an arrest we'll have it sewn up so tight that not even Billy Big Bollocks will be able to squeeze his client out of it.' *Or Andee Lawrence,* she added silently to herself.

CHAPTER FORTY-ONE

'Julia,' Annie exclaimed in surprise as she came into the kitchen. 'I didn't know you were here.'

'Sorry, I – I wanted to talk to you when no one else was around. I saw David go over to the Byre . . . '

'What is it?' Annie asked, trying not to sound impatient. She was waiting for Andee to arrive; David had agreed to talk to her and right now it was all Annie wanted to think about, so if this turned out to be Julia worrying that Henry was going to leave her for Chrissie . . .

'I keep thinking,' Julia began, hesitantly, 'or remembering – you'll remember it too, I'm sure – about the time you told Geraldine that if David ever screwed up again you'd call off the wedding.'

Annie blinked in confusion.

'Then he did screw up a few weeks later and I – I'm afraid,' Julia said brokenly, 'that Henry or Dickie found Karen in David's room that night and because they knew about your threat they decided to make sure she could never tell.'

Annie stared at her, dumbfounded. If she'd just understood that correctly . . . But no, she couldn't have.

'I also keep wondering,' Julia whispered, 'if it actually might have been Chrissie who found her and she's who told Henry and Dickie what had happened. I'm not sure. I mean, I don't know, but I think she was involved.'

Annie's head started to spin. Henry and Dickie might have been involved in some way, but surely it was plain crazy to think that either of them would actually kill a girl because *she,* Annie, had threatened to walk out on David.

And as for Chrissie . . .

Chrissie's text about not telling the police any more than they knew flew into her mind.

'Please don't look at me like that,' Julia implored, squirming slightly. 'I'm just telling you . . . '

'Have you ever mentioned this to Henry?' Annie interrupted.

'God no! I wouldn't dare, and anyway I don't know if I'm right. It's just . . . I'm sorry, maybe we should forget I ever said it.'

Annie looked round as David came in the door.

'I should go,' Julia cried, jumping up and grabbing her phone. 'I'll see you later.'

As she left David said, 'Is she OK?'

Realizing she needed to think this through before she could repeat it, Annie said, 'Uh, yes, she's fine.'

'Good. Any sign of Andee yet?'

Seeing how tense he was, and anxious, her mind quickly returned to all that he'd been through, all that was still to come, and she went to put her arms around him. 'She's on her way,' she said softly. 'Should be here any minute.'

By the time Andee arrived David was in the sitting room, standing at the window staring across to the woods where Henry was at work with the groundsman, Eli Russell, clearing debris from last night's storm. Though his back was turned Annie knew very well how uptight he was, how difficult he was finding it to summon up the words he needed to tell his story again. Maybe the second time around would prove easier, although knowing what she did now that was hard to imagine.

Andee went to sit on one of the sofas, with no tablet or tape-recorder as David had requested, while Annie perched on the leather-topped fire-fender with her phone held in both hands.

Without turning around, David said, 'I'm going to get straight to what happened. No embellishments, no names, just the bare facts of what went down and why I requested and was granted an early discharge.' Cassie flumped at his feet, but for once he didn't seem to notice her, he was too bound up in what he was about to say. Annie wished she could spare him the pain of it, but he'd insisted he should be the one to tell Andee.

'It was my first tasking in what's now known as the 16 Air Assault Brigade,' he began tonelessly. 'We were HALOed in – parachuted in – thirty miles from a Central European border town, middle of winter, snow ice, freezing temperatures. There were six of us, our mission to locate and bring out four missing operatives from another unit. Intel reports had it they'd been captured by the MUP – Serb Secret Police – and were being held at a location either in, or close to this border town.

'We stashed our gear, changed into Serb military kit and trekked the thirty miles to town, passing burned out villages and shattered, displaced people along the way, every one of them going into a state of panic as soon as they saw us. It was our first look at how terrified they were of the Serbs. When we got to our destination trying to engage with the locals – what was left of them – was a challenge when we were dressed as we were, and didn't have the language. But there were some braver souls among them, one who agreed to act as a translator, and that's when we found out that a serious ethnic cleansing programme was underway.

'Later, after we were there, when 1 PARA went in on an official mission . . . ' He took a breath. 'You might remember seeing the dozens of mass graves on the news, and torture chambers that were so beyond sick I don't even know what to call them. We saw it all, and collections of porn that were so barbaric in nature that evil can't begin to describe it. It was like going into a version of hell that no normal human being could ever survive, or properly recover from.

'The place was swarming with traffickers, many of them MUP, others from . . . God knows where they were from, some ex-military, mercenaries, civilians . . . It was lawless and terrifying and we were already seriously doubting our targets were still on this side of the pearly gates. We didn't even think that our own chances of getting out of there were good.

'It was through our terp – interpreter – that we learned about the police HQ where people were taken to be questioned and were never seen again. Almost everyone who had a daughter had either sent them into hiding, or had already had them snatched. Some were pregnant by Serbs, another form of ethnic cleansing. Young boys were taken too, either to be shot, or trafficked through a local government building that had been turned into a brothel.

'This diabolical hellhole was where we found one of our quarry, not as a prisoner, but a deserter. He didn't know where the others were – I don't know if anyone ever found them. All I can tell you is this guy didn't care. He'd joined the other side and during the time we were there one of our number went over too. You might think that shocking, given how tightknit we had to be as a unit, depending on each other for our very lives, but he'd always been unpredictable, volatile, too ready for action . . . DOB we used to call him behind his back, Devoid of Brain. None of us thought he'd get through selection. He wanted to kill very badly and very brutally if he could. We all knew that about him, and tried never to get on the wrong side of him.

'His defection meant that any cover we had was blown. It was time to retreat and fast, but on our way out of town we were ambushed and two of us were captured. We were driven by armed militia to the brothel. I was sure we were going to die a horrible death . . . I still think that was the plan, but it turned out they wanted some sport first. The soldier with me was stripped, beaten senseless and thrown back out into the snow. I was taken down to the basement . . . The smell of putrefying flesh made me gag and that made them laugh. The strangest thing was they hadn't searched me. They'd hardly even roughed me up yet, but they were drunk, and this was their turf, and they had AK47s, so what did they care?

'At first I thought no one else was around. The place was quiet, at least in the basement it was, upstairs there were all kinds of sounds that didn't leave much to the imagination about what was going on and none of it was good. In the dim light I could see wire mattress beds with leather straps attached and assumed I was destined for one of them, but then I heard a scream from somewhere deeper in the basement and I was shoved towards it. We got to an open cell where a naked girl of about fourteen had been strapped to an iron bed. She was already badly beaten, her face was swollen, her body covered in welts . . . There was so much blood between her thighs she could have been haemorrhaging, then I saw the gun next to her and realized how it had been used.' He took a moment, swallowed and pressed on. 'There were two men in the cell with her, one was our very own rogue, clearly enjoying his new role as much as the fact that I'd been captured. He offered me a bottle of slivovitz – a kind of brandy – to help get me in the mood, he said. I declined and a pistol was jammed against my head. Better to drink than to die, so I reached for the bottle, but the game had already moved on. They were eager for me to rape the girl, to get a taste of what I was missing.' He took another breath and pressed his fingers to his eyes as though to blot out the horrific images he was conjuring. 'The trigger was cocked, and I was certain I was about to die . . . They were laughing . . . I was never in any doubt that they meant to shoot me whether I did it or not. I knew I couldn't. I was incapable . . . They thought this was hilarious, and hit me over the head with the butt of the pistol so I was on my knees. Then Radcliffe – the codename we'd given our DOB – suddenly grabbed the gun and put it to the girl's head. He told me to do it or he'd shoot her. He was grinning up at me like he was truly enjoying the moment. Do it, he kept shouting at me. Do it, motherfucker. Then with no warning at all, and still looking at me, he blew out her brains.'

Annie's heart contracted as she felt the same terrible shock she had the first time she'd heard it. She could see that it had affected Andee too, but neither of them spoke, simply waited for David to continue.

'I completely lost it,' he said. 'No plan, no thinking, I just threw myself at him, got him round the throat and I wasn't letting go until I was sure he was never going to breathe again. I don't know why no one shot me, I only know it took three of them to drag me off. I was shoved towards the door; everyone was shouting, waving their arms, getting seriously worked up, but I had no idea what they were saying. Radcliffe was clutching his throat, trying to tell me I was going to die. He kicked the girl like she was a pile of rubbish. I reached in for my Browning, aimed it straight at his head and shot him dead.'

When he stopped Annie wanted to go to him, to try and ease the ordeal of having to relive this hideous episode of his life twice in as many days, but like Andee she simply waited quietly until he was ready to go on.

'The rest of the patrol had arrived,' he said. 'That's what all the shouting was about. They burst in as I fired, neutralized the other three before any of them could even raise a weapon, and then we got the hell out of there.

'A few days later we were back at base being debriefed. It went on, weeks of interrogation about what we'd seen, who was involved, and how it had ended. It was intelligence that would go right up to the PM, and later be shared with NATO commanders before the Kosovo Intervention.

'Radcliffe's family were told he'd been killed on active duty during a highly sensitive mission, so avoiding having to say where he'd been, and the rest of us were instructed to take leave before returning to base to await further orders. I knew I'd had enough, that I wasn't cut out for this, that I didn't even want to stay in the army, so I requested an early discharge and after a lot of discussion behind closed doors and up and down the chain of command it was granted, on condition I never spoke about what had happened. If I did they'd have no alternative but to convene a court martial for murder.'

His eyes went to Andee, bleak and anguished and yet even faintly ironic. 'So, there you have it,' he said. 'Not an edifying tale, no winners or losers, just another covert operation that went wrong in that hideous conflict where the atrocities committed have to go down as some of the worst in history.'

A silence followed as all he'd told them lurked like ghosts in the shadows.

In the end, Andee spoke in a clear voice as though to break the lingering spell. 'And you think,' she said, 'that this horrendous experience is responsible for tipping you over the edge one night when you were drunk, to the point where you became so confused you killed an innocent girl?'

His expression was stony as he said, 'I don't know what I was capable of back then. The nightmares, they were so mixed up, one minute I was throttling the girl, the next someone was blowing my brains out . . . Sometimes, in my head, I was even attacking my mother. I was a lot more messed up by what I'd seen, by what I'd done, than I think you realize, than I think I knew myself. Experiences, events can get twisted up in your mind, and if . . . ' He let the sentence hang.

'Do you recall having nightmares the night Karen died?' Andee asked.

He shook his head. 'I hardly recall anything,' he reminded her.

'Well, we can't deny the fact that you had sex with her, but as for killing her . . . If she died in that room, and we don't actually know that she did, I'm going to say it's most likely to have been an accident. She fell and hit her head . . . Do you have any memory of someone coming into your room, of anything else happening?'

Again he shook his head. 'I don't even remember the sex, but as we know that doesn't mean it didn't happen.'

'No.' Andee sat with that for a moment, until David said, 'You understand, if you're going to use my mental state as a defence, the threat of a court martial for murder hasn't gone away. I killed that man, and I meant to. I don't even have any regrets, but I don't want to serve a life sentence for it.'

'Yes, I do understand,' Andee assured him, 'but the army would have a lot of explaining to do for not acting on the case when they should have and I'm sure they won't want that out there in the public domain. But I'm not yet seeing a reason for it to go any further than this room. Where Karen Lomax is concerned there is no proof of murder, only the much stronger possibility of accidental death. So what we need to ask ourselves next is who brought Karen to the farmhouse, to your room, and who took her away later?'

Annie immediately opened up her phone, her hands starting to tremble. 'I have a text here that you need to see,' she said. 'It came a while ago and I forgot about it, but . . . Here it is. I've already shown it to David. It's from Chrissie Slater.'

Andee read the message.

So sorry for what David's going through. I promise I didn't tell them any more than they already knew. Call if you need to chat or just fancy getting out.

She looked up at Annie. '"Any more than they already knew?" What does that mean?'

'I've no idea,' Annie replied.

'Same,' David said when Andee looked at him.

Passing the phone back, Andee took out her own. 'Can you send that to me please, together with Chrissie's number?'

After doing so, Annie said, 'There's something else. I haven't told David this yet, there hasn't been time, but Julia was here earlier . . . ' As she recounted the conversation, aware of how wrong and yet horribly plausible it sounded, her eyes were mostly on David. Even before she'd finished he was shaking his head.

'That's crazy,' he declared. 'My father and Henry! Because you said you'd leave me if I messed up again? No, sorry. They'd have known we could sort things out . . . For Christ's sake, why would Julia think that?'

'Maybe,' Andee said, 'she doesn't have it entirely right, but it's perfectly possible they know more than they're admitting to. After all, someone brought Karen to the farmhouse, and if it wasn't you, it was quite probably the same someone who got her out again. So, here's a suggestion? Your father had nothing to do with it, but maybe your brother and Chrissie Slater did?'

David was still unwilling to accept this. 'Henry wouldn't have killed her,' he protested, 'and why would he bring her to the farm?'

'I don't know the answer to that,' Andee replied, 'but there seems to be a good chance that Chrissie Slater might.'

For some time after Andee had gone David and Annie sat together talking through everything that had been said, and what it could mean for them as a family, even as individuals, until David finally asked the question she'd known was coming.

'Do you really think Henry might have . . . ? That Julia could be right about him, even if she isn't about Dad?'

Knowing how devastating it would be for him to believe such a thing of his brother, she said, 'No, I don't think he killed her. He wouldn't. He might be difficult at times and tetchy, but he doesn't have it in him to end someone's life, especially for something as ridiculous as me threatening to break off our relationship. I honestly don't think Julia believes it either, she's just trying to get to the truth the same way we are.'

'By accusing her own husband of murder?'

'Try to imagine how hard it was for her to do that.'

Casting her a look he said, 'Yes, very hard when she thinks he's cheating on her. Maybe this is some sort of payback.'

'Oh, come on, you know she's not like that. No, what I think is more likely is that Karen fell and hit her head on one of the bedposts, or the fireplace, maybe the windowsill, and when Henry came in to get you up in the morning he saw her lying there, panicked, decided he had to get her out of there before you woke up, but he couldn't do it alone.'

'So he got Chrissie to help him?' As his eyes closed she knew exactly what he was thinking, because she was thinking it too, even picturing it. Henry and Chrissie driving fifteen miles to a deserted railway hut where they'd abandoned a young girl's body, in order to try and protect a brother who was still suffering the destabilizing effects of a horrific mission.

'Even if we're right,' David said, 'and God knows I hope we're not, it still doesn't explain why she was at the farmhouse, or how she got there.'

CHAPTER FORTY-TWO

Natalie and Leo Johnson were at their desks in the incident room when Natalie's mobile rang. Seeing it was Andee she braced herself for she-knew-not-what and clicked on. 'Hello, my friend,' she said wryly, 'what can I do for you?'

'I think it's more what I can do for you,' Andee replied. 'Can you meet me at Christina Slater's on the moor?'

'Why?' Natalie asked warily.

'I'm about to forward you a text. Call me from the car when you're on your way and we'll discuss.'

Moments later the text arrived, and as Natalie read it she felt her pulses quicken. 'OK, seems your old boss is prepared to share more than I'd expected,' she commented to Leo, and forwarded the message for him to log. 'I'll need Ms Slater's address to put in the satnav.'

Calling it up he sent it to her phone, then checked to make sure it was taking her on the easiest rather than fastest route. 'You're good to go,' he told her. 'I'll ask for details when you get back.'

By the time Natalie reached the top of Porlock Hill she and Andee had discussed what they most expected to come from the visit to Chrissie Slater's, and since it was likely to be further questioning at the station, or possibly even an arrest, Natalie now understood why Andee had called her.

Spotting Andee's Mercedes in a lay-by just past an ancient AA box, she slowed down, as arranged, for Andee to lead the way to the isolated property. It was probably no more than a mile away, but felt like three with all the twists and turns and unmarked junctions; Natalie just knew that in spite of the GPS she'd have got lost trying to find it on her own.

Chrissie Slater was already at the door when they drew up outside her ivy-covered home, and since Andee had explained who she was when she'd called to set up the meeting, there was no need for prolonged introductions on that front. However, seeing Natalie getting out of her car clearly threw Ms Slater quite badly: to a point that it looked for one minute as if she was going to refuse to let her in.

Natalie smiled warmly. 'Sorry to spring this on you,' she said, 'but I'm sure you won't mind if we have a little chat.'

'No, of course not,' Chrissie assured her, recovering quickly. 'It was just a surprise to see you.' To Andee she said, 'You didn't mention it when you rang. I thought you were working for David's lawyer?'

'I am,' Andee confirmed, and with no explanation for why she'd invited Natalie to join them she stood aside for Natalie to go in ahead of her.

Natalie took the place in as they went through to a large, cosy room with an oak beam ceiling and welcoming hearth, and made herself comfortable on a chintz sofa while Chrissie fetched a tea tray from the kitchen. Since she was gone only minutes it was clear she'd brewed a pot in advance and had simply added another mug to those she'd already set out.

As she poured and offered biscuits, Natalie took her through the statement she'd given two weeks ago at the station, making everything seem quite relaxed, just dotting a few i's, crossing a few t's – until finally she scrolled to the text behind the reason for their visit.

Passing the phone over she watched colour seep into Chrissie's face, a hot, mottled flush that spread down over her neck and into the collar of her pink linen shirt as she read her own message.

When she failed to look up, Natalie said, 'What does it mean, exactly, Mrs Slater, you didn't tell us any more than we already knew?'

Sweat began beading on Chrissie's upper lip and tears were shining in her lustrous eyes as they flicked between Andee and Natalie. She looked as trapped as if they were physically pinning her to a corner. 'I guess Annie showed you this,' she said.

Since there was no reason either to confirm or deny it, Natalie simply waited for her to go on.

'I knew as soon as I sent it,' she said, 'that I shouldn't have, but there's no way to get your messages back.'

Natalie was still waiting for her question to be answered, but in the end it was Andee who broke the silence. 'What more do you know, Chrissie?' she pressed gently. A different technique to Natalie's, but, whatever worked was OK by her.

Chrissie took a tissue from her sleeve and dabbed her eyes. 'It's quite simple really,' she said. 'I got up in the early hours, on the night . . . You know, when we were all at the farmhouse. I needed the bathroom, and when I was on my way back to bed I saw someone at the end of the hall. It was dark, I wasn't sure who it was . . . I thought maybe she needed the bathroom too, but then she opened the door to David's room and I got a glimpse of her before she went inside.'

Natalie was staring at her hard. 'So, who did you see?' she prompted.

Chrissie shook her head.

'Was it Karen Lomax?'

'No, I . . . ' Her eyes went first to Andee, then to Natalie. Looking as bemused and upset as she clearly felt, she said, 'It was Annie. Annie Crayce.'

Andee and Natalie were back in the lay-by close to the top of Porlock Hill, where Andee had just jumped into Natalie's passenger seat and quickly slammed the door behind her to shut out the wind.

'Well, I have to admit I didn't see that coming,' Natalie commented, gazing through a line of winter-bare trees to the roiling sea beyond.

'Do you believe her?' Andee asked.

'Do you?'

'I don't know. I'll need to speak to Annie. She was supposed to be at a baby shower that weekend, right?'

Natalie nodded, and connecting to Leo, said, 'Have you double-checked . . . '

'I've just sent you an attachment,' he interrupted hastily. 'You need to see it.'

'Is it about Annabelle Crayce?'

'No, why?'

'I'll come back to it,' and opening the attachment she blinked in shock as she realized what she was looking at.

Apparently today was a day that kept on giving, for she hadn't seen this coming either.

Deciding it was too early to share the new information with Andee, she said to Leo, 'OK, good work. I'm on my way back. Meantime I want you to double-check Annabelle's Crayce's alibi for that weekend.' Ringing off, she said to Andee, 'Thanks for bringing me in on this with Christina Slater. I realize it hasn't gone quite the way you expected it to, but you know I'm going to need to speak to Annie Crayce.'

'Of course. Do you want to go there now?'

Impressed by the offer, given the very different light now being cast on David Crayce and his wife, Natalie mulled it over, weighing it with the new information from Leo and her lack of trust in Christina Slater's eyesight. Deciding Annie Crayce was less of a priority, she said, 'You go, and maybe after you've spoken to them you'll bring them both to the station?'

'That will depend on what they say, but you already know that. Am I allowed to ask what Leo just sent you?'

'I'm afraid not, but I accept I owe you so I'll try to get back to you by the end of the day.'

CHAPTER FORTY-THREE

Annie's eyes were ablaze with angry shock. 'Chrissie said she saw *me*?' she cried, reeling from what Andee had just thrown at her, what Chrissie had claimed. 'You've got to believe me, I was in London that night.'

'Actually, I do,' Andee responded, 'but you won't be surprised to hear that the police are double-checking your alibi.'

'Let them. I have nothing to hide. I was at a baby shower with Laura. The friend who . . . '

'Honestly, I'm not doubting it,' Andee assured her, 'so let's move on to the bigger question, which is: what is Chrissie Slater hoping to gain by saying it was you she saw, if she knows it wasn't?'

Annie turned to David as if he might have the answer, but he simply shook his head, clearly also at a loss. 'We've got no way of knowing if she saw anyone at all,' he pointed out, 'but given that we're fairly certain Karen was there, I'm asking myself, was that who she saw?'

'And mistook her for me?' Annie said, dubiously.

Andee said, 'Karen was blonde, as are you, and it was dark.'

'Even so, I was nearly ten years older, and a lot taller.'

Annie's mind was racing now, running into all sorts of possibilities and obstacles. 'Chrissie would have had time to talk to Henry before you got to her house,' she mused. 'But it hardly makes sense for them to try and implicate me when they have to *know* I wasn't there.'

Andee was looking at David as she said, 'I need to ask if you've talked to your father about any of this?'

Before David could answer, Annie said, 'We don't want to upset him. After he had that turn at the police station we're worried the stress will bring on something worse.'

In spite of appearing to understand, Andee said, 'I'm afraid you'll have to talk to him at some point, or the police will get there first, and the doubts that have come up about him and Henry might be easier coming from you.'

David gave a scoff of laughter. 'How is it ever going to be easy to hear that we think he might have been involved in covering up, or even causing a death?' He shook his head decisively. 'I for one don't believe Dad had anything to do with it. I'm not ready to believe it of Henry either, but I'm slightly more willing to go along with him covering up a death than causing one.'

'They were so drunk that night,' Annie added, 'if Karen had a fall and hit her head . . . They'd have panicked when they realized she was dead, so instead of reporting it, as they should have done, or at the very least waking up David, they decided to hide her. It might have seemed like the right thing to do at the time, and only after, once it was too late, did they realize what a monumental mistake they'd made.'

Andee didn't argue, simply said, 'I'm afraid whatever happened and whoever was involved in getting Karen out of the farmhouse, it still doesn't tell us how she got there.'

Annie and David looked at one another. She could see he was still no more able to answer that than she was. In the end, she said, more to Andee than to him, 'Do you think Chrissie might have brought her there?'

'Either her, or Henry,' Andee replied. 'But why? If it weren't for David's DNA being identified I'd be thinking that the accident, if that's what it was, happened in Henry's room. Indeed, it might have, there's nothing to place her in David's room, or anywhere else in the farmhouse come to that, and there certainly won't be after all this time.'

'Are you saying you think Henry might have . . . But it was David's DNA?'

'What I'm saying is I think we need to wait for the police to contact you. Something's going on with them and I got the impression it's pretty significant.'

Feeling a jolt of nerves go through her, Annie said, 'Is there any way of finding out what it is?'

'I doubt it. I have some good contacts in CID but at this stage of an investigation they're not likely to give me anything that might jeopardize things, unless they decide there's something to be gained from passing it on to you. If that turns out to be the case I'll get in touch right away.'

After she'd gone Annie went to the fridge and took out two beers. 'I'm starting to feel scared,' she admitted, handing a bottle to David. 'If Henry and Chrissie are behind it . . . '

Getting to his feet, he said, 'We can't tie ourselves up in knots trying to work it out. Let's do something productive, like looking at the state the business is in and what can be done about it.'

'Are you serious?' she asked, in spite of knowing he

was. Maybe he was right, they needed the distraction, and with the future so uncertain they really ought to get things into some sort of order to help her and whoever was left running the place with her to decide on a way forward.

CHAPTER FORTY-FOUR

Although certain Leo's fact checking was sound, Natalie was barely through the door of the incident room before she said, 'You're absolutely sure this alibi doesn't check out?'

'One hundred percent,' he confirmed.

'OK, we need three search warrants, the farmhouse . . .'

His eyebrows shot up. 'After all this time? What are you expecting to find?'

'No idea until we look, but I think the info you sent me gives us very good grounds to pull every one of those places apart, which we'd have done sooner if there had been a single chance of a magistrate signing off on it.'

'Right, but I'll have to put something down.'

'OK, go with the Nokia phone that was never found, and wasn't there also a handbag?'

'They won't still be there . . . '

'Just do it. And remember, we need the element of surprise in this, so if your old boss calls . . . ' She thought about that. 'If she calls, direct her to me.'

Still looking worried, he said, 'Is it a good idea to spring it on the old man? We don't want him keeling on us . . .'

'We'll do the farmhouse first, and get one of the family to be with him if we need to move on to his place after.

Now, I'm off to talk to Gould about extra manpower to help with the search.'

It was close to ten the following morning when Natalie, Leo, Gould and four uniformed officers drew up outside the farmhouse in three separate vehicles. Had it been possible to pull a bigger team together they'd have gone into the properties simultaneously in the hope of preventing word of the search from spreading across the moor, but Natalie was OK with starting here. At least Noah Shields was at Chrissie Slater's staging a little follow-up chat, so he'd know if anyone got in touch with her, and as for Dickie Crayce's cottage, she was going to worry about that when, if, she had to.

Sitting beside Gould in the passenger seat of his BMW she watched Leo and the uniforms trying to establish if anyone was at home. It seemed strange to be seeing the place for the first time when it had been the focus of so much speculation and attention, although it wasn't too different to how she'd imagined it. Perhaps it was a little more rambling, with three separate roofs all at different levels, and a good many windows of varying sizes and opacity. In the greyish hues of morning sunlight and nestled in the bowl of a wide, low valley of fields and scrubland it had its appeal, provided all the old farm paraphernalia and rusting barns were overlooked – however she accepted some people went for that sort of thing.

There didn't seem to be anyone at home, for no doors or windows were opening in response to Leo's and the others' calls and knocks. Even the adjacent stables looked deserted, although the surrounding land was apparently home to a few dozen horses and donkeys – residents, presumably of Julia Crayce's sanctuary. Nice of her to take them in, and Natalie was sure they appreciated it, but she couldn't imagine wanting to live up here herself, two legs or four.

'So, where's your ex these days?' Gould suddenly enquired.

Thrown way more than her expression showed, she thought, *Where the hell did that come from?* And: *Of all the times to ask*. 'Not so far away, as it happens,' she replied, still watching the activity around the farmhouse. 'Dartmoor.'

'Oh. As in . . . ?'

'Yep. Didn't you know that?'

'No. What got him there?'

'Armed robbery that went wrong. A security guard lost his life.'

He inhaled deeply, sounding as though he might be regretting having started this.

'He was a decent bloke when I first met him,' she said. 'If the Troubles, Iraq, the whole bloody hell of it all hadn't driven him to drugs and booze, he might still be.'

'Are you still in touch?'

'No. That part of my life is behind me,' and seeing Leo on his way over she got out of the car.

'There might be someone in the stables,' she pointed out as he reached her.

'I'll send one of the lads. The back door is unlocked so we can go in that way.'

'OK, I'll be right behind you.' Slipping back into the passenger seat she appraised Gould of what was about to happen and added, 'Care to join us?'

'Thanks, but I've got calls to make, but before you go, tell me exactly what you're expecting to find?'

'You mean apart from the missing phone and handbag?'

His eyebrows rose.

'Probably nothing,' she admitted, 'but once they find out we're here, it might rattle the family enough to get us to where we need to be.'

He glanced at her, she smiled and leaving the car again she went off to start a careful, but extremely thorough search of the farmhouse. This might include bringing up floorboards or knocking plaster off walls, or sticking hands up chimneys, but at this stage there was no knowing what it might entail.

It was just after midday when one of the search team shouted from an upstairs room that he'd found something. Astonished, and certain it was going to turn out to be nothing, she hurried along a dim hallway and met the young officer as he reached the foot of the stairs. Leo was moments behind him.

'What is it?' Leo demanded.

Natalie, already in gloves, was checking it over, holding it up to the light and pressing it carefully.

'It was in here,' the uniform told her, presenting a small case as if he were some sort of magician.

Natalie glanced at it and then at Leo.

'Could it be Karen's?' Leo asked, nodding towards the Nokia phone Natalie was inspecting.

'There's no way of telling until we get it charged up, but remember they were popular back then, so it could belong to any one of the family.'

'It'll still be interesting to find out what's on it.'

'More interesting,' the uniform told them, 'is this,' and pulling a small book out of the case he handed it over opened to the page he wanted the DS to read.

Natalie did so, and as her heart rate accelerated she

instructed Leo to contact Noah Shields right away with a very specific directive, and leaving the uniforms to put everything into evidence bags she returned to Gould in the car.

After detailing the discoveries, she took a moment, as though catching her breath, and looked back to the farmhouse, still taking in the unexpected turn of the day. It was too easy, she was thinking, had happened too quickly, and yet it *had* happened. 'I never imagined,' she said. 'When we got here this morning . . . I thought we'd be here all day and still have nothing.'

'Well, look on the bright side, at least you don't have to turn the old man's place over now.'

She shook her head slowly, glad of it, yet still not quite able to process where they were and how they'd got here. 'It's like it was waiting for us,' she stated, almost to herself, 'as if someone knew . . . Maybe not knew, but . . . Why didn't we see it before? It was there, staring us right in the face and we didn't see it.'

Dryly, he said, 'Wood and trees come to mind.'

She threw him a glance. Should she tell him how much faster they'd have solved this if one of the detectives had done their job properly, or remind him that it would have been wrapped up twenty years ago if it had been handled as it should have been then? Maybe not right now, she had other things to think about, not the least of which was the text she'd just received from Andee Lawrence.

Any news? FYI I don't believe what Chrissie Slater said about Annie Crayce being at the farmhouse. Both Crayces willing to come in when you're ready. Can we talk?

Showing the text to Gould, she said, 'If it were anyone else I wouldn't call. As it's her . . . What do you think?'

He didn't take much time to mull it over. 'Do you know where she is right now?'

Natalie shook her head.

'Well, just in case she's at Hanley Combe, if I were you I'd pretend not to have seen the message until later on today.'

Pleased that he agreed with her instinct, she got to work tracking down everyone's whereabouts, while he summoned the necessary backup to assist them from here – always remembering that this was a shooting family.

CHAPTER FORTY-FIVE

Annie was sitting at the circular table in the middle of the Byre with the other directors of the shooting school – David, Dickie, Henry, Julia and Hans. This wasn't the usual location for a board meeting, but, with no clients or customers coming and going thanks to the demonstrators still grouped at the gates, they'd relocated from the banqueting room to be close to the fire.

Though Annie felt decidedly uncomfortable with the way they were making a show of carrying on as if Karen's murder had been solved and they had no more to worry about, she was going with it, because to resist wouldn't have felt right either. After all, she and David couldn't go on fixating on what sort of game Henry was playing with Chrissie Slater, or if he was playing one at all. Maybe Chrissie had acted alone, although the logistics of it all surely meant that Henry must have been with her.

The agenda for today had been drawn up by David last night and emailed to everyone first thing, so that anyone who wanted to add a point of discussion could do so before the meeting began. Annie and Julia had raised the need for an increased marketing spend due to the recent downturn, while Henry had suggested bringing in a PR firm to help rebuild the company image when the time was right.

He appeared so relaxed, so unaffected by the position he was in, seemingly unaware of how far the suspicion had swung towards him and Chrissie.

Hearing a car pulling up outside, Annie looked at the others. Not one car, but several by the sound of it. Everyone was frowning in puzzlement; the shop was closed and any visitors who turned up at the gates were greeted by Saul, their temporary security guard, who hadn't made contact to let them know he'd just let someone through.

Since there were no windows in the Byre facing the courtyard, Dickie got up to go and see who it was, and taking advantage of the impromptu break Julia popped over to the coffee machine to start up a fresh brew.

Annie's eyes were on David's as they waited for Dickie to come back, but she couldn't tell what he was thinking. She wasn't even sure what was going through her own mind, only that she was experiencing a horrible sense of foreboding, as if by calling this meeting to make everything seem normal, they'd tempted fate to shut them down completely.

'We're all in here,' Dickie was saying as he came back in the door, and Annie saw right away how pale he'd become. Then she realized who was following him in and her heart gave a sickening jolt, for she couldn't think why Andee would have brought DS Rundle with her.

'Annie, David,' Andee said. 'I just ran into DS Rundle at the gates.'

Annie looked at the detective, her mouth turning dry, her heart beating too fast, as David said, 'Has something happened?'

Rundle said, 'I wasn't expecting to meet you again so soon, Mr Crayce, but here we both are . . . '

'What's going on?' Annie demanded, putting a hand on David's.

Henry said, 'This is all looking very serious, Detective. How can we help you?'

'It's a good question,' Rundle replied. Instead of answering, her eyes searched the room, going from one to the other of them, and only came to a stop when they found Julia standing by the coffee machine, watching with wide, unblinking eyes. 'Mrs Crayce,' she said blandly.

Julia coloured, and tugged at her pearls as she said, 'Yes? Well, that's Annie as well, but . . . ' She broke off as Rundle started towards her and Annie watched, dumbfounded, as the detective said, 'Julia Crayce, I am arresting you for the murder of Karen Lomax. You do not . . . '

'What are you talking about?' Julia cried in a panic. 'I didn't kill her. Is this a joke? Henry, this isn't funny.'

Henry's face was ashen, uncomprehending, but he said nothing, didn't even move as Rundle finished reading Julia her rights and gestured for her to lead the way out.

'No, don't touch me,' Julia almost shrieked. 'You can't do this. I didn't do anything . . . '

'It'll be easier if you come quietly,' Rundle told her.

'I'm not going anywhere. You've made a mistake. Henry, tell her . . . '

Henry still didn't move, he hardly seemed to be breathing, as Rundle said, 'There are officers outside, Mrs Crayce, I can call them in to assist arrest, or you can come with me . . . '

'I told you, you've made a mistake,' Julia shouted, wrenching her arms from Rundle's attempt to grasp her.

'Why do you think I did it? Who told you? They're lying . . . Annie, tell them I didn't do it. You know I didn't.'

Torn between shock and confusion, Annie could only watch as Rundle spoke into her radio and a moment later two uniformed officers, both female, came to take over the arrest.

It was awful, surreal to watch Julia – *Julia?* – kicking and struggling, doing everything she could to stop them carrying her out of the Byre. No matter how hard she tried to resist them their hold on her was too firm for her to fight herself free even though she jammed her feet to the doorframe and writhed around like a child. Annie watched in disbelief as her precious pearls scattered all over the floor and Julia howled as if they'd broken her neck.

The sound of her screaming and begging continued, lessening in volume, until the doors of a vehicle outside were closed and she was driven away.

For long moments no one moved, simply stood in the aftermath of it all, until DS Rundle said to Henry, 'We obtained a warrant to search your house. You weren't there . . . If you want someone to escort you over there now . . . '

Annie was looking at Dickie, and afraid he might be about to pass out she rushed to catch him before he fell. David was faster, caught him and moved him to a chair.

'It's all right, Dad,' he soothed. 'You're OK. Take a breath. Someone get him some water,' he shouted.

Annie ran for it, brought it back and saw that Henry was on his knees next to his father.

'Is it your heart, Dad?' Henry urged. 'Can you speak? Oh God, is he having a stroke?'

'Move aside,' Rundle said firmly, and taking over she

began administering all the vital checks until Dickie murmured, 'I'm all right. I just . . . ' He coughed and signalled for another drink.

Annie cupped her hands around his as he sipped, trying to take in the madness of what was happening, the suddenness of it all – and how, after everything they'd been through, all the questioning, emotional turmoil, David's arrest, his time in prison, his reliving of nightmares that should have remained forgotten, this was what they'd come to.

While David went with Henry and DS Rundle to the farmhouse, leaving dear, long-suffering Hans who was probably going to leave tomorrow, to lock up the Byre, Annie and Andee took Dickie back to the main house. He was starting to recover from the initial shock of Julia being taken away, but Annie knew how grateful he'd be for some company and a brandy, so she didn't waste any time in pouring him one as Andee sat him down in the kitchen.

'You too?' she offered.

Andee shook her head. 'I'm driving. I just wanted to make sure you were OK before I left.'

'But you can't walk away after what just happened,' Annie protested. 'We're all still reeling. We need to know . . . ' She threw up her hands. She could hardly get her thoughts together, had no idea where to begin.

Andee said, 'I'm still not fully in the picture myself, so it might be best if we talk in the morning.' She nodded towards Dickie, who was looking pale again. 'You'll have even more questions by then, as will David and Henry, and with any luck I might have more answers. Right now, I need to call Helen Hall and Hugo Blum, because your sister-in-law is clearly going to need a lawyer.'

Feeling the shock of it shaking her again, Annie said, 'Yes, of course. Will you let us know if there's . . . I'm not sure . . . Oh God, I can't seem to think straight . . .'

'It's OK,' Andee soothed, 'you need some time. We'll speak later.'

After she'd gone Annie sat with Dickie, listening to the sound of him breathing, rhythmic and soft, making him seem less likely to collapse, although he was clearly still in a state of shock. She remembered how Julia had tried to pour suspicion on him, had wanted everyone to think he'd been helping David by hiding Karen's body, when all the time she'd apparently known exactly what had happened. Although Annie still had few details, DS Rundle had told them before she'd left for the farmhouse that they'd found Julia's diary from that time and shockingly, incredibly, Julia had not only written it all down, she'd actually kept it. Why? Who actually hung onto to something like that? What had she expected to do with it? Had she subconsciously wanted it all to come to light?

If she hadn't kept it Annie was afraid that the truth might never have been discovered, and that someone, most likely David, would have gone to prison for a crime Julia had *known* he didn't commit.

'I don't understand it,' Dickie said quietly. 'Why would she . . . ? It's not only the girl, Karen, though God knows that's the worst of it, it's what she allowed to happen to David. I thought she cared for him like a brother; she always looked up to him, seemed to think everything he did was special, better than anyone else could do. Henry too.'

Deciding not to tell him how Julia had tried to drag him and Henry into it by salting suspicions that had made a horrible sort of sense, Annie said, 'Someone needs to go and break it to her mother, if it hasn't already happened.'

Dickie nodded. 'We've known them for so long,' he murmured, 'since before Julia was born. Bob, her father, and I went to school together. I remember when Celine gave birth, such a cute little thing she was, and Bob doted on her. Then one day he left. He didn't even say anything to me, he just went, leaving Celine and that dear girl . . . We'd always been like family, all of us . . . She was the daughter me and Geraldine never had, our boys were the sons Celine didn't have . . . ' His bewildered eyes went to Annie. 'It's not making any sense. Why would she do something like this?'

Annie shook her head. 'I guess only she knows,' she replied. 'Unless it's in the diary. If it is, the police will also know by now.'

'Will they tell us?'

'I don't know, but it'll surely have to come out at some point.'

His eyes moved away distractedly; he was clearly still unable to take it in. After a while he said, 'Have you called your parents?'

'Yes, they're on their way to collect Max and Sienna to bring them home. It wouldn't be right to break something like this to them when they're at school. They'll have a lot of questions, same as the rest of us.'

With a sigh, Dickie put a shaky hand over hers. 'What'll matter most to them is that their father isn't going to prison.'

'Of course, but they're very fond of Julia.'

'As are we all.' Looking at Annie again, he said, 'Do you believe that David doesn't remember anything about that night? That those hours are mostly lost to him?'

She nodded. 'Yes, I do. How about you?'

'Yes, I believe him, but as we still don't know where, or exactly how the girl died . . . '

Understanding what he was trying to say she squeezed his hand, letting him know that her thoughts were the same as his, but for now they could only continue to wonder what had really happened to Karen that night.

CHAPTER FORTY-SIX

Natalie was in the custody area listening to what Helen Hall was telling her, and trying to figure out what the hell to do about it.

'I realize it's unusual,' Helen conceded, with an ironic tilt of her auburn eyebrows.

'*Unusual*!' Natalie echoed incredulously. 'More like unlawful.'

'Not unlawful,' Helen assured her, 'just a different way of getting to what you want. My client is adamant that she'll talk to no one but Annabelle Crayce. If you'll allow that, I believe you will receive a full confession.'

With an ironic tilt of her own eyebrows, Natalie said, 'The diary tells us pretty much everything we need to know.'

'Ah, but are you sure it's not the work of a fantasist?'

Knowing she should have seen that coming, Natalie gave an amused sigh. 'It isn't,' she replied confidently, 'but OK, if I can get the go ahead for Annie Crayce to be present your client can have her way, provided you and I are also there. Otherwise it'll be out of the question.'

'Thank you,' Helen smiled. 'I have a few calls to make, but I'll be just outside when you've got clearance to continue.'

As the lawyer left Natalie scrolled to Gould's number

and relayed Julia Crayce's request – or was it a demand? The damned woman was in custody, for God's sake, was quite possibly a murderer, and she was issuing orders like she was the one in charge.

'You're kidding me,' Gould retorted. 'She doesn't get to call the shots . . . '

'I've already been there, and believe me I agree with everything you're about to say, but now I've had a minute to consider it, I'd like to find out why it's so important for Annie Crayce to be there.'

'So why do you think it might be?'

'I've got no idea, but what's the harm in playing it her way?'

'Ask me that when it's over. What did you decide about searching her mother's place? That was the third warrant, right?'

'It was, but as that diary's pretty explicit on just about every count we have what we need, so there's no reason to go upsetting the occupants any more than we already have. Unless circumstances change, of course. Noah Shields went to see Karen's parents right after we found the diary.'

'Yes. How did they take it?'

'Would you believe, they think they might remember Julia popping into the wine bar in the early evening, but they can't be sure now if it was that actual day.'

'But it could have been when she arranged to meet Karen?'

'It's possible. She doesn't say so in her diary, but we might get some information from her old phone. If it is her phone. So, I'll tell Helen Hall she can bring in Annie Crayce?'

'OK, do it. I'll be watching the video feed. This is one I don't want to miss.'

CHAPTER FORTY-SEVEN

Annie wasn't entirely sure she'd just heard right; she was even on the brink of asking Helen Hall to repeat what she'd said. 'But why does she want me to be there?' she demanded, looking at David, who was watching her worriedly. Quickly she put the call onto speaker.

'All I can tell you,' Helen replied, 'is that she's refusing to talk to anyone but you. I've already explained to her that a detective will have to be present, and so will I for her sake, and she's agreed, but only on condition that you're there too.'

David said, 'Is this actually allowed?'

'I've had the go ahead,' Helen assured him. 'I should probably mention, by the way, that a mobile phone was also found with the diary. They thought it might have belonged to Karen, but apparently it's Julia's.'

'Is there anything on it?' he asked.

'I don't know. If there is, it might come out during the interrogation.'

'Have you found out yet what led them to think it was Julia in the first place?' Annie wanted to know.

'Ah yes, Andee got it from DS Rundle. Apparently it was as simple as her alibi not checking out.'

Annie frowned as she searched her memory. 'Wasn't she eventing that weekend? In Wiltshire?'

'There was some kind of equestrian competition going on, yes, the one she told the police she'd taken part in, but when a follow-up call was made to verify her claim it turned out she was not personally entered for any of the events.'

'So, it wasn't an alibi at all,' David said.

'Apparently not. The police should have been quicker on that, of course. I'm told the detective who made the first call has been spoken to about it. Anyway, the fact that there was a problem got them looking at the case from another perspective, which led to the search that turned up the diary. Now, is your brother with you, by any chance?'

'No, he's at the stables with our children,' Annie replied. 'They're doing all the things Julia normally does at this time of day.' Even saying those words disoriented her, pulled her into a place that felt strange and separate, somewhere that had nothing to do with them – as if the shock of their changed lives was making itself felt all over again.

'How is Henry?' Helen asked.

'Not good,' David replied. 'None of us slept last night.' They'd all stayed here, at Hanley Combe, her parents included, but in spite of talking most of the night they'd been unable to piece it all together, much less deal with the painful conflicts of emotions as they came and went, each rise seeming worse than the last.

'I'm sure it was a difficult night,' Helen sympathised. 'You'll need answers, all of you, so will you come to the station, Annie?'

Glancing at David, she said, 'Do I have a choice?'

'Of course, but it would be helpful to Julia if you agreed.'

Why would she want to help Julia? It was hard to imagine why Julia thought she could.

'You can say no,' David told her softly.

Realizing that though she might want to, her conscience wouldn't allow it, Annie said, 'What time do you want me there?'

'As soon as you can make it. Text when you arrive and I'll meet you in the front office.'

As Annie rang off David said, 'Are you sure?'

'No, but . . . ' She shook her head. 'I don't know what the but is, it's just I don't think I'd feel right if I turned her down.'

Regarding her tenderly, worriedly, he said, 'Do you want me to drive you?'

She was about to say yes when she remembered the children would want at least one of them to be here when they got back, probably him more than her given how insecure they still felt about him being taken away again. There were also the demonstrators at the gates to consider, whose numbers had again been swollen by press since word had gone out that the police had taken someone away from Hanley Combe late yesterday afternoon. Speculation was still rife as to who it was – all bets were on David – which told them that Julia must have hidden as she was driven through the crowd. Or perhaps she'd been in a vehicle with tinted windows or even no windows at all; Annie didn't know because they hadn't seen her go.

'You should stay here,' she said, stepping into his embrace and feeling it envelop her. 'I'll be fine. I'll call as soon as . . . I guess when I have some news.'

CHAPTER FORTY-EIGHT

An hour later, after being briefed about her role by Helen and DS Rundle, Annie was led into the interview room where Julia was already seated. A jolt of shock went through her to see how ravaged Julia looked, bloodshot eyes, tear-streaked cheeks, pale, bitten lips, hair mussed as if she'd been tearing at it through the night. As she looked up from the table where her cuffed hands were clutching each other tightly, Annie saw straightaway how fearful she was, and desperate. It was as if she were silently begging Annie to put an end to this, to make it all go away and take her home. Annie could hardly bear to look back at her, yet nor could she tear her eyes away. A part of her, the part that still lingered in their previous world, in good and happy times, wanted to go to her, to tidy her hair and straighten up the awful grey T-shirt she'd been made to wear – to give her some pearls and make her back into who she used to be.

'Annie, thanks for coming,' Julia said hoarsely. 'I knew you would.' Her voice was scratched and frail, seeming to come from someone else, not the lively, almost childlike woman she'd always been. *It had been a front, a charade to protect the stranger sitting here now about to be charged with the murder of an innocent girl who'd probably never harmed anyone in her tragically short life. What the hell had happened?* Annie wasn't even aware that Julia had known Karen Lomax, or not to the extent that she could have brought all this about.

She followed DS Rundle's direction to a chair facing Julia across the table. The detective sat next to her, which felt odd, wrong even, for it made it seem as if she were aligning herself with the opposing side and she wasn't sure she was ready for that yet. Helen Hall took her place beside Julia. While Rundle identified everyone present for the recording, Annie was staring at Julia's hands in their ungainly steel bracelets, shaky and thin – and so familiar with their neat, short nails and veiny backs it was almost dizzying. She looked at her face again and told herself this was *Julia* whom she'd known for more than twenty years. Julia, who'd been such a good friend and wonderful aunt, who'd loved them all and cocktailed them up at the end of the day. Julia who'd nursed Henry, married him, and become an actual part of the family instead of someone they'd always considered to be as good as.

DS Rundle began. 'Julia, you've requested that your sister-in-law, Annabelle Crayce, be present for this interview, so can you start by telling us why it's so important to have her here?'

Julia's bony fingers twisted around each other as, looking at Annie, she said, 'I need her to understand . . .' She stopped, and started again. 'I have to tell you what happened, why I did it.'

Wasn't that as good as a confession, on top of whatever was written in the diary? Did they really need more? Annie knew that she did: she wanted reasons, explanations, a way of understanding what had made Julia do this – how she'd spent the last weeks with them, seen what they were going through and had never spoken up.

'It was you,' Julia told her, causing Annie to tense with shock. 'You and David.' Her voice stumbled into a sob and Annie watched, dumbfounded, as Helen passed her a small pack of tissues.

'Can you explain that, Julia?' DS Rundle asked, not unkindly.

Julia's eyes were brimming with tears. 'They didn't realize, they didn't care,' she answered, staring at Annie as if Annie surely knew what she meant.

'What about?' Rundle prompted.

'They didn't *care*,' Julia cried, 'that forever, since I was a child, David and Henry meant everything to me. They were my *brothers*, they came to the stables to ride horses with me and took me to their parents' farm to help with the lambs. They knew I was shy, so they helped me to make friends with their friends. They taught me how to swim in the lake that's part of Hanley Combe now; how to climb trees and hunt for rabbits or squirrels or deer. They taught me how to shoot and I was a better shot than both of them, which made them laugh and feel proud of me. I was one of their family, I loved their parents, even more after Daddy left, they were so kind to me then, and caring. Mummy used to say I hope you end up marrying one of those boys, Julia, then Geraldine will have her daughter, and I'll have my son. I knew it was what she wanted more than anything. It was what I wanted too, with all my heart, to be a wife to David or Henry, but most of all to David. He was always the nicest to me, he made me feel important, funny, clever, like I mattered. He has that way with him, we all know that, but I knew I was special to him. He told me so; he said 'You're special, Julia,' and I know he meant it, because he kissed me after and it was a first kiss for both of us. He chose *me* for his first kiss.' Her eyes flashed as she threw this at Annie, and Annie could only wonder how old they'd been at the time, probably no more than early teens, and Julia had obviously remembered and treasured it in a way David apparently hadn't.

'So later,' Julia said wildly, 'when Henry met Laura and told me that he thought she was the one, I could bear it, even though I didn't want to share him with anyone. But I realized I couldn't have them both, and to marry David had always been mine and Mummy's dream. She deserved to have something come good for her, she was so unhappy after Daddy abandoned us, so I began making plans . . . I chose my dress; it was beautiful . . . You've seen it, it's the one I wore when I married Henry. I chose the church for the wedding. I thought we'd have the reception in a marquee at Crayce farm and David would surprise me for our honeymoon . . . I had everything worked out, and I couldn't wait to tell him when he came home on leave, but then he met you.'

Annie could only stare at her in disbelief and even pity, for how deluded she'd been, for how much heartache she'd caused herself with her thwarted adolescent dreams.

'I didn't mind so much about you at first,' she continued, lifting both hands in search of her missing pearls, 'you were just a girl he'd picked up in the pub. I thought he'd soon forget you and it would all be over, but it didn't happen that way. He went to London when he left the army to be with you, and then he brought you back to

Exmoor. Henry hadn't done that. He stayed in London when he married Laura. He didn't flaunt it in my face that he'd found someone else, but David . . . He behaved like I didn't exist anymore, or I just didn't count. And why would I? He had you and Hanley Combe and everyone loved you, treated you like they'd known you forever. All our friends became your friends, his parents thought of you as a daughter . . . I couldn't bear it. It's why I agreed to marry Roger, to try and get away, to prove it didn't matter, but it did. I thought about you all the time, wondered what you were doing; I hated not seeing any of you, even if it hurt when I did. So, I ended up leaving my stupid marriage and going back to Mummy's.

'But it was still the same. I don't know if you all meant to shut me out, but it's what happened. It was like I was no one – oh Julia, she'll be off with her horses, she won't want to come for a drink, or surfing or wherever you were all going. If you saw me you'd always ask, but even if I came I felt like the odd one out, the one who never really got the in-jokes, or had a proper place in your couples world. *You* were the nicest to me, but David . . . He was so cruel.' She struggled to catch her breath, pressed her fingers to her lips, as though to stop any more words spilling out, but they came anyway. 'I tried to make him understand that it ought to be me he was marrying, and he said I was crazy, it would be like marrying his sister and I had to stop kidding myself and get on with my life.'

Shocked by how Julia had seen herself back then, so insignificant and unwanted when that wasn't how Annie remembered it at all, she felt a stirring of guilt inside. She wondered if David had ever known just how devastated Julia had been when he'd rejected her, stopped noticing her even, but was sure he hadn't, for he wasn't deliberately cruel. It would have upset him greatly to know that someone who'd always meant so much to him was suffering because of the way he'd treated her.

'I think it was then,' Julia said, 'when he told me to get on with my life, that I first decided if I couldn't have the life *I* wanted then he couldn't either. I didn't know what I was going to do, how I was going to spoil things for him, but I made up my mind that I would. I'd lie in bed trying to think up ways, going over and over ideas while I was riding, and even when I was asleep because I'd dream about it. And then one day it was like everything fell into place without me doing anything at all. I didn't plan it, I couldn't have. It just . . . It was like a sign.' A single tear dropped onto her cheek .

'I was in the wine bar one Sunday afternoon,' she continued. 'I was waiting for Henry and Laura. I'd seen them earlier at the farm. They were down from London for the weekend, and when I asked if they'd like to meet for a drink they said yes, why not? We made the arrangements, but in the end only Henry turned up. Ryan, their little boy, got sick and Laura didn't want to leave him, not even with Geraldine. I didn't mind, I was more than happy to see Henry on my own. I was lonely after my marriage had broken up, I felt such a failure at everything, and I thought it would be nice to have him to talk to, the way we used to before . . . When it was mostly just us two, or three if David was there.'

Gently steering her back on track, Rundle said, 'What do you mean, everything fell into place?'

Julia sniffed, tossed her head and wiped her cheek with the back of a hand. 'It was while I was waiting, before

Henry came in, that I overheard Karen talking to her friends. You must remember what she was like,' she said to Annie. 'Pretty, but loud and raucous, they all were. They had reputations . . . and that day she was saying what she'd like to do with three men, all at the same time. It was outrageous, the kind of thing I'd never have been able to put into words myself, even if I thought it. I didn't realize at first she was talking about Dickie, David and Henry. When I did I was shocked. It made me want to slap her, to tell her to shut up, but of course I didn't. Henry was there by then; it was him coming in that told me who they were talking about, because someone said, "Oh my God, it's one of them," and there was Henry coming in the door. I wanted to leave right away, but he ordered a drink and so we had to stay until he'd finished it. They kept looking over at him and giggling, and he was kind of flirting with them, you know, smiling and raising his eyebrows, that sort of thing. We didn't speak to them at all, apart from to say cheerio when we left.'

She took a breath, and then another, as if trying to get herself to clear a hurdle before continuing.

'For the next few days I kept thinking about Karen and what she'd said about wanting to sleep with the three of them, and it made me remember what I'd heard you tell Geraldine at the time David was having his . . . problems. I thought it was terribly cold-hearted and unforgiving of you to say you'd call the wedding off if he ever messed up again, but I could tell you meant it, and if you did call it all off it would get you out of David's life.'

Annie's throat turned dry. Here was that same conversation, same excuse all over again, first to try and explain why Dickie and Henry would have tried to protect David, now to . . . To what? To absolve herself of whatever she'd ended up doing to Karen?

'It came to me how I might make you leave on the day that everyone got together for a drink in town,' Julia ran on, sounding vaguely detached now, as if she weren't responsible for any of it, simply part of a fateful whim, an onlooker even. 'I was out exercising one of Mummy's horses while she was eventing in Wiltshire when I saw their cars heading for town. I didn't know where they were going, only that they hadn't invited me . . . I was left out again and it upset me so much. You have no idea what that feels like, Annie, have you? None at all, because no one's ever turned their backs on you or pretended you weren't there. Life has always been wonderful for you, and *you* were always wonderful to me.'

Annie was dumbfounded. How could she even try and respond to such a bewildered accusation?

'I followed them as far as I could on horseback, but then they disappeared, so I rode back to the stables and took the car to go out looking for them. By the time I got to the wine bar it was after six. Someone said they'd gone up to the moor and Karen shouted out that was what she'd heard too. She brought me a drink, and I remembered what I'd overheard when I'd been there with Henry. I told her there was probably going to be a party after the pubs shut, and we'd all be really pleased if she came, but that we should keep it our secret because we couldn't invite all her friends as well. She was OK with that, said she understood, so we arranged that I'd pick her up at the bus stop on Old Moor Road around ten.'

Annie was almost physically recoiling now, wanting this to stop. That poor, unworldly girl, so trusting and excited and with no idea of what she was letting herself in for; she wondered if even Julia had fully understood it then. Surely she hadn't set out to kill her?

'I didn't really have a plan,' Julia said, 'I didn't know whether I could make anything happen or not, but in the end it was almost like it was meant to be. I took her to Mummy's first. The house was empty, Mummy and Aunt Ruth were overnighting in Wiltshire, so I said we should have a few drinks to get us in the mood. She definitely wanted to do that, she'd even brought a bottle of rum and a few cans of coke. She drank it all.

'I rang the farmhouse, I don't know what time it was, late, maybe twelve, but no one answered. I had no idea what was happening there, but I felt sure Dickie, David and Henry would be back by now, and it was probable that at least some of the others were with them. I thought if Karen and I just turned up saying we'd heard there was a party it would seem strange, especially for her to be with me, but I couldn't see them making a fuss. They'd probably be too drunk to anyway. Then I had another idea. I said that when we got there we should go in through the back door and straight to David's room, because it wouldn't be good for anyone to see us. The others, Henry and Dickie, would come in after, once they knew she was there. So, she put some more make-up on and I gave her the perfume you used back then, Annie, *Diorella*. She sprayed herself all over, even between her upper thighs. I'd never seen anyone do that before.'

So David, in his drunken state, had thought it was her, Annie realized, and though Julia couldn't have known in advance that she'd find him practically out cold, she'd apparently banked on him responding to a familiar scent.

'When we got to the farmhouse I went in first,' Julia said, still not seeming fully to connect with her words, 'through the back door. There were some lights on, but I couldn't hear any music or voices coming from the sitting room, or anywhere else. I told her David was probably waiting in his room and I led her upstairs. She staggered a lot and kept bumping into things and giggling, but I don't think anyone heard us. When we got to David's room I knocked and pushed the door open, just like he was expecting someone to come in. He was already in bed, and asleep by the look of him. I told her not to worry that I was sure she'd know the right way to wake him and when she did she should just do the things she thought he'd like most. Meanwhile I'd go and find Dickie and Henry.

'After I left the room I went to tuck myself into one of the window seats on the landing. I wasn't sure whether I should burst in on them at some point so he'd know I'd found them together, or should I just leave her there for someone else to find them in the morning, and go home. Then I realized if I left she'd end up telling everyone I'd brought her, and I couldn't let that happen. Then it struck me that whatever I did she was going to drag me into it. I couldn't think how I'd been so stupid as not to see it before. By then I could hear something happening in the room, so I put my hands over my ears. I didn't want to listen to him having sex, it seemed wrong.'

Annie felt as though the ground was shifting beneath her: everything about this was beyond any normal comprehension. What on earth were DS Rundle and Helen Hall thinking – surely they were finding it as crazy as she was.

'After a while, when things had gone quiet,' Julia continued, 'I crept back into the room, hoping David might have crashed out again, and he had. So had Karen. I woke her up and whispered that we should go. I helped her to dress, but when we got to the car she said she couldn't go home because her parents thought she was at her friend's for the night. I said it was all right, she could stay with me, but when we got back to Mummy's and I tried to make her swear she'd never tell anyone I'd taken her to the farmhouse she started shouting at me, saying I'd lied to her, that I was a pervert, a pimp . . . she called me so many names. I tried to calm her down, but I couldn't. She said she was going to tell everyone what I'd done, and that if she ended up pregnant she'd blame David. It was terrible. I didn't know what to do with her. Then she threw herself at me, like she really wanted to attack me. I pushed her away, not hard, it didn't seem hard, but she tipped backward over a chair and her head cracked against the Aga as she fell to the floor. It was awful, horrible. I was so scared. I couldn't believe what had happened. She just lay there, not moving. Blood started seeping out over the flagstones and her eyes were open like she could see me, but she wasn't looking at me.' She pushed her hands to her mouth as if to stifle a sob, as if she were still the young woman who'd found herself at the heart of the treacherous web she'd spun.

'I didn't know what to do,' she wailed. 'I tried to wake her up; I kept telling myself it would be all right, she would come round, but she didn't. I rang 999, but then I hung up. I realized I'd have to explain why she was with me, what she'd done and what I'd done. I knew everyone would hate me if they found out why I'd brought her to the farmhouse, that I'd have no friends, my life would be over, even Mummy might turn against me.' Her breath hiccupped as she gulped for air.

Helen Hall passed her a glass of water, and Annie watched it dribble down her chin as she drank. It was clear she was trapped in the midst of that ghastly scene, as were they all.

Gasping again, and speaking shakily, she said, 'I sat down at the table with my back to her, trying to think what to do, who I could tell. I thought about saying she'd broken in and I'd caught her and frightened her, and that was how she'd come to fall. I decided that was what I must do, I even picked up the phone again, but then I remembered they'd want to know how she got here – and worse than that, if she'd actually been with David they might find evidence of it when they examined her. Everyone would want to know then how she'd got to the farmhouse, who had invited her, and it was sure to come out eventually that no one had. Not even him.

'I had no idea if anyone had seen me pick her up at the bus stop, if she'd told her friends where she was going, or if anyone at the farmhouse had seen or heard us coming and going. As it turned out no one had, but I didn't know that when . . . when I decided to hide her. It was a chance I had to take, and in the end it was OK because no one ever even questioned me, or came looking for her anywhere around the moor.'

Long moments ticked by as she fell silent. It seemed she had no more to say, but there was still so much more they needed to know.

Finally, Natalie said quietly, 'You've written in your journal that you took her to the railway hut in a horsebox. Is that true?'

Julia's head fell forward as she said, 'I thought – we – I meant to bury her, I even made a little cross to put on her grave – not a big one that anyone would see, it was small enough that it would probably blow away in the wind, but it seemed only right to give her something before I left. But I'd forgotten to take a spade. So, I got her out of the horsebox and dragged her into the hut. I would have carried her, but she was too heavy . . . I didn't know what else to do. I knew she'd be found eventually. I didn't think it would take so long . . . I wanted to ring up and tell them where to look, but I was afraid they'd trace my call and ask how I knew. So, I just waited, dreading what would happen next, feeling certain they'd find out it was me, that I'd go to prison, everyone would hate me, but they never did.'

After another awful silence, Natalie said, 'Why did you write it all down, Julia? You must realize we might never have been able to prove your involvement if you hadn't?'

She shrugged awkwardly. 'It's what I do, keep a diary,' she said, eyes once again filled with tears, 'and I suppose it was a bit like a confession, or a way of making it real even though I didn't want it to be. I didn't want her to die, obviously, it was never my intention. If I could have brought her back, or made it so I'd never ever talked to her in my life, I would have, but I couldn't. So, it was like if I wrote it down it would kind of keep her alive. Once I'd done it I knew I had to throw it away, burn it, make sure no one ever saw it, but I couldn't make myself do it. It felt like I would be killing her all over again. I know that sounds strange, but it was as though the words I'd written were binding me to the truth, binding us together, and if I tried to destroy them she would come back to destroy me.'

Annie could only wonder what the others were thinking. How could she come to terms with what she was hearing.

Julia said, 'I didn't read my journal for years. Sometimes I could go for months and forget it was even there, but then Mummy told me, just before Christmas, that she wanted me to clear my old room for the decorators to come in. So, I packed up the journals along with everything else and took it all to the farmhouse.' Looking at Annie she said, 'The day you were in the attic searching for your diaries was the same day that I read my own for the first time since I'd written it. It was in my hand when I spoke to you on the phone, even though I told you I might have to go to Mummy's to find it.

'I tried to make myself destroy it then, but I still couldn't. I don't understand it; it's like it's stronger than me, won't let me do anything with it apart from reread it or keep it.' She gave a dry, sobbing laugh. 'I suppose it was my conscience stopping me, or some spiritual power working for Karen.'

Natalie said, 'The phone we found was yours. Can you tell me what happened to Karen's?'

Julia's head stayed down as she nodded. 'I threw it into the Nutscale reservoir with her handbag the day after she . . . she died. Hardly anyone ever goes there, so I thought it was the best place to hide them. If they were found no one would connect them to me, because there was no reason to.'

Deciding she'd heard enough, that she really didn't want to sit through any more, Annie got to her feet.

'Annie! Please! No!' Julia called after her. 'Don't leave me here. Annie!'

Closing the door behind her Annie stood against it,

tears half-blinding her as she listened to Julia still shouting for her, begging her to stay, while Helen and DS Rundle tried to calm her. But there was no going back, and there never would be, not for Julia, not for her and certainly not for Karen.

CHAPTER FORTY-NINE

As Annie made her way towards the custody officer's desk a voice said softly from behind her, 'Annie.'

Turning she found, to her relief, that it was Andee. 'I didn't realize you were here,' she said, collecting herself.

'I was watching the interview with DCI Gould. When I saw you leave I thought I'd come to see if you're OK.'

Grateful for it, Annie dried her tears with her fingers, still feeling disoriented, almost disconnected from herself. 'It's so . . . I can't . . . ' she stammered. She clasped her hands to her face, not sure how to continue. 'To do what she did to Karen . . . How could she? And to have lived with it all these years, to have let David go through what he did, to try to blame Dickie and Henry . . . I hate myself for even listening to her . . . '

'Please stop,' Andee interrupted gently.

'But the thoughts I've had about Henry . . . ' Not able to deal with them right now, she said, 'I need to call David.'

'Of course. But why don't I drive you home? You can come back for your car tomorrow.'

Accepting she was probably too upset and distracted to drive herself Annie dropped her keys back in her bag and let Andee lead the way outside.

'You know,' she said, as they headed down to the coast road, 'I'm not sure I'll ever be able to forgive her – not just for Karen, that's a given – but because of what this is going to do to her mother and aunt, and because I'm afraid she'd really have let David go to prison for life if the police hadn't discovered her alibi was false.' Groaning in despair, she let her head fall back against the seat. 'How am I going to face Henry?'

'You will, and he'll understand, if you want to tell him, that is. There's no reason to.'

'And what about Chrissie? I was convinced she had something to do with it.'

'We all were.'

Turning to look at Andee, she said, 'Why did she say she saw me?'

'Because,' Andee replied, 'I believe she thought she did. She also thought that keeping it to herself was helping you and David.'

Stunned all over again, Annie said, 'You mean she thought we'd done it together? For God's sake!'

'I haven't spoken to her myself,' Andee said, 'but a detective did yesterday, while the farmhouse was being searched. He got her to open up more.'

Still struggling with her conscience, Annie said, 'I've thought the most awful things about her and Henry . . .'

'It happens at times like this,' Andee told her gently. 'Everyone suspects everyone else, they don't know who to trust anymore, we even start to see those we love the most in another light.'

Realizing how distressingly true that was, Annie eventually made herself say, 'I particularly hate myself for the times I doubted David. Aren't you supposed to know when someone you love that much is being truthful or not?'

Wryly, Andee said, 'I'm not sure whether that would be a blessing or a curse.'

Taking the point, Annie allowed a small smile as she considered the pros and cons of it. In the end she said, 'Did I make this up, or did I hear it somewhere: "Anyone can say anything, but you have no way of knowing if it's the truth"?'

'I'm not sure I've heard it before,' Andee replied, 'but it's truer than almost anything I can think of.'

Annie's eyes closed as, for no apparent reason, the fog in her mind cleared, allowing through the memory of Julia speaking the words – Julia who'd known better than anyone how easy it was to pretend and to lie, with the sweetest of smiles on her face and the darkest of truths in her heart.

CHAPTER FIFTY

There were still press and protesters at the gates of Hanley Combe when Annie and Andee drove through, although far fewer since yesterday, and Annie could already see David waiting on the veranda, in full view of the cameras. Everyone knew he wasn't the killer now, nevertheless she was in no doubt that her homecoming was being captured for publication and transmission as part of the ongoing story.

As she got out of the car he came down the steps to meet her, and she all but melted against him. 'Are you OK?' he asked, clasping her shoulders and looking worriedly into her eyes.

'I'm fine,' she assured him. 'Still shell-shocked, but I think my head's starting to clear a bit now. How about you?'

'I'm good. Your parents are still here, and Dad and Henry arrived a few minutes ago.'

'Have you told them anything yet?'

'Everything you told me on the phone.' Since that amounted to just about all of it, Annie said, 'How's Henry?'

'Calm, but in truth, I'm not sure.' As Andee came around the car, he said, 'Thanks for bringing her home. Will you come in?'

'That's kind of you,' she replied, 'but I think I should

leave you together as a family.' After hugging Annie she added, 'You know where I am if you need me. Call any time.'

'Thanks,' Annie responded. 'For everything.'

With a fond smile Andee got back into her car and after she'd disappeared with a wave through the gates David and Annie walked hand in hand into the house.

Everyone was gathered around the kitchen table, each of them looking stunned and bewildered, even Quin appeared shattered. Annie's eyes found Henry's first, and as she tried to speak an onrush of tears drowned her words.

Coming to her, he wrapped her in his arms, and said softly into her hair, 'It's OK.'

'But you . . . '

'I know what she said and I don't blame you for what you thought. Anyone would have in the circumstances.'

She looked into his eyes and pressed her fingers to his mouth as she whispered a thank you. Then she turned to Dickie, who drew her into his own embrace.

'It's been a terrible time,' he said gruffly, 'for all of us. Let's just be thankful it's over, shall we?'

Knowing it was very far from that for all sorts of reasons, Annie simply hugged him, understanding his need at least to make a start on putting it behind them.

Next she turned to the children, who threw their arms around her, clinging tightly and all talking at once, until over their heads she asked Henry, 'Have you seen Celine yet?'

'I was there earlier,' he replied. 'Dad and I will go again later.'

'How is she?'

'Trying to be stoic, you know how she is. It's good she

has Ruth there, and Helen Hall has sent someone to help deal with the press, at least as far as statements are concerned.'

'Do you think David and I should go over?'

'Yes, when you're ready. She might find it difficult, all things considered, but I think it will mean a lot to her to know that you're not bearing a grudge.'

Surprised, Annie said, 'Why would we? It wasn't her fault.'

'No, of course not, but she's a mother, she'll no doubt feel responsible on some level the way most mothers do.'

Knowing that to be true, Annie said, 'I think it's important that we get through this together and make sure she and Ruth don't feel shut out.' Realizing this was where it had all begun, with Julia feeling left out, she felt a wrenching sadness and guilt in her heart. It was too late to repair that now, way too late, if they even knew how.

'I'd like to go and see Celine too,' Harriet said, 'when the time feels right. You'll let me know, won't you?'

'Of course,' Henry promised.

'Have you talked to Chrissie since the arrest?' Annie asked him.

'Only briefly. I know she wants to explain in person why she thought it was you she saw that night.'

Deciding she could wait to hear it, Annie leaned against David as he came to stand beside her and found herself looking at their beautiful daughter, whose ludicrous teddy bear escapade had started all this, or at least had brought it back into the light. To her surprise, just as she was about to speak, Sienna voiced her very thought.

'There are people we're forgetting,' she stated, looking around the room to include everyone. 'Karen's parents.

Can you imagine how they must be feeling now? It might have happened twenty years ago, but she was still their daughter, and their only child. I think we should find a way to reach out to them, don't you?'

Later, after Henry had driven himself and Dickie over to the Hare and Hounds – would they ever be able to think of it as anything else, and without hearing Julia's voice say it? – and Harriet and Francis had gone for a walk with the children, Annie passed David a cup of tea and said, 'We still haven't properly talked about what happened to you on that terrible mission.'

'I know,' he sighed, 'but now really wouldn't be the time. I'm just sorry you ever had to hear about it.'

'If I had known earlier it would have explained a lot, but I'll leave it there, for now, and I'm not going to wonder what they'd have done if you had been forced to use it as a defence. However, I will say this, I view the military quite differently now to the way I did before.'

'It's not perfect,' he conceded, 'far from it, but to be honest, I'm much more worried about Henry at the moment and how he's going to deal with things.'

Feeling the concern pulling at her too, she said, 'He already had quite a complicated relationship with Julia. Can there still be one when she's in prison? Will he even want there to be?'

'I don't know, but he cared for her, a lot. We all did, we always have, and I don't really know yet how much it's changed. And if I don't, how is it for him?' He sighed and rubbed a hand over his unshaven jaw. 'He told me not so long ago that it felt right to be with her and at the same time wholly wrong, because she was still like a sister. I think that's why he never properly settled into the marriage, or treated her as well as he could have and she probably knew the reasons but didn't want to let go. So, there was a lot of love there, but a crazy, mixed up kind that wasn't good for either of them.'

'And what about Chrissie? He doesn't seem to have a particularly straightforward relationship with her?'

'I know, but there's a better chance he could have one now that he doesn't have to feel so conflicted over Julia. That's if they both want it, of course.'

'Do you think they might not?'

'I don't know, with her marriage only recently breaking up and now all this . . . I guess they could be a comfort for one another. We'll have to wait and see.'

Annie's thoughts moved on, flitting through so much that it was hard to keep track of where they were going, until cupping her face in one hand, he said, 'Shall we post-pone any further discussion and go upstairs for a lie-down?'

Guessing that was probably all they'd be doing consid-ering how exhausted they both felt, she let him lead the way. For the next hour at least, she'd like to think no more about Julia but knew it would be impossible when everything she'd heard that morning was still echoing around in her head and churning her emotions. She realized she was already feeling the strangeness of Julia not being there, the emptiness of the space she'd left behind, the knowing that she wouldn't be coming back. In spite of everything she was going to miss her, and worry about her and how she was surviving in the kind of world that could hardly be more alien or terrifying to someone like her.

'I understand,' she said to David, as they lay quietly together, 'that being in prison is no more than she deserves, given what she did, but I'm finding it hard not to feel sorry for her.'

Pulling her closer, he said, 'Nothing's ever as black and white as we'd like it to be. Just because she did something wrong, very wrong, doesn't mean there wasn't a lot of good in her too.'

Knowing that there had been plenty, she said, 'Should we go to see her, or write to her, do you think?'

After giving it some thought, he said, 'Maybe in time, but it's not our priority right now.'

Knowing what was, she closed her eyes and decided the discussion about that could wait, would have to, since they had no idea yet how to handle it. It was simply something that had to be done, and soon.

CHAPTER FIFTY-ONE

Aside from the detested paperwork, Natalie had often found solving a case to be almost dispiriting, depleting even. The victory could feel pyrrhic, in spite of knowing that the right person had been brought to justice. Naturally, it was a joy when that person was a paedophile or psychopath, a lowlife drug pusher, domestic abuser, or human trafficker, but when it was someone like Julia Crayce the sense of achievement didn't register very high on the job satisfaction scale. Putting that mildly eccentric and nervy woman in prison was never going to bring Karen Lomax back, nor would it serve any useful purpose in Julia's life, although Natalie knew it wasn't about that so much as punishing her for what she'd done.

And punishment Julia Crayce surely deserved for the way she'd misled and used the girl, then abandoned her in a disused railway hut. Should she also be punished for her death? It was the question that kept niggling at Natalie along with: had it really been an accident, as Julia had described both verbally and in her diary? Or had she actually meant to kill Karen? There was no doubt Karen's death was more expedient for her than having the girl free to go about telling the world what had happened.

And the diary entries of the time were no actual proof of anything; they could as easily have been made up to mitigate the offence, should it ever be discovered, as they could have been a true record of events. It wasn't possible to know exactly when they'd been entered in spite of August 8th, 9th and 10th being written at the top of the pages. Those that followed dated from August 18th, so the crucial entries must have been made before that, but how was anyone ever to know if they had been an exercise in deception rather than an outpouring of shock and guilt? She wondered if Julia had hung onto the diaries not because she couldn't bring herself to throw them away, but so they could be used in the way they were now, should it ever be necessary. If so, that would make her cunning and manipulative to a point that would transform her from a slightly whacky posh bint into a cold-blooded killer.

Natalie had only to think of the way she'd tried to plant suspicion on her husband and father-in-law, and how she'd let David Crayce go to prison for something she'd known he hadn't done, to feel a little more convinced of the latter.

Whatever the truth, she guessed it was academic now, for Julia had already pleaded guilty to manslaughter, along with other offences relating to concealment of the body, prevention of burial and obstruction of justice. There was neither the manpower, nor will, nor budget to take the case any further.

Now, as she rode along in the back of a taxi on her way to Andee Lawrence's she was fully aware that Andee – having once been a detective herself – had a good understanding of the feelings of doubt and even despondency that could follow in the wake of a case. It was undoubtedly part of the reason she'd organized this dinner, as a kind of cheer up after the event. Natalie was truly grateful for that, while the other part of Andee's motive, another kind of altruism, was currently holding her in the fluttering grip of a teenage-style anticipation.

'OK, here we are,' the driver announced, coming to a stop outside the smart Georgian end-of-terrace residence.

After paying and shooting him a daggered look for his presumptive appreciation of her appearance, she smiled to herself and went to knock on the door. As she waited she held her head high, refusing to feel nervous, or worried about being late (she wasn't), but unable to stop the annoying waves of self-consciousness that seemed to be enjoying themselves immensely at her expense.

'Well, take a look at you,' Andee declared, her eyes widening with surprise and approval.

Natalie put her shoulders back in a showy way meant to cover her embarrassment, while hoping she looked sexy rather than tarty in the bright red bodycon dress she'd bought especially for this evening.

'You look a-maze-ing,' Andee told her.

As Natalie crossed the threshold she pursed her lips at the corners, in mock disbelief, but she couldn't have been more thrilled by the compliment. 'You're not looking so bad yourself,' she informed Andee, who, in her opinion, was never anything short of gorgeous.

With a laugh Andee closed the door and led the way through to her and Graeme's study. 'Just a little chat before we join the others,' she said, 'if that's OK with you?'

Happy to follow her, Natalie quipped, 'And would it be about another information share, by any chance?'

Andee twinkled guiltily. 'Kind of,' she admitted, 'but it's

not about Julia Crayce, at least not directly. There's a phone number I need from you.'

Natalie's eyebrows rose with interest, and when Andee told her who it was for and why, she said, 'I know you could have found it for yourself, so is this you seeking my approval?'

Andee didn't deny it. 'If you think it's the wrong thing to do, I'll be guided by you.'

'Well, I see no problem with it,' and taking out her phone Natalie messaged over the details.

After thanking her, Andee said, 'Now, before we go in, I was wondering how much Gould already knows about your past. Not that I'm intending to spill it out with the green beans, you understand . . . '

'He knows the dreaded ex is in Dartmoor and why. That's probably enough, don't you think? And please don't ask if I'm really over it, because I am, very, and I'd rather we weren't having this conversation. But since we are, I'm prepared to admit there were times I was in danger of letting my personal life get in the way of certain judgements where David Crayce was concerned. Do you think I should apologize to him?'

Wryly, Andee said, 'It's possible he's already seen more of you than he'd like to, so I wouldn't rush it, if I were you. I'm not even sure it's necessary. Have you been in touch with any of the family since Julia's arrest?'

'As a matter of fact, I had a call earlier today from Henry. He wants to know if there's anything we can do to help keep sightseers and vandals away from Julia's mother's property.'

'Oh dear, it's still happening, is it? So, is there anything you can do?'

'You know how short staffed we are, but I'm going to visit Celine Tulley tomorrow to have a chat. It's not fair that she should be made to suffer for something she had no hand in. Presuming, that is, she didn't know what happened at her home while she was in Wiltshire eventing during that fateful August weekend in 1999.' Natalie paused.

Regarding her closely, Andee said, 'That sounds as though you think she might have known.'

'If she did we'd never be able to prove it, but thanks to the miracle of modern science blood traces have been found on the flagstones in her kitchen that we're expecting to match Karen's. If they do I'm bound to ask myself if Mrs Tulley might have known a long time ago how they got there, if she even helped to clear up after the "accident".'

Andee's interest was clearly piqued.

Natalie said, 'Do you really think Julia disposed of the body on her own? Don't worry, this is off the record, I'm just interested to know your thoughts.'

'Well,' Andee responded carefully, 'I have to admit, it does seem unlikely, but if she had help wouldn't she and whoever it was have managed to bury the body?'

'Possibly, but not definitely.'

Andee's eyes narrowed with suspicion. 'There's more to this,' she stated knowingly.

Natalie smiled at having her mind read. 'We came across that diary with almost no trouble at all,' she said. 'Admittedly it was packed away in a sealed box with others in the back of a wardrobe in a guest room, but that's hardly a failsafe hiding spot, so I keep wondering if it was *put* there for us to find.'

Andee frowned. 'By Julia? She wouldn't have known you'd search the farmhouse.'

'No one would for certain, so you could say it was a way of tempting fate, to put it there. If we didn't search and she got away with it, she'd tell herself it was meant to be so she had no need to do any more and whoever went to prison deserved to be punished for the way they'd treated her. However, it's also the room her mother most likely uses if she stays over, and if she decided to smuggle a box containing the diary into the wardrobe, along with several similar boxes, it might save her from coming to us to tell what she knew about her daughter.'

Andee's eyes lit with surprise.

'And when you add to that some of the diary entries,' Natalie continued. 'Not that they're saying Mummy did anything specific, but there were lots of comments about how grateful she was to Mummy for her advice, and how she wouldn't be able to cope if it weren't for her. It was all written during the time of the search for Karen, and Julia, being as highly strung as she is, would no doubt have been in a terrible state, so she'd have needed advice and someone to lean on. Who better – and who could she trust more – than her own mother?'

Andee shook her head in disbelief and mounting dismay. 'I guess it could make sense,' she said. 'But if you're right . . .'

'I'm not going to try to prove it. It's just what I think.'

Andee was clearly still mulling it. 'I can see why, and with us both being mothers, I suppose we're aware of how far we'd go to protect our children.'

Wickedly, Natalie said, 'Don't tell me one of yours has offed someone and you've gone and stashed the stiff.'

Andee's eyebrows arched. 'Would I tell you if I had?

Anyway, I hear they found Karen's bag and phone in the reservoir.'

'And totally useless they were, but I guess it had to be dragged, just in case Julia changes her plea at some point and it wouldn't surprise me if she does. She's nothing if not unfathomable and unpredictable. Now, if it's all the same to you, I wouldn't mind a drink.'

'Of course,' and gesturing for Natalie to go ahead Andee pointed her to the sitting room, where voices could already be heard.

'So, the last time I was here,' Gould was saying to a very striking, neatly bearded man who Natalie presumed was Graeme, 'was when you and Andee . . . ' He stopped and Natalie heard Andee smother a snort of laughter at the way his eyes almost popped out at the vision of his normally much more soberly dressed DS coming into the room. 'W – well,' he stammered, 'you look . . . ' He searched frantically for the right word with everyone hanging on in rapt anticipation of what it might be. 'Different,' he said, and Andee groaned out loud.

'Oh Gould,' she chided. 'Can't you do better than that?'

'What?' he asked, seeming bemused, but still hardly able to take his eyes off Natalie.

'Hello, sir,' she said, 'you look . . . ' She searched the air as though she might catch her own right word and ended up with three. 'Just the same,' and everyone laughed, Gould the loudest and longest which made it even funnier.

Apparently thrilled they were off to such a good start, Andee introduced Graeme, and once all their flutes were filled with champagne they drank a toast to new friends and old. Only when Andee went to pick up a tray of hors d'oeuvres did Natalie spot her sending a quick text.

Although she guessed who the recipient was and expected nothing to be said about it, she felt pleased when a while later Andee showed her the reply.

Please thank DS Rundle. We've arranged to go on Monday. Annie and David xx

CHAPTER FIFTY-TWO

As David brought Annie's car to a stop outside a house on an estate they'd never visited before, he turned off the engine and sat quietly staring down the street of smart detached properties in their open plan squares of garden. There was no one around, it was the middle of a working day in suburbia, with only the rhythmic sound of the tide soughing over a pebbled beach in the near distance to accompany high flying jets gliding through a scurry of white cloud above.

Beside him, Annie was checking the texts she'd received during the drive here.

'From Max and Sienna?' he asked, when she passed her mobile over.

She nodded. 'They think we're doing the right thing and they're wishing us luck.'

After reading his children's words he said, 'Are you OK? Are you sure you want to do this?'

Surprised, she said, 'It's me who should be asking you that.'

His expression was solemn, strained as he said, 'I'm sure,' and turning to the back seat, he ruffled Cassie's head before lowering a window and getting out of the car.

Annie waited for him to join her on the pavement, then led the way along a perfectly straight path to a pillared front door wondering if anyone was watching from inside, or from another house nearby. Before she could reach for the shiny brass knocker a petite, fair-haired woman of around sixty opened the door, almost as if to prevent them from making a noise.

'Mrs Lomax,' Annie said, feeling awkward and afraid this wasn't going to go well, in spite of having been told when she'd rung that it was OK for them to come.

'Please call me Jess,' the woman said, and smiled in a way that allowed Annie to relax a little. 'It's so kind of you to call by. You didn't have to, I told you that on the phone, but we're ever so grateful. You must be David,' and reaching past Annie she shook his hand, seeming to feel nothing of the animus he and Annie had expected. 'Come in, Eddie's through here,' she said.

A slightly balding man with deep brown eyes and a tremulous smile came to the door of the sitting room to greet them. 'Mr and Mrs Crayce,' he said, 'It's very . . . '

'Please call us Annie and David,' David insisted, taking the man's hand to shake. 'As my wife said when she rang, we wanted to come and tell you in person how very sorry we are for all you've been through.'

'But it wasn't your fault,' Jess declared, ushering them into the room and directing them to a pale green linen sofa. 'You've got no need to be sorry.'

'He's offering condolences,' Eddie told her gently. 'Thank you, David and Annie, it's very thoughtful of you. I'll admit it's been a hard journey, and a long one. Karen was our everything, you know, I suppose that's how it is when you only have one, even if she was having a wild phase . . . ' He coloured slightly and Annie knew that David would be sharing the embarrassment. 'It doesn't mean we loved her any less,' Eddie continued, 'we just worried about her more, and now with all this bringing it back . . . '

'We knew she got up to things,' Jess confided, hands clasped tightly in her lap. 'When they were looking for her, during the time she was missing, people said some awful things about her, called her names, us too for being bad parents. Well, I suppose we were given what happened, but it was still . . . '

Coming in gently, Eddie said, 'Go and get the tea, babe. Or would you rather have coffee?' he asked Annie and David.

'Tea will be lovely, thank you,' Annie replied. 'Can I help?' she asked Jess.

'Oh no, don't worry, it's all done. I just got to pour on the hot water. You sit there, nice and comfy.'

After she'd gone Eddie smiled fleetingly at them both and returned his gaze to the door his wife had left through. 'It's been very hard for her,' he confided. 'Very hard. We never expected to have answers, we'd given up and then, out of the blue . . . We were in Cape Verde when they rang, but we came straight back. We'd never have been able to settle there knowing what was going on here, but there wasn't really anything we could do, except wait. And then, well, it was a big shock when the detective came the other day to tell us who it actually was. We're still having trouble taking it in; I expect you are too. Worse for you, I'm sure.' Without giving them a chance to respond, he went on, 'The police told us they found her handbag and phone in the reservoir. We asked if we could have them, but it was a silly idea. They'd been in the water so long, and what were we going to do with them? I told Jess, it's best to keep thinking about the good times, before it all happened, and there were lots of them, not only when she was young . . . Well, she was always that, but right up until we lost her, she was a lovely girl in all sorts of ways.'

'Here we are,' Jess announced, backing in through the door with a large tray of tea and cakes.

Going to take it, David set it down on the table and asked if he could pour.

The Lomaxes seemed touchingly pleased that he'd want to, and both asked for milk and sugar as if they were the guests.

Stirring his tea, Eddie said, 'I'm sorry they got it wrong about you, David, you know, when they arrested you. That couldn't have been easy.'

Before David could answer, Jess said, 'I've got to admit, when they told us they'd taken you in and then charged you it was the biggest shock for us. We never dreamt . . . I mean you and your friends, your family . . . I kept remembering your dear mother and thinking of how it would have been for her if she'd thought it was you, her son, who'd hurt our girl. But it didn't turn out to be true in the end, did it? Thank goodness. Yes, thank goodness.' Her hand was over her heart. 'The police have told us what happened that night, you know when Karen got taken to the farmhouse . . . How there was supposed to have been a party going on . . . She could be a silly girl at times, headstrong, you know, too full of herself really, but . . . she was young.'

'It wasn't her fault,' David said. 'Her only . . . '

Eddie continued. 'We always had a soft spot for your parents, you know, your mother in particular. Not that she came into the bar often, but she was a good person, you could tell that about her as soon as you met her. What I would call a no-nonsense sort of woman with a ready sense of humour. We sent a card when she passed, but I don't expect you remember it. It must have been a difficult time for you all, and I suppose it is again now, although in a different way, so I'd like to say how sorry we are for that too.'

Wondering how two people who'd suffered so much could be so understanding of other's pain, so generous of spirit and free of malice or need for revenge, Annie found herself struggling for the right thing to say.

'At least she's admitted to it,' Jess went on apparently not needing a response, 'so we've been spared going through a trial. I don't expect that makes it any easier for her mother, though, does it, or for any of you? Have you seen her since they arrested her?' She coloured and said, 'I'm sorry . . . '

'It's all right,' David reassured her. 'The answer is no we haven't seen her. Her mother and aunt have been, and my brother.'

'Her husband?'

He nodded.

Jess shook her head sadly. 'Poor man. I don't expect he ever imagined it was his wife who'd done it, any more than we did. She was always so . . . nice. Friendly . . . I remember her quite well, actually. Loved horses, didn't she? Used to wear pearls, or every time we saw her she did. It goes to show how deceiving appearances can be.'

'The important thing for me and Jess now,' Eddie continued, 'is that we have some closure. Believe me, we never thought we'd get it. We'd given up hope, hadn't we, doll?'

Jess nodded. 'And you coming here like this has helped a lot. It makes us feel like . . . Well, like we matter, that it's not all about Julia and what she did, the way the press would have it right now. You recognizing it's also about Karen means a great deal to us.'

'A great deal,' Eddie echoed. 'Not that we haven't been getting on with things,' he assured them. 'We've got the deli now, a couple of streets away, and we like living here in this house. We have some lovely neighbours, real salt of the earth types, but it was always hanging over us . . . Who did that to our girl? What sort of person could just dump her like that? Was it someone we knew?'

Caught unawares by the sudden silence, Annie tried to think what to say, but David was ahead of her.

'The part I played in what happened . . . '

'Oh, it's OK, the police told us all about it,' Jess came in quickly. 'We know it wasn't your fault . . . '

'But . . . '

'No, really, we're not blaming you. And we don't want to dwell on the bad things, or why she was there that night, if you don't mind.'

'No, of course not,' he said. 'I just want you to know how sorry I am.'

Eddie smiled, 'We appreciate that, David. That's very big of you. Thank you.'

Annie could hardly bear this; it might almost have been easier if they'd been angry, resentful, accusatory even, but they were so sweet, unassuming and sensitive to the feelings of a man who many wouldn't think even began to deserve it. Her voice shook slightly as she said, 'Our children have asked if they can host a little celebration of

Karen's life. They didn't know her, of course, but . . . ' She stopped as Jess suddenly broke into sobs.

'Oh, that's so kind of them,' Jess gasped, bringing a tissue from her sleeve. 'Fancy them offering to do something like that. I— I don't know what to say. Eddie, isn't that the loveliest thing you ever heard?'

Clearly overcome too, he said, 'It is. Please tell them how much their kindness means to us. We hadn't even thought of doing anything like it ourselves.'

David said, 'They're away at school during the week, but they come home on Friday evenings, so if you let us know what dates work for you . . . It'll be just us, me, Annie, our three children and you two.'

'And anyone else you'd like to invite,' Annie added.

Jess and Eddie looked at one another. 'Maybe it'll mean more if we keep it simple,' Jess suggested. 'We have your phone number now, so we'll call or text when we've made up our minds, if that's OK.'

As Annie and David drove back to Hanley Combe their hands were linked over the gear shift as they thought back on the past half an hour and how deeply moved they'd been by the Lomaxes obvious grief and humbling kindness. They were truly special people who seemed not to know the meaning of ill-will or vengeance, who were even prepared to call Julia by name when so many in their position wouldn't have been able to bring themselves to utter it. Annie was certain she'd be one of those people, for the mere thought of one of her children being treated the way Karen had and then abandoned to the elements would be enough to make her feel murderous, never mind bitter or vengeful.

'I hope,' she said, as they drove into Hanley Combe, 'they bring some photos of Karen when they come. It would be nice to see her through their eyes, don't you think?'

David nodded and brought her hand to his lips. 'Why don't you call and ask them?' he suggested. 'I think they'll like that. Sienna will too, given it was her idea to hold the celebration.'

As they pulled up next to the Defender, Quin came hurtling down the steps to his father, throwing himself in for a swing. David scooped him up and gave him such a bruising hug that Quin shouted, 'Surrender!'

Smiling as Cassie bounded from the car to join the fun, Annie wandered inside and went to hug her mother. 'I'm not sure people come much sweeter than the Lomaxes,' she said, putting down her bag and taking the cup of tea her mother was about to drink from.

'So it went well?' Harriet asked.

'It did, and the children's suggestion was very warmly received. They're going to let us know a date that'll work for them.'

Coming in through the door Quin was saying to David, 'Grandpa says I need a haircut, so when we go can I have a fade and taper like Max? That's what he's having when he comes home and I want to be first.'

With a laugh David ruffled his already tousled hair and said, 'We'll see about it tomorrow.'

'Cool. Can we go and do some shooting now? Uncle Henry's over there and he says I'm getting really good.'

'In a few minutes,' David replied.

'OK, I'll meet you there,' and after throwing himself at Cassie for another boisterous hug, he zoomed off across the lawns to find his latest long-suffering instructor, aka his Uncle Henry.

'Now we're alone,' Harriet said quietly, 'it might be a good time to give you this.' She took an envelope from her pocket and when Annie saw it was from the prison she almost told her mother to put it away again. 'It came just after you left,' Harriet told them. 'I can always throw it away, but I thought you should make the decision.'

Annie looked at David.

'It's addressed to you,' he said, 'so it has to be your call.'

'If I read it,' she said, 'then I want you to as well.'

He nodded agreement and went to take a beer from the fridge before they sat down at the table together.

Dear Annie,

I know you probably don't want to hear from me and I understand that, really I do, but I find I am talking to you all the time in my mind, so I thought I'd try writing some of it down and sending it to you. I hope that's OK.

Would you believe me if I told you that I'm truly sorry for all the upset I've caused? I hope so, because I am. I know it must be awful for all of you, especially Mummy and Aunt Ruth, and Henry seems to be finding it quite difficult too. I think he might actually have really cared for me, you know. I was never very sure of it, but at least he's been to see me and he's said that he might come again, he isn't sure yet. I asked him if he's going to divorce me, but apparently he has no plans to at this time, which surprised me in a good way. Maybe he'll wait for me, we'll see. I could be away for quite a long time, several years they say, so perhaps it's too much to ask. I expect it's more likely that he'll get together with Chrissie now I'm no longer there to stand in the way. Better not to think about how I'd feel if he does, there's already so much that upsets me terribly, best to take one day at a time, my lawyer says.

The lovely thing is, he's promised to keep the refuge going, even if it means bringing someone in to help run it. I've given him lots of suggestions, people I know he can trust, so hopefully one of them will work out.

I wonder if you're missing me at all, or do you just hate me now and feel glad I'm never going to walk through your door again? No more 'cocktail me up, sweetie,' and certainly not in here. It's going to be a very long time before I can have a glass of wine again. Will it make you laugh if I tell you that the thought of that has just made me cry?

There have been quite a lot of the old waterworks since I was brought to this place, but my cellmate, Daphne, doesn't like it much, so I try to keep them to myself and remind myself that it's all meant to be. If it weren't I suppose David would be in prison instead, and I know you really wouldn't want that. I've been thinking about writing to him to say I'm sorry. Do you think I should? Mummy says I probably ought to wait for things to settle down before I start bothering him, and Henry says it's a bit late for that, and of course he's right. Brutal, but right.

I would love it if you came to visit me some time. I realize you won't want to yet, and maybe not ever, but if you do ever fancy a little chin wag with me it would make me the happiest person alive. You're very special to me, Annie. I wish I'd realized that before I tried to break up your relationship with David all those years ago, but I didn't know then that I would come to love you a lot more than I ever loved him or Henry.

If I don't hear back from you I won't write again, because I don't want to pester you. Actually, I'm not sure I can promise that, because it's doing me some good to feel that I'm talking to you, so maybe you will hear from me again. It could be a long time, or it could be soon, I guess that depends on a lot of things that I can't foresee right now.

Please send my love to the children – if you're still saying my name – and to everyone else. Most of all I send love to you, Annie, my dear sister-in-law and best friend.

Julia

As she finished reading Annie turned to David, too thrown for the moment to know what she was thinking, much less feeling. His face was set, showing her that the letter hadn't impressed him very much.

'It's all about her,' he commented, passing the letter to Harriet, 'and what little remorse there is doesn't ring true. She says the words, but I don't think she's actually feeling them.'

Annie shook her head in dismay. 'She didn't mention Karen's name once,' she said sadly. 'I wonder if she even thinks about the Lomaxes and what this has done to them?'

David said, 'It's them she should be apologizing to, not me. If you do write back, maybe you could suggest it –

although on second thoughts, why should they have to bother with her? I'm sure they'd rather forget all about her, as if that were even remotely possible. Tell her to get some help with empathy and genuine regret, because both have clearly completely passed her by.' Tilting the bottle to his mouth he drank deeply and walked outside to the veranda, Cassie close on his heels.

Annie waited for her mother to finish reading the letter and said, 'What do you think?'

Harriet sighed. 'I agree with David, she's not expressing herself well, quite poorly in fact considering all the heartache she's caused. Maybe she hasn't fully engaged with it, she might not even be capable of understanding the depth of other people's feelings. I wouldn't have said that about her before, but I suppose I've never had any reason to consider it until now. Anyway, things are still raw, there hasn't been time for the shock to wear off, so any decisions about visits or writing should wait. Even Henry's not sure he's doing the right thing in going to see her, but he says not going doesn't feel right either. It's different for her mother, of course, and her aunt. I'm sure they'll always go, but I think you and David should put it out of your minds and come back to it when you're ready.'

Thinking that was good advice, Annie gave her a hug and followed David outside.

He'd lit the chiminea and was sitting on the swing seat gazing out at the far horizon, where the sun was starting to set over the stark swathes of moorland. Down at the lake sprigs of yellow daffodils were clustered around the base of the trees. Early tulips were coming into bud too, along with crocuses and violets. Annie looked up as a pheasant clucked and fluttered from a nearby hedge, and the sound of gunshot told her that Quin was blowing clay pigeons to bits over at the stands.

Going to sit with David on the swing seat, she linked an arm through his and rested her head on his shoulder. She could feel the strength of their bond as if it were physically wrapping around them, as if it were an actual part of the way he smelled, a mix of soap, gun smoke, and tangy fresh air. She could tell as he turned his face into her hair that he was inhaling the scent of her too. It was something they often did and yet hadn't in a while; it was good to feel it happening again.

'I guess you realize,' he said, 'that the fact I was ever a suspect in a murder is probably going to haunt us, and the children, for a long time to come?'

Afraid that was true, she said, 'We won't let it win. We're stronger than anything they can throw at us, and as long as we have each other and the rest of our family and friends we'll be able to face it.'

He kissed her head and rested his own against hers as they continued to gaze out at the slowly darkening sky, listening to gunshots and birdsong and the sound of Cassie's tail thudding on the deck as she chased rabbits in a dream.

Tugging her phone from her jeans as a text arrived, Annie said, 'It'll be Sienna, wanting to know how we got on today.' But it wasn't, it was from the Lomaxes, so she held it out for David to read too.

If it's all right with you can it be the Sunday after next? We were also wondering if David's dad would be able to come. I think his mum would like that.

With a laugh David pressed his fingers to his eyes.

Knowing the laugh was at himself for the tears, Annie moved in closer to him and felt the heat from the fire warming them both.

'I've had an idea,' she said, watching a sparrowhawk riding the thermals, 'after the celebration for Karen why don't we take the whole family away for a while? I think it would do us all some good to relax and recharge before we start again.'

Finishing his beer, he said, 'I could ask what about school, but if this virus that's dominating the news ends up finding its way here, and I think it will, it's possible we won't be able to go anywhere.'

As the sobering prospect of that settled in her mind she turned to gaze out at the moor, bleak and beautiful, mysterious and forever untameable. She pictured the valleys and peaks she knew well, the forests, streams, farms, pubs, hamlets and cliffs. It was magnificent and alive in so many ways that it was hardly possible to imagine them all.

Catching a movement in the corner of her eye, she looked down towards the lake and was surprised and pleased to see a stag taking a drink at the shore. In the twilight it seemed almost mystical, part of another world, its muscular bulk sleek and elegant and gleaming as if burnished in the dwindling hues of the day. She thought of the other stags she'd seen in recent weeks, as full-bodied and contained as this one, and wondered if they were one and the same. When this one turned around and seemed to meet her stare across the dampening lawns, unblinking and still, she decided to believe they were. She willed it to stay a while, to allow her to feel their connection, and it seemed in no hurry to leave.

From David's stillness she realized he was watching the beast too, and in this enchanted moment it was hard to imagine a virus wreaking havoc throughout the world, much less finding its way here to their beloved moor. If it did, it would be tomorrow's nightmare. For tonight, with the sound of Henry's and Quin's chatter as they made their way in fading light back to the house, and the glimpse of Dickie putting on his coat to walk over from his cottage, they were safe and well at the heart of all that was familiar. At the weekend Sienna and Max would come home; their family would be together, and with so much to love about this strange and special part of the world, why would they want to be anywhere else?

ACKNOWLEDGEMENTS

First and foremost, I want to thank Claire Morse BSc. Hons, Senior Forensic Scientist for guiding me through the eye-crossing labyrinth of her world that is such an important part of this book. In particular the subject of familial DNA. Thank you so much Claire for our chats and for answering my emails so swiftly and in a way that this complete airhead of a non-scientist could get to grips with. Of course if there are any mistakes they will be entirely down to me.

I also want to express an enormous thank you to Caroline Froud of Avon and Somerset Police for advising me on arrest procedure, investigation, and interrogation. There is so much to take in, and huge potential for getting it wrong, so if I have at any point please know the mistakes are mine – or I have used some poetic license in order to better serve the story.

It was extremely inspiring spending time at the Lady's Wood Shooting School near Chipping Sodbury to help me create a setting for Hanley Combe. A huge thank you to Chris Hanks, manager and senior coach, for so much patience, information and instruction in his field of expertise. It was a real eye-opener for me being in a world full of guns, game and gaming estates – not to mention an education in terminology that Chris so effortlessly guided me through. (I should probably say here that I didn't handle a gun or shoot anything myself, not even a clay – I'm guessing it will be important for some readers to know that.) I'd also like to thank Helen Cutter of Lady's Wood for making me feel welcome and answering some questions on Chris's behalf. Most of my family, and many friends, are looking forward to returning for a clay pigeon shoot and maybe even a flurry as soon as COVID is no longer a part of our lives.

I also want to say a very warm thank you to Simon Murphy and Caroline Hykiel of the Notley Arms in Monksilver, Exmoor. A truly fantastic pub for both food and accommodation in this stunningly dramatic part of the world. Wonderful hosts. We can't wait to go back.

It seems no book of mine is complete these days without a huge thank you to my dear friend, Ian Kelcey, who gave me the idea for this story and then, in a legal sense, guided me through it. What a fascinating world you inhabit as a criminal defence lawyer. Thank you so much for sharing some of your stories, experiences, and expertise.

Read on for a sneak peek
at Susan's next book

I Have Something to Tell You

Available September 2021

Tom was already packed for his week in London, his holdall still open on a rack in their dressing room waiting for last minute items to go in. Jay hadn't wanted to check if it was more than he usually took for three or four nights away, but she had, as subtly as possible, and to her relief it didn't look as though he was planning to go for any longer than he'd said.

She hated herself for being so mistrustful and insecure, but it seemed there was nothing she could do to stop her suspicions in spite of him giving her nothing to feed them.

Apart from those chilling words, *I have something to tell you.*

What had happened to make them go away? Or were they still lurking, gathering force in the silence, and he just hadn't yet found the right way to break them free?

You can't say that to someone and then not deliver.

She couldn't go on hiding from it either, although she seemed to be doing a good job of trying.

'You're going to have a busy week,' she commented, wandering into the bedroom where he was sorting through some papers on the bed. 'Do you think your guy's guilty?'

'Actually no,' he replied, stuffing files into his briefcase, 'but it's coming down to a case of her word against his and she presents a lot better than he does for all sorts of reasons.'

'Such as?'

'She's well-spoken, he isn't; she's a smart dresser, he's not; she's young and pretty, he's also young, but overweight and no pin-up. Frankly, being the physical slob that he is, it'll be hard for any jury to believe the act was consensual.'

'So, you're expecting to lose?'

'We'll try hard not to, because I happen to think he's telling the truth.' Setting aside his briefcase his expression became sardonic, even sad as he looked at her standing in the doorway, hair loose, feet bare and wearing old yoga pants and T-shirt. 'You've got a busy week of your own coming up,' he remarked. 'I'm guessing your chap won't get bail.'

'Snowballs and hell come to mind,' she sighed, going to take the hand he was holding out to her. She looked down at their entwined fingers and back to his upturned face, not exactly handsome, but strong, striking, as familiar as her own and yet sometimes as impenetrable as a stranger's.

'So, what's it about?' she said softly. 'What do you have to tell me?'

Sighing heavily, he pulled her to stand between his legs. 'Please try to hear me out before you jump to conclusions,' he began.

Jumping right into one, she pulled her hand away. 'It's *her,* isn't it?' she said, stepping back. 'I knew it would be. I've been trying to tell myself . . .'

'Jay, you need to listen. It's not what you think . . .'

'So, it's *not* about her?'

'Well, yes, it is, but . . .'

Her eyes blazed with pain and fury as she glared at

him. 'I knew to my core you hadn't given her up,' she spat. 'I tried to believe you . . .'

'Stop it! Just stop,' he cried, trying to grab her hands again, but she snatched them away. 'You don't know anything,' he told her, getting up from the bed, 'and you won't unless you let me speak. I need to tell you what's happened, how shocked I am by it and worried, and yes, guilty, but I swear I didn't see it coming.'

'Oh, so you're the victim here? Is that what I'm supposed to think?'

'That's not what I'm saying. If you'd just calm down and let me tell you . . .'

'I'm calm. I'm here, but I don't want you to touch me. Not until I know what this is about.'

'You're making it very difficult.'

She turned her head away, furious, frightened, but somehow making herself breathe in and out, forcing a connection with the more adult, rational part of herself. 'So here we are,' she said tartly, 'talking about Ellen Tyler *again*, in our bedroom, and the phrase "there are three in this marriage" comes racing to mind, so I . . .'

To her astonishment, he snatched up his briefcase and walked out of the room. 'There's no point trying to talk to you while you're being like this,' he growled, heading for the stairs.

As she listened to him going down, she tried again to control herself, to stop allowing her dread of where this was going to prevent them from getting there. She needed to know what it was about, only then would she be able to start dealing with it.

Can't wait to find out what happens next?

The gripping new novel from Susan Lewis
is available to order now . . .

EXCLUSIVE ADDITIONAL CONTENT

Includes an author Q&A and details of how to get involved in *Fern's Picks*

Fern's Picks

Dear lovely readers,

I'm delighted to say that this month's book is *The Lost Hours*, by the wonderful Susan Lewis.

Susan Lewis has written over forty books. Her novels are known for their twisting plots, emotional moments and fully-realised characters, and *The Lost Hours* is a perfect blend of dark and domestic.

It tells the story of Annie Crayce and her husband, David. They have a loving marriage, with three beautiful children and a thriving family business. Their lives are perfect – until the unthinkable happens. New DNA evidence suddenly places David as the prime suspect of a murder committed twenty years ago. As the police investigate the cold case, so does Annie, but it all comes down to a few lost hours she can't solve . . .

This is a gripping story about a close-knit family and deeply-held secrets that will stay with you a long time. I can't wait to hear what you think!

With love

Fern x

Look out for more books, coming soon!

For more information on the book club, exclusive Q&As with the authors and reading group questions, visit Fern's website **www.fern-britton.com/fernspicks**

We'd love you to join in the conversation, so don't forget to share your thoughts using **#FernsPicks**

Fern's Picks

A Q&A with Susan Lewis

Warning: contains spoilers

What inspired you to write *The Lost Hours?*

This book was actually inspired by a true story of how a family was torn apart by the shock of familial DNA coming to light so long after a murder. The awful twist at the start of the book is quite close to how things happened, but after that it becomes its own story.

DNA evidence is at the heart of this novel. What sort of research did you have to do to write a story about this?

I consulted a great deal with a forensic scientist who guided me through it all and helped me to simplify many of the technical terms for ease of reading.

Family is such an important theme in this novel. What made you want to write about this large and complex family?

David and Annie just came to me as I began to write, and the closeness they share with the other members of the family was integral to the story. I set it in a shooting school simply because it was different. I'd never even been to such a school before I began my research. I still don't handle guns, but many of my family members are keen clay pigeon shooters now.

Fern's Picks

Who was your favourite character to write about in *The Lost Hours*?

I loved David. I'm not sure why he worked so well for me, but I definitely wouldn't mind meeting him!

The novel is set in the beautiful landscape of Exmoor. Have you spent much time there yourself?

We go to Exmoor as often as possible. It will be our one little vacation this year (just one night for my birthday in August). We'll stay at The Notley Arms – as featured in the book.

***The Lost Hours* features Andee Lawrence, who readers of your books will be familiar with from other novels. What is it about her character that draws you regularly back to her?**

I always feel safe in Andee's hands, and from what readers say I think the feeling is shared. I didn't set out to feature her in so many books, but she's definitely taken on a life of her own.

The novel has a lot of twists and turns. Did you know what had really happened to Karen Lomax when you started writing?

Yes, I did!

Can you tell us anything about your next book?

My next novel, *I Have Something to Tell You*, is another book inspired by a true story. Jay Wells is a criminal solicitor called in to defend Edward Blake for the murder of his wife and they become very close while he is in prison awaiting trial and she investigates the case. The police are convinced he did it, but she is not.

Fern's Picks

Questions for your Book Club

Warning: contains spoilers

- **Who is your favourite character in the book?**
- **What does the setting of Exmoor add to the novel? Did you enjoy the landscape?**
- ***The Lost Hours* is all about a large and complicated family. How does the book explore family?**
- **Did you have a favourite moment or scene in *The Lost Hours*, and why?**
- **While you were reading, did you believe David was guilty, or innocent?**
- **Did you see the twist coming? Was the ending what you expected?**
- **How do you think you would act, were you in Annie's shoes?**
- **Can you remember what you were doing, twenty years ago today?**
- **Have you read any of Susan's other novels? Which one is your favourite and why?**

Questions for
your Book Club

Fern's Picks

An Exclusive Extract from Fern's New Novel

Daughters of Cornwall

Callyzion, Cornwall. December 1918.

I leant my head on the cold glass of the train window, drinking in the outside scenery. Bertie had described all this to me time and time again. He had insisted on reciting all the romantic names of the Cornish station stops.

'As soon as you are over the bridge, you come to Saltash. The Gateway to Cornwall.'

'Why is it called Saltash?' I had asked.

'No idea. Then after Saltash it's St Germans, Menheniot, Liskeard—'

I interrupted him. 'I'll never remember all those names. Just tell me where I need to get off?'

'I'm getting to that, Miss Impatience.' He inhaled comically and continued. 'Saltash, St Germans, Menheniot, Liskeard and then Bodmin. I shall be waiting for you at Bodmin.'

'Will you really?' We had been lying in the tiny bed of our Ealing home. 'I'm not sure I have had anyone wait for me anywhere before.'

'What sort of blighter would I be if I didn't pick up my beloved fiancée after she's travelled all that way to see me?'

'You'd be a very bad blighter indeed.' I smiled.

He held me closer, dropping a kiss onto my head. 'I can't wait for you to meet my family. Father will adore you. Mother too, though she may not show it at first, she's always cautious of new people. But Amy and you will be great friends. She's always wanted a sister. Brother Ernest can be a pompous ass but he's not a bad egg.'

'It'll be wonderful to feel part of a family again.'

'You are the bravest person I have ever met.' He squeezed me tightly, his arms encircling me. 'My stoic little squirrel.'

At this point, I am sorry to say I had already told a few lies to Bertie about my upbringing. Needs must sometimes.

Fern's Picks

'My parents were wonderful,' I fibbed, 'and I miss them every day, but I feel they would be very happy for me now.' Shameless, I know.

'Do you think they'd approve of me?' he asked.

'Oh Bertie,' I smiled. 'They would adore you.'

In the peace of my carriage, I searched my little bag for my handkerchief, angrily wiping away hot tears as, with a jolt, the mighty train wheels, powered by coal and steam, started to slow down.

The train guard was walking the corridors as he did before arriving at each station.

'Bodmin Road. Next stop Bodmin Road.' I readied myself to disembark.

Standing on the platform, I watched as the train chuffed its way down the line and out of sight on its journey towards Penzance. The Cornish winter air blew gently on my skin, and I took in lungfuls of the scent of damp earth.

Bertie had told me that it was warm enough down here to grow palm trees.

'You are pulling my leg.' I had laughed.

'No, I'm telling the truth. We have one in our garden. I will show it to you.'

I picked up my bag and walked past the signal box painted smartly in black and white, towards the ticket office where a sign with the word TAXI pointed. Even now, the half-expected hope that Bertie would be waiting for me made me breathless with longing. I imagined him running towards me, his long legs carrying him effortlessly. His strong arms collecting me up easily, lifting me from the ground so that my face was above his. The look of love shining between us.

'Excuse me, Miss.' A man with a peaked hat was walking towards me. 'Would you be Miss Carter?'

'Yes.'

'I thought so. You looked a bit lost on your own.' He had a kind face, but not too many teeth. 'Welcome to Cornwall.'

Available now!